I0612624

DYSTOPIA FROM THE ROCK

A COLLECTION OF SHORT STORIES

DYSTOPIA FROM THE ROCK

EDITED BY ERIN VANCE & ELLEN CURTIS

BOOKS

Library and Archives Canada Cataloguing in Publication

Title: Dystopia from the rock : a collection of short stories.
Names: Vance, Erin, 1992- editor. | Curtis, Ellen, 1993- editor.
Description: Edited by Erin Vance and Ellen Curtis.
Identifiers: Canadiana 20190053828 | ISBN 9781926903965 (softcover)
Subjects: CSH: Short stories, Canadian (English)—Newfoundland and Labrador | Canadian fiction
  (English)—21st century
Classification: LCC PS8329.5.N3 D97 2019 | DDC C813/.01089718—dc23

Copyright © 2019 Engen Books
Candles in the Tree © 2019 Michelle Churchill
The Island Outside the War © 2019 Lisa Daly
Carry Her Home © 2019 Diane Lynn McGyver
Game Plan, Authentic New Island Experience™ © 2019 Ali House
In the Rising Flame © 2019 Samuel Bauer
The Schedule © 2019 Shannon K Green
Blood Red Horizon, The Other © 2019 Jon Dobbin
A Flood of Sorts © 2019 Heather Nolan
Future Imperfect, Future Tense © 2019 Lauralana Dunne
The Ninth Wonder © 2019 David Rimmington
Young Republicans, The Views © 2019 Matthew LeDrew
Watcher © 2019 Garreth Mitton
Eggshell Revolution © 2019 Matthew Daniels
Cash Grab © 2019 Chantal Boudreau
Family Business © 2019 Corinne Lewandowski
The Lost Generation © 2019 David Wright
Jianghu © 2019 Jed MacKay
In Dangerous Company © 2019 Christopher P Walsh
Trickster Sings the Blues © 2019 Katie Little
Kaida of the Eastern Shore © 2019 Finnan Beaton
Escape from Selenous Valley Retreat © 2019 Andrew Pike
Rudeworld © 2019 John Haas
Final Edict © 2019 Peter J Foote
Anchored © 2019 Jeff Slade
Unsettled © 2019 Elizabeth Whitten
The Match © 2019 Ryan Belbin
The Market, The Last One Standing © 2019 Nicole Little
Afterword © 2019 Erin Vance
Forward © 2019 Brad Dunne

NO PART OF THIS BOOK MAY BE REPRODUCED OR TRANSMITTED IN ANY FORM OR BY ANY
MEANS, ELECTRONIC OR MECHANICAL, INCLUDING PHOTOCOPYING AND RECORDING, OR
BY ANY INFORMATION STORAGE OR RETRIEVAL SYSTEM WITHOUT WRITTEN PERMISSION
FROM THE COPYRIGHT HOLDER, EXCEPT FOR BRIEF PASSAGES QUOTED IN A REVIEW.

This book is a work of fiction. Names, characters, places and incidents are products of each author's
imagination or are used fictitiously. Any resemblance to actual events or locales or persons living or dead
is entirely coincidental.

Distributed by:
Engen Books
www.engenbooks.com
submissions@engenbooks.com
First mass market paperback printing: March 2019
Cover Image: JJ King

Engen Books thanks JJ King and Sci-Fi on the Rock for helping make this collection possible.

CONTENTS

Introduction
Brad Dunne

If you read enough dystopian literature, you'll soon realize that there are, in fact, many ways in which the world can go to s**t.

In the title that is perhaps synonymous with the genre, *Nineteen Eighty-Four*, George Orwell imagines a world of state tyranny achieved through omnipresent surveillance and propaganda. Big Brother is always watching. The government enforces their own version of the facts (2+2=5) and anyone who thinks differently is guilty of "thoughtcrime." Indeed, *Nineteen Eighty-Four* is a bleak vision of perpetual war and a complete erasure of individuality. You don't exactly have to read between the lines to see Orwell thought too much government was a bad thing.

On the opposite end of the spectrum, William Golding shows us that a world without government isn't so great, either. In *Lord of the Flies*, a group of well-educated boys quickly revert to their primitive lizard brains after crash landing on a deserted island. They briefly give democracy a shot, but this soon deteriorates into a might-is-right tribalism where the strong prey upon the weak and everyone dances around a pig's head impaled on a pike. The prep schoolers thus demonstrate Thomas Hobbes' maxim that life in its natural state is "nasty, brutish, and short."

Clearly, while an excess of rules can crush the individual, as Orwell shows, the individual also needs modern society's guardrails to survive and flourish. Or maybe boys just aren't very good at this whole law and order thing.

Speaking of which, the most popular dystopian work *du jour* is arguably Margaret Atwood's *The Handmaid's Tale*, which has been adapted into a successful TV show. Atwood is currently penning a sequel, to be released this year. Here we see a patriarchal society, called the Republic of Gilead, that has reduced women to vehicles of procreation. Atwood shows us a world in which men use a literalist, fundamentalist interpretation of the Bible to politicize and control women's bodies. In addition, racial minorities are segregated, and homosexual men are tortured and killed. Men who challenge the status quo are strung up for all to see as deterrents.

Not to be outdone, female despots are also represented in dystopian fiction. I would argue that Ken Kesey's *One Flew Over the Cuckoo's Nest* is a kind of dystopia, at least on a microscopic level, wherein a group of emasculated men languish under a matriarchy. Nurse Ratchet rules over her psychiatric ward like a despot by weaponizing the feelings of shame and insecurity of her wards. When Randle McMurphy, famously portrayed by Jack Nicholson, challenges her authority, she has him lobotomized. The story is an attack on institutionalism and the psychiatric practices of its time.

These examples thus far have largely been characterized by external forms of control. Be it governments, institutions, or sociopathic bullies. But there are also dystopias that are defined by a tyranny of the appetites. Control that comes from the bottom up. In Aldous Huxley's *Brave New World*, the upper class consume *soma* to achieve a near-constant dream-like state. In Ray Bradbury's *Fahrenheit 451*, people's attention spans have been so degraded by television and smut that books are considered dangerous because they are so bewildering to these scrubbed brains, and therefore must be destroyed. These futurist dystopias are clearly warning of the potential problems that excess can cause with the on-going technological revolution. Conversely, post-apocalyptic dystopias show us what can happen in resource scarce worlds, like *The Road*. Or even something like *Soylent Green* ("It's people!").

"Dystopia" literally means "bad place" in Greek. It is an antonym to "utopia," which nowadays is used to describe an ideal society. Interestingly, "utopia," coined by Thomas More for his 1516 book of the same name, actually means "no place." More's fictional island is one of peace and prosperity, but it is clear by his play on words that he doesn't believe such a place is capable of existing. Dystopian literature takes this observation a step further and shows us that not only is the perfect society impossible to achieve, it is dangerous to do so. In many of the examples I used earlier, we can see how dystopian stories take a current societal trend and extrapolate it into worst a case scenario. They are fictional case studies. Ideally, we would consume these stories and avoid their pitfalls. Too much government is bad, but no government is equally bad. An ascetic and repressed culture is bad, but too much stimulation is equally bad. Too many resources vs. not enough. You get the idea. Like Goldilocks, we can analyze these stories and deduce a happy medium where possible.

Unfortunately, that doesn't appear to be the way things are playing out nowadays.

Despite Orwell's warnings, we are increasingly monitored by governments and our data is bought and sold by corporations. Despite Huxley's warnings, we are over reliant on medication to tranquilize our anxious minds in these anxious times. Publishers are folding as people would rather Netflix and chill than dive into a book, magazine, or newspaper. Women's reproductive rights are still a battleground even in first world countries. The mentally ill continue to struggle for proper support (here in Newfoundland, our main psychiatric hospital is older than Canada). The planet is collapsing while the wealth gap between the haves and have-nots is increasing, and the powers that be would rather blot out the sun than reduce current levels of consumption. Perhaps *WALL-E* was the most prescient with its vision of us as dehumanized bags of milk floating through space having escaped a ravaged planet while robots tend to our every need.

Kurt Vonnegut said that "During the Vietnam War, every respectable artist in this country was against the war. It was like a laser beam. We were all aimed in the same direction. The power of this weapon turns out to be that of a custard pie dropped from a stepladder six feet high." What are we to do in the face of what seems like a tidal wave of epic collapse tearing towards as we wait for these various other shoes to drop?

Personally, I subscribe to the maxim that it is better to light a candle than curse the darkness. Slovenian philosopher Slavoj Zizek argues that the reason so many revolutions fail is that they didn't do the prior work of imagining a world that is different from the old one. What ends up happening, then, is that the new regime starts imitating the old one. Like when the pigs finally takeover in Orwell's *Animal Farm* and quickly abandon their supposed morals. "Some animals are more equal than others." Meet the new boss, same as the old boss. As consumers and producers of literature, we must do the heavy lifting of imagining a world other than our own.

And so, we read and we write. We create things like this anthology you're holding in your hands right now. Call me corny, but I believe each of these stories are a spark that could light the way through these dark times. To me, the fact that dystopian literature is trending is actually a positive thing. It means that, on some conscious level, we as a society are recognizing the problems and are groping towards some kind of solution(s). What I find particularly encouraging is that the fact that budding readers seem especially drawn to the genre. Young adult fiction is obsessed with dystopia. Will the generation who grew up on *Divergent* and *The Hunger Games* save the planet? They may be the only chance we have left.

Brad Dunne
author, After Dark Vapours

Michelle Churchill

A native Newfoundlander raised in Nova Scotia, Michelle is the mother of two incredible children. From 2015 to 2017, she volunteered on the planning committee for *Sci-fi on the Rock*, Newfoundland's premier science-fiction and fantasy convention.

Michelle made her publishing debut in 2018's *Chillers from the Rock*.

Her first novel, *The Last Tree*, debuts in December 2019 from Engen Books.

Candles in the Tree

They gave us fair warning at least.

We thought we were safe on the east coast, thousands of kilometers from the accident. It was on the other side of the continent for goodness sake. Accident was the official word. Cruel irony or malicious purpose? We'll never know. Those that did are long since gone.

My girls were watching cartoons on TV that morning. Who even does that anymore? We all have those streaming services now. But for whatever reason they were watching TV, real TV, when the programming was cut short for the announcement. I had stepped into the kitchen to make coffee when my eldest stormed in accusing her little sister of changing the channel.

The news bulletin: three cities gone!

Gone!

Wiped off the map forever. Just gone. An accident, the announcer said.

I couldn't turn it off; it was too unreal, too impossible. My husband came home from work before lunch. No one could focus at the office, so it made no point to stay. We spent the rest of the day glued to our phones, until the cell service crapped out because that's what everyone was doing.

The world mourned. We mourned people we didn't even know. Though, that's not how it works. There was always someone's second cousin, friend of a friend, neighbour's sister-in-law that had been there. Gradually the circles grew smaller to include people we knew, people we cared about.

We gave to fundraisers, attended services, and gave away toys and clothes. Anything to fill the void, make it better. As if recycling bags of the girls' clothes from last summer was really going to make up for the millions lost.

The real impact trickled out slowly at first. The price of fruit and vegetables went up considerably. Then there was no more orange juice. My eldest wasn't happy about that.

My husband lost his job, and I went back to work at a coffee shop surrounded by 20-somethings. We cut back: sold our mini-van and bought a small car. Just in time for me to lose my job. After some mega fire or whatever, coffee went up to $38 a cup. My husband got another job, said it was all a blessing in disguise. Chocolate bars cost $22 a piece—way out of budget— some blessing.

Importing food became expensive and near impossible to find. Stores were closing, and importers went bankrupt. Local farms couldn't keep up with demand. The government offered a buyout on lawns. Some scheme to turn suburbia into one big homestead.

One morning a tractor came and tore up our front and back yards. They removed the lilac tree we planted when we bought the house and the kids' swing set. The girls watched in amazement as the tractor tore up the earth and planted patches of the neighbourhood. My husband was the one who jumped on the idea first. Good thing he did; a month later, the government made the program mandatory. Our neighbours who hadn't sold their land were forced to give it up, with no compensation.

Grouchy neighbours were all around. Cabbage for breakfast, lunch, and supper didn't help moods or stomachs either.

Bees were gone, but they called that years ago. Same with the polar bears.

Seagulls were a surprise though. None of us saw that one coming.

At first, five cities were gone. Then came the fall out, and fires brought that up to seven, then twelve.

Diseases not seen in centuries started to return. There weren't enough vaccines. School was closed, and the girls took classes on the internet. My husband lost his job, again. This time we all took up work tending the neighbourhood.

Our street got chickens. The girls loved raising baby chicks. After twelve weeks, I told the girls they could have the day off. Let their dad take care of the chickens. They still refused to eat supper that night. Though, they didn't grumble when I made homemade soup the next day.

Another accident, so they told us. Some research facility deep inside the earth. I don't know what they called it, every announcer pronounces it differently.

None of it mattered now: cabbages, chickens, nothing.

Rolling blackouts: to buy time, we had lights only one hour a night, then thirty minutes, then fifteen minutes, then none. Then total blackouts; the laptop was just a paperweight now.

It was like camping every day. We survived the cold, but not everyone did.

Spring brought hope with warmer weather and longer days. Then that hope was gone too.

June, my husband's old Scout radio, announcing what we all knew deep inside.

Good Bye!

Power gone, the time bought to solve whatever had broken with our world. We all tried so hard, gave what we could, paid with the lives of so many friends and families. None of our suffering mattered; it wasn't enough.

The best minds couldn't save us. No one could save us.

We were alone.

The Great Good Bye.

They gathered the world's leaders, those who remained, and those who survived. They brought in the world's best doctors and psychologists. They spoke in every language using quiet reassuring tones – the same way my husband spoke to the girls when he wanted to pretend that he was brave.

A global DNR, Do Not Resuscitate. They were pulling the plug on all of us. One day to say goodbye, rather than let us all suffer slowly.

We didn't tell the kids, but they asked what was going on. We needed to say something.

Christmas!

The tree was still in the basement, and we took it out. My husband dragged it upstairs. I opened the boxes of bows and decorations. Even let the youngest put on the glass bulbs; she always wanted to do that. From the cupboard, I emptied our ration of candles. I always wanted a tree with real candles. It was never practical, but now, it didn't matter. Now for once we would have real candles in the tree.

Lisa Daly

A native Newfoundlander, Lisa is an archaeologist, historian, professional ballroom dance instructor, crafter, and avid baker.

Previous non-fiction writing credits include essays *Sacrifice in Second World War Gander* and *An Empty Graveyard: The Victims of the 1946 AOA DC-4 Crash, Their Final Resting Place, and Dark Tourism*.

Lisa will act as a guest editor for the Summer 2019 *Flights from the Rock* collection.

The Island Outside the War

There is a tradition on the island of seeing the body. Children will challenge each other, daring others to prove that they are not afraid. They are all afraid, but the challenge must be met. In groups of fours and fives, they will sneak down to the shore. They are all certain they will get in trouble, so they make excuses, tell stories, and try to hide the truth from their parents.

The adults know. They pretend it is forbidden, but they know the importance of this rite of passage and continue with the charade.

The kids all know of a small boat, sometimes a dory, sometimes a rowboat, hidden in one of the gentler coves.

The adults know about this boat as well. They carefully maintain it so that it looks abandoned but still ensures that it is safe.

The kids pile into boat while one of the bigger kids, one of those who must lead the way, push them off the rocks and into the water, before jumping in themselves. They reach over and touch the cold water, looking at the smooth rocks below. They splash each other, or take turns bailing out rainwater. For many of them, it is their first time in a boat without parental supervision.

The adults who live closest to the water can usually hear their laughter. The excitement always overtakes the kids as they hit the water. When the shouts and giggles make their way from the cove, the adults send word to each other, checking to see which kids are going to the wreck, which kid is leading, and who still has not gone. It is a great privilege to be the parent of the guiding child. That family will get extra rations and the child will be given a gift. Something useful, of course, but extravagant, like a bicycle. The other families will be given something extra from the butcher and the baker. The child with the new gift will be congratulated and will be inducted into the world of the parents on their next birthday.

After the initial excitement, the kids will remember that they are supposed to be sneaking around and will quiet each other down. The older kid will help and will remind them of their mission. Oars will be gathered, and rowers chosen, sometimes two children to an oar, especially if the water is rough. Outside of the cove, the rowers stop talking, focused only on pulling the boat through the waves. The seas will push the little boat around, rocking it back and forth, forcing them to continuously check their bearings. Their goal is a buoy, not too far from the shore, but further than most have travelled without an adult.

The adults signal out to the ocean, and the fishermen know to keep at least some lookout for the little red light, especially on nice days. Once the laughter is heard, the lamp is lit and there are a few minutes until the kids leave the cove. The adults know to avoid the wreck, to tuck their own boats into different coves, or fish on the other side of the island. The kids are never caught out on this adventure.

The kids never wonder why, on the open ocean, they never see another boat. Usually the harbour is full of boats, pulling nets and jigging fish, calling to one another, but not now. Now it is only the wind across the bow, the waves against the planks, and the grunts of effort as the children row. It seems on these days there is never a whale to seen or even a seagull to be heard. But the kids do not think of this. They are all too nervous with the anticipation of getting to the buoy, of being out here when they know they shouldn't be.

The adults are all watching from their homes. Some are close enough to need nothing, but others peer through binoculars, crouched near the front window. No one dares leave once the call has gone out in case the kids see them on the road and lose their will. They know all it takes is for one child to become too afraid and the boat will turn back.

As they near the wreck, the older kid tells them to draw in their oars. With no adults to be seen, if they drop one, they might end up stuck out here for who knows how long, and none of them want that. As the boat nears the buoy, they all hold their breath. Beneath them they can see pieces of twisted metal. They carefully put their oars back in the water and slowly move the boat forward, following the debris.

This is the worst part. So often the kids will be so focused on rowing that they will be surprised when they come upon the wreck. At least once a year, a child will drop an oar in the water. Sometimes they will manage to retrieve it. Other times, they will drop the other trying to get the first. Then they must sit there, drifting until sundown when a fisherman will happen upon them. Once every few years, something tragic will happen. In trying to get the dropped oar they will capsize. Or, when they see the first piece of metal, they will all run to one side, all wanting to get a look, and the boat will turn over. If they are lucky, they will climb back in the boat, or manage to sit on the overturned vessel, floating until sundown. But even then, cold and wet, they usually succumb to the elements.

As the boat moves forward, they all look down at the metal wonder. They recognize some of the things, like the big cannons on the deck. No, that's not right. They don't look like the cannons, old and thick with corrosion, that can be found around the island. They look too sleek and shiny. Too different. But still somehow the same. As they get closer to the buoy, they almost forget why they came out in the first place. They have never seen so much metal in one place, and this, even under water, is so much different than what comes out of the forge.

The older child speaks as they come make their way along. They tell a story of explosions and fire, of things called bombs that can destroy whole towns in the blink of an eye. They tell the young ones about people at war, and how they come out broken – not like when the blacksmith caught a piece of metal under his glove, and not even like when the butcher was kicked by cow and lost his eye – no, these stories are of people who lost limbs and parts of their faces. The stories are embellished over the years, but still cannot fully portray the horrors they try to describe. Men and women who are caught in war come out missing something else beyond body parts; they are missing their souls. The child tells of people who have seen war and who are come back little better than walking corpses, doomed to haunt the land until they can finally die, and even then, might very well haunt the place where they died. They tell of how this metal monster brought the evil of war to the shores of the island and used the cannons – they explain that they are called guns – to sink the fishing boats, kill the people of the island, and even shake the island itself with their force. This always makes some of the little ones cry out. It is never said, but always wondered if these guns could sink the island and everything they know.

The adults know this part of the story is true.

As they near the buoy, the older child gives the warning. Leaving the island means going back to war. Leaving the island means the risk of coming back incomplete. Leaving the island means you may never fully come back. So, the island has made sure everyone had to stay. Trying to leave the island, trying to go back to the buoy, will have consequences. The island wants no more war, and will reach up and grab you, keeping you near the island forever.

The war was awful. Entire countries were ripped off of the map. No where was safe. It lasted generations and moved across continents. People tried to flee, taking only what they could carry, but the war was everywhere. In desperation, some took to the seas in ships too derelict to be used as war machines. One such ship limped across the ocean until a storm tore her to pieces. Many were lost, but many survived, picked up by a passing naval ship. The allies, the enemies, it didn't matter. They were safe, for the moment. Until a ship from a combatant nation attacked. Never free from fighting, the war ships fought, until the aggressor capsized. The crew of the first ship, at the begging of the refugees, picked up the survivors. Together, allies, enemies, casualties of war, tried to find somewhere to be safe worried about being found by another ship. With such a mix of passengers, would they be attacked? After months of traveling together, they found an island. Small, uninhabited, and out of sight of the mainland.

With those words, the kids arrive at the buoy and look down. Below them is a body, floating up from the metal monster below. Ropes hold the body to the deck, wrapped around the legs, torso, neck, and one arm. The other arm is free, floating toward the children. Reaching for them. Asking for help. Or maybe trying to pull them down into the water.

All agreed. This would be a new home and they would keep the war away from it as long as possible. They sank the ship where the waters just started to get deep. Shallow enough that it could serve as a warning. The first body belonged to an older man who died of natural causes in the first days. They lashed him to the deck before they sank the ship.

They made a home for themselves. Salvaging materials and supplies from the ship, they made a new and simple start. They provided for themselves as best they could, but the cold climate made growing some things, like wheat, difficult. So, twice a year, a ship leaves the island, traveling as far away as possible under the cover of night, before turning to the mainland. The ship will trade artisanal goods labeled from countries still on maps. Canned and pickled foods mostly. While it is not fresh, produce is rare in many places, and these luxuries are sold to buy other rare necessities, like salt and flour. On these trips, information is gathered. What countries have fallen, what countries have taken over, and most importantly, if the war is still happening. Loaded with supplies, the ship returns, making sure no one follows and finds the island.

The kids are silent as they watch the body floating on its tether. They talk in whispers. They embellish the story and talk of other stories of people who tried to leave. They wonder if this is one of those people. The body is too far away to recognize. Could it be a cousin or an uncle who talked of leaving but never came back? Every family had such a story, though the family often omits that it might be a great uncle or a distance cousin. They all vow to stay near the island. They will never venture beyond the buoy. They will never be taken by the ship. They will never become the body on the ship.

The island has seen peace for generations. Supplies are limited and carefully rationed. No one lives richly, but no one starves. It is a precarious existence that relies on secrecy. If the children, when they become old enough and brave enough to take a boat, were to travel too far, they would find themselves in view of the shipping lanes. Every child must go see the body. Every child must hear the warning. The ritual mostly takes care of itself, because there will always be an older child who will lead the younger ones, ready to scare them by telling the story. And, unknown to them, it will bring them into the secret and into adulthood.

With reluctance and relief, the children row back and tuck the boat in the quiet cove, tiredly working together to pull the boat back up on the rocks. They arrive quietly, their mood heavy while they all reflect on the day. They wander back, ready with falsehoods to tell their parents, but the parents never ask. They spread the story to their friends, encouraging others to go to the buoy, to see the metal monster, to see the body.

The only big problem is the body. Once, early on, when the first body rotted away, and the children born to the island started to explore, they would go too far, putting the entire community at risk. So, the story was created, but the body was needed. Every few years, as the current body starts to break away, another is chosen. Sometimes the island is fortunate, and someone dies by accident or nature. The kids are brought to the other side of the island for a celebration, while some of the adults bring the body to the ship and tie it down, leaving one arm free to wave at the world. Sometimes, there is no body available. Someone is chosen, often by lottery. They start to talk about leaving the island, and one day, they simply vanish. If they leave a spouse behind, they get to move into the house above the cove and their only job is to keep vigil for the laughter of children, to light the red lamp, and tell those on land.

Diane Lynn McGyver

Diane is a novelist from Cole Harbour, Nova Scotia. To date she has written two novels, *Shadows in the Stone* and *Scattered Stones*.

"Carry Her Home" represents her first piece of published short fiction.

Carry Her Home

Thick grey clouds drifted slowly across the sky as if morning could wait another day. They blocked the rising sun and cast an eerie darkness upon the land. Soon they'd disperse the cold bitter rain and force Grace to seek shelter.

Scanning the horizon to the south, she watched the swell of the ocean gently rise and fall. The memory of being tossed overboard by a large wave rekindled the terror of leaving home. Long before she hit the water, she had known she and her father should never have left Nova Scotia. He didn't admit this truth until after they were stranded in Killarney, Ontario, and he realised they'd never make it to Thunder Bay.

She blinked several times to stall the tears, adjusted her pack, and drew a deep breath before continuing on the worn road. Deep cracks in the pavement threatened to twist an ankle if she didn't take care to step over them, and large erect chunks of grey asphalt forced her to walk in a zigzag pattern.

Grace stopped at the edge of the pavement and looked to where it began again twenty feet away. A shallow gully separated the end from the beginning. She glanced north to where the Northumberland Strait slapped the shoreline. Her father had told her stories of his travels between his province and New Brunswick, and he said at that time, he could not stand on the TransCanada and see the Strait. It all changed after the meteor struck Antarctica and sea levels rose dramatically.

She pulled the tattered map from her pack and stared at the

section she had left exposed. The old map revealed the width of the isthmus separating the two provinces with Port Elgin being on the Northumberland coastline. Now the small community lay under water. She followed the blue lines of the highway east and stared at Amherst. Her father had said it had become an outpost after the disaster and was no longer a friendly town. She had to go around it during the night and avoid the people who lived there.

A raindrop fell on the paper, and she looked up to see the clouds had grown darker. She had to find shelter.

Shoving the map into her pack, she scrambled down the side of the gully, crossed the small stream of water at the bottom and scampered up the other side. She walked quickly, avoiding the deep potholes and jagged broken pieces of pavement. Her target was a small grouping of trees in the distance. There, she could set up her tarp and wait out the rain.

The rain didn't stop until late afternoon. By the time Grace shook off the excess water from her tarp and packed her things, only a few hours of daylight remained. She set out on a steady march, hoping to reach Amherst and be well past it before dawn. The clouds thinned, and the rising gibbous moon promised enough illumination to guide her.

In the dying light, she pulled her father's journal from her pack and reread the instructions.

Shortly after you cross the bridge, you'll see a small lighthouse and the sign welcoming you home, if it's still standing.

A few hundred feet away – just past the bridge – she saw a derelict car in the middle of the road. Her steps slowed as she scanned for movement. From this distance, she saw the smashed windshield and the crumpled engine bonnet. The car still held its shape, so the impact hadn't been that brutal. The farther she walked, the more rust appeared, and her steps returned to the march. The vehicle had been there forever.

Once across the bridge, she approached the car with casual

caution. Though certain no one sat inside, fear tickled the back of her neck. Her pace slowed, and her eyes roamed over the car quickly, looking for movement of any form. A few feet away, she stopped and listened. Nothing. She stepped forward quietly, craning her neck to see the contents.

Torn upholstery and smashed windows greeted her. Peering inside, the human remains made her jump. The driver slouched across the centre console. Its head rested on the passenger seat. The skeleton had been stripped of every living cell and its shirt. The ruddy colour of the ribcage blended into the cloth seats.

Relief swept through her. She had grown accustomed to travelling alone, and no longer desired companions. It felt better this way. She need only look out for herself and run with no thought of what she left behind. Thinking for the safety of two had burdened her father and led to his death.

Grace quickly examined the interior for useful items, but it had been picked clean, just as the bones had been.

It didn't matter; she had everything she needed and everything she could carry. Anyways, it felt odd stealing from the dead even if her father had said it was okay. *The dead needed nothing the living could use*, he'd said.

She walked away from the car and looked towards the welcome sign. The only letters remaining of Nova Scotia were V, I and A. *Via*, she spoke in her mind. She would reach home via this route.

The remnants of a small building lay scattered on the ground in a pile of rocks to the left of the tattered sign. The remains of the lighthouse.

She walked beneath tall steel poles that creaked in the breeze. A small section of green sign still clung to the metal.

She referred to the journal again. *Stay on the TransCanada*, her father had written. *Lean to the right and go in the ditch if you can. The town will be off to your left and will be avoided if you stay true to this road. Go quickly and quietly.*

She read the words in her father's voice and it felt as though he walked alongside her. A tear slipped down her cheek and she wiped it away. She had to be brave.

The sun set, hoarding its light for another day, and she zipped her jacket closed. A cool breeze blew off the barren land into her face. She turned her head and listened for distant sounds carried on the wind that would indicate human activity. When none came, she hastened her steps. In a few hours, she'd be past the town and then rest until dawn.

In the dim light, she made out the edge of the road and the tree tops against the sky. A short time later, she spotted a light in the distance. She switched to walking on the pavement as it made less noise than the gravel sidewalk. Other lights became visible where her father had said Amherst lay.

Her breath quickened. Her feet wanted to run, but she knew it unwise to do so. She'd make too much noise with her pack jangling and she'd tire easily. She also wouldn't detect sounds that might warn her of danger. So, she kept walking, watching the lights, glancing at the road to ensure she didn't trip and hoping she'd soon pass the town.

An unseen force knocked the wind from her lungs and threw her to the pavement. Before she saw her attacker, he pushed her down face-first and applied pressure to her shoulder blades to keep her there.

"Who are you?" a male voice growled in her ear.

"Grace," she wheezed, struggling to catch her breath.

"Last name."

"McDonald."

"Home."

"I don't understand the question."

"Where do you come from?" He applied more pressure to her shoulders.

"Margaree Harbour."

"Cape Breton?" His grip softened.

"Yes. Now get off me." She wiggled her shoulders, and he released his hold. Scrambling to her feet, she stepped away to put space between them.

He looked no older than sixteen, but he stood taller by a few inches. His camouflage pants and jacket concealed him well in the dim light. He wore a black stocking hat, and his face sported black paint. His stance indicated that he was ready to fight if she aggravated him.

She had dealt with men meaner looking than this boy, so she stood in a relaxed pose though she trembled inside. "Who are you?" She tightened her jaw to project a stern voice.

"My friends call me Hammer." He smirked. "But my enemies call me their worst nightmare."

"What should I call you?" She folded her arms to still her shaking hands.

Half a grin played on the corner of his mouth. "Thor."

She huffed and stifled a chuckle. "Last name?"

"Gillanders."

"Home?"

"Amherst." He waved his hand towards the twinkling lights in the distance.

She had assumed this but when the word escaped his mouth, her heart rate increased. Her father's warning replayed in her head.

Thor glanced behind him, then looked back at her. "What spooked ya'?"

Damn. She had to learn to hide her emotions better. "Nothing. Just got a chill."

"Thought you saw something." He eased his stance. "Where ya' headed?"

"Home."

He raised an eyebrow. "To Margaree Harbour? Alone?"

She lifted her chin in a show of defiance. "Of course."

"You'll never survive Truro. The gangs have taken over."

Truro? Her father had made no mention of danger in that town. "How do you know of this danger? Have you been there?"

He shook his head. "I've heard stories from my people. The only way you'll make it to Cape Breton is to bypass it to the north."

She thought about the map in her pack. She'd studied it many times for fear she'd someday lose it. She could take the #6 Highway north and skirt the North Shore, but that would mean passing through Amherst.

"You'll have to travel along the mountains because the shore is underwater."

"The #6?"

He nodded. "It's rough going with lots of bridges washed out."

"You know this from your people's stories?"

"Yes. They explore the province still, looking for supplies."

"You never go with them?"

He shook his head. "I am forbidden."

She watched him carefully, weighing his words. Forbidden conjured several images. None of them good.

"Because I am too young," he added.

Sensing time ticked away, she steered the conversation towards them parting. She hoped their meeting would end on friendly terms, and she'd be on her way. "So, I should turn off the highway and head for Wentworth. It will be safe until then?"

"That would be a wise decision. There is a road that goes to Pictou. There you'll find safe passage, perhaps even a boat to deliver you to Cape Breton."

"You know a lot about the route for someone who has never travelled it."

He peered into the darkness and slipped his hands into his pockets. When he looked back, he said what his mind had prepared: "It is best to study the maps in case of an emergency."

"A wise idea." She prepared to take her leave. "Thank you for the valuable information. I wish you the best." She stepped to the side.

"You are leaving?"

"Yes. I wish to make camp a few miles up the road."

"Can I walk with you a while?" He turned to face the road east. "I will not slow you down."

"If you wish." She walked slowly, glancing at him, wondering if he wanted more than friendly conversation. "The company is nice."

"New faces are rare in Amherst. It's interesting to talk with someone different."

She smiled. He was lonely. "How many people live in Amherst?"

"The council says 823."

"Council?"

"Our leaders. They keep order and ensure everyone has shelter, protection, and enough to eat."

"It is good you have them. Many places I've been live in chaos."

"Where did you come from?"

"Killarney, Ontario."

He stared, wide-eyed and mouth open. "It is incredible you survived alone."

"I wasn't alone at first." She looked at the ground, regretting her words, knowing the question that would follow.

"Who were you with?"

She drew a deep breath, steeled her emotions, and answered, knowing also his next question. "My father."

"Where is he now? Did he...?"

The unfinished question sat like a razor on her ear. "Yes. Several miles south of Montreal." She held back the tears and thought of cleaning mackerel on the shore near her old home, unwilling to replay her father's death scene in her mind.

"I'm sorry."

And there was the familiar response. Flat. Meaningless. "How is the weather this summer? Has it changed drastically since other summers?"

"It has been the same since the meteor struck the South Pole. It feels like fall every day as if every day is October 1st."

"Thor, you're out late tonight, son."

The voice startled them both, and they came to an abrupt stop.

A dark shadow approached. As he neared, Grace saw he was a grown man, taller and thicker than Thor.

"Uncle Malcolm, I didn't see you there." Thor's voice shook.

Malcolm stopped two feet away. He stared down at Grace curiously, his eyes wide to see her in the dim light.

Goosebumps exploded on her arms and a cold shiver raced down her spine. Unlike Thor, this man showed no sign of friendliness.

"I'm often not where you might find me." Malcolm adjusted his dark toque. "Have you invited our young guest home?"

"She's in a hurry to reach her own home." Thor spoke as if pleading his case to an angry father. "I was only walking a bit to see her on her way."

"There's nothing to hurry about." He gazed up at the starlit sky. "Decent people shouldn't travel so late." He returned his eyes to Grace. "It would be rude of us to not invite you to our house to rest and eat."

"Thank you, sir, but as Thor said, I'm in a hurry, and I don't wish to bother you."

"It's no bother." He grinned. "I insist you join us for a late-night snack. In the morning, you'll be on your way, refreshed from your rest."

She glanced at Thor who fell silent. She found it difficult to read his expression in the dim light, but his voice earlier had suggested concern. "I must respectfully decline your offer. I really must be go—"

"It's not an offer." He leered towards her. "It's an order." He grasped her arm and compelled her across the abandoned highway.

"Uncle, please, let her go." Thor fell into step beside him.

"I am not in the business of letting opportunity walk away." He frowned at the teenager. "And neither should you be. Have you claimed her?"

"No, she belongs to another. We have no right to—"

"Then I lay claim." He stopped abruptly. "Because I have

the right given to me by council."

Grace tugged on her arm to free herself, but the man held her firmly. "Let me go." She lowered her voice and released the command as a growl as her father had taught her. "If I do not return, they will look for me. When they find me, you'll regret you ever laid eyes on me." She clung to the idea that she was one of the chosen ones, that her protectors would kill anyone who harmed her. This story gave her strength, but only if she believed it. Her father had spent many hours telling her of the rare gift she possessed, one protected by her clan. They were searching for her now to deliver her home safely. Deep down, though, she knew it was a lie, one created to incite courage.

Malcolm stopped and reconsidered her. "Who are *they*?"

"The deadliest of them all. The McDonald Clan of the Highlands."

He laughed, first with mild amusement, then with unbridled passion. When he finished, he wiped his eyes. "I've known some McDonald boys. Got a few living within Amherst. They're far from the *deadliest*."

"Obviously, you've not met the Highland McDonalds." She planted her feet and scowled. "If you release me now, I will not tell them of this assault."

He thrust his face an inch away from hers. "I'm not into catch and release, dearie. I play for keeps."

The stench of his breath wafted over her face, eating at her defences. She could fight him off, try to escape now or wait for a better opportunity. Glancing at Thor, she wondered what he would do if she knifed his uncle. He said he wanted to let her continue her journey, but he might change his mind if she injured a family member.

Malcolm jerked her forward and Thor followed them. They travelled down a well-beaten path towards the collection of town lights. Before they reached them, they took a path leading along the outskirts. In the distance, she saw a looming shadow. As they neared, she found the outline of a building. Darkness consumed it.

"Get the door, boy," Malcolm growled.

Thor ran ahead and opened the door to the small house.

Malcolm dragged her inside where he lit a flashlight to guide them down a set of stairs to the basement. There, in the corner, rested a cage large enough for a human to sleep and stand. Here is where he threw her.

Grace landed on her hands and knees with a thud. Before she rose, she felt a strong tug on her pack, and she whirled.

"No!" Thor said in a hefty voice. "I claim the pack and everything in it."

She watched him snarl at his uncle with his arms akimbo.

A wry smile crossed Malcolm's face. "Take it. It will remind you of what you've lost."

Thor stepped forward and, with his back to his uncle who could not see his face, half smiled and winked at her. He eased the knapsack from her shoulders and held it tightly. "It will remind me of what I have gained." He turned and left the cage.

Malcolm swung the door shut. The clatter of steel smashing against steel echoed in the small basement. He snapped the lock in place, then grasped the bars. "I'll be back later to educate you." He smirked and turned to Thor. "Come. I must make my appearance at the square. Not a word about this find, boy, or I'll throw you to the wolves."

Thor glanced back at Grace as he followed his uncle up the stairs. His coy smile suggested his actions didn't align with his thoughts.

The thud of a closing door drifted to her ear followed by silence as the men left the house. Consumed in darkness, she reached out, found the bars and gripped them tightly. She pushed and tugged, testing their strength. They remained solid. Feeling her way to the door, she fingered the lock, jerking it back and forth. It too held strong. Imagining the placement of the bars, she threw her weight against it. A sharp pain exploded in her shoulder, but the door didn't budge.

As she rubbed her shoulder, she formed a plan. They hadn't searched her, so they hadn't found the knife—the only weapon

she carried—beneath her jacket. She looked up, not remembering if there was a top to the cage. Reaching up, she felt only air.
She recalled the lighter she had picked up the day before and
pulled it from her pocket. The small flame illuminated the piece
of wood covering the cage. It was crudely fastened with wire
ties.

To reach the top, she had to scale the door. She placed her
foot on a horizontal bar and lifted herself up to take a closer
look at the ties. They appeared weak, but dozens of them held
the board in place. She'd have to work fast. Wrapping her arm
around a bar to secure her balance, she held the lighter with one
hand while the other worked on the wire ties. Stronger than she
initially thought, it took more time than she had estimated to
break them with her knife. Still, she moved onto the next one,
then the next one.

Her arms ached from the awkward position, but she continued. With each snap of wire, she drew closer to freedom. She
soon learned the weakest spot of the wire and moved quicker.

Two dozen wires later, she heard the scrape of a door. Her
heart beat louder and her breath caught in her throat. Lowering
herself to the floor, she hid the lighter and placed the knife in
the sheath beneath her jacket, a place she could grab it quickly.

She pressed herself to the far side of the cell and waited.
Malcolm was a big man, but even big men bled out. She tilted
her ear towards the door and listened. In the silence, she heard
footsteps touch the stairs softly as if they sneaked, not entered
their own house where they'd scuttle down the stairs without
thought to sound.

She held her breath as the footsteps neared. A dim light
struck the bottom step, a dimmer light than Malcolm's. When
the shadow appeared, concealed behind the light, she saw it
smaller than she anticipated.

"Shh," came the voice. The light approached the cage and
shone on her.

She held up her hand to block the glare from her eyes. "I
can't see." When he moved the light to the floor, she saw Thor

staring at her with an uneasy expression.

"We have to move fast." His breath came quickly. "My uncle will only be at the square a short time."

"Do you have the key?" She sprinted to the door.

"No, but I have a crow bar." He held up a long metal rod and pushed it into the metal loop of the lock. He clutched the bar with two hands and pulled it downward.

Grace watched, hoping the lock would snap quickly. She glanced into the young man's strained face and wondered why he had disobeyed his uncle and returned to set her free. Surely, he risked something, perhaps his life, to help her. Why? What was she to him?

His grunting grew louder, and the flashlight slipped from his grip, hit the floor and went out. He cursed in the darkness.

She flicked her lighter and illuminated the floor.

He grabbed the flashlight, banged it on his knee and the light came to life. "Hold this." He held it out to her. "Quickly." He glanced towards the stairs.

She grasped the light and shone it upon the lock.

He went to work again and with two hands solidly on the metal rod, he snapped the lock. After ushering her out, he closed the door, making it appear it secure. "Stay near. Be quick. Be silent."

She sprinted after Thor as he climbed the stairs and went to the door. He extinguished the light, then paused to look outside before exiting the house.

"Silence." He clasped her hand and led her away.

His hand felt strange in hers, yet she held it tightly as they crouched low and followed a narrow path into the trees. They had not gone far before he stopped and released her. A breath of light shone on the ground, and she realised his hand covered the flashlight to conceal it. When the light found a large shadow, he picked it up and gave it to her. It was her pack. She slipped it on quickly and watched him gather his own pack.

He was leaving Amherst? She tried to sort out his plan. Where did he plan to go? With her? Why would he risk everything for her?

"Here." He thrust a thick, three-foot long stick into her hand. "Don't lose it."

"What's it for?" The end felt heavy and looking closer, she found a dark wad of material stuck to it.

"I don't have time to explain." He pulled her along. "Can you see enough to follow?"

"Yes." He was a mere shadow, but the clear sky provided enough light in the thin trees for her to see him.

"Good. We have to get to the river quickly."

Thor moved swiftly and at times, she stumbled over twigs and stones to keep up. The pack bounced against her back and branches slapped her face. She pushed herself to run faster as the distance between them grew. Her legs strained and her heart beat so fast it pounded in her ears. Occasionally, he glanced back to see if she still followed, but he never slowed, running as if the grim reaper stalked his every move.

Avoiding capture by his uncle had motivated their swift flight but after travelling more than a mile at this speed, it seemed pointless as he could never catch up to them; he probably didn't even know she had escaped his cage yet. He'd only close the gap between them if he travelled by means other than foot, which in this narrow trail meant either by dirt bike or horse.

She glanced at the trail behind her and saw nothing. Taking her eyes off the trail for that brief second meant she didn't see the tree root, and she tripped over it. The short-lived free fall through space ended with a hard thud against the ground. She rolled several times, then sprang to her feet with the three-foot long stick still in her hand. Gasping for air, she took one step and pain shot up her leg. Looking down, she saw a large scrape on her lower right calf. Blood dripped from it.

"We can't stop." Thor paused only long enough to pull her forward. "We're almost there, and then you can rest."

A long, mournful howl echoed in the air. Several more followed.

Grace stared into the darkness, then looked at Thor. The

starlight revealed a ghastly expression, one that sent a ripple of terror through her body. "What is it?"

"Coywolves." He jerked her forward. "Run."

She tried to ignore the pain and keep moving, but she couldn't keep up with him. Pushing herself hard, the ache grew. Wherever their destination, it needed to appear soon before she collapsed. Several hundred feet later, she heard the howling and yapping of fast-moving animals behind her. She had seen coyotes many times. Although they could be dangerous when a lone person travelled the woods and encountered a pack, they seldom bothered two or more people. Still, she had never heard of coywolves. Were they wolves or coyotes?

The yapping grew nearer, and Thor stopped. He held up his stick and flicked a spark below it. The thick wad of material on the top burst into flames.

"Come quickly." He ushered her forward.

When she reached him, he touched his flame to the end of her stick to ignite it. "Why do we need torches?"

"To fight those." He pointed to from where they had come. "Watch your back." He grasped her hand and moved quickly along the trail. The flame fanned out behind him, but remained lit.

Sudden movement on the path made Grace look back. What she saw stole her breath. The large wolf-like animals looked like coyotes supersized. Twenty feet away, the beasts slowed to a trot. She counted four. The one in the front bared its teeth in a low growl while the other three howled at the gibbous moon.

Thor slowed his pace and pulled her closer. "Coywolves."

"Your uncles?"

"Yeah." He glanced at her uneasily. "He doesn't care about recovery. His goal is not to let us escape. He uses it as a deterrent." He swung his torch behind them. "They fear fire. It will keep them at bay."

"How long will the torches last?" She clung to him and positioned her torch between her and the animals.

"About twenty minutes."

"How long will it take us to get to the river?"

"Five."

"Do they fear water?"

"No." He winced. "But they will not cause us harm in deep water if we are in a boat."

"We have a boat?"

He smirked. "Of course. They will lose our scent in the water."

A small drop struck Grace's nose. A second drop hit her cheek and ran down her chin. "Rain," she mouthed. It would douse their torches, leaving them exposed.

"Hurry, but not too quickly." He urged her forward. "If they sense fear, they may attack even if we carry fire."

For several moments, they staggered and stumbled through the brush, dividing their attention between the trail ahead and the coywolves trailing them. The animals reduced the distance between them and the flame and snapped at the air as if to draw fear from their intended victims. The pitter-patter of rain increased, striking the leaves on the trees and dripping to the forest floor.

Grace stared at her torch, wishing the rain would ease long enough for them to be in the boat and on the river. But her wish went ungranted, and a flash lit up the sky. Her arm ached from holding the torch, but her white-knuckle grip kept it a loft. The tension building in her body and the growing pain in her calf exhausted her breath.

"We're here," he said. "Stand your ground. Take this." He thrust his torch into the hand he had held.

She kept glancing between the beasts that approached slowly, Thor pulling a boat from the bushes and the dying flames at the end of the torches. The steady rain dripped down her hair and into her eyes and with no hand to wipe them, her vision blurred. "Hurry!" she cried. She heard him struggle to pull the boat free from the bushes.

The lead coywolf remained ten feet away. It stood firmly on its front paws and lowered its back end, all the time snapping and snarling at the air. The three following it replicated the stance and joined in on the yelping.

The sound pierced Grace's ears, sending tremors down her neck and stirring her gut acids. It shook her eardrums like the sound of gunfire on that horrible night her father died. It mixed with the lightning and then the thunder, recreating the nightmare on the street outside of Montreal. Her life for the past several months flashed before her eyes: being stranded at Killarney, never reaching Thunder Bay where her mother had gone before the meteor had struck, the horrible clashes for food, the bloody and maimed victims, her father as he faced death to allow her to escape...

Her plans hadn't involved being attacked by coywolves. She needed to get home to find whatever family remained. She had to keep the promise she made to her father. Ignoring the pain and ripples of fear threatening to shake her knees from beneath her, she braced herself for the imminent attack. The two torches jutted out from her midsection, ready to strike the pack leader. She curled her lip and let out a roar of her own, hoping to drown the sounds assaulting her ears.

A faint splash told her the boat had reached water, but she didn't remove her eyes from the lead coywolf. His stance had changed, and he looked ready to attack. Her mouth drained of spit, and her howl sounded dry and cracked.

"Ready," said Thor, breathless. He took his torch from her hand. "Slowly. Back up." He held the torch in front of him as far as he could reach.

Grace did the same, watching her flame slowly die in the rain. When the lead coywolf leapt into the air, she braced herself and did what her father ordered her to do to live: go for the kill. She drove the torch into the open mouth of the animal and plunged it deep into its throat.

The coywolf dropped to the ground, squirming and yelping in pain. Gone was the instinct to attack, replaced by the desire to survive.

She withdrew the torch and found it extinguished. Before

she had time to think, the three remaining coywolves attacked. She struck the one who turned on her across the snout with all her might. It yelped but came back for more.

Thor slashed at the two beasts before him, scorching their noses. It did not deter them, and they snapped wildly at him. The torch slammed down on the snout of one of them, and the animal yelped and jumped back. He wound up and swung the torch across the jaw of the other. Sparks flew into the air and the rain quickly doused them.

The coywolf recoiled, turned and raced away into the night.

Grace held her fireless stick as a golf club and heaved it forward. It struck the beast across the throat, quieting its yapping. It drew back, shook its head, then leapt into the air. Again, she struck the animal with a mighty swing, sending it crashing into the trees.

The dying flames of Thor's torch was the only light illuminating the scene before them. Darkness crept in from the shadows and forced him and Grace towards the water's edge.

She glanced back and saw the bow of the boat resting on dry land and the stern bobbing in the gentle flow of the river. If she jumped for the boat, she might escape. But she couldn't leave Thor. The image of the coywolves leaping into the boat, too, erased the thought of jumping for it. They could never fight the beasts in the boat. They had to ensure the animals never got on board it.

A sharp yelp made her turn. Thor had beaten the spirit out of the final coywolf standing and continued to pummel it until the embers of his torch completely disappeared.

She grabbed his arm. "Let's go."

He turned to run, but the coywolf she had sent into the bushes had recovered and leapt at his leg. The pair rolled across the ground, the animal's teeth deeply buried into his flesh. Thor cried out, swinging his stick wildly.

Grace flung her pack from her shoulders, unzipped the top pocket and pulled out the red-handled flare gun. She flicked off the safety and pointed her last shell towards the shadows wrestling in the bushes. Her father had taught her how to shoot years ago, but flare guns were not as accurate as a regular gun. Manufacturers had constructed them to hit the sky, and who could miss that target?

The end of the gun followed the rolling bodies, her finger twitching on the trigger. She waited, hoping she didn't wait too long for a good shot. Suddenly, the coywolf sprang back as Thor's club struck its jaw. Before she released the shot, it clamped onto his leg and started dragging him away.

She held her breath, stilled her shaking hands and pulled the trigger. The sharp pop was followed by loud yelping. The flare struck the coywolf in the chest and burst into flames. It sizzled and snapped, lighting up the night.

Grace lurched forward and pulled Thor to his feet. "Come on!" She lugged him to the boat and flipped him inside. Grabbing her pack, she took one last look at the scene before her. The three severely wounded coywolves yelped and whined in unison. A shadow on the trail behind the flare caught her attention. It was the lone beast that had run off, returning to finish what it had started. She turned, threw her pack into the boat and pushed off.

Thor grabbed an oar and pushed them further into the stream where the current caught the boat and pulled it away.

The coywolf stood at the water's edge, yapping and snarling, but it did not follow.

Grace grasped the other oar and helped guide the boat to the centre of the wide river, far away from the shore in case other beasts awaited them. Hearing breathing strained with pain, she looked at Thor. His pant leg was torn to shreds, exposing the gash from sharp teeth. Even in the dim light, she could see the blood oozing from the wound.

She placed her oar inside the boat, then dropped to her knees before him. Pulling her pack to her, she dug inside for the makeshift first aid kit. It didn't contain much—a small bottle of rubbing alcohol, a few pieces of gauze to act as dressing, two rectangular lengths of clothe for bandages, and half a dozen safety pins—but it would help stop the bleeding and keep the injury clean.

"Your flashlight," she said. He handed it to her and she shone it on his leg. The damage made her freeze. She'd never treated a wound this serious.

"Do the best you can." His weary breath fell upon her forehead.

His battered face had aged since she met him. "Why did you do it?" The question nagged her since he had arrived in the basement to rescue her. She placed the remaining gauze over the wound, then poured rubbing alcohol on it to clean the cut. She held it in place until it stuck to the damaged skin.

He gasped in pain and spoke between clenched teeth. "I couldn't stand by and let him keep you prisoner."

"But he was your uncle. You lived with him." She wrapped a long strip of cloth around his leg to keep the gauze in place and to keep the dirt out.

"Only because he had claimed my mother." He lowered his eyes.

"What about your father?" She regretted the question as soon as it left her mouth. The question had been asked of her too many times, and she knew the pain it ignited.

"He died the year of the meteor."

"You leave your mother behind?"

He shook his head. "She died last fall from the flu."

Grace paused to study the man who still held the spirit of a boy. His dark hair, wet and dripping with rainwater, concealed even darker eyes beneath. When he looked up, she saw something she hadn't seen for a long time. A smile played at the corner of her mouth. "Why didn't you claim me for yourself?"

"My uncle would have challenged me." He frowned. "And when he won you, I'd be outcast. I'd have no place to go."

"Is that why he wanted to keep me secret? So others would not challenge *him*?"

"Yes. There are men bigger and stronger than Uncle Malcolm who would desire a girl like you."

"A girl like me?" She clipped three safety pins in place to hold the cloth.

"Young. Healthy. Beautiful." He looked out onto the water.

Her face grew warm, and she returned her things to her pack. "I'm hardly beautiful," she mumbled. "Darkness conceals the flaws."

"Maybe." He smirked.

"So, where will this river take us?" She turned off the flashlight to save the batteries and to better hide their position on the river.

"Towards the Bay of Fundy. There's a trail several miles downstream that will take us across the north side of the mountain range."

"Are you going all the way to Margaree Harbour?"

"If you'll let me."

It had been so long since she had company, she felt uncertain about the idea. Her first reaction was to leave him at the first chance, to strike out alone. It suited her better. Then again, he had saved her life, returned her freedom. The least she could do was give him a chance at finding a new home. "I'd be happy to have the company. You're not worried about the fierce Mc-Donald clan?" She smiled, wondering if he remembered the threat she had made to his uncle.

"They strike fear in the hearts of many, but I want to join them."

"I'm certain they will have a boy like you. Young. Healthy. Handsome." Her face warmed again and this time, *she* gazed upon the water.

A bashful grin lit up his face, and his voice grew soft. "When I first heard of the clans rising again, I was worried, but"—he caught her gaze—"then I saw it as a good thing."

Confused, she studied his face. He wasn't joking. "What news have you heard?"

"That the clans are growing strong and securing the province, returning law and order. They have reinstated the name New Scotland over the land they have secured. Rumour has it, the gangs in Truro fear them."

"The McDonald Clan?"

"All the clans of old. The McDonalds and MacNeils are leading them."

Incredible. The stories her father had told in desperation were supposed to be only wishful ideas. Thinking back to when they had left Margaree Harbour, she remembered the words her grandfather had spoken to her father, his son. Gramps had been a master of the sea, had built his own home and had never let his Gaelic slip into the past. He had whispered secrets about a gathering, but she had no idea of what sorts.

A smile creased her lips. Home lay near. The only thing that stood between her and it were the gangs of Truro. Alone, her chances were slim but with Thor Gillanders as a companion, the task didn't feel so formidable.

The rain increased, but it didn't dampen her spirits. Somewhere in those dark swirling clouds above shone a ray of sunshine. She'd find it and let it carry her home.

Ali House

A native Newfoundlander, Alison is a graduate of the Fine Arts program at Sir Wilfred Grenfell College (MUN), and past recipient of the Golden Crescent Wrench Award. Her short story, 'The Price of Beauty' won the December 2018 Kit Sora Award.

Her first novel, *The Six Elemental*, was released in October 2016.

She is the only person to have short fiction published in all of Engen's open-call short story compilations, including *Sci-Fi from the Rock*, *Fantasy from the Rock*, *Chillers from the Rock*, *Bluenose Paradox*, and *Kit Sora: The Artobiography*.

Her second novel, *The Fifth Queen*, was published in March 2019.

She currently resides in Halifax, Nova Scotia, where she works in arts administration and spends more time than a person should in and around theaters.

Game Plan

As John half-listened to his co-workers talk about how their lives were so much better under The Emperor's rule, he imagined how wonderful it would be once the Resistance swarmed the palace and killed them all. He had spent the past four months working in the palace, making friends with the other employees, and proving himself to be trustworthy, but secretly he had been placed there by the Resistance. It had been exhausting to keep up the charade for so long, but he was fuelled by his conviction that the world would be a better place once The Emperor was dead.

Although he was too young to recall how life had been before The Emperor took control of the government, the elders remembered. They told stories of democracy and freedom, where people were allowed to choose where they worked, where they lived, and who they loved – when citizens could go for a walk without worrying that they might be arrested for no discernable reason. Nowadays everyone's life was controlled by The Emperor, except for those within the Resistance, who hid from the prying eyes of the militia and spent most of their time plotting to bring down The Emperor and end his tyrannical rule.

The elders had been hesitant about John's long-term plan, not wanting to wait so many months for action, but he had convinced them that it would be necessary. The more time he had, the more trusted he'd be, and the easier it would be to infiltrate the palace's security.

And, good as his word, he had done just that. He'd memorized layouts, cultivated relationships, and learned what time would be the best for an attack. Tonight he would put the final part of his plan into motion. Tonight he would taste success.

Although he had a job on the palace cleaning staff, he'd made friends with many of the security workers, and a few weeks ago they started inviting him to their after-work gatherings. When their shift was over, they'd go to an unoccupied room in the basement to drink, laugh, and talk about how great life was for them. They believed wholeheartedly in The Emperor and his master plan and enjoyed the power they received as part of the palace security staff. Although it disgusted John beyond belief, he played along, smiling and laughing, and pretending to be one of them.

Tonight, however, he was done with playing. He waited an appropriate length of time before snapping his fingers and declaring that he'd left his coat in the employee room. He informed the group that he'd be back in a few minutes and not to drink everything without him. They laughed and went back to their discussion before he'd left the room.

That was the easy part. The employee room was on the first floor, but he had to make it to the third floor without being spotted. Earlier he'd lifted Everett's key-card from his pocket, since Everett had worked here the longest and had the highest security clearance. Providence seemed to be on John's side as Everett's key-card had no trouble unlocking the door to the third floor. The hall was empty as he made his way towards the electrical room, and one quick wave of the key-card triggered the sensor and unlocked the door.

Most of the palace's electricity was wired through this room, including the security fences. John slipped inside and quickly got to work, first turning the electricity off before setting about destroying the wires and fuses. The Resistance fighters were hidden outside, waiting for the hum of the electric fences to go quiet so that they could charge into the palace and kill their oppressors.

He wished that there were windows in the room, so that he could see the fighters charging. The security teams had grown soft, confident in their secure surroundings, so they would be easily overpowered. Without electricity, the palace wouldn't be able to go into panic mode and every room, and every person, would be accessible.

As much as John wanted to be out there, fighting amongst his people, he knew that he had to make sure the electricity stayed down. Maybe someone would come in here and find him, and maybe he would be killed, but if the Resistance succeeded, his death would be worth it.

"Simulation over. Kill count is one hundred and fourteen, including The Emperor. The palace has fallen."

Kline removed the VR helmet and let out a substantial sigh. Even with an accelerated time rate, spending four months in virtual reality was a long time.

"Great job, sir," a young man said as he walked over to take the helmet. "We've had fourteen others try the simulation and none of them came close to succeeding."

"Of course not," Kline said, fighting the urge to roll his eyes. If you wanted something done right...

There were four computers along the far wall and in front of each was an employee quickly extrapolating the data from the simulation.

"This will be very helpful, sir," the young man continued, putting the helmet back on the equipment table. "We thought that we had covered all the bases, but you've done it again. We had no idea that someone would risk going undercover for so long."

"You'd be surprised what some people are capable of when they truly believe in something."

The young man smiled. "I'd be surprised if there was another person on this planet who was as capable as you. You have an incomparable mind and an awe-inspiring ability to solve any problem."

Kline couldn't help smiling at the compliment. "That's what makes me The Emperor." He straightened his suit and walked towards the door. "I know that you still have data to extrapolate, but I'd suggest that we immediately obtain backup generators for the security fences and palace grid."

The man nodded enthusiastically. "Long live the Emperor."

Kline held back a satisfied laugh. Yes, long live me.

Authentic New Island Experience™

Looking for an exciting place to travel? Why not visit New Island Ltd.! Formerly known as Newfoundland, trust us when we say the only thing that's changed is the name! Experience our stunning vistas and breath-taking views, while enjoying the Authentic New Island Personalities™ that the island is known for. Wander through one of our many small towns and admire the natural scenery while getting to know the local characters. Or, if you're looking for a more modern experience, visit the bustling city of New St. John's where you can grab a pint with a pal and dine on the finest local delicacies!

Worried about your daily consumer allowance while on the island? Don't be! Purchase a Local Traveller's Pass to cover all your basic needs or get more bang for your buck with a High Roller's Pass. Or upgrade to an Unlimited Pass and consume as much as you desire! Whatever your needs are, we have a Pass for you!

See majestic ocean creatures on a whale watching boat ride or travel north on an iceberg tour! Hike the magnificent mountains of Gros Morne Park or discover the magic of Lanse Aux Meadows! Get 'Screeched In' and eat as much Jigg's Dinner as you can handle! New Island Ltd. has it all!

There was a brief moment of silence as the commercial ended, the jingling tune fading into nothingness as the logo for New Island Ltd. appeared on the screen. The logo remained for a few seconds before changing into an image of rolling waves beneath a cliff. The jingle started up again and the commercial repeated itself for the seventh time.

As much as Dana hated the commercial, she couldn't handle the silence of the apartment. She needed some kind of sound in the background, and this was the only channel that didn't cost any money to watch.

If Jocelyn had been here, she would have told Dana to turn the television off before that jingle drove her insane. She also would have told her to stop crying so much. All those tears would surely dehydrate her, and she'd run the risk of going over her daily water allowance.

But that was the problem. That was why Dana couldn't stop crying.

Jocelyn wasn't here.

©

"How ya' gettin' on?"

Dana snapped back into reality. The lush green forest she'd been dreaming of was replaced by the hard, plastic truth of the Valley Mall food court she was currently sitting in. Grass, leaves, and sunshine quickly transformed into Some Nice™ restaurants and Best Sort™ shops that populated malls all across the island.

Turning to her right, Dana looked up at the smiling brunette whose cheerful voice had shattered her daydream.

"Are you Jocelyn?" she asked.

The brunette nodded. "Sorry I'm late. There was a hell o'va line up at Timmy's. Should'a known better than th' think there wouldn't be a line up at th' mall." She took a sip from the cup in her hand and sat down across from Dana. "So, yer lookin' for a roomie?"

Nodding slowly, Dana wondered what she'd gotten herself in to. When they'd spoken over the phone to set up the meeting, Jocelyn hadn't sounded so... small town.

"And you're looking to move out of the boarding house?" Dana asked, trying to keep her voice pleasant.

Jocelyn smiled. "Yup. Gotta feel some freedom under me wings. Them women running th' boardin' houses got eyes like hawks. Can barely take a breath without one of 'em knowin'."

Dana tried to return the smile, but she knew it must look forced. "And the price of rent won't be a problem?"

She nodded again. "I gotta job at th' Some Nice™ Bakery on West Street, sos I can afford th' rent. I assumes all th' taxes are included? Water, electricity, police, fire, whatnot?"

"They are. We get a bit of a break, because there are two apartments in the house, so we share the city maintenance and local maintenance taxes with the other tenants. Also, the landlord's an old family friend who babysat me when I was younger, so he was able to give me the family rate instead of the unmarried woman's rate."

"Ah, that's why th' rent's so affordable," she smirked. "Heck, I'd let someone babysit me now if it'd get me a deal like tha' one."

Dana couldn't help laughing. It seemed that Jocelyn had a sense of humour, which was encouraging. "Would you like to see the apartment?" she asked. "It's only one block away."

Jocelyn's eyes widened. "You lives near th' mall? Whatta grand deal. I'd love ta see th' place."

Dana stood up and gestured for Jocelyn to follow her.

She barely said anything during the walk, as Jocelyn didn't stop talking about what it had been like to move from Rocky Harbour to Corner Brook. Every word was pleasant and absolutely dripping with her North-coast accent. Dana wondered if the accent would lessen after a few years of living here or if it'd stay that way forever. As much as she didn't want to give up her apartment and move into one of those boarding houses, she wasn't sure if she could handle listening to that every single day.

They quickly reached the apartment, which was on the second floor of a former two-story house. "So, what'd happened ta your old roomie?" Jocelyn asked as they made their way through the apartment. "Oh, sorry," she said, stopping in her tracks. She paused and took a moment to compose herself. "So, what happened to the person you were living with? Why did she move out?"

It took Dana a few seconds to comprehend what had just been said. The un-accented words sounded as if they should be coming from someone else's mouth, but there was nobody else around.

Jocelyn laughed. "Sorry about that. You know what it's like growing up in a Designated Small Town. All accent, all the time. It's a hard habit to shake."

"Wow." Dana was truly taken aback. "You sound so normal now. Not that – I mean – it's just that... Oh, god..." She put her head in her hands. She needed to stop talking.

"It's okay," Jocelyn said, her voice light and cheerful. "After eighteen years in a DST, it's hard not to put the accent on whenever I'm in public. I always get paranoid that tourists might be within earshot, and I've made it this many years without getting fined for 'ruining the illusion'." She dramatically rolled her eyes.

Dana laughed, feeling the tension melting away. "Sorry. I grew up in Corner Brook, so I've never had to deal with laws that strict. I can't imagine what it's like."

"Honestly, it's like anything else – you get used to it. But it's refreshing to live somewhere that you can relax. Performing 24/7 is *exhausting*." Jocelyn sat down on the couch. "But I was asking about your previous roommate. Do you mind talking about her?"

She shook her head. "Erin... Erin had been friends with me

since junior high. When we moved in here, we knew that it was only a matter of time before her boyfriend proposed and she'd get married and they'd get a house to live in. Sure enough, a few months later, he did, and they started wedding planning. Then, a few weeks ago, about two months before the wedding, his relatives in Nova Scotia contacted him, saying that they were willing to sponsor his move off the island. The only problem was that they couldn't afford to sponsor two people. He didn't want this opportunity to pass him by, so he called off the wedding, did up the paperwork, and moved away. After that, Erin married the first decent guy she came across and moved out. They've got a house up on Glenhaven Boulevard."

Jocelyn let out a slow breath. "Wow. That sucks."

"Yeah. Makes me never want to get my hopes up. About anything."

"Well, if it helps my application, I don't plan on getting married any time soon." Jocelyn smiled.

Dana returned the smile. "It definitely tips the scales in your favour."

©

Jocelyn moved in a few days later and the two of them quickly grew close. At first Dana found the way that Jocelyn unconsciously slipped into her old accent a bit much, but she knew that it wasn't done on purpose. Jocelyn was a genuinely nice person, and Dana was glad to have met her – even with all of her Designated Small Town tendencies.

"You've got to play the game," Jocelyn said, tapping Dana playfully on the nose.

Dana frowned and waved Jocelyn's hand away. She'd come home from her date early, having decided that enough was enough two hours in. She'd been hoping her roommate would offer commiseration, but apparently that wasn't to be the case.

"I don't want to," Dana complained, walking over to the

couch and falling onto it dramatically. "Dating is stupid."

"It won't kill you," Jocelyn replied, crossing her arms. "You know, you always have to make things more difficult than they actually are."

Dana frowned again. She wasn't the person who'd thought of mandatory dating for all citizens, or the person who'd included it in Govern-Corp's Tourism Laws, so how was she the difficult one? It wasn't her fault that the guy she'd gone out with tonight had been utterly wrong for her, so why should she be punished for not wanting to go out with him again?

Jocelyn sat down next to her. "The Rom-Cops will be easier on you if you look like you're making an effort. You don't have to get married, just date him for a few months before making up an excuse to dump him, and then move on to the next guy."

"But it's so stupid..."

"You know that if you don't go on a date at least once a week, you'll be fined. And you've already got two fines on your record. A few more of those and they'll get suspicious and investigate you, which wouldn't be good for either of us." Jocelyn gave her a knowing look. "Do you want to end up in a detention centre for the rest of your life – or worse – all because you didn't want to go on a few stupid dates?"

Dana sighed. "I know, I know. I'm just tired of it all."

"Well, grab a cup of Some Nice™ coffee, get your second wind, and suck it up."

She gave Jocelyn an unimpressed look. "I cannot believe you just said that."

Jocelyn smirked. "You can take the girl out of the DST, but you can't take the DST out of the girl."

It would be wise to take Jocelyn's advice, and Dana knew it. Jocelyn knew how to look like she was following the government's rules while secretly maintaining her own agenda. Her pleasant attitude and friendliness with tourists had been noted by Govern-Corp, and whenever she'd 'accidentally' stepped out of line, they'd been much more lenient with her than they would with any other citizen.

Citizens living in DSTs were paid to act like charming locals for the tourists, and with the high cost of living on New Island Ltd., not many of them could afford not to. Living in a DST meant being constantly aware of the Quality Control Agents who patrolled the whole island, writing up anyone who was caught out of character or causing trouble for Govern-Corp.

It sounded like the worst kind of life to Dana, who'd surely be in a detention centre by now if she'd been unlucky enough to be born in a DST. Corner Brook was the perfect size for her – too big to be a quaint small town, but too small to be as bustling as the capital city. They still had to be friendly and nice to all the tourists, but not at the same level as those in DSTs.

"But he talked through the entire movie," Dana groaned, unable to let the subject drop. "It's been so long since I've been to one, and he had to ruin it with his incessant chatter."

Jocelyn laughed. "You could have simply avoided the movies next time."

"Ugh. When you say things like that it sounds so... rational." She sat up and put her head on Dana's shoulder. "I just wish that I could date who I wanted."

"The mandate of Govern-Corp is to promote the prosperity of New Island Ltd. and all its citizens through a rich tourism trade, which includes creating a safe, non-political environment where tourists from all over the world will not feel uncomfortable." When Jocelyn finished quoting policy, she kissed Dana on top of her head. "At least they can't govern us inside our home."

A smile appeared on Dana's face. "Yeah. At least we have that."

Outside these walls they could never be anything more than friends, but in here nobody could tell them that what they felt was wrong.

"Have you ever wondered what it would be like to live normally?" Jocelyn asked softly. "Before Govern-Corp purchased this island and the Tourism Laws were passed?"

"All the time," Dana replied honestly.

"What if it were possible? What if we could?"

She straightened up. "What are you talking about?"

Jocelyn leaned in close and her voice went low. "Vineland."

Dana was confused. "You mean, what the Vikings called this island back in 1000 AD? Are you talking about the Viking settlement at Lanse Aux Meadows? That's even more tourist-themed than Rocky Harbour."

"No," Jocelyn shook her head. "The new Vineland. Surely you've heard the rumours. No Tourism Laws, no taxes or fines... It's the promised land."

It sounded vaguely familiar to Dana, but in a fairy-tale kind of way. Vineland was a fantasy for adults, a long-abandoned settlement that had been reclaimed by people sick of living under Govern-Corp's rules. It was supposed to be like the good old days, before Canada sold the island and all its resources to Govern-Corp for a tidy sum, and it was most likely a complete and total fiction.

Anyone who talked openly about going there was never heard from again. Some dreamed that those people had actually made it to Vineland, but Dana wasn't so optimistic. They had most likely 'disappeared', like the majority of the island's unhappy locals. Troublemakers didn't last long on New Island Ltd.

"Vineland's a fantasy," she replied. "It doesn't exist."

Jocelyn gave her shoulder a squeeze. "Ah, there's that pessimism I love so much."

"If it existed, I'm sure Govern-Corp would quash it. They'd destroy something like that twenty times over."

"But," Jocelyn was getting excited again. "It would actually be in their best interest to have a place like that. Somewhere for the rabble to go, to stay away from tourists, and stop us from being so contrary in front of them. The existence of Vineland benefits everyone."

Her enthusiasm was infectious, but Dana couldn't stop worrying.

"Still..." Dana said. "It's illegal to move without alerting Populace Control. What if they find out what we're doing and have us arrested or put in some dark hole for the rest of our lives?" There were more than enough stories about locals who didn't obey the Tourism Laws and had to be rehabilitated, or sent to detention centres, or forced to work in mines, never seeing the sunlight ever again. Did she really want to risk her comfortable life for something that didn't exist?

"And what if we're very, very careful and we don't get caught?" Jocelyn's eyes pleaded with her. "Haven't you ever wanted more than this? Haven't you ever wanted to live on your own terms?"

Dana frowned. Honestly, she'd never thought of a life other than this one. Sometimes she'd dream about what it would be like to live somewhere not ruled by Govern-Corp, but it was a pipe dream – something that would never happen. She didn't have rich relatives who could sponsor a move off the island, and she'd never be able to save up enough, so why bother dreaming about it?

Although she still had her doubts, Dana had a feeling that Jocelyn would try to find Vineland no matter what. If she agreed to this crazy plan, then at least she could try to keep Jocelyn safe.

Maybe they'd discover that Vineland actually did exist. And if it didn't, at least they'd still be together.

Dana sighed. "You have to promise me that you'll be careful? That we'll be careful?"

Jocelyn's eyes lit up. "I promise."

It was all going according to plan, until Jocelyn fell ill. One day she was fine, and the next she was in the hospital with Viral Strain 14. Dana had no idea how it happened or how she'd avoided getting the virus as well, but even though the doctors explained that VS-14 only affected a small percentage of the population, Dana was too paranoid to be comforted.

Had Govern-Corp somehow realized what they were planning? Had Jocelyn said something to the wrong person? Asked the wrong question? Drawn attention to herself?

They'd spent the past five months slowly gathering supplies and information, even going on camping trips in Gros Morne to account for the purchase of certain items, like lamps and bedrolls and backpacks. Dana didn't think that they'd done anything out of the ordinary, but how could she really know?

It was possible that she was overthinking this. Jocelyn's illness could very well have been natural. It might have happened no matter what.

Then again, it wasn't unusual for Govern-Corp's enemies to come down with life-threatening illnesses. There were twenty-three Viral Strains on record, and almost every person who'd passed away from them had been known trouble-makers. Had Jocelyn's name found her way on one of Govern-Corp lists? Was Dana's name also on a list?

Jocelyn had tried to calm Dana's fears, but both of them knew that Jocelyn would never leave the hospital. As the hours passed, she grew sicker and sicker, and nothing the doctors did seemed to make any difference.

Throughout Jocelyn's quick and deadly illness, Dana had to pretend to be a friend and was only allowed to visit during general visiting hours. Whenever she complained about how unfair it was, which was a lot, Jocelyn would smile and tell her to "play the game." More than ever Dana wished that there wasn't a game to play.

She hadn't been there at the end, which was one of her biggest regrets. She should have tried harder or made up some kind of lie. Even though she knew that Jocelyn wouldn't want her to take unnecessary risks, Dana wished that she'd been there.

She could still hear Jocelyn's last words to her, echoing inside her head. "Be happy," Jocelyn had said, but that seemed impossible now. Dana had no idea what she was going to do without her. All she could manage was to sit in the apartment they'd once shared and cry.

Her gaze fell on the two backpacks in the corner of the room. If things had gone as planned, Jocelyn and she would leave for Vineland next week, but now that would never happen.

It would make sense for Dana to stay here and continue her life, but in the moment that Jocelyn took her last breath, everything had changed. Dana didn't want this. She didn't want to live in a world where she couldn't hold her partner's hand in public, where she had to hide her feelings and pretend to be 'normal', all because some corporation was afraid that her actions might cause controversy. She wanted to live somewhere where she could stay by her partner's hospital bed day and night, where she didn't have to be so afraid.

Wiping the tears from her eyes, she stood up and walked over to the backpacks.

©

This was the part Dana was most afraid of. This was where everything could go terribly wrong.

There weren't many other cars on the highway this late at night. With the high cost of gas, vehicle registration, and licence fees, most people couldn't afford to drive. The only reason Dana had a car was because her parents had gifted it to her before retiring in Twillingate. She'd never bothered to drive it before meeting Jocelyn, but it had become integral to their plan.

Outside Corner Brook, she stopped at a gas station along the highway to purchase a snack and fill up the tank before continuing on. She felt strangely calm, but as she took the turn towards the Port au Port Peninsula, her stomach filled with a horde of nervous butterflies.

Twenty minutes after the turn off, she reached the spot. Taking in a deep breath, Dana pressed down on the gas pedal. She turned the wheel sharply to her right before slamming on the brakes and swinging the wheel to the left. The car sped across the highway and drove off the road, heading for the trees. As the car bounced and jumped over the uneven terrain, Dana was glad she'd tightened her seatbelt, although that didn't stop her head from taking a nasty bump against the door. Luckily the airbags deployed as soon as the front of the car crashed into a tree.

When it was all over, Dana sat in the car for a few minutes, trying to pull herself together. Her body felt sore and shaken, but she could still wiggle her fingers and toes, and her arms and legs worked. Her head hurt, but at least it was still on her neck.

Unbuckling her seatbelt, she opened the door and spilled out on to the ground. There were so many aches and pains that she was afraid to stop and list them, lest she be here for days. Pulling herself up onto her feet, she leaned against the car for a few seconds before moving on with the plan.

Opening the back door, she pulled off the blanket covering the two backpacks and removed everything from the car. If the information Jocelyn had gathered was correct, then she should have more than enough provisions to make the journey. She rolled up the blanket, shoved it into one of the backpacks, and shut the door.

When someone inevitably found her car, hopefully they'd

assume that she'd gone off the road accidentally, wandered into the woods while disoriented, and died of exposure. It was common for people to crash while trying to avoid hitting moose or other animals. Besides, who would fill up a gas tank before purposefully crashing their car – especially at these prices?

After checking that there was nobody else on the highway, she turned on her flashlight and looked towards the woods. Vineland was supposed to be hidden in there, somewhere. Hopefully it was. Hopefully she wouldn't die out here alone.

There was still time for her to give up, to stop this crazy plan, ditch the backpacks, and stay with the car. Someone would find her and bring her back to Corner Brook. She could go back to the life she knew and learn to cope, learn to adjust. Learn to settle for less.

But Dana didn't want that. She didn't want to bow down to a corporation that cared more about lining its pockets than the people who worked for it. She wanted revenge, she wanted happiness, she wanted freedom...

She wanted more.

Shouldering the backpacks, she walked towards the woods.

Samuel Bauer

Samuel Bauer is a proud mathematician, Shad alumni, and part-time storyteller.

Sam is one of only a handful of authors to be featured in all current *From the Rock* volumes. His previous stories include *The Locket, Precious Pieces Unknown, Dark Peaks* and *Nucklavee*, the latter two of which were in the bestselling *Chillers from the Rock* anthology.

In the Rising Flame

"Our world was birthed in flame. Make no mistake about it, children, it was birthed in flame. The atomic flames of the bombs, those flames of our own making mixed with the flame of the Earth itself."

The priest looked out over his flock, sweat dripping down his face in the hot Central American summer. He continued, "And the Flame is our strength! The flame that fuels our own fields, that keeps the northern winds from plunging our world into darkness and cold. It is only by the grace of Cariociecus that we do not plunge into the cold or become slaves of the heathens to our southern border!"

Goyo kept his head down and mopped the sweat from the back of his neck. The church was stiflingly hot, the sacred flames filling the air with soot that only occasionally slipped out of the windows.

"Our lives are luxurious to them, children! We are untainted by bestial desires, to things unmentionable in our holy places! They blaspheme the flame with blood, children!"

Goyo glanced out the window. He had been in here for about an hour, judging by the clouded sun. He wanted to get back to work; he was behind on his quota.

"So, follow me in prayer, children! So we may remain ever by the fire!"

The priest urged his flock to stand and led them in a prayer. The words sprang unbidden to Goyo's tongue; ever since the subjugation of Guerrero ten years ago, not a day had gone by that he hadn't needed to recite it.

"Nos sometemos a la llama, permitimos que nos purgue a nosotros y al mundo. Que el dios encarnado nunca nos eche de su abrazo."

Goyo shuffled out of the small church, pulled on his broad hat, and began to make his way home.

Approaching the farmhouse, he stuck his head in through the kitchen window. Esteban nodded, and continued weighing the crop. Goyo reached in and grabbed the whip from where it sat beside the sink. He unfurled the short thong of leather and started towards the poppy fields.

The tip traced errant, almost invisible paths in the soft ground of the field as he walked between the knee-tall flowers. The bulbs had been slit earlier in the day, and the opium had dribbled down it, coalescing like candle wax in large globs. He swished the whip absentmindedly as he watched one of the women scrape the white globs into a bag.

What was her name? Goyo couldn't remember; the slaves always came and went. He just thought of her as reliable. Her cuts were always that perfect depth: deep enough so the opium flowed freely, but shallow enough that it wouldn't pool in the bulb, wasting precious product. He gave her an almost friendly tap on the back with the end of his whip. She moved a little faster. She had been with Goyo for many years now. She even remembered his wife.

He could tell when he passed out of her section of the field. The slave here, a young boy from up north, had only just arrived, the scars of a soldier's training still red and inflamed. He cut too deep, both damaging the flower and leaving opium in the bulb. As he came to the boy, franticly trying to scrape every last morsel of product into the bag, he delivered a harsh blow to the back of the neck, causing the kid to yelp in pain. The biopsy scar that traced from the nape of his neck to the middle of his collarbone on the right became redder, the whip inflaming the tender flesh.

He would have to get the woman to tutor this one.

And so he continued through the fields, his hat deflecting the sun from his eyes until it dipped below its brim.

Goyo's arm was sore by the time he found his way home by the dusk's dim light. He rubbed the base of his fingers of his right hand between his left thumb and forefinger, feeling the coarseness of the calluses that the whip had built up there. Lighting a lamp in the dark kitchen, he made his way over to where Esteban had left the logbook. In the ebb and flow of the light, he inspected the numbers, written in Esteban's scrawl.

He was still a good ten kilos short of his quota, even with the amount he made up for today. His lip curled in a snarl at the newer slaves, the ones who cut too deep or too shallow for the opium to flow well. But then he caught himself. Ten kilos was a lot, even for the best of them, even for the woman. He contemplated stretching the load, diluting the fluid with something of similar qualities, but he dismissed the idea; that had always been his wife's contribution, and he did not know it well enough to risk both his and Esteban's wellbeing. Up until now, he had been lucky. For the past three years he had no need to cut the product. He rubbed his eyes. The year had been too dry, too hot. His production had been down. He wracked his brain for something he could have done differently, but there was nothing. He couldn't afford the cost of watering the crop manually, neither the misters themselves or the physical act of pumping the water. Like everything else in this place, he was trapped.

Resting his hands, he shuddered out of exhaustion.

Shannon K Green

A gifted author with a talent for the strange, Green has been recognized in both the genre community and the contemporary literary community for his pursuits. In the past, he has been shortlisted for the 1996 Arts and Letters Award, and later won the 2015 Audience Choice Steampunk Newfoundland Showcase.

Green's short fiction had appeared in *Fantasy from the Rock*, the bestselling *Chillers from the Rock*, and *The Hamthology*.

The Schedule

It was another pleasant day in the valley that Sunday. Televisions could be heard through the open windows of television rooms in most of the suburban homes in the neighbourhood; from other houses, the sounds of people playing various musical instruments could be heard. Just a perfect day to walk your animals in the park. Which is just what Ruby and Jack were doing, one leading a husky on a leash while the other was being led by little black cat.

The husky stopped to sniff everything it passed, occasionally lifting a leg to mark a tree it favoured but for the most part it wandered lazily behind Ruby. Jack, on the other hand, seemed to sprint from tree to tree chasing the sounds of squirrels and song birds in the upper branches. From time to time he would raise his arm until the leash would extend rigidly into whatever tree the cat was scaling. The couple took this walk every Sunday, as scheduled, but they enjoyed the trail that led them by the playground where they could see the children play and fantasize about having children themselves one day.

Across the park, a young couple was picnicking on a stretch of freshly mowed lawn, watching children play in a nearby playground. "Mitchell! Leonard!" the male called to two young boys. "It is now eleven thirty-five!" he said with meaning in his voice.

"Coming, Papa," the two boys said in near unison, marching obediently to a red and white striped blanket to accept sandwiches from their father. Only the children ate, it was just eleven thirty, after all. The adults would eat between noon and twelve thirty.

"Ruby, we should start heading home now," Jack said as calmly as he could manage with the cat dragging his arm into the sky again. "You did hear what time the man across the park said it was?"

"I heard," she said calmly, not changing her stride. She picked some sort of flower from a bush nearby, laughing when Jack gasped. "For heaven's sake, Jack, we're not children anymore. Why should we be frightened about straying from the schedule?"

"We have to follow the schedules as laid down by the Princess. The schedules provide the structure on which society is based. If the schedule falls into disarray then we might have…"

"Naps in the daytime. Meals at night. Cocks that crow for sunset. Total chaos," she concluded the credo for him. "I know that's what we've been taught, but remember that time last year? The time we were an entire hour late for bedtime last July? What ever happened to us for that besides being tired the next day? Nothing, same thing that happened to everybody else when they go off their schedule, I bet."

Jack looked at Ruby, gauging how serious she was about testing her theory, a theory she had been pushing him to test since the night their clock had stopped, and they had taken the extra hour before going to bed. He did not like the look in her eye as he turned away to start the homeward march; he knew they would be late for their own meal unless he carried the cat back to their apartment as it was.

"Jack, I have never heard of anybody being punished for not following their schedule precisely; their work rota, yes. And you'd expect to be punished for not showing up to your job. Never for staying awake longer than they should be. Not for visiting the washrooms at the wrong time. And never for eating late on their day off. Sure, there's always the odd tale told of somebody who vanishes after days of completely neglecting their assigned tasks, but they're just stories told to frighten us into following the rules. Can we please just walk and enjoy the day while the sun is out?"

"The Princess provides us with the schedule, the schedule provides us with order and productivity. If we break the schedule, then we disobey the Princess, and the Princess is the law," he retorted in a hoarse voice while pulling at the cat's leash as it began to scale another tree.

Ruby, now pulling at the leash as the dog started to follow Jack, asked, "Well, if the Princess cared about us, where was our punishment for the late night? Why wasn't I punished for skipping my break at work? What was the punishment for me skipping my last shopping day?"

"Ruby, we must be back to the house to eat during the appropriate time. If for no other reason, then for the fact that I am hungry and my shoulder hurts from walking this accursed cat we were saddled with when we requested a second dog."

"If the cat is so accursed, then why did you accept the license?" she shouted.

"Because I was told that would be our punishment for your minor infractions!" he shouted. "Because we could only have our second choice because you often took too long at the table and in the washroom on our off days. That's why I took the blasted cat. And if we don't get home and eat and get the dishes done, then we'll be turned down again!"

Ruby ran to him shouting, "Turned down again? Turned down again for what?"

"For a baby," he said with tears in his eyes. "We were turned down last year for staying up too late that night. The only reason we were given a second chance at all is because I had pictures of the broken clock."

From the corner of his eye Jack saw the dog bring up short and turned to face Ruby. She stood, face ashen and mouth hanging open in shock. "You mean she watches all the small things? Even the things we can't control?" she asked.

"Yes! That's what they've always told us and it's true. The Princess watches, the Princess sets the schedules and we have to follow the schedules, absolutely have to. Any deviation from what the Princess has decreed is punished," he nearly screamed. "We have to get home, we have to follow the schedule. If we hurry, we can just make it in time, but we really need to pick up our pace. I'll carry the cat, you drag the dog if you need to."

Suiting action to words, he scooped up the cat and began to briskly walk the path back towards their apartment. Satisfied when he heard Ruby taking a similar pace behind him, happier when she made it to his side. The pace Jack set, the fastest they would be allowed outside of exercise times, made conversation difficult and the pair said nothing until they were in their home preparing sandwiches for their lunch.

Spreading mustard onto a slice of bread, Ruby asked, "So what you're saying is that every time we've been turned down for something it's because one of us didn't follow the schedule?"

"No, not in every instance. Sometimes the Princess just wants us to follow a schedule we don't know along with the one we do know," Jack responded while he set the table. "I think we were turned down when we requested the dog first because it wasn't on Her schedule for us to get the dog then. Or maybe because there were no dogs available at the time. The Duchess made an offhand comment, Friday as I arrived at work, that we had to better follow the schedule if we hoped to be approved for a child."

"In that case, you might be mistaken, it could just be her ladyship's typical reminder to be on our best behaviour on our days off."

"Well, she stopped at my desk afterwards, reminding me that Schedule reviews would be happening soon and that I should be sure we followed ours to the second. It seemed more like a gentle nudge in her direction than one of her platitudes." He looked up from the napkin he was folding. "Do you think I'm reading too far into it? Or not far enough?"

Ruby brought the completed sandwiches to the table, where the pair spoke the ritual words: "Thank you, Princess, for this bounty which we eat at the appointed time. As with everything, all at the proper time, and never before."

With the ceremony completed, Ruby resumed their conversation. "I'm sure I don't know, Jack. You've always done your best to follow the plan, I guess I'll have to try harder." She began eating as tears started in her eyes. "Why did we have to be born into this? Why are we forced to follow the endless Schedules of the Princess? Why can't we just live our lives freely as I've heard people did before She rose to the throne?"

Jack gently took the hand closest to him and gave it a little squeeze. "Would you rather we were in the Prince's realms? By all reports, he still sets his duchies and baronies against each other. Forcing them to fight on the plains before his castle for no other reason than that it amuses him. Or maybe you'd prefer to live with the Knave, scrounging for everything you need at the borders of other realms. No, dear, we follow the Schedule, we obey Her rule, and we live in peace," he said in a shaky voice. "What other option do we have? There's nowhere else we can go, nowhere else to go." He dabbed her eyes with the napkin he had folded so carefully only a few moments before. "Don't cry now, dear, you finish your food and I'll do the dishes. Our schedule says we have the afternoon free until six when we're to eat again."

Rather than quieting her tears, as Jack had hoped, Ruby began to sob loudly. "Not even time in the schedule to have feelings like a human being." She buried her face in the napkin as Jack consulted the clock on the wall and began clearing the table. With the remains of the meal tidied away, he returned to Ruby and held her until her tears had ceased.

Ruby decided to nap, to gather herself after the revelation she said, and was snoring quietly in the bedroom when Jack checked on her. Normally Jack used the allotted Sunday afternoon free time to exercise or fix something around the apartment -- there was always something in need of repair it seemed

– but instead he opted to settle in the chair in the living room to read. He found he couldn't quite focus on the pages before him, often having to skim back as much as two pages to make sense of the passage he was reading. Eventually he let the novel fall to the floor as his eyes closed. Seconds later his snores joined hers in the Sunday afternoon stillness of their apartment.

He awoke feeling fuzzy headed to the sound of thunder in the darkness of the room. Glancing about as his head cleared he had a double moment of panic: darkness told him it was well beyond their appointed dinner time; thunder said rain and he was sure they had left at least some of the windows open. Springing from the too comfortable chair he shouted, "Ruby, check the windows, it sounds like another storm coming through" and ran into the kitchen, turning on the light as he went. The time on the clock brought him up short as the thunder repeated itself in a pattern to predictable to have been caused by a storm: ten o'clock. Fully three hours beyond the cleanup time for supper, almost their scheduled bedtime in point of fact.

The thunder repeated itself as Ruby emerged from the bedroom, her hair sleep tousled and the seams of the pillow case visible on her face in the harsh fluorescent lights of the kitchen, "Jack, it isn't even raining?" she said in a puzzled voice. And repeated itself, as the colour drained from her face.

The pair faced each other in the harsh kitchen light, each framed in a doorway as the thunder repeated itself for a third time. "Jack Ball, Ruby Ball, born Ruby Red," a voice intoned from the hallway. "You have been noted as being tardy. Open the door for inspection by agents of the Princess."

After a count of what could be no more than thirteen seconds the knocking was repeated a fourth time. "Jack and Ruby Ball, open the door in the name of the Princess and prepare for inspection. Failure to do so will result in immediate exile from the Princess Kingdom."

Jack opened the door as the knocking resumed with more force. Through the portal, he saw an upraised foot at the end of a knight's leg. "Thank you," the body at the other end of the leg said as it strode into the room.

"Everything right on schedule here, Sir," Jack said frantically. He glanced about the room and hoped it appeared true. "We ate early in the time slot and finished the dishes."

A pale face between the pulled low dark hat and piled high dark collar atop the severe uniform said simply, "I am here to judge that, sir" and entered the room. He strode rapidly through the apartment, a loop starting which took him through each room before concluding where he had begun, at the front door.

"See sir, everything in order. All done according to the schedule of the Princess," Jack said as Ruby nodded.

"And it will soon be time to prepare for bed, sir," she added.

"Jack Ball," the uniformed inspector began. "Ruby Ball, born Red. You have been found to be tardy, repeat offenders of lateness, and have lied to an official of the Princess."

"What!?" Ruby shouted as Jack said, "How can you stand there and make such..."

The figure in the uniform continued, "Your repeated infractions have been noted by the Observers and my inspection confirms these actions." The pair began to wail as the figure produced a small screen showing them still images of the pair asleep in separate rooms at the appointed meal time. "You will now come with me to begin your exile." He took each of them by a hand as two other similarly suited agents entered the apartment to retrieve the cat and dog.

The five humans and two animals exited the building walking into the back of a school bus, and drove for approximately one hour, in silence, before halting beneath a sign. The first knight, the only one who had spoken to the Balls, stood and faced them saying, "This is where you begin your new lives. You will have twenty-five minutes to exit the realm of the Princess. I wish you the best of luck finding homes in your new realm." His speech finished, the other agents ushered them off the bus, passed the leashed animals to the couple, and closed the bus doors.

Jack looked up at the sign before them. It was a large triangle with four words written in varying scripts in each of the corners. The corner closest to them read "Realm of the Princess", in a flowery script. The upper right-hand corner bore the words "Realm of the Prince" in a harsh angular script. In the upper left-hand corner, it said "Realm of the Knave" in an uneven script.

From the bus, the knight watched them. Ruby, clutching the cat to her chest looked to Jack. Jack tugged the husky closer on its leash and looked back at Ruby. He put his free arm around her and drawing her into a one-armed hug. As they stepped forward, he ordered the bus to return to the depot. He had no care where they went as long as they left at their appointed time.

Jon Dobbin

A native to the St. John's metro region, Dobbin tied for first place in the 2017 *48-Hour Writing Marathon*, sponsored by THE Creative Learning, Thrive, and Engen Books. He describes himself as "the father of three, the husband to an amazing wife, an educator, and a tattoo and beard enthusiast."

Dobbin made a splash last year with "The Chosen" and "Man of Fire" in *Chillers from the Rock*.

His first novel, *The Starving*, debuts in May 2019 from Engen Books.

Blood Red Horizon

"The end is nigh," Ennis said, tossing aside the cardboard sign he was reading from.

Their footsteps echoed through the narrow alleyway, wading through the refuse that had collected over the past ten years. The city was empty… more or less. It had been abandoned when it all started, when it all seemed hopeless. No one came back to the cities. Rioters, looters, survivors: all took their turn riding the old place, leaving nothing but detritus and sorrow.

"Base is sure about this, Sarge?" Eastman said, pushing his tall and lanky frame up alongside. In the old world, Eastman would have been scouted for college basketball, would have been a hit with the girls, and was sure to make mommy and daddy proud. Now he was just a new recruit along for the ride.

"As sure as they can be, Private. Rumours, hearsay, and gut feelings are all we got anymore."

"Yeah, but, where did we get this info?" Eastman talked in a slow, prodding way, a drawl that always ended in an inflection whether it was a question or not.

Ennis shrugged. "Not my pay grade, kid." He took the lead again, extending his stride to put a little distance on the youngster. "Besides, if you're worried the info is good, we'll find out soon enough." He could hear Miller and Moore chuckle from the rear.

They were a four-man team, always four. It was a round

number that felt good, made base all tingly. Eastman was a late replacement for Bandis, their long-term burner that was KIA on the last mission, a long walk into downtown that turned into a fire-fight and a fast run the other way. There were squads like them all over the country, doing the same work and fighting the same fight. This city was their jurisdiction though; base did the research, located threats, and Ennis and his crew were sent to char and mar.

"Two blocks out, Sarge," Moore said, folding up his map and buttoning it into his pants pocket. Moore wasn't someone who Ennis would have picked as a soldier, or whatever it was they were doing out here, but as the world changed more people stepped up where they were needed. For his part, Moore pulled more than his fair share of the weight.

Ennis motioned for them to stop in front of a derelict old brownstone, the windows boarded, and trash piled high on its entryway. "We're about ten minutes out," he said, his eyes scanning the street. "Do an ammo check and load up."

This hadn't always been the deployment for the others, but Ennis had always been here. This was home. Under the muffled sounds of the weapons check, he scanned the city he had known as a boy. He'd walked these streets in the old world, felt them under his young feet as he ran alongside his mother and father. The street they were travelling on now had been an easy walk to his father's barber. It'd been a small brick fronted shop on the corner that smelled like mint shaving cream and cologne. The owner, and only barber on staff, was an older man named Clyde. He had a small smile that emerged from his wrinkled features at the sight of young Ennis, his pale blue eyes twinkling at the young boy. He always gave Ennis an orange lollipop when he visited with his father. His favourite flavour.

Cities everywhere were the same: abandoned, used up, dead. Even the best cities in the world, Paris, London, New York… none lasted. Humanity's idea of safety in numbers was severely questioned. Ennis' city, like the others, succumbed. The buildings fell to disrepair, the streets eroded and cracked, and cars abandoned and rusting in the filth.

Above all that, the saddest thing to Ennis was the death and decay of the formerly lush parks where he'd played. There had been a park just across the street from his old house. Nothing fancy, just some green space with a swing set, a slide, and a teeter totter. He only had one memory of that place, an image of him cutting through the air on a blue rubber swing, its chains squeaking its sorrowful disdain of its work. He could remember his strawberry blond hair floating around his eyes, the wind whooshing past his ears and his mother laughing. On his first mission to the city, he had checked to see if the park was still there, but its trees were barren and withered, its grounds ashen and gray. All the city parks were like that now: dead.

It was probably for the best, Ennis thought, checking his own clip before slamming it home. Locked and loaded.

"Okay, let's do this by the book. Two by two; Miller, you're with me up front. Eastman and Moore take rear. Keep an eye out for any lookouts. When we reach the target, I'll breach."

The target was a bombed-out shell of what used to be a pharmacy, the sign hanging off the side of the door with a stylized mortar and pestle graphic still visible. Ennis knew this place. The big window that had once showcased some of the treats that could be found inside was now gone, and a makeshift covering made of flotsam and jetsam took its place. Its brick exterior was marred with graffiti, age, and disrepair, but it still stood -- more or less.

They halted across the street, huddled tight to the corner of a building that dwarfed their target. There were broken windows as far up as Ennis could see. They scanned the streets and buildings looking for any signs of life.

"Looks clear, boss," Eastman said from the rear, his skinny neck stretching to get a better view.

Ennis nodded. The building didn't seem like it'd seen any activity since the window had been replaced.

"No signs of renewal either," Miller said with a cough, followed by a phlegmy spit.

"Okay. Eastman, stay behind a half step and get your burner ready. Moore, I want a five count. By the book, gentlemen."

1.

Ennis led them across the street at a jog, their slapping footsteps echoing in the deserted city. They fell in behind Ennis and Miller at metal framed, glass door. It was boarded over like the broken window and Closed was spray-painted over the boards in a faded white paint. Droplets of white were frozen in mid-escape from the haphazard letters. The door wouldn't budge.

2.

It took two earth quaking kicks from Miller to dislodge the door in a flurry of splinters and dust. As the door cracked open, Ennis tossed two hissing smoke grenades into the dark room beyond. They covered their faces with their scarves.

3.

Ennis swung his rifle around the corner of the entryway, the gun's stock held tight to his shoulder, its scope brushing his eye. He moved quick, taking in the whole of the room in the red tint of the rifle's sight. It was a squat room, cluttered by fallen shelving units and broken glass. As he moved, the smoke slowed its escape from the tin-like grenades and began to settle in the room, a harsh gray fog that wafted before Ennis' line of sight.

The store had been picked clean long before it was battered. In the back of the room, the wall was pocked with holes where custom shelves once rested; it was now gouged and crumbling. Graffiti tagged the walls that were still intact, fluorescent swirls that broke away from the fog and formed words and images all around him.

4.

The sound of the swift movement of his team's feet as they fanned out took up the whole room. They scanned the room, fingers on their triggers, with the hiss of Eastman's flamethrower overpowering the silence. They waited for movement, waiting for a sign of life or a sign of resistance.

Nothing.

5.

"Clear," Ennis said, lowering his rifle. The smoke creeped around him as it floated toward the open door. The gray light that spilled into the building shed very little illumination on the wreckage. Miller had moved further into the pharmacy, kicking away refuse as he did. The sound of his heavy breathing could be heard under the clang of his steel toed boots on the fallen metal shelving.

The hiss of Eastman's flamethrower ended with a *whomp* as he cut the gas flow. "What does this mean, Sarge. Do we head home?" the young man said, his voice hopeful.

"It means we keep looking, Private." Ennis' voice was low as he moved to follow Miller further into the room. "Moore, review your map, make sure we're in the right place. Miller, let's see if there's a back door to this place."

It took Ennis and Miller the better part of an hour to clear a way to the far side of the room, giving enough time for the smoke to air out. Before they were done, both Ennis and Miller were sweating and panting, their scarves long since pulled down from their mouths. The large, solid counter that had once separated the pharmacist from the remainder of the store was cracked and split, but remained standing in front of broken and fallen shelves. The medications that had once rested on those shelves were long gone, likely stolen in the early days after the Incident.

"Sheeiit," Miller spat a gob of goo and wiped his forehead.

Ennis saw it as well, leaning his shoulder into the wall, his rifle hanging at his chest. Hidden by the wreckage of the store, probably right where the pharmacist stood drinking his morning coffee, was a large hole in the floor. It fell through the basement and into the earth underneath; it was cavernous. The stench of dirt and mold wafted out of it, and water drops could be heard echoing, while a tinge of gray light touched the blackness from somewhere beyond. Sheeit.

Moore whistled at Ennis' ear. "Big hole."

Ennis nodded.

"We going in?"

Ennis sighed. "I think we'll have to." He rubbed at the back of his neck. "Eastman, bring over that burner."

Eastman plodded up between them, holding the barrel of the flamethrower toward the sky. With his other hand, he brought up a flint cup, clicking the two stems together to ignite the pilot light on his weapon with another subtle *whomp*.

"Okay, junior, give us a quick blast. Make sure there's no one waiting for us."

The flame streamed from the gun, a wave of heat hitting Ennis like a brick to the chest; he raised his hand to shield his face and looked away. The room filled with a stark orange light that cast their shadows, angular and distorted, onto the walls of the former pharmacy. With a whoosh, the flames cut out. Silence followed.

Ennis listened for any reaction, any response. There were no screams of pain, no cries for help. "Clear," he said. "Good job Private."

The entrance was a steep, but passable, embankment. Each man took his turn navigating down by skidding the broad-side of their feet in the dirt. Miller stumbled, a foul look clouding his features. The cavern turned out to be nothing but a short hallway of dirt and mud. There were several supports lining the dirt walls as the four men made their way toward the ever-present light they had seen from the surface.

It only took ten minutes of walking before they came to the end of the tunnel, and a steep set of stairs. Though the stairs seemed to have been cobbled together from scrap wood, they were much more inviting than the embankment they had encountered at the other end. Ennis hoisted and readied his gun, signalling the others to do the same. He gave a quick hand motion: two by two, same as before.

Miller and Ennis entered the gray light first, their eyes squinted against its sudden brightness, but it was the heat that astounded Ennis. The sun hadn't given off that kind of heat in quite some time and yet a persistent blast of heat surrounded him, sweat popping out from his skin. They took up position at the top of the stairs, covering for Eastman and Moore, but there was no one in sight.

Before them was a garden, fresh and bright. They were harassed by new scents, perfumes they hadn't been exposed to in years: the mossy smell of aged trees, the pungent whiff of flowers in bloom, and the miasma of manicured grass.

It was the grass, its freshly cut scent that triggered Ennis' memories once more. Not as a boy, but as a young man walking the sidewalks of his city. A push mower in front of him, he plied his business and trade to the neighbours and the elderly. He'd make handfuls of change that would help him buy comic books or video games, or, if he saved his pittance, he'd be able to buy a new hockey stick, maybe roller blades. All the while his father watched on, a good-humoured grin upon his thin face.

"A greenhouse," Moore said in a whisper. "A bloody greenhouse."

Glass and clear plastic surrounded them, contrived from more scrap materials. Ennis thought it was a miracle that it stood up to a stiff breeze, and here it was as big as the building they'd just exited, bigger even. Large enough to fit fully grown trees, innumerable lines of crops, and patches of flowers that were composed of so many colors that it seemed to bewilder the eye. They all stood there, awed.

"What does this mean, Sarge?" Eastman said, his quivering voice quiet in the open space. "What do we d--" He was cut off by an arrow slicing through his throat. Maroon blood leaked from his neck, and a gurgling noise escaped his slackening lips. Eastman dropped to his knees, one hand grasping at his throat, the stem of the arrow between his fingers.

"Contact! Contact!" Ennis let out a burst of fire from his rifle and backed himself up towards the stairway. To his side, Miller and Moore let loose their own weapons, a blind salvo at nothing. More arrows came their way; Ennis could see them now as he moved backwards. Black lines outlined on the background of the gray sky, blurred by their motion, they flew high into the air before landing around the three men, most landing well in front of them. Moore grabbed the back of Eastman's flak vest and dragged him toward the stairs, Miller's M-60 thundering to life, covering everyone's route to the safety of the entrance.

Eastman was dead. His prone body propped up on the stairs, blood still leaking from his wounds. Miller moved in next to them, an arrow lodging into the dirt just above his head as he sat.

"F*****g Enders," he said, panting.

"Moore, get his burner. Miller, give me some cover. I'm going to try to spot these fools."

Miller checked his gun, slapped down the top cover and stood, his machine gun roaring to life as he turned. Ennis crawled up the steps on his stomach, his weapon sight nuzzled against his eye as he scanned the greenhouse for signs of movement. When the arrows began to fly again, he spotted them, red-tinted through his sight: three featureless people hidden in the branches of the trees near the far side of the greenhouse. He took aim at the closest robed figure. He was pulling back his bowstring again, an arrow notched. Ennis fired once, his shoulder bucking a little with recoil, and he watched as one red-tinted figure fell from the tree.

"They're in the trees." He was getting to one knee and tried to yell above the deafening sound of Miller's pig. Moore crawled up next to him, Eastman's flamethrower strapped to his back, and his rifle in his hands. Miller began to move his fire to the small wooded area, his whole body shaking, and Moore followed suit. The trees were being torn apart, their branches waving and dancing, raised high in a sign of defeat. Two more robed bodies fell from on high, their limbs splayed in grotesque angles.

Miller's belt finally expired with a sharp click and he began to reload, his big gun leaving an uncomfortable silent echo as it rang quiet. He went to work slinging a new belt from an ammo box through it. Moore and Ennis stopped as well, reloading, and scanning for any more enemies. The three archers lay still, their bodies covered in bark, branches, and leaves. The trees themselves looked ready to slump over and die with the bodies at their roots.

Ennis stood and walked into the garden once more. Blood stained the grass where Eastman had died; it looked black against the vibrant green. "Moore, light this place up. Start with those trees."

Miller slapped down the top cover of his M-60, and made to follow Moore into the garden. A shadow from above gave him pause and he swung his gun upwards. A spear pierced his chest, the weight of the man wielding it driving him into the ground. Ennis looked up to see two more men tear open the plastic covering of the greenhouse and jump down. He scrambled into the garden, trying to put distance between himself and the attackers; he fired blindly into the air, but hit nothing. Moore had stopped at the noise but fumbled between the flame-thrower's gun and his own rifle. He was of no help.

Enders. Lunatics, zealots obsessed with the end of the world. In the old days they could be seen pacing the streets with signs proclaiming the end of the world, cursing and yelling at those around them. "Repent," they'd say from beneath their spittle-soaked beards. They were loners, dismissed as crazy and given a wide berth. But they became sick of waiting for the world to end. Impatient with the timing. Now they'd gathered together to help it along.

Ennis swung the barrel of his rifle in an arc towards Miller. The Ender was still on top of him, spear forgotten as its shaft trembled back and forth embedded in big man's chest, a knife now in his hand. The Ender looked the part: Unkempt, in mud-stained robes that were lashed around him with gray rope. His hair was greasy and it fell across his face and tangled with his length of curling beard. The man's mouth of crooked teeth was open in a grimace. His milky white eyes focused on Miller.

Ennis fired three shots into him. The Ender let out a short grunt. He tripped in Miller's legs and fell.

Moore cried out, his voice distorted in pain. Ennis turned in time to see the remaining Enders stab at him with the sharpened sticks they brandished as spears; Moore's weapon had been lost in the struggle. Ennis rushed forward and knocked one of the Enders to the ground. He brought his rifle up and squeezed off several rounds into the man's chest. Ennis adjusted to aim at the last attacker but felt a sting on his wrists and heard a loud *twhack*. His hands went numb. He dropped his rifle.

The Ender charged Ennis, leaving Moore to drop to his knees holding his stomach. With a slobbering grunt, the Ender jabbed at Ennis with his spear, quick, testing pokes. Ennis backed into the garden, timing the assault. Ennis acted. He moved into the Ender, dodged the spear, and grabbed it between the man's grip. With a yell of exertion, Ennis planted his feet and twisted his hips, tossing the man to the ground. Ennis dropped his knee on the Ender's face. The man went limp and Ennis took the spear.

Ennis turned back to Moore. "You alive?"

A wet cough was his answer.

"Come on, Moore, let's get this over with before more show up." He leaned over and picked up his rifle, slinging it back into place before gripping Moore's bicep.

"I don't know, Sarge, I'm not sure ...." Ennis could feel the strain in Moore's body as he tried to stand, only to fall back on his backside. "Enders got me good." Moore coughed again.

A large pool of liquid had gathered around Moore, the harsh scent of chemicals rising above the floral smells of the garden. "Ugh, you're leaking," Ennis said, taking a look at the flamethrower.

"In more ways than one," Moore laughed, a low chuckle that turned into another barking cough.

The sound of soft footfalls in the grass drew Ennis' attention to another half-dozen Enders heading his way. He fired toward them in a quick burst. He hit nothing but halted their progress. He grabbed Moore again, slid him under one of his arms and hoisted him to his feet. He made for the stairs.

Arrows flew past and thudded into the ground behind them. A sharp pain flared through Ennis' calf, and he fell to the ground, Moore tumbling next to him. The footfalls quickened.

Ennis cursed as he tried to stand. The arrow hadn't gone all the way through; it stuck out from his leg at an obscene angle. He levelled his rifle from his knees.

The Enders had begun to run towards their wounded prey. Ennis put the sight to his eye once more and readied to fire when he heard a small clicking sound at his side. He looked over to Moore. He was lying on his side in the lush grass, blood oozing from his pale lips. Moore had Eastman's flint cup in his hand, clicking the stems together.

"You better get moving, boss," Moore smiled around the leaking blood.

Ennis cursed and started to hobble away in a fast limp. Each step brought a new level of pain. It was taking too long, Ennis thought. Maybe Moore had died before he could spark the gas. He tried to turn when he heard it, the whoosh of fire catching in rapid succession. He felt the heat, then the impact. The explosion gave him a hard push that sent him into the air. Before the world faded to black, he could see the greenhouse light up in orange hues. A spectacular sunset in a world of gray skies.

Thump, click, thump, click. The sound of hollow wood being stomped upon woke Ennis, his head pounding, his body aching.

Thump, click, thump, click. Ennis was strapped to a bed. Thick nylon bindings wrapped around his chest, arms, and legs. His wrists were handcuffed as well. He didn't bother struggling; it would be a waste of energy. Instead, he listened to the sounds of the house and outside of it. Aside from the thumping, it was silent. A subtle call of a bird, the gentle gust of wind, the delicate creak of the building settling.

Thump, click, thump, click. The sun broke through the window of the room. It was the brightest sun he'd seen since the old days. Almost too bright. Ennis tried to keep his eyes closed, but the light spilled through them and forced him to keep them open.

Thump, click, thump, click. It was a small room, and while the white walls gave it the illusion of more space, Ennis could tell the difference. It was Spartan: bed, bed pan, and a small table that nuzzled next to him. It was mostly a blank space.

Thump, click, thump, click. The creak of a door opening somewhere behind Ennis made him flail and twist to try and get a view at who else was in the room.

"You really did a job on my garden." It was a slow voice, deep and calm. "It's a pity, you know, it was such a nice, soothing place. It meant so much." Thump, click, thump, click.

A face leaned into Ennis' perception, normal and completely unexceptional. It wasn't handsome, the oval face that stared down at him, with its cat-eye glasses hanging by its ears. A stubbled chin jutted out under a half-smirk, and salt-and-pepper hair fell around the face at random. "You and your friends were really a bother, you know that?"

Thump, click, thump, click. He walked into full view: a small man dressed in a blue button up shirt under a beige, corduroy suit jacket. Chest hair poked out from under his collar, and his shoulders slumped as he placed his hands in the pockets of his tight jeans. He leaned heavily to his right side, even his smirk turned that way.

"Who the hell are you?" Ennis struggled to stretch his neck and keep the man in his sight. His voice croaked in the effort.

That half smile again, his hand floated to his chest. "Moi? Vincent Acer. I'd shake your hand, but…" He waved his hand toward the bed.

"You're no Ender," Ennis said, letting his head drop back to the bed. "Let me go, let me get back to my work."

"Ender." He furrowed his considerable eyebrows. "Is that

what you call my associates?" His shoulders bounced as he chuckled. "Cute. They really are a funny bunch, aren't they? Loyal though. Dedicated. Real believers." *Thump, click, thump, click.* He walked around the foot of the bed. Acer's gait was marred by a heavy limp, and Ennis stretched his neck once more to get a better look. His right foot was clad in a thick-soled boot in contrast to the flat sneaker he wore on his left. The boot reminded Ennis of Frankenstein in those old monster movies his father would make him watch on Halloween.

"Oh, this?" Acer pointed to his boot. "You noticed. This is a very special boot. One of a kind, really. You won't find anything like this in the world anymore. I'm fortunate to have had it before the world changed. Lucky, I'd say. It's helped me do a lot." Acer's eyes drifted away from Ennis, one hand rubbing his upper arm gingerly. Ennis grunted.

"I don't look like much, do I?" Acer turned back to Ennis. "Not to someone like you. But, consider this: look at all I've done since the collapse. I've gathered together the ragtag remnants of society, those that weren't quite stable even before then. I've given them purpose, a goal to work towards. Renewal, not only of the planet but of its people."

Ennis shook his head. "You're as insane as your friends."

"I'm helping the world turn itself around. I'm creating. You're the one who's destroying."

"Creating," Ennis spat. "You're ending the world, people will die!"

"And the world will be reborn. Its people will be reborn. Just as it was foretold."

Thump, click, thump, click. Acer was gone, leaving Ennis to fill the plain white room with his screams.

It felt like days of Ennis being strapped to the table, of being tended on by Enders who hand-fed him and let him use the bedpan twice a day. Their brain-addled, slack-jawed faces surrounded by greasy beards and unwashed flesh stared down upon him with so much hate he could feel its heat in the air. Under their malodorous breath, they muttered things. Things about him, about the garden, about Acer. One Ender even screamed, "The end is nigh," as he exited the room. Otherwise it was just the white walls and the terribly bright sunlight. Acer didn't make another appearance.

Ennis struggled; he rallied against his bonds in desperate convulsions that did little more than to burn or gouge his own flesh. His wrists in particular felt like raw meat as the handcuffs bit into them, but his blood made them slick. He attempted to slip them, to shimmy his hand out, but it wouldn't work. His wrists hurt. He felt weak and tired. He passed out.

His sleep brought no dreams, but as he woke, his memories filled his headspace. He was nineteen, a community college dropout, and he was going to war. His father, Duncan Ennis, stood on the white porch to watch him go, his premature wrinkles caused his smile to look more like a grimace. His mother, Abigail Schofield Ennis, was already inside; her tear-soaked wails could still be heard by the two men in her life.

The bus wouldn't be there for another half hour or so, but he stood underneath the skies of home studying the stars that had looked down upon him his whole life.

"You packed up there, boy?" his father drawled as he rocked on his heels, hands buried deep into his khaki pockets.

Ennis took a look at his belongings: one green, canvas duffel bag and a small black carry-on bag he had borrowed from his parents. He was travelling pretty light. Uncle Sam provides. "Yes, sir."

His father put one thin hand on the railing of the porch and leaned on it, the edge of his gray cardigan creeping up over his bony wrist, a hint of faded blue tattoo ink peeking out. His eyes narrowed as he looked upon Ennis. "You sure this is what you want, son?"

Ennis cast a glance towards the sky once more and, removing his standard issue beret, he ran his hands through thick black hair, ruffling it, letting it breath. "Yes, sir," he said, meeting his old man's gaze.

A sob from inside caused his father to turn and look, a new smirk on his face. He turned back and met eyes with his son. "I better go check in your mother," he said with the shake of his balding head. Ennis and his father shared a short, but true, laugh then. A laugh that echoed in the bare night.

Then his father was gone, the creaking metal screen door slamming behind him, leaving Ennis alone with his thoughts and the sounds of the night.

Ennis wondered again about what had happened to Duncan and Abigail Ennis during the collapse. Part of him hoped they perished in the initial fury. He'd hate to think they were exposed to this life. To the life after.

It wasn't as simple as a phone call anymore. Communications, electricity, most anything mechanical were the first things to go. There was panic in the streets, riots, death. And then a sudden calm. Acceptance, Ennis supposed. Everyone accepted life differently though. Some chose not to accept it. Others chose to take it.

At first, they thought a foreign power had set an EMP bomb. That invasion wouldn't be far behind. The military bulked up. Nothing happened. Eye witnesses started to come forward, came to seek shelter in the safety of the army, navy, Air Force. They claimed they saw a battle between a man and a giant snake. That when the golden-haired man died, the power went. Unbelievable, but it didn't matter; the invasion may still be coming.

A year or two later, someone noticed rapid growth of plant life. Of replenishment on a large scale. A good sign. It turned out that Al Gore was right all along, but now the human race couldn't keep destroying the planet. It was making a comeback.

But it grew too quickly, spread too easily, and people started to die. It wasn't obvious at first, nor was it obvious to Ennis even now, but someone connected the dots. The plant life killed. The more of it, the less people. That's when burner units were put together. They were meant to keep the plant life in check, but it was a new world and not everyone agreed.

The days didn't end in that room. Perpetual sunshine was made brighter by the too white walls. Ennis languished. Where he first hated the sight of the Enders and their two daily trips, he now accepted them. Knew their tics and habits, could predict their mutterings; would often join with them. It got to the point that if the Enders were late at all, Ennis would defecate himself. He barely noticed until they were cleaning him instead of manoeuvring a cold bedpan underneath him.

During one of the Ender's daily visits, as the Ender was removing the bedpan, Ennis made a lucky grab for the man's wrist, stretching his own gouged and bruised wrist to do so.

This Ender was a tall, gaunt man, his beard falling out in patches. He was one of the silent ones; he didn't mutter or hum or scream. He just did his job, his sad blue eyes unfocused and uncaring.

The man froze in place. No panic, no fear, he just stood statue still. His pale eyes focused on the table in front of him, and Ennis could see his mouth twitch at the corners.

"Let me go," Ennis said, squeezing the man's wrist as tight as he could. He wanted him to look at him, to acknowledge his presence, to speak. The gaunt Ender just stood in place. His mouth had stopped twitching. "Please," Ennis moaned, straining against his bounds.

The man turned his distant blue eyes to Ennis, his hair balding but sticking out on the sides. He laughed. A rolling, wheezing, smoker's laugh that erupted from his red-rimmed lips in spurts until it filled the room, took up the air. He was insane, but then, they all were. The Ender's wrist felt cold and clammy, his skin rough. It felt like his muscles were curling and twisting against his grip.

Ennis let him go. The man continued laughing as he left the room, laughing while he walked away, the sound deadened by the closed door. Maybe he would laugh forever, Ennis thought; maybe he'd laugh until he choked.

Later that day, or maybe some other day, Ennis couldn't say for sure, two Enders entered the room. Neither was laughing. One held a gun on him, Moore's old rifle by the looks of it, an AR-15 full auto; the other undid his bindings. When the Ender was finished, he jumped back, keeping out of reach of Ennis, and the other man tensed and held the weapon so hard it shook. Ennis rose to sitting, rubbing his wrists, feeling a grimace grow on his face.

The Enders backed out of the room, their wild eyes locked on Ennis as they made for the door. Once outside the room they took flight, their footsteps echoed down a long hallway.

Ennis was slow to get to his feet. His joints ached all the way down to his feet, and he was cold. He hadn't felt the cold as he lay prone, but it hit him now. He shivered as he realized he was only wearing a small pair of underwear. He stumbled around the room, looking for anything to cover himself with. He found some clothes: a pair of beige trousers, a white sleeveless tee, and a red, plaid shirt that turned out to be too small. He left it unbuttoned. The trousers had the opposite problem, and he slung a pair of suspenders that were left in the pile about his shoulder. Underneath everything was a pair of brown, leather boots that he slipped on. They were comfortable and fit well.

He approached the door cautiously. The Enders had left it open a crack, and more light spilled in through it. He pushed it open, a gradual creak in the otherwise silent building. It was the garden again, green and bright and lush. It fell in huge leaves over crumbling archways, while vines grew around and through stone walkways and flowers stood out in bright explosions of blue, yellow, and red. Ennis covered his face, trying to diffuse the array of scents that harassed him, and walked through the green space. The sky cleared as he walked deeper and deeper into the garden. It was blue again, just as it had been in the old world. The sun cracked the clouds, a sight he couldn't help but stare upon, his eyes watering as he squinted against

Dystopia from the Rock

the brightness.

Ennis walked and walked. He let his hands fall to his sides, his fingertips brushing the tall grass. He walked until the sun was falling and the sky turned a blazing red under a bruise purple sky. In the distance, Ennis could see a structure, small and slight against the horizon and made for it. It was a statue, tall and piercing the landscape. He couldn't quite make out what it was meant to be. It could have been a person, a creature, a continent for all he knew. Whatever it was, it was crawling with vines, and birds (actual birds) jostled one another for space, cooing and tweeting as they did.

At last he stood before the statue, stood at its very base, a thick concrete block that looked cracked and old. Ennis tried to look up at the statue, tried to discern what it was, what it meant. For a moment, he thought it looked like a hulking beast breaking out of the ocean, waves surrounding its legs. Then, as the moonlight began to strike it, it looked like a snarling wolf, gnashing and growling. A moment later and it seemed to be a triumphant warrior, hands held to the sky, one armoured foot resting on its fallen enemy. Ennis closed his eyes then, trying to banish the images away. He fell to his knees, feeling the cool grass as he did, his hands scratching at his forehead and eyes. He didn't want to look at the statue again, every part of him fought against it, told him not to look, but he couldn't help it; he stared up at the statue for one final time. All he was met with was an ominous, towering shadow with the blood red horizon sinking into darkness behind it.

The Other

The voice boomed around him in the steady cadence of a prayer, or a chant. It was garbled, but it was there, plain and unmistakable. It droned. His head shot up and he stood from his seat, a mix of fright and readiness. It was for nought however; he sat back down, slumping his shoulders in his brown leather jacket.

He was in a waiting room. A vast waiting room with hundreds, thousands of others. There were people wandering, sitting, sleeping, and dying. Screens inset in the walls blinked from news bulletins to hospital directions to standard emergency procedures. *What to do in case of a biochemical attack.* He had to get outside, see the real world, and touch real earth, ground, dirt.

There was a bag next to him. Ben Maddox was written on the luggage tag that hung from its black leather handle. Was that his name? He wanted to look inside but forced himself to wait. Get out first, he thought; take a look at it under some natural light. He grabbed it and moved toward the doors.

The voice continued all around him, disembodied but constant. It was the drone of recorded directions, some monotone nurse calling out orders over and over again for eternity.

"Anyone seeking medical emergency -- gunshot trauma -- please report to section 4A. Anyone seeking medical emergency -- knife or blade wound -- please report to section 4B."

The voice intoned. His pace increased.

A security booth blocked the exit. A fat and worn looking

man sat inside, his pouched eyes red and creased with veins stared out of the plexiglass, drilling curious holes into him as he approached.

"Sir," the portly man said, pressing a button and locking the exit doors with a loud *Ka-chunk*. He turned on him, could feel the burning coals behind his eyes. "Sir, I'll need your name." The guard's voice crackled through the round speaker that was lodged into the thick glass he sat behind.

"I..."

"Place your right hand on the window, palm first sir," the guard said with a sigh.

He hesitated. His name, what was his name? It was on the tip of his tongue. He put his hand flat on the window. Buttons and words appeared around his hand in florescent green. Orange circles moved around his hand. A picture popped up, some words he couldn't read.

"Ben Maddox?" the guard said, his red eyes flicking back and forth from his face to the picture.

The luggage tag. Ben nodded.

"One moment, Mr. Maddox," the security guard said, typing something into the computer. A strange whirring sound began to surround him. There was a sliding sound, a whoosh of something slipping against hardened, scratched plastic and a dull thud. "Please remove the parcel from the slot sir," the guard said in his robot voice.

Ben looked down. Below the thick plexiglass that protected the guard, a thin piece of black plastic hung there, like the opening on a vending machine. He sighed and reached inside, his hand feeling around, partially expecting a can of soda. His hand landed on something cold and heavy; he could feel the small bumps of a grip and he curled his fingers around it, removing it from the window. A gun. A small handgun, and dangling from the trigger guard was a plastic bag with two clips of ammunition.

"What the hell is this?" Ben said, holding the gun at arm's length, his head swivelling from side to side, expecting a platoon of hospital security to jump him at any moment.

"I'm sorry, sir, we didn't have a weapon on file for you. Either you arrived with no firearm or a loved one removed it for you. What you have there is a standard issue pedestrian firearm." The guard paused, his eyes shifting. He put a hand up to his mouth, blocking it from view of anyone looking save Ben. "I've used one myself. It serves its purpose, though it is a little cheap." The guard winked, hit another button and the doors unlocked. "Have a good day, sir."

Ben dropped the gun in his bag, too many questions running through his aching head. He shoved the gun into his bag and moved through the doors, picturing 54 Anders' Crescent.

Looming buildings sprawled into the sky, breaking through a canopy of smog. Neon coloured ads danced on their surface, offering flavours and products in Dolby Surround and digital hi-res. At the limit of the hospital's entrance, a smiling doctor, black with hair greying at the temples, offered kind and compassionate care for children, loved ones, yourself.

Ben gaped at the digital landscape he'd stepped into, a million voices blending into one buzzing gnat that assaulted his ears with nonsense. Visions of digital perfection attacked him, pleading behind smiling, dead eyes for him to buy something, to do something. Unconsciously, he closed his empty fist and turned it to the right. The noise got quieter, the video fading. He turned his fist again and the ads disappeared, their noise with them. Ben stood alone on the sidewalk, his bag hanging at his side, no noise aside from the steady churn of traffic and people, who skirted around him; aware but unaware of him.

He closed his eyes tight. This was not how he pictured the city where he lived in the small house on 54 Anders' Crescent. His home, surrounded by grass and trees, could not be in a place like this.

Ben walked away from the hospital, pushing through a wave of people, sighting a bus stop. He fell to the bench and tried to make sense of things. It didn't work. He could feel his heart thump into his ribs, could feel his breathing increase. His grip on the leather-bound straps of his small duffle tightened. He didn't even know the name of this city.

Check the bag. Startled, Ben looked around him, trying to make eye contact with the person who whispered in his ear. They all passed him, each giving him a sidelong glance in return.

Check the bag. He jumped up, twisted around. His fists clenched. More people began to move around him, tried to keep their distance. No one was speaking to him.

He pulled the bag onto his lap and unzipped it. At the top was his new pedestrian issue gun. Ben took it out and slid it into his jacket pocket. Underneath the gun was a phone, nothing fancy, but usable. He found the power button in the side and held it down. The screen came to life, loading. He put it aside while he looked at the rest of the contents: a business card for **Sound/Fury** -- where all your dreams come true; a pair of jeans; a sweater; a charger for the phone. There was a thin leather wallet slid into a side pocket; Ben took it out and unfolded it. A credit card stood in the front card slot with some small bills in the back.

Ben pulled out an ID from the wallet. Benjamin M. Maddox stared back at him. That was him. Was it really him? He didn't remember if he had looked into a mirror before he left the hospital. Did he look like this? Six-foot-two, balding, white with a five-o'clock shadow, and cold blue eyes. Was that him? He rubbed his chin; at least they got that part right. He shoved the ID back in its place and put the wallet in his back pocket. It felt right there.

He sighed and repacked the bag. There were two dings from the phone, and he gave it a look. Two green boxes floated on the screen, covering the background, a pale blue skull in a black field. One was from Lisa; the other was a private number. He tried to open the phone, but a four-digit password screen appeared, blurring the blue skull. He fumbled at some random four-digit numbers, each one prompting a slow vibration but never moving from the locked screen. He put the phone in his pocket.

The only thing he had of any substance was the business card. Ben turned it over in his hands. What type of business was **Sound/Fury** anyway? How could it make your dreams come true? The address was slanted on the bottom of the card, embossed in such a way that you could only see it when you moved it at just the right angle, in just the right light. It meant nothing to him, his mind was blank. He kept it in his hand as he started to walk again, determined to find something that would jog his memory, something that would give him an answer.

A yellow cab darted in and out of traffic and slowed to a stop on the sidewalk right next to him to a cacophony of squealing tires and honking horns. Ben stumbled away from it, his hand darting into his jacket pocket, feeling the grip of his gun. The cab's window rolled down, a stream of profanity flowing from it. Ben could see a chubby man yelling out of the other side of the car, his fist waving in the air. Ben stood transfixed, looking upon the scene until the driver finally stopped his tirade with the renewed movement of those behind him. He looked through the passenger side window, raised his eyebrows, and flashed a genuine smile. "You Maddox?"

Ben relaxed his grip on the pistol and bent down to see the man more clearly. The car was fairly clean, its gray interior spotted with cigarette burns, but there was no garbage in the front or back seat. It smelled like flowers, but not real ones. It smelled like flowers imagined by perfume companies.

"Maddox. Maddox. I'm looking for Maddox. Someone told me to come by here and pick up someone named Maddox. That you? Said he'd have a green bag, you have a green bag." The little man shrugged, tapped his fingers on his steering wheel and leaned out towards Ben. He was a handsome man with a steel gray shadow on his cheeks and jaw. His nose was large and crooked, and when he smiled a glint of gold flashed from his teeth. His hat, a baseball cap, sat back on his mess of greasy curls, exposing his forehead.

"I'm Maddox." Ben moved closer.

The cab driver's face lit up. "Maddox! Come, come. Get in, I will take you anywhere you want to go." He pressed a button and the back door began to open, inviting Ben in. "I'm Mehul," the driver said as Ben sat in the back, placing his duffle bag on the seat next to him. "Where do you want to go?" the cabby said, looking over his shoulder and swerving back into traffic.

"Who sent you for me?" Ben asked, sliding his seatbelt across his chest. "Take me to them."

Mehul waved his hand. "I don't know them. My dispatcher called this in." He pointed to the radio in the front dash. "Said it would be easy money. Lucky me huh?" He swerved into the other lane, a distant horn heard behind him.

"You don't know who hired you then?" Ben played with the business card.

"No. Just was told to pick up some guy with a green bag." Mehul's big brown eyes flashed in the rear-view mirror, looking into Ben's own.

"Do you know where 54 Anders' Crescent is?" Ben kept watch in the rear-view.

"54 Anders', 54 Anders'?" Mehul rolled it around for a few more tries. "No. I don't know that place. You sure it's in town?"

"I don't know," Ben said, looking out the window at the buildings slide by. This wasn't his city. He played with the business card, could feel the small letters and their ridges as they slid through his fingers. "What about this place, can you take me here?" He passed the card over the seat.

Mehul grabbed the card with two fingers and then turned it around to get a look at it. His eyes shot up to his mirror again, wide now and staring at Ben. "You sure, boss? This ain't a very nice place."

Ben nodded, of course. Nothing would be that easy. He leaned his head onto the window, the cool glass refreshing on his skin. The streets passed by in a blur. Stabilizers and propulsion engines began to fire to life all around him and the car began to lift from the ground, a mechanical knock interrupted the silent transition from wheels and road to boosters and air.

"Don't worry about the knocking," Mehul said, his hands plastered to the steering wheel. "Just needs some oil is all."

Ben ignored this and looked out the window at the city and people as the car took flight towards **Sound/Fury**.

The sprawl of downtown crested the horizon, holographic giants bent and swayed to unheard music, beckoned and flirted, and shook and shook against the gunmetal sky. Ben stared at a tawdry, static frilled goddess whose enormous eyes seemed to meet his own, her car length fingers urging him to come to her, biting her sofa sized, bright pink lips. He turned his head and was thankful that the ads could not materialize inside vehicles; a safety feature.

The radio blared the somber tones of a reporter listing the most recent victims of a school shooting. Youth in schools, between the ages of twelve and sixteen, had just landed in most targeted group of gun violence to no one's surprise. School-aged children six to eleven came in at a paltry fourth place. Ben turned his attention away when the DJ started to talk about the effort to ensure more teachers and school staff had weapons in the future. Guns saved lives.

"You okay, boss?" Mehul peeked at him from the corner of his eye, his face still mostly facing the road.

"Fine." Ben chanced another look at the giantess he saw earlier, but now her hologram was of a woman being ensnared by tentacles. He looked away once again.

"Okay. We gonna land now, boss." Mehul flicked a switch and the familiar knocking sound returned, a terrible crunching of metal on plastic that gave him a swift and unrelenting headache. Mehul put rubber to asphalt, landing with only minor shudders and jostling. A small hatchback passed them a moment later, honking furiously its driver extending a middle finger to Mehul. The cab driver just laughed and extended his own.

Despite their intrusive landing, there were few cars on the road, and Mehul drove them at a leisurely pace. In this part of town, it was too early to be the wasp's nest of activity that would develop in a few hours. First the vendors would appear, their homespun ads offering all types of treats for the mind, body, and soul. Next would be the party people, already drunk or stoned, tripping out of their mind and covered in neon plastics that left little to the imagination. Last were the hustlers, the thieves, the gamblers. Those that wanted to exploit, take advantage of those lost in their medicated worlds. Ben knew this as much as he knew he didn't enjoy that scene. His mind kept flickering back to the house on Ander's Crescent.

The cab pulled up in front of a red brick building where a long black awning stretched over the doors and partially concealed the two bouncers from the rain that had just started to fall. On the front of the awning, emblazoned with gold and white highlights, was **Sound/Fury**. The two bouncers eyed the car behind their dark black sunglasses, their fingers probing their ears while they spoke into their sleeves.

"How are you being paid, you know, to chauffeur me around?" Ben said as his door opened on its own. He looked out past the rain and at the bulky bouncers that stood before the entrance.

"Hourly." Mehul smiled and slipped a toothpick between his lips.

"Good. Think you could stick around here until I come out?"

"Sure. That won't be a problem, boss." Mehul flashed his self-satisfied grin.

Ben stepped out and stretched his legs. Once he was clear, Mehul pulled the car up to the curb and turned it off. Ben barely heard the muffled music filled with horns and strings that floated out of the car as he walked to the door.

"Hey," one of the bouncers said, his voice deep and rich.

"You can't park that there."

Ben could see just how big the bouncers were as he approached. Both men looked like linebackers, but instead of football pads, they had black flak vests to cover their bulging shoulders and broad chests. They looked calm, confident, and they had spotted him doing something they didn't like. That was strike one. Ben winced.

"You're not open?" Ben chanced a smile. "No biggie, I'm here to speak with your boss." He flashed the business card he'd found in his wallet.

"Mr. Franklin is expecting you?" The first guard was shorter than the other guard, was black, but he was just as wide and laced with muscle as his companion. He stood in front of Ben blocking the door. Ben nodded and stopped. Up this close, he noted both guards were strapped with semi-automatic pistols.

"Boss," the first guard spoke, turning his head away from Ben. "We got a guy here says you're expecting him." He paused for a moment and nodded, moving away from the door. As he did, the other guard stepped up; Ben didn't move.

The taller bouncer had a smirk that meant anything but humour. Ben could feel the heat of the man's withheld aggression as he stared down on him. Ben put his hands in his pockets, gripped his pistol, and waited for things to go south.

"You got ID?" the first bouncer said as he returned.

Ben handed him the ID from his wallet. "Think I'm too young to drink?" He tried a laugh.

He removed his sunglasses and looked Ben over once more. He pocketed the ID, "You'll have to leave that piece you're carrying with us." He pointed to Ben's jacket pocket.

They stared at each other for a moment; Ben tried to weigh his options and realized he didn't have any.

"This thing?" he said, slowly pulling the gun from his pocket, not ignoring that fact that the bouncers had their hands resting on their own. "This thing is just a loaner. A standard issue pedestrian. Couldn't hurt a fly."

The bouncer took it from Ben's extended hand, relaxing the

grip on his own. "Mr. Franklin will see you now."

The club grew up around Ben as he walked through the doors. A large dance floor was laid out before him, its black tiled floors empty. On the perimeter were two large bars with trendy looking bartenders behind them preparing for the coming night, their work echoing in the empty room.

The tall bouncer followed him in. His smirk subdued some, he pointed up the stairs that climbed around the walls. "Top of the stairs."

The stairs were a black metal, diamond cut and hollow, so that they clanged with each step he took. The matching metal railings were cool to the touch and, while they were very sturdy, did not instil confidence or safety in Ben. The bartenders slowed their chores and watched Ben as he climbed the stairs, curious but not shocked.

At the top of the stairs was a set of matte black double doors, the walls around them painted in a contrasting red. Another large bouncer stood there, this one wearing a suit jacket buttoned up to hide his flak jacket and weapon. This bouncer gave Ben a curt nod and opened the door, standing out of the way as Ben made his entrance.

The office was a sober contradiction to the dance floor he'd just left. Lining the deep brown walls were pictures, certificates, and licences. A leather couch sat at the end of the room next to the door, a glass coffee table in front of it littered with magazines. At the far end of the room was a large desk. The contents on top were neat and organized. Behind the desk, slouching in his chair and hands joined on his stomach, was a tired eyed man who yawned as Ben noticed him.

"Hello," he said in a deep, confident voice. He was a California man, Ben thought. Tanned and smiling with his perfect white teeth over his square jaw. But he was aging. Greying. He was a melted wax candle of what he once was, sagging and undone.

Franklin unfolded himself from his chair and stood leaning on his desk. "Care for a drink, Mister?" He gestured to a wet bar that was set up behind him.

"Maddox," Ben said. He felt very thirsty all of a sudden. He nodded. "Please."

"Have a seat, Mr. Maddox." His smile tightened, and he turned to the bar to mix a drink. The tinkle of ice in glass seemed far too loud and Ben grabbed at his coat pocket for the missing gun, surprising himself.

"So, Mr. Maddox, to what do I owe the pleasure of this visit?" His blue eyes peered over his green jacketed shoulder.

Ben was aware of the darkness around him. He was aware that the room was in a near dimness everywhere but the desk. The proprietor of **Sound/Fury** was also in the dark. Ben shrunk himself back. He slid into the shadow, out of the slanted light of the window, and the small circle of light created by the desk lamp. His heart thudded in his chest.

"I came here for answers," Ben said, watching the other man's back.

"Ahhh, answers. Isn't that something we all want?" A laugh on his words. "For instance, I'd like to know who you really are, and why you're really here?" He turned, a glass of ice and brown liquid in one hand, a gun in the other. "I only know one Maddox and you aren't him."

Ben became very still. He could feel his heart regulating itself, could feel his breathing relax into a casual rhythm. He was calm. Ready. "I was really hoping for that drink."

"I only drink with people I know." Franklin motioned to the chair in front of his desk with the gun. "Please take a seat."

Ben moved to the chair and sat down. Franklin did the same.

"Now, tell me who you are and what you're doing here."

"Ben Maddox. I came here because I found your business card in my wallet and I thought you might have some answers for me."

"Maybe. Maybe not. The question is can you provide me

with answers or not," Franklin said as he took a sip of his drink. "Here's how it's going to work: I'm going to ask you a question. If I like the answer, I'll let you go. If I don't like the answer, I'll shoot you. I'm not going to kill you, but I'm going to keep pulling this trigger until I get my answer."

Ben's mind was screaming in panic, but his body remained calm. This man knew a Ben Maddox, but not him. Was it some kind of terrible coincidence that he walked into here? Ben Maddox and 54 Anders were the only things he was sure of. What if they were wrong?

"So, please," his captor said, "tell me who you are and why you are here. Think about this very carefully." Franklin jabbed the gun at him with every word.

"Listen up, Franklin. You know who I am and what I can do. I'm here for what's mine and I'm going to get it." Ben was startled and turned to see who else was in the room. No one was there. He turned back to Franklin. The other man was wide eyed, his mouth was agape.

"Who the hell are you?" Franklin stood and locked back the hammer of his gun.

Ben's mind was racing. He wanted to put up his hands, wanted to tell the guy to calm down, that he'd leave, that it was all a big misunderstanding. His mind said that, but his body didn't. It was a numb feeling that came over him, a paralysis that he attributed to fear. Until he picked up the chair next to him and threw it in one swift movement.

It felt like he was watching a movie, a video game that someone else was controlling. A gunshot went off when the chair first went flying, but Ben was already in motion. He ducked in front of the desk and pushed it backward into Franklin. Another shot went off, high and wide. Ben kept moving. Fast. Faster than he thought he could. One hand shot up to meet Franklin's gun hand. Ben's other hand slammed Franklin in the stomach in two rapid successions. The bar proprietor crumpled to his knees. Still holding Franklin's arm, Ben punched him in the nose. He dropped the gun to clutch his face with both hands.

Ben brought up his leg and kicked Franklin in the solar plexus driving him backwards into the wall, his breath laboured and wheezing.

That's when the door busted open, and the bouncer by the door entered. "Boss? Everything all right?" he said, his hand on his gun.

Ben dropped, picked up Franklin's gun and rolled from behind the desk into a kneeling position. He fired once and the man dropped twitching on the floor.

"What the hell?" Ben said, but nothing came out of his mouth.

"Sorry, kid," that new voice again. "I'm at the wheel now. You may want to take a breather, this won't be pretty."

Ben tried to scream, to rage, to argue but nothing came out. He tried again and again and again. He screamed until his world was nothing but darkness.

"Please," someone said with a terrible squeak. "Please don't hurt me."

Ben rubbed at his eyes, trying to clear them. As the world came into focus, he saw the bloody face of a handsome, effeminate man crying black tears of eyeliner. One of his eyes was swollen and red, and there were scratches and abrasions all over his face. His brightly coloured lips were swollen, cut, and bleeding. Ben almost didn't recognize him as one of the bartenders that he'd seen when he first walked in. Now he was holding his upper torso off the ground by the collar of his mesh shirt. He dropped him. The bartender fell flat, his green Mohawk bouncing with the impact, and he started to crawl away, his body wracked with sobs.

"What...." Ben stood and looked at the carnage around him. Bodies were scattered around the dance floor. A dissonance of groans and sighs filled the room, bounced off the walls and echoed in Ben's ears. He was breathing hard, and there was a sharp pain in his left shoulder. He looked at his blood covered hands and saw that they were swollen and cut. They hurt to open or close. Ben looked at his left shoulder and saw a small hole through his coat, and some dried blood at the entrance.

"I've been shot," he said to the small bartender who was still crawling away from him. "I've been shot!"

The bartender cringed and dropped into the fetal position, covering his head. Nausea fell over Ben like a blanket. He wavered on his feet and looked up at the ceiling to avoid the blood and misery around him. He was greeted with more bodies sprawled on the staircase and the railing. He turned his head and vomited. The young man before him yelped.

Ben wiped his mouth with the corner of his sleeve and made his way up the stairs and to the office. He sidestepped unconscious and wailing bouncers and walked into Franklin's office. It was more of the same: two more bodies lay atop the initial man he saw himself shoot when he was helpless in his own body. Franklin was laid out on his desk, his stomach moving up and down in shallow, wet breaths.

Good, he's alive, Ben though. Franklin jumped with fright at seeing Ben again, his whole body spasming. One arm covered his face while the other hung uselessly at his side.

"I'm sorry. I'm sorry. Please," Franklin said, his voice weak. Bubbles of blood grew in his mouth.

"What happened here?" Ben stared down at the broken man, into his broken eyes.

Franklin gave him a strange look between the fingers of his still working arm. "You happened here. It was you. It's always you, but you were gone. You were gone and now you're back. You shouldn't be back. You can't be back." Franklin shut his eyes tight and turned to his side. Ben reached out his hand to touch Franklin, to draw him back into the conversation or shake some sense into him. As Ben raised his hand, Franklin let out a wild shriek, convulsed, and fell from the table.

"You can't be back. You can't be back," Franklin repeated over and over again, his voice rasping and unsteady.

Ben shook his head; did he do this? He looked around the

room, there had to be cameras. He grabbed a blood-soaked tablet from Franklin's desk and left the room. On his way to the door, he saw the lead bouncer that had stopped him earlier. He was in a pile on the floor, holes riddling his body in a direct centre mass grouping. He was not breathing. Ben turned him over and searched his body. He removed his ID and the handgun he had gotten from the hospital and moved towards the door. He just wanted to leave, to escape.

The night air was cool and refreshing coming from iron-tinged scent of the club. The neon light singed his corneas and he blinked away. No bouncers stood guard and no police were waiting for him. He looked to the right and saw his cab still where he left it. He breathed a sigh of relief.

"We know what you did," a voice filled his head and he froze, expecting to see a cop bearing down on him, gun pointed at his head. He turned, but there was nothing. "We know what you did, and we can help." Out of the corner of Ben's eye he could see a flash of color and movement. He turned, pulling his gun.

A tall woman stood before him. Tall and beautiful. She was wearing a smart business suit in strange neon colors that attacked his eyes and forced him back on his heels. Her smile was large around her perfect teeth, her pink lips stretched in a flawless heart shape. It was her blue skin that threw Ben the most, her blue skin and neon orange hair. Her eyes were a dead black. "Let us help you. We can defend you." A shield appeared on her arm, shining in a non-existent sunlight, her smile turning devilish.

"How do you know?" Ben asked the strange apparition before him.

"Call us." A number flashed in Ben's mind. Flashed and multiplied and scrolled through his brain. "Call us and we'll set everything right." She brandished a balance scale in her free hand, the pans on either side tipping back and forth so that they were never aligned. "Call Grohl, Hawkins, Mendel, and Smear. Barristers-at-Law for all your legal needs." The woman smiled and winked, lifting the scale high into the air. Ben turned his wrist and she disappeared.

Mehul cursed as Ben fell into the backseat. "What the hell happened in there? You okay?" His big brown eyes scoured the rear-view mirror, crawling over Ben's changed appearance.

"Yeah, I'm okay. Get us out of here, would ya'?" Ben felt exhausted, but his mind was firing on all cylinders. Mehul wasn't the only one confused about what happened in there. "Mehul, think you could find me a hotel, something a little discrete?"

"Yeah, boss, I can do that." The car started driving away from the **Sound/Fury**, getting up to speed to merge with the steady stream of traffic. Still no sirens, no sign that he would be caught, or punished. He took his ID out of his front pocket and looked at the face in the picture. The unkempt, unshaven face of a balding man looked back at him, leaning back in a permanent grimace of discomfort or anger. Who was he really? He stared into Mehul's rear-view mirror, stared at the dark eyes that looked back out at him and he was frightened.

A familiar knocking sound jostled him out of his thoughts as the car took flight once more. Ben looked out at the city below.

Heather Nolan

Heather Nolan is a singer, songwriter, photographer, poet and author born and living in St. John's, Newfoundland.

In 2017, her poetry was longlisted for the CBC Poetry Prize.

Her short fiction has been featured in *The Overcast*, *Secret East Magazine*, and *Wet Ink Magazine*.

Her first novella, *This is Agatha Falling*, debuts in March 2019.

A Flood of Sorts

I decided one evening to flood the family home.

"Look, Mother, the ceiling is swollen with water," I goaded.

There was no reply at all. Mother took a long, seductive draw from her cigarette, and continued reading the magazine on her lap.

I made for the stairs. On the second floor, I splashed down the carpeted hallway that was already mossy with water to the spare bathroom. Spinning the taps into full force, I stood back to watch the sink fill with satisfaction. The water slid over the sides of the porcelain bowl in a steady shining sheet.

"Look, Mother, at how the rains fall inside the room."

There was no flinch until three drops of water fell in a neat triangle across the pages of her magazine. With the dramatic flourish of a woman who dislikes being interrupted, Mother glared up at the cracking ceiling. It was beginning to sag under the weight, and there was a river in the making down the stairwell.

A contemptuous glance befell me, a sharp and thrilling attack of eye contact.

Mother was like a wild animal. Each time she moved, it was with a precision and purpose so calculated, that to see a muscle flinch was to take part in the ancient ritual of fear of predator and prey.

Overhead, the sounds of devastating volumes of water could be heard lapping against the walls.

"Listen, Mother." My voice was shaking with excitement. "Do you hear the sea?"

Without breaking her steely gaze, Mother was on her feet. In a great whirl of her dressing gown, she made for the basement stairs to the storm cellar. I pranced behind like a delighted jester, glorified by the success of my trick.

Father was already waiting there in the dark, smoking quietly with an expressionless face. Mother lit candles with the heat of her raging eyes.

Seagulls could be heard overhead, crying far above in the fresh sea air. The waves crashed over the cellar door.

"I'll go out hunting soon," said Father, his eyes unfocused. "To keep us fed."

I continued to prance about the room, twirling and leaping like a circus performer.

For thirty days and nights we cowered in that storm cellar, we three. Each day, Father would say, to no one in particular, "I suppose I should go hunting. We'll need something to eat." He ate his biscuits and sardines silently while he planned this expedition beneath the sea.

Mother glared at me with absolute concentration, unaware of how I delighted in watching the energy drain out through her heated eyes. I rejoiced secretly with every new wrinkle that formed across her seamless face. I watched her prized skin pucker and crease as she anxiously counted food rations over and over again, and it gave me purpose.

I was building an ark. Once the damp air was regulated by the slow easy breathing of sleep, I gently lifted the candle from the floor by Mother's side and shone its glow upon the darkest corners of the cellar. She had fallen asleep with one arm draped across the heavy green army canister, the other withering hand resting on the clasp.

I sifted through the rubble, producing broken relics

of wood shop projects that Father had never completed. I collected the warped chairs from the old dining set, ruined by weather when I had left them outdoors overnight years before; the disassembled crib that I had occupied as an infant, peeling pink paint coming off in great flakes; scraps of wood; sections of a fence never erected; and several old bicycle tires. There was a torn garden hose that would serve to lash these materials together. I found a great thick stick with handsome knots of sturdy oak wood that would serve as my staff. I took to carrying it around the cellar with me. I would be the captain of this vessel of forgotten things.

I returned the candle as Mother began to stir, and my broken treasures were cast back into shadow. Mother and Father had become very predictable and woke within minutes of each other. Neither looked at me or at each other, merely shifted slightly in their seats and stared blankly ahead. Mother carefully opened the army canister and began her concentrated morning count of the rations. Raising a weak hand, she offered crackers to Father and I. The sardines had either run out days ago or were on a more severe rationing schedule; I never did get close enough to find out. My stomach was uttering threats against the frail body draped over the food supply, but I wordlessly accepted my breakfast. It took Father several minutes to stand and lean over to the outstretched hand, and once he collected his package, he fell back in exhaustion. Mother's arm collapsed from the effort of remaining outstretched.

Mother began to speak to herself, a mantra so jumbled and incomprehensible it passed as a low hissing. Father did very little and continued to try and light his pipe though he had run out of tobacco some weeks prior. The ground around his upturned milk crate was littered with burned-out matches like a territory marking.

On the thirtieth day in the cellar, once Mother had fallen into a fretful sleep, I carefully dragged my raft into the outer rings of the candle's glow. Father watched me with a vacant expression.

I decided it was time. Positioning the raft before the storm doors with my staff of strong wood in hand, I thrust the doors open and the waves rushed in. I stood proudly on my vessel and the mighty tongue of the sea lifted me up and paraded me from the dank cellar, past the shipwreck of my childhood home and through the town down to the shore where I held my court.

Mother and Father washed up onto the beach and cowered before my vessel, the tide lapping at their feet in contempt.

"Look Mother!" I cried for the whole town to hear. "See how the seas are creeping under the doormat?"

Father bowed his head. Mother trembled. The waves made offerings, and fish presented themselves upon my deck in gratitude.

My citizens lined up along the beach to receive the sermon.

"Brothers and sisters of the Ark," I called. "The seas have called upon me to bring justice to this land."

The people began to cheer and dance, crowding around the raft, leaving a wide berth around Mother and Father in disgrace. I joined them in the dance of victory; a crude animalistic celebration of dominance, enormous roars of delight launching from my throat and echoing back from the writhing crowd below.

I beat my staff against the raft several times, ordering silence. The frenzy halted, a hush falling over the beach. The people leaned forward as one, awaiting the great secrets that I would whisper to them.

"First, my brothers, the punishment." Cheers erupted from the crowd, and they began to dance again.

As I gazed down upon my grovelling parents, my

heaving chest began to deflate. The fear that swam in Mother's eyes; the pleading softness of her face that so resembled affection. The fragile way Father's hand clutched her shoulder. They had aged thirty years in our month below the sea, shedding years of hardness along their edges.

Mother broke eye contact and sank her prized nose into the wet sand just as I felt the rotting wet wood of my great staff crumble in my hand. The wood had been decaying from within the whole time, leaving a façade of strength on its handsome outer bark.

Lauralana Dunne

Dunne has proven herself to be a force to be reckoned with in Canadian writing circles over the course of the last year.

In December 2018 her short story, 'Venus Flytrap,' was featured in *Kit Sora: The Artobiography*.

Dunne joined the 2018-2019 Board of Directors of the Writer's Alliance of Newfoundland in October 2018, an organization which contributes to a supportive environment for writing in the province and fosters public recognition of Newfoundland & Labrador writers.

Her first novel is expected in early 2020.

She describes herself as a slayer of imaginary monsters.

Future Imperfect

The blade's angle caught the morning light. Jexdon watched with fascination as the dark red that pooled in his palm stretched and scraped against the scissors before curling around his fingers. He straightened the ribbon to inspect it, then released it, watching as the decoration bounced back into a thick spiral.

He grasped the third strand and slid the blade along it three times to get the desired effect.

Jexdon set his scissors down with a satisfied nod, surveying the lumpy, brown package with a critical eye. It was less than impressive, if he was being honest. The crinkled paper was standard issue, belying the importance of the event ahead of him, and making him feel foolish for the sleepless nights he'd endured. Despite being an excellent student, he'd been woefully unprepared for the difficulties of manipulating the waxed paper. The crisp folds had devolved into nothing more than bent creases. Still, it was a passable for a first attempt.

The mismatched colors were what irritated him the most. He had requested a deep blue for the ribbon, the color he envisioned his mother's eyes were, instead of the mismatched browns that his own held. But the delivery drone had displayed an error message when it arrived. The dark red had been the only option left - a strange color for a celebratory event - but Jexdon had keyed in his authorization without hesitation, deeming it worth the cost in credits. He'd been lucky anything was left.

Jexdon laid the package reverently in his carrier, carefully fastening the flap securely as if his hard work would attempt to escape somehow. His stomach rolled at the idea of it breaking.

A gentle rapping on the door snagged his attention. The House Mother stood at the entrance to the dorm, hands clasped together with a serenity that always eluded him.

She inclined her head towards him. The grey of her uniform cut a stark line against the white of the room. A neutral color, darker than his own outfit, yet it commanded his attention so thoroughly that he had to remind himself to exhale in the silence.

"It's time."

Jexdon nodded, swallowing against the nervousness that had lodged in his throat.

She stopped him at the door. Cool fingers clasped his chin and tilted his head this way and that. When the House Mother finished her inspection, she allowed him a small smile. The rare gesture did not go unnoticed. "You're going to do great."

Jexdon blinked away the sudden wetness that blurred his vision. "Will I see you again?" His voice crackled with repressed tears.

The House Mother's smile faltered. She was younger than the others, faster with a word of praise or encouragement than the older ones, so Jexdon had developed a preference for her. He knew it was against the rules -- the idea of an unsanctioned attachment -- but sometimes he felt as though she returned the feeling. She had always been a source of warmth in an otherwise emotionless environment. He felt raw at the idea of saying goodbye to her.

The House Mother folded her hands in front of her. "Your new House will provide all that you need, Jexdon. I am confident that our paths will cross again as is necessary, Ministry willing."

Jexdon nodded quickly. It wasn't an admonishment, but it wasn't a rejection either. Squaring his tiny shoulders, Jexdon extended his hand. "Until we cross again."

The House Mother clasped the offered hand. "Until we

cross again."

To his surprise, she didn't let go right away. "Just remember," her low voice barely reached his ears, "it's not always your friends who smile at you. Take care of yourself, Jexdon. No one else will be strong for you."

Confused by the sudden warning, Jexdon stood motionless ever after she had released his hand. The House Mother gestured to the hall. "Don't keep everyone waiting." Her features had schooled themselves back to neutrality, her voice settled back into the demure calm he was accustomed to. There was no sign of the warning that had just slipped past her lips.

Jexdon nodded and hurried from the dorm. He ignored the hollowness in his chest, ignored the voice that whispered to his back, "Happy Seventh, Jexdon."

The sound of chatter could be heard throughout the halls. Jexdon trailed the voices to the courtyard, slowing his pace before arriving at the entranceway. It was important not to appear too eager in case anyone was watching him. He paused a moment on the threshold, resting a hand on the statue of the House Mascot for luck.

The large goat statue, affectionately referred to as Cans, kept watch over the courtyard with a blank expression. A symbol of adaptation and survival, the hooves of the massive creature had been worn to a shine from decades of stubby fingers rubbing the effigy in times of trial. Today had been no exception. Jexdon could see where the new smudges marred the mirror-like surface from earlier genuflections, where others had said their farewells when exiting the dorms.

Jexdon rubbed the front hoof -- clock-wise, counter-, then clock-wise again. Three times for luck. Straightening his spine, he slowly descended the steps.

Nervous babble ricocheted off the stone walls as the Sevens filed into the waiting mechambulator. Several House Mothers descended to conduct the chaos, pointedly ignoring the dark heads that peered down at them from the surrounding windows.

Jexdon joined the queue and took one long last look around. The high walls of the House were immaculate, unchanged since they had first been built, radiant against the sun bleached, golden yellow of the courtyard. Despite living here the last three years, Jexdon had never thought of it as homey. Now, with the unknown stretching endlessly before him, it seemed like the most comfortable place on Earth.

Jexdon reached the front of the queue and bid a silent goodbye to the House. He couldn't help but wonder which Six would take his bed.

Jexdon slid into a window seat. Antonneia, another Seven, was seated next to him. She perched there wordlessly as she assessed where everyone was sitting, cradling her carrier carefully in her lap. He was able to catch a glimpse of iridescent green ribbon before she shifted in her seat. Irritation at her forethought sparked against his insides, but he was able to smother the jealousy a heartbeat later.

Instead, he watched as Antonneia's anxiety bubbled to the surface around her schooled expression. She picked nervously at her shoulder strap, her eyes looking everywhere but settling nowhere. Jexdon felt sorry for her despite his previous annoyance.

"Have you gotten your new House Assignment?"

Antonneia jerked at the sudden question. The other Sevens around them conversed with a nervous energy, but their row had been quiet until now.

Antonneia dipped her head at Jexdon. "Nano Mexico. You?"

"New Floridia."

"Ah."

The enormity of the situation swirled in Jexdon's stomach, threatening to make him lose his morning's rations. He concentrated on his breathing.

Antonneia quirked a half smile. "At least you'll be able to see the ocean."

Jexdon nodded. It was the first thing he had thought of.

New Floridia was located along the coastline, but the toxicity levels were much stronger there. The worst cases of sun sickness were usually a result of New Floridians forgetting to reapply their UV shield.

"At least you'll get to enjoy the sun," he replied.

Antonneia nodded in acknowledgement. Nano Mexico was far enough away from the contamination zones that the atmosphere was still tolerable. She would be able to walk around without specialized equipment.

A departure bell clanged a warning. The door pod slid shut, then activated its vacuum seal with an intense *thunk*. Silence fell, a tense nothingness punctuated by several clicks from those who had forgotten to secure themselves in their seats.

Jexdon could hear expulsion from the air jets. There was an internal grumbling as the mechambulator began to tilt. Thin spider-like legs unfurled from the undercarriage and dug into the sand, pushing the tram off of the ground.

The mech tilted back and forth as it fought to balance on its long legs. Jexdon's heart hammered in his chest, and he closed his eyes against the churning in his stomach.

"This is always the worst part," Antonneia muttered next to him. Her tone sounded bored, and Jexdon couldn't tell if she was putting on a brave face or not. "If they actually made a stabilizing system specific to the mech's hydraulics, it would be so much smoother."

Jexdon swallowed against the nausea expanding in his throat, forcing his eyes open. "Maybe you can petition the Capital to do that." He offered a weak smile, feeling it turn into a grimace as the tram gave a final lurch.

Antonneia tossed her head. "Maybe I'll do it myself," she retorted.

Jexdon blinked in surprise. Did she have her Profession Indoctrination already?

Another warning alarm sounded, this time for the courtyard. Jexdon's ears protested the continual noise as the clanging sped up. A warning to those out in the open: take cover.

Several of the Sevens around him clapped their hands against their heads, trying to relieve the discomfort.

Air hissed around them angrily as the mechambulator pushed through the atmospheric barrier. There was an audible *pop*, and the force of the blowback launched them forward.

The enormity of the moment seemed to grow the longer the silence stretched.

Unceremoniously, the mech scuttled past the protection of the envirodome and into the desert.

Jexdon squinted at the sand. He was unprepared for how much brighter it was. Here, the ground had no protection from the harsh sun. Nothing lived out here. The sand was bleached bone-white, and it reflected the unforgiving light so brightly that Jexdon squinted his eyes against the sun spots. He cast his gaze around for the window's shield when something caught his eye.

A long shadow stretched towards them, away from the sun, as a second mechambulator came into view. Everyone quieted as the approaching mech moved to the side to allow them to pass.

Dozens of Threes had their noses pressed to the glass, watching as the Sevens scuttled by before they continued towards the envirodome's decontamination lock.

The House slid down into the horizon. Jexdon forced his gaze forward, keeping his expression a mask of indifference as the only home he knew disappeared from sight.

The Seven in front of them twisted in his seat, a mass of curly red hair popping up over the chair back as he peered down at the two of them. "Where are you two headed?"

Sebastian's skin was shockingly pale under the tram's lights. Jexdon knew his coloring was an anomaly. Pale-skins succumbed to sun sickness before they reached adulthood, so Government had been trying to extinguish their genetics for years.

Antonneia gave a self-satisfied smile. "Engineering Lab in Nano Mexico." Jexdon decided she was definitely downplaying her boredom.

Sebastian looked appropriately impressed. He slid his gaze to Jexdon and waited for an answer.

"New Floridia. No Indoctrination… yet."

Jexdon didn't dare say what he was hoping, what he had hoped when he had first set up in the Three's dorm -- that once he met his Birth Mother he would stay on to Indoctrinate with her.

Sebastian looked at Jexdon through half-lidded eyes. "I'm Indoctrinated to Scientists."

Jexdon blinked. No one was Indoctrinated to the Scientists before they were an Eight.

"Seriously? You?" Antonneia looked skeptical.

Sebastian lifted his arm and wiggled his wrist. A new ID bracelet caught the light with the movement, and Jexdon and Antonneia gaped at the sight. "I already spoke with my Birth Mother. They didn't want to waste any time getting me to In-doctrination." Sebastian smirked at them and turned around, plunking down in his seat with aplomb. Conversation over.

Antonneia snorted. "Good luck," she muttered ominously.

Jexdon didn't ask what she meant.

The rest of the trip was uneventful. Jexdon quickly became tired of watching the surrounding desert -- its giant cracks ooz-ing different colored ground sludge -- so he rested his head against the shielded window and dozed.

He woke from the *thunk* of the mech hitting the ground. He looked around, bleary-eyed, to see everyone fixated on the windows. The only sound in the tram was the protesting of the mech's legs as they curled back up underneath it.

A chime sounded to indicate that it had settled completely, then the door opened with a whoosh. As one, the Sevens stood and wordlessly filed out in an orderly fashion.

Jexdon gaped at the turmoil in the arrivals bay. Multiple mechambulators had arrived at the same time, their insides spilling excited Sevens onto the tarmac. Teams of Directors waited next to the parking spaces with clipboards and light sticks to direct the traffic.

Sebastian surveyed the scene with a low whistle. "Is Transfer Day always this busy?"

"Is that pertinent information, Seven?"

A Director had joined them without notice. A permanent frown was etched onto his face, and he scowled down at them from behind a hooked nose.

Sebastian straightened under the scrutiny. "I couldn't say what is or isn't pertinent information, Director."

Jexdon held his breath, waiting to see how the director took it, but he ended up looking impressed despite his dour expression. "You must be Sebastian. 3694-7?"

Sebastian nodded at his ID number.

"Come with me, please. Your transit is waiting."

Sebastian threw them a cocky grin over his shoulder and followed the Director without another word.

Antonneia pursed her lips, watching him leave.

"Do you think he'll be okay?" Jexdon blurted, despite himself.

Antonneia shook her head. "Do you?"

Jexdon searched for the correct response. "I think he will be a valuable asset."

Antonneia side-eyed him speculatively and said nothing.

A second Director walked to where their House Sevens had gathered. He wore the same as the first, but his expression was much friendlier as he looked around. "Capra Aegagrus! This way please."

Excited murmurs rolled through the group as they shuffled out of the bay and into the main structure.

The building was the most impressive thing Jexdon had ever seen. Splashes of color adorned the walls, a stark contrast to the pale grey he was used to. Even the floors were punctuated with thick, rich carpets that rolled endlessly down the corridors.

Countless people, more than he had ever seen before, flitted in and out of his peripheral vision. Hundreds of citizens of all ages milled about, either gathering in clusters of similar

House colors, or in uniformed clothing denoting the difference between the professions.

The commotion faded behind them as the Director led them down a corridor. He stopped in front of a large meeting room, gesturing with his clipboard for them to enter. "Remain here until you are called," he instructed. He waited until they began filing in before returning to the main hall.

The first Seven, Aveh, entered and whistled appreciatively. "Sebastian will be miffed he missed this," she announced in an attempt to be humourous.

Jexdon felt she more than missed the mark.

Everyone filed in excitedly, their awe increasing when they spied the large refreshment table set up in the middle of the room. With a chorus of whooping, the Sevens descended on the food.

Jexdon held back, his stomach still in knots from the journey. It had only gotten worse upon their arrival. The commotion in the arrivals bay, Sebastian's leaving, and now having to wait for an undetermined amount of time... The thought of eating nauseated him, and he wanted a clear head when he met his Birth Mother. The idea of getting sick during their meeting terrified him.

A few others held back as well. They planted their shoulders against the bare walls and watched the rest of the group at the table.

Jexdon did the same, crossing his arms as if that would somehow settle his nerves.

He was surprised to see Antonneia reclining next to him, assessing everything with a steady gaze. She slid her eyes to his and smirked. "Good call, Jexdon. I'm surprised you didn't fall for it."

Jexdon frowned at the backhanded compliment. He had no idea what she was talking about. "It?"

"Yeah. 'It'. The trap." She waved a hand dismissively. "The Director said to wait. He didn't say to eat... But I obviously don't need to explain that to you."

The Seven in front of them, Williver, cast a furtive look at Antonneia, then hurriedly discarded his food and joined the others against the wall.

Jexdon remembered the House Mother's warning and kept his face neutral. "No, you don't."

Antonneia inclined her head and remained silent. Her attention focused on the rowdy Sevens at the refreshment table. Conversation over.

Jexdon continued leaning against the wall, one of a few left in the room. Each time a new Director appeared, calling the next Seven by their ID, Jexdon had carefully reigned in the hope that it was his turn. It didn't matter, he told himself; the fact that he was still here was a good thing. He was sure it meant that he didn't have to catch a transfer out, unlike the Sevens who left before him.

Antonneia had been one of the first who was called. She'd dipped her head in acknowledgement -- whether it was to him or to everyone as a whole he couldn't tell -- and followed the Director without so much as a backward glance, her hand planted firmly on the top of her carrier. Jexdon had stood in silence ever since.

A whoosh of the automated door announced the arrival of yet another Director.

"Number 8624-7," she announced, looking at her tablet.

The room was tense with silent disappointment. Jexdon straightened into a standing position. "Here." His voiced betrayed the dryness in his mouth. Belatedly he licked his lips.

The Director looked up from her tablet. Calculating eyes took in his tired expression, and the hand that rested too-casually on his carrier. Jexdon noticed the look and clenched his muscles to keep from fidgeting.

"This way please."

Jexdon nodded and followed her from the room. The door whooshed shut behind him after he passed the sensors. He knew without asking that it would only open from the outside.

The Director had already settled her attention back into the tablet she was carrying, tapping it and muttering under her breath as they walked. She was so absorbed in her work that Jexdon had a brief moment where he worried that she had forgotten he was there.

The heels of her issued boots clicked against the polished floor, the only sound around them as they moved. He was careful to keep pace with her as they entered a new wing of the building. The only time he faltered was to gawk at a fountain in an enclosed courtyard. The craftsmanship was masterful -- or so he assumed, based on its complexity -- but it was the running water that kept his attention. A precious resource, the difference between life and death in many of the domes, and here it was only being utilized by the inedible greenery that greedily gulped its nutrients from the air.

The walk was a brief eternity. The Director slowed when they arrived at a lobby, and Jexdon felt apprehension rise in his throat. Checking a note on her screen, she made a point of looking carefully at the engraved plaques on the doors around them.

"Wrong floor," she grunted, flicking her head with annoyance. "Figures."

Before Jexdon could respond, she marched to a metal door and waved her hand over the sensor. There was a grinding of gears, a loud complaint at the sudden forced movement, then the door slid open with a ding.

The Director stepped into the small room and looked at him expectantly. Jexdon hurriedly stepped onto the plush carpet, the texture springing back against the thin soles of his shoes. He took a few extra steps, feeling the resistance, until he noticed the Director staring at him. Instantly he stilled.

"Press the button," she commanded in a bored tone.

Jexdon blinked at the rows of numbers. "Which one?"

"Eleven," the Director huffed, somehow irritated that he didn't know this piece of information beforehand.

Jexdon reached out and touched the disc, watching as the light around it glowed at the contact. The doors slid shut with another ding.

Jexdon grabbed the metal railing as his stomach lurched, grateful that he had ignored the food. The floor rose beneath his feet and they shot upwards in silence.

The Director looked up from her screen. "First time on a lift?"

Jexdon nodded, feeling miserably unprepared for the experience. She chuckled. "You'll get used to it."

"If you say so," he managed to get out before pressing his lips together. He was too miserable to enjoy the hint that he would be staying on.

Another ding announced the halting of the lift. The doors opened as effortlessly as before, and Jexdon scrambled back out into an identical lobby.

"Fourth unit on your left," the Director instructed, dispelling the notion that they hadn't moved at all.

Jexdon nodded and quickly walked down the hallway on shaky legs.

The units were surprisingly far apart. He reached the first one, but the doorway to the next one was barely a sliver down the hall.

"One. Two. Three. Four." Jexdon counted out loud to ensure he wouldn't mess it up.

He paused when he reached the fourth door. His stomach fluttered in time with his heartbeat, trembling erratically as he attempted to slow his breathing. "No big deal," he muttered to himself wryly, steeling his spine. "It's only the beginning of the rest of your life…"

He lifted his fist and knocked on the door three times. *1… 2… 3…*

It was the loudest sound in the world. The silence after each knock roared in his ears, and Jexdon half-expected the ceiling to fall down around him.

Three was his lucky number.

Three for the number of years he'd waited for this moment.

Three for when he was first transferred to House Aegagrus, and the number of days he had been punished when he was caught sneaking back on the transfer.

Three for the number of units he had to pass to get here; the number of Birth Mother's already meeting their Sevens, and the number of Sevens who came to the hub to meet them.

There was a hollow ache in his chest that grew as the silenced stretched, then he heard a muffled, "Coming!"

The door whooshed open, and Jexdon was immediately face-to-face with a pair of appraising eyes.

Brown, like the color of his left eye -- not blue like he had envisioned all these years. She was older than he had anticipated. Her hair was more grey than black, and wrinkles were deep lines in her face around her mouth and where her eyes crinkled. At least she laughed frequently, he thought, unlike the smooth-faced House Mothers that ran his lessons.

She stepped aside for him to enter and he did so quietly. The door whooshed shut noisily.

She -- his mother -- inclined her head. "Jexda, is it?"

"Jexdon," he corrected, his voice halting on his name, as if he'd never spoken it out loud before.

"Ah," she nodded, as if the name meant something. "Did you have a good transport?" When he nodded, she smiled in way that didn't quite reach her eyes. "You're welcome to take off your coat if you'd like."

Jexdon fumbled for the clasps on his House blazer. His hand brushed against the cross-strap of his forgotten carrier. He flipped the top flap open and carefully removed the package inside.

"This is for you," he said, shyly.

"Oh!" Her expression was carefully neutral, a perfect match to her tone. "Thank you very much."

Deft fingers tugged at the paper. The ribbon that Jexdon had so carefully curled that morning fell unnoticed to the floor. The wrapping quickly followed suit, drifting down after it as if balancing on a breeze.

Jexdon watched her anxiously. Carefully cushioned and miraculously unbroken -- the fired lump of clay had survived the transport. Two small hand prints were stamped onto the top of the piece. 'Jexdon, 8624-6' was scrawled underneath.

Two weeks ago, when he had made it, it had somehow seemed larger than life. Now, looking at it through her eyes, Jexdon felt a twinge of embarrassment at how poorly it had come out. Not only was it misshapen, but he could make out several distinct fingerprints within the lumpy clay.

"It's great," she said at last, handing it to him carefully. "I think there's an empty spot for it on the shelf behind you."

Jexdon could barely control his elation. At best he had expected her to set it down next to her, as if laying it down would somehow alleviate the awkwardness of their first meeting. But on a shelf, anyone could see it on display... Holding the gift with both hands, he carefully set it on the edge of the shelf she'd motioned to. He fidgeted with it a moment, making sure that it caught the light just so, before taking a few steps backwards to survey his handy work.

His elation immediately crashed into despair. His gift was surrounded by blobs of clay. Some were worse than his, but most were better, and each one boasted two small handprints that were pushed into the clay when it was fresh. The entire shelf was covered in them.

Jexdon turned to see his Birth Mother putter towards the eating area, filling an elongated cistern with drinking water.

"Did you want to stay for a cup of tea?"

Future Tense: Logistical Experimentation System

Charlie lay prone on the hard metal table. A bright light shone above him, nearly blinding him with the unfiltered white light. He was unable to move, his limbs useless and heavy around him as he struggled to sit up in the glare of the hanging lamp.

He assessed his situation, his soldier's training keeping him calm against the terror that clawed its way up his throat.

Quiet room. Sterile environment. Total blackness beyond the light above him.... He didn't know where he was or how he got there, but he knew that Command would have activated his tracking device once he missed his checkpoint report. Augments and cyborgs captured squadrons frequently. He just had to wait. As soon as Command-

There was the sound of clicking. Evenly spaced, it miraculously tapped out the counter-rhythm of his pulse. The sound grew louder, coming closer, and Charlie cast his eye around desperately to find a means of escape.

Waiting was the easy part. Staying alive was the challenge.

"You're awake." The voice was smooth and feminine. All-encompassing, it nagged at Charlie's senses until it settled in his skull with a resounding shock. Human. The voice was definitely human.

Charlie stared as she came into view. Petite and angular features could barely be seen around the giant lenses secured across her face. The curve of the glass magnified her eyes, distorting them past recognition to the point where the colors of the iris and pupils bled together.

She gave a curious smile. "This won't hurt a bit," she murmured almost soothingly, voice tinged with an amusement that escaped

Charlie. A blade came into view, an elongated scalpel, angled so that its needle-like edge was positioned just in front of his pupil.

"Stay still…"

The tin whine of air raid sirens cut through the stillness. Charlie gasped and launched into a sitting position, flailing his arm blindly in an attempt to locate the light.

He flicked the switch, eyes squinted, as the flash stuttered twice before an audible *click* announced the secure connection.

The bare lightbulb illuminated the small bunker. The dim light reflected dully off of the subterranean walls. It took a moment for him to pull himself from the nightmare and collect his bearings.

With a grunt, Charlie unplugged himself from the REM generator and bounded to his feet. Two quick taps on the console had the screens booting up in a wave of light. Several heartbeats later, everything was displaying in the system, and Charlie logged into the alarm grid to see what had set off the warning, quickly keying in the code to shut off the siren.

The lights continued to flash noiselessly around the console. The satellite image panned across the screen, then dragged northwest, zooming across the wooded area that separated him from the warning trigger.

Charlie whistled appreciatively, noting the size of the red zone that had cropped up on the radar. It took up half the screen and was expanding at an exponential rate. It would reach him in the next few hours.

"Perfect," he muttered.

In response a light activated on his ID bracelet, a steady pulse of blue that traveled up the circuit wrapped around his bicep and into the device that rested in his ear. Charlie stifled a groan.

"Good morning, Charles," the calm, disembodied voice greeted him. Machine-generated, slightly too deep to be completely androgynous, the inflections were incorrect enough to cause a tinge of annoyance in Charlie's brain. "Did you sleep well."

"Did you?" Charlie shot back, grabbing his pants and dancing into them. "You're welcome to take another nap. I don't mind."

"I do not sleep, Charles. You know this."

For what felt like the hundredth time this week, Charlie silently cursed the interface program. Command had insisted that he use it during his mission, but so far he had found it more of a distraction than anything. He felt his task was too important to divide his attention babysitting the Artificial Intelligence... well, Artificial Lieutenant, technically speaking. Not that that made him feel any better.

Charlie grunted noncommittally and stuffed his feet into his boots. "Any update from Command, AL?"

There was a blip of silence, a stutter of static that repeated in his left ear while he secured his supplies in his carrier. Sometimes it took a while before AL could interface with the satellites.

"The line is silent."

Charlie frowned, the slowly growing red on the screen snagging his attention. Whatever it was, it was between him and where he needed to go.

"Try again."

"The line is silent."

Charlie tapped his thigh in irritation, eyes fixated on the screen. "Can you connect to the satellites at all?"

"Affirmative."

"Only Command is silent?"

"Affirmative."

"Can you confirm the red zone?" When AL remained silent, he clarified, "North by northwest."

"Processing..."

Charlie swung his pack over his shoulder and grabbed his sniper carbine, snapping it into his holster so that the barrel hung down his leg. He popped open one of the compartments attached to his belt and took stock of the shots he had available: taser and metal. Perfect.

"Satellite assessment has returned. Red zone is spreading unchecked."

"Helpful," Charlie muttered, rolling his shoulders. "Tell me something I don't know."

"Before songbirds went extinct, they had been known to mimic the calls of birds of prey in order to scare off predators."

Charlie's eyebrows shot up into his scalp. "What?"

"Apologies if that is a fact that you already knew."

Charlie lifted his arm and stared at his ID bracelet, as if the interface could somehow see his incredulousness. He debated a quick retort but knew that the sarcasm would go undetected.

"At this rate the forest fire will reach the bunker in 3.2 hours."

"Forest fire?"

"The red zone."

"You really buried the lead on that one, AL."

Charlie frowned at the screen. He had heard the thunder from the lightning storm last night, had found the bunker hidden away just as dark had fallen, but he had hoped that rain had accompanied it. Apparently not. It had been weeks since it rained.

"I do not have arms, Charles. It is impossible for me to bury anything."

Charlie rubbed his face in exasperation. God, how he wished that Command hadn't saddled him with this blasted Intelligence. "Can we wait for the fire to pass?"

"Negative. Atmospheric conditions are not ideal. Temperatures are too extreme."

"Of course they are." Charlie tapped the keys several times, scowling at the map as it zoomed back out. The only choice was to backtrack the way he had come. The fire was between him and his destination, so he needed to pinpoint the best place to wait it out.

"Query error. Restate command."

"I wasn't talking to you." Charlie bit back a string of curses. He had long since learned that swearing at it was more frustrating than cathartic. The same way he had given up correcting it with his proper name. "When was the last sweep conducted?"

"Sweep has not been conducted for 5.2 hours… Initiating scanner… No life forms detected."

Not good. Not good at all. Not only had he not found any survivors, but he likely would not find food at this rate - especially if the wildlife continued to flee before the encroaching flames.

Charlie shrugged into his coat. The issued brown camouflage fit like a glove once he zipped up the closure, the material stretching around the tubing that kept him connected to AL - connected to Command the further he went into enemy territory.

"Keep scanners active. Scan at forty-five minute intervals."

"That will pinpoint Charles' location."

"*Charles* will be moving." Charlie flicked the light switch, plunging the bunker back into darkness. Except for the rumpled sheet on top of the mattress, it was impossible to tell that anyone had ever used the room.

"Where is Charles moving."

Charlie tapped the keys once more. The screens began to power off, the last one, the main one, dimming before finally flickering into darkness. He watched as the rugged coast of the isthmus faded from view.

"Somewhere to wait out the storm."

Charlie zipped along the backroads on his AT Cycle, the hum of the propulsion discs doing little to calm his nerves. He had narrowly missed the blockade on the main drag.

A new checkpoint had been set up long the mainway, augments and BOTs keeping watch of every vehicle that approached to check in to the area. It hadn't been there last week when he had burst out of the belly of the beast, somehow managing to find a working taser stunner to help him escape from the Base, his confinement cell hacked by Command to bypass the locking mechanism.

Charlie had stayed in the area longer than was safe, waiting to meet up with the team who had infiltrated the base, but they hadn't appeared. His orders had been clear: find any survivors and transport them to Command. Now, thanks to nature and a turn of bad luck, he had to backtrack to previously secured territory. Only this time, the mechanicals had branched out from their stronghold and were creeping towards the north.

"Augment approaching," AL's calm voice announced in his ear.

Charlie geared down his Cycle and let the remaining force carry him into the underbrush. The prickly leaves obscured his location from the approaching BOTs. He used a thick finger to move a twig away from his eye, the tendril snapping easily from the force, and Charlie frowned at the dry husk. It wouldn't take long for a fire to devastate this area. He was almost at the isthmus -- the place with the most access to water which offered the most secure location. Once he was there, he would be able to relax.

"Incoming."

AL's voice nearly made him jump out of his skin. Charlie jerked, brushing against the mostly dead bushes. They snapped and crackled from the movement as the BOTs whizzed past on their pulseboards.

Charlie held his breath, frozen in place as he watched them disappear down a dip in the road. There was silence for a brief moment, then the sound of the electro-pulse grew louder as it came closer.

"S**t!"

Charlie used his toes to push out of the trees and back onto the road. Unholstering his gun, he aimed while he attempted to start up his Cycle. He struggled with the engine, trying to get the spark to heat the battery source. "All Terrain my a-" There was a pop as a bullet whizzed by, flying past Charlie's ear and embedding itself in a trunk.

Charlie opened fire as he kicked down the Cycle's ignition. A roar answered his effort, and the ATC sprang to life, nearly bucking him off in the process.

He used his thighs to grip the saddle and keep his balance. The wheels hummed to full strength, the propulsion launching him down the dirt road.

He fired several shots behind him, but the BOTs avoided them easily, zigzagging across the road in random patterns. One bullet ricocheted off a boulder, bouncing back towards the engine of the first electro board. A split second before it could bite into the metal, a forceshield slid into place to protect it. The bullet crumbled into pieces when it connected, disappearing faster than the blue light that had appeared without warning.

Charlie slid the sniper muzzle back into his leg holster. Great. That was just great. He turned his full attention to the road ahead, checking his six in the side-mirrors to clock the position of the BOTs.

Their machines were better. They had more strength and gadgets, with more capabilities -- but that meant that they were heavier, too. Charlie knew he could outrun them. All he needed was a long stretch of road and he could speed past their tracking and wait out the approaching fire in a cave on a beach somewhere. If only the blasted trees had been farther apart, he could ride his Cycle into the forest and move around unencumbered.

"Life form detected."

Charlie nearly skidded into a wipeout. "What!"

"Scheduled scan initialized. Lifeform detected."

Charlie gritted his teeth. Of all the luck. He had been looking for weeks and now the scans detected something. "You're killing me, AL."

"Negative. Charles is operating within designated parameters."

A chuckle rasped out of his throat despite himself. "Where is the lifeform located?"

AL paused. "Lifeform is 6.8 kilometers south of Charles's

location… lifeform is humanoid…"

Charlie swerved to avoid a large puddle, assessing from the dip in the road that the sudden drop was deeper than it looked. "Figures." He checked his side mirrors, noting the position of the BOTs behind him in the distance. "I spend weeks looking for soldiers, only to find one just as I'm about to bunker down…"

"… Life signs are faint… Lifeform is eight years, four months, twenty-eight days, six hours, twelve minutes, and sixteen seconds… seventeen… eighteen…"

This time Charlie skidded to a halt. The Cycle protested the sudden braking and seized up, skidding along the ground until it came to a stop a few feet away. Charlie watched from where he stood after jumping off the saddle.

"AL. That can't be right. You're telling me you found a human *kid*?"

"Affirmative."

"We're in a warzone!"

"Affirmative."

Charlie's brow frowned as the hum of the BOTs' boards came closer. He had to act fast…

Pushing the Cycle closer to the approaching BOTs, Charlie removed his boot and tossed it down on the ground. He pivoted and dove behind a tree, pressing his back against the trunk as the sound of the BOTs' approach grew louder.

Pulling his coat out of the way, he popped open the cartridge attached to his belt and thumbed two electrobullets into his palm. He considered a moment, then added a third one for luck.

The approaching boards went silent. Charlie peeked between the branches to see the BOTs assessing the fallen Cycle. Two heavy sets of footsteps thumped against the dry dirt road as they dismounted and moved closer to inspect it.

Charlie waited until they were closer, until their constructed legs paused unknowingly in the puddle he had narrowly avoided, then he swung out from behind the tree. Acting quickly, he lobbed the charged capsules into the water. There was a flash of light as the charges made contact with the water.

Blue lightning arched along the surface of the water, snaking up around the bare metal legs and attacking the command centres in their chests. The first BOT had continued forward, inspecting the boot that Charlie had left to confuse them, so it didn't get the full strength of the charge. The second BOT, both feet immersed, dropped to the ground and immediately became still.

Charlie launched himself forward before the first BOT had time to react. Gun drawn, he fired several rounds of headshots while it was distracted from the first attack.

The bullets hit their mark. The clink of metal against metal was a sharp staccato in the silence. The BOT was knocked back several steps from the force of the bullets, its navigation system scrambling to catch up from being shocked. Better than a dream, Charlie watched as it tripped over its own foot and fell backwards into the puddle. The water, still electrified from the extra charge, made short work of its command system, and an uneasy silence settled around Charlie as the two machines remained offline.

Charlie dusted off his sock and pulled his boot back on. He kept one eye on the fallen BOTs as he laced it up, not moving towards them until he was satisfied that they were no longer a threat. He eyed their boards appreciatively. They would be slower moving, but more secure because of their shielding capability. They were the better choice... unless they had trackers in them...

Charlie circled the boards. On the outside there was no obvious marking, nothing that led him to believe that Humaphobes would be tracking the transports -- *could* track the transports if he used them.

He prowled closer--

--And stopped dead in his tracks when he heard the static. "Unit 641... what... r position?"

A bead of cold fear ran down his spine. Charlie raked his eyes over the console until he located the dimpled mesh box that acted as a speaker. He took an uncertain step forward, trying to decide between speaking and shutting it off.

"Unit 641. Report!"

Charlie reached out to toggle the switch, deciding to kill the box before it could alert anyone else to the area.

A clipped laugh caused his finger to hover uselessly in the air. "Charles? Are you there?"

It was the same voice. The same soft voice that haunted him in his sleep while the whir of torture devices hissed in the background. The feminine syllables hung between them, dissipating into the empty air.

"Time to come home, Charles. I miss yo-"

Charlie punched the toggle into the off position with a force hard enough that the switch snapped and crumpled into the speaker.

"Humanoid life sign is diminishing," AL's pragmatic voice interrupted his anger. Spurned into making a decision, Charlie stalked back to the AT Cycle and revved it back to life. He shook off his anger, throwing a leg over the saddle.

"Transfer the co-ords to the Positioning System." Charlie inched the Cycle forward while the propulsion systems came back online. With a grunt, he grabbed one of the shield generators and broke it off the side of the board. He threw it into the Cycle's magnetic compartment, then sped off towards the blip on his dash's PS.

Charlie was immediately glad for his choice of vehicle. It zipped effortlessly across the dry dirt, backtracking slightly the way he had come until a spot in the thicket opened up and he veered into it. Ignoring the looming cloud of smoke on the horizon, he put all of his energy into concentrating on his driving, steering himself between the trees, avoiding any rocky outcroppings that could cause his ATC to flip.

The foliage shrunk and became sparse the farther he traveled. The ocean breeze buffeted his face over the shortened trees, their growth forever stunted by the rough wind that whipped along the shore. Charlie concentrated on the tiny blip on his radar, straining to push his vehicle faster as it came closer, the pulse of the blue dot slowing in conjunction with the passage of time.

He had no idea how a human could appear out of nowhere. Charlie had combed every area of the peninsula before he had left -- while he had escaped -- covering all of the terrain that AL needed so that there were no gaps in its scan. The compound was half a day away, so they couldn't have stumbled out here...

The driftwood caught his eye first. Charred and broken, old pieces of board floated with the tide as they washed towards the rocky shore. Charlie frowned and scanned the rest of the beach.

There was no sand. Only countless rocks, their different shapes and sizes slick with the saltwater spray that crashed into the shore. AL had picked up the previous storm chatter off the coast, so it looked as though the winds had finally arrived, but it seemed as though the rain had dried up before it could reach the island.

An off-shore storm... Charlie snapped his attention back to the pile of driftwood. There, out past the undertow, a large piece of wreckage still floated with the tide, a round shadow resting on the smooth board.

Charlie veered toward the ocean, killing the Cycle just short of the water's edge. He tapped a code into the dash, switching the programmed terrain from land to water, and coasted over the water's edge just as the secondary propulsion jets kicked in. He revved the engine and sped towards the bobbing head, reaching it just as a rogue wave crashed into the battered board, capsizing it.

Charlie swore. Grabbing a retractable cable, he clipped around his wrist and jackknifed into the ocean.

The strength of the undertow grabbed at him, pulling his arms and legs in opposite directions. He forced his eyes open in the brine, blocking out the accompanying sting as he searched frantically under the oily waves.

The empty board stuck the side of his head, jerking his attention to the right, barely spying the tossed head of hair sinking lower beneath him.

With a strong kick, Charlie curled downward -- if that even was the direction -- and dove after the falling body, breaking free of the undertow into calmer depths.

Unceremoniously, he grabbed the head of hair between the thick fingers of his gloves, yanking the unconscious face closer to him so that he could sling an arm over his shoulder.

Pinning the tiny waist against him, he flicked the retractor on the cable around his wrist, feeling the sharp jerk as they were pulled back towards the surface.

With a grunt, Charlie threw the human onto the back of the Cycle, hurriedly wiping the oily brine away from its mouth and nose.

Human. Female. And she most definitely was not breathing.

"C'mon," he muttered, hoisting himself up into the saddle next to her. He pressed against her chest with a massive gloved hand. "Breathe."

"Human requires oxygen," AL's pragmatic voice announced, making Charlie want to rip the implant out of his eardrum.

Charlie pulled her chin down to open her mouth, compressing her chest again.

"Human requires oxygen."

"Dammit, I know that," he yelled at the disembodied voice.

Charlie clenched his hand into a fist and pounded it against the girl's chest. Grimy water shot from her mouth and dribbled down her chin, pooling in the hollow of her neck. Charlie pounded on her chest twice more -- three times in total -- and winced when he felt the snap of a bone breaking.

The girl gagged. Gasping for air, clawing at her neck, Charlie quickly turned her over and held her in place as she spewed the contents of her lungs back into the ocean.

When she was finally done retching, she clung to the Cycle

with a moan, holding herself still on the hovering vehicle, concentrating solely on sucking the sea air into her starving lungs.

Once Charlie was convinced that she had enough strength to keep herself secure, he grabbed the handles and turned the Cycle towards the shore.

"Let's get you back on solid ground," he told her.

"Are there any bunkers nearby?" he asked AL, for what felt like the twentieth time.

The dry air around them was punctuated now and then by a chill breeze. Not only did it have the misfortune of being terrible weather for drying off, but it was absolutely excellent for fueling the oncoming firestorm.

The girl -- Ella she had repeated, pointing to herself -- had fallen asleep as they sped away from the wooden wreckage, but not until after he had somehow convinced her through a series of hand gestures and exaggerated smiles that he wasn't going to hurt her -- which was a blessing as far as Charlie was concerned. It had become immediately obvious that she had no idea where she was, and that she spoke little-to-no English. Keeping her safe until he could get them to the mainland was paramount, a situation made ideal if she were to stay asleep as long as possible.

"No bunkers located in the surrounding area." AL's response was starting to sound like a broken message stream.

"You're killing me, AL."

"Negative. Charles' functions are operating within their normal parameters. Parameters have been adjusted to reflect current hydration saturation levels."

Charlie's mouth cracked into a grin. "Hey, AL, you just made a joke!"

"If you say so, Charles."

Charlie scanned the area as the AT Cycle zipped in between the trees. They needed to get out from being out in the open. "Are there any cave systems on file?"

"Affirmative."

Charlie nearly geared down on the spot. "Show me on the radar."

There was a buzz of visual static, then the map zoomed out to show several interconnecting caves along the shoreline. The kind that were small enough to be completely submerged when the tide came in.

Useless.

"Anything on land?" he ground out from between clenched teeth.

The map blipped offline for the scan, then loaded back to their current location, highlighting an area about forty kilometers east of them.

"That'll do," he muttered, veering the Cycle in that direction.

They reached the cave well before dusk arrived. Charlie was able to scout the area to his satisfaction, scanning and visually inspecting the immediate vicinity before he felt secure enough to kill the engine.

There was always a twinge of apprehension once the saddle's vibrations stilled. Almost as if the immediate window after the engine died meant that he, too, would share the same fate.

Nothing happened.

The cave was deep enough that he could stash the Cycle without fear of it drawing attention from passing patrols. Charlie parked it across the entrance, dragging tree boughs and bushes in front of it, filling in the opening of the cave to make it look like a blind. Hopefully nothing would be scanning for humans this close to the base. And just to make certain… Charlie interfaced his bracelet's signal with the Cycle's power system and activated his shielding device.

It was a massive drain on resources, and Charlie knew it was a bad idea. So far, he had been lucky. None of the patrols had scanned his life sign, but he couldn't risk his good luck running out. Not while he was watching the kid.

The activated shield pitched to a soft whine that echoed back within the cave. Charlie effortlessly lifted Ella from the Cycle and set her on the hard ground. He pulled a single, thin blanket out of the saddle's compartment, draping it over the shivering girl. He frowned. Her clothes and hair were sodden, and he wasn't doing much better himself. He didn't notice the cold as she did, but they both needed to dry off if they wanted to get warm.

She didn't look like someone who was accustomed to the cold. She was probably on an escape vessel from a warmer climate -- one that wasn't equipped to deal with colder weather or storms. Charlie knew he wouldn't get the whole story until he found a translator up along on the continent, but there was no way a child was the only escapee on board. Her family had to have been with her...

A metallic beeping interrupted his thoughts. Creeping forward, Charlie crouched behind the Cycle, peering out between the woven branches of the blind. He couldn't see anything at first glance, then the sound repeated to the left, louder and more insistent.

There was a whir, and two BOTs rolled into view.

The scanners had picked up the shipwreck.

They were far enough away that Charlie couldn't make out the smaller details, barcodes or assignment coloring, but close enough that when a red eye scanned the surrounding area, a pulse of light slicing outwards like a phantom laser beam, Charlie ducked down with a silent curse and waited, unmoving, for the upcoming firefight.

Everything remained still. There were no alarm bells, no sirens or blasting in their direction. Instead, there was a metallic chirp between the BOTs as they conversed, then the crunching of twigs as they rolled away.

Charlie waited another minute before poking his head back into the lookout hole.

There was no sign of the BOTs. Nothing but the sound of

the shield's hum, and the scrap of dry branches as they rubbed together in the breeze.

Relief flooded through him. He undid his coat and let it fall to the ground with a wet thump, unholstering his rifle and inspecting it to make sure the sea sludge hadn't caused any damage.

He sat cross-legged next to the lookout, balancing the muzzle across his knees, finger at the ready on the trigger just in case.

They would wait out the rest of the search parties -- either until the shield died or the firestorm reached them -- then head back to the ocean and scoot past the isthmus to the mainland.

Two, maybe three days tops, and they would be back with the rest of the humans.

Charlie rolled his shoulders, straightening his back to get comfy. Three days was nothing. He could wait.

A hacking cough grabbed his attention. He must have dozed somehow while sitting at the blind. Without his REM generator it was impossible for him to log his down time, impossible to achieve a sustainable state of rejuvenation in a short period of time, so Charlie was in a state of confusion when his attention narrowed to the presence behind him.

Carefully, he slid backwards to check on the girl. "Ella?" he whispered, carefully giving her a shake.

"Papa," Ella groaned. Her eyes cracked open, two brown irises peering out at him past her narrowed eyelids. She took stock of her surroundings and pressed her eyes closed, deflated.

Charlie's heart went out to her having experienced the very same scenario himself, waking from a terrible dream only to find out that it was actually reality.

"Hey," he said softly, giving her another shake. "Wake up, kid."

Ella opened her eyes again. "Charlie," she croaked, clutching the sheet around her as a shiver wracked her body. "Warm."

Charlie frowned. She had started to shiver, but heat had blossomed on her pink cheeks, contradicting the signs being chilled.

The girl had spiked a fever.

"Okay," he told her, giving her shoulder an awkward pat. "It's gonna be okay."

Moving back to the front of the cave, he peered out into the dusky forest.

Patrols would be everywhere by now. Once the wreckage had been detected, that would be it; the entire area would be on lockdown. He had counted on being able to stay put until the fire had cleared the BOTs out, allowing them to move unencumbered across the island.

He slid his gaze to the Cycle. It still whined with power, the barely-detectable vibrations ticking against his eardrum when he got close, but a quick glance at the meter showed that the machine was almost out of juice.

Charlie rubbed his jaw in thought. He was going to have to get creative.

"AL, are there any fuel stations nearby?"

"Processing… Affirmative. Fuel levels are unavailable."

"What does that mean?"

"The current level of the fuels in the stations are not available.

Charlie bit the inside of his cheek. "Is there a way to detect them?"

"Negative."

He frowned. He was definitely going to have to get creative.

He rolled his shoulders, wracking his brain. The BOTs had to rest somewhere. And the two he'd encountered on the isthmus had their own vehicles, so they had to get fuel from somewhere…

No, not fuel. Energy.

"AL, are there any charging stations nearby?"

"Affirmative. Charging stations are currently online and operating within normal parameters."

Charlie felt himself grinning like an idiot. "Location?"

"CABOT Base Bunker."

His enthusiasm faltered.

The Cybernetic Android Battle Operating Tactician bunkers were centuries old. Carved into the cliff faces themselves, facing out over the Eastern Ocean, they were a standing relic to a war that time had nearly forgotten. That is, until they had been repurposed as combat centres for the Base that had been built above them. The very Base that Charlie had just escaped from.

He shifted his balance between the balls of his feet, just as Ella was caught up in a fit of coughing that reverberated off the back of the cave.

The Cycle's shield was about to fail. If any patrols picked up on their life signs, they were dead. If he tried to rush them to the mainland through the firestorm, they were dead. If he brought them to the base to secure a better mode of transport -- one that could travel over water for an extended period of time -- they were... less dead.

With a sigh, Charlie secured his rifle back into its holster.

"I broke out once before," he told Ella, scooping her up into his arms. "Might as well break back in just for fun."

The Cycle gave out after twenty minutes of riding. Cursing its ineptitude of driving with a shield, Charlie cradled Ella in one arm while keeping his rifle at the ready in the other, stalking through the trees along the edge of the road in order to stay out of sight.

So far, he had not encountered a single patrol. A fact that did not sit well with Charlie. AL constantly scanned the area, but there was never anything to report.

Ella became warmer as they travelled. Charlie had ripped open the saddle's compartment for any hint of medication for her, but nothing had been available.

"The nearest charging station is just over the next rise."

Charlie trudged on, his legs adjusting as he began what felt like a nearly-vertical incline.

Shattered shells of houses lay in rubble around him. Their brightly-colored paint had tarnished under the unchecked sun, the pieces of wood intermingling like faded confetti.

He kept his eyes peeled as he scanned the area, constantly calculating the distance to the cover of trees that had grown over the abandoned dwellings. So far so good.

"Incoming," AL's voice contradicted in his ear.

Charlie ducked behind the rusty hull of a wheeled box just as two video drones zoomed past overhead. He stayed crouched, waiting to see if they would to circle back. When they didn't, he eased them back out into the street.

"That was close. Any sign if they detected us, AL?"

"Negative. Drones are reporting to the advancing firestorm."

Charlie slid his gaze along the horizon, noting the dark plume of smoke that was fast approaching. The undertow here was too strong. There was no way they could survive in the ocean until it passed.

Ella coughed weakly in his arms, her breath rasping past her lips.

"How much farther to the station?" Charlie frowned as he noted the girl's deteriorating condition.

"Charging station is located on the other side of the elevation."

"...On the cliff face?"

"Affirmative."

Not good. The incline was steep, and cover would be a scarcity at the higher elevation. If any more drones passed overhead…

"Humanoid life sign is diminishing," AL continued neutrally.

"What?"

"Humanoid life sign is diminishing."

"How?"

"Foreign contamination a possible factor. Toxicity levels have increased beyond acceptable parameters."

Charlie cursed. Clearing her airways at the beach hadn't been enough. Whatever sludge she'd ingested, whatever oil and sewage that made up the ocean, had seeped its way into her body. They couldn't wait out the firestorm. Ella didn't have three days left.

He thought back to the bunker he had left yesterday. He had left supplies there untouched: rations; bullets; spare clothing. Nothing that could help her. The only place he had seen medic supplies recently...

"AL, locate the nearest Base entrance."

"Nearest Base entrance is one hundred metres to the left of Charles."

Charlie strode in the direction outlined, counting his steps out loud to make sure he didn't miss it. The dull glint of thick metal caught his attention. Charlie shifted a pile of rubble with his foot to uncover a heavy manhole cover set into the face of the cliff.

Reluctantly, he holstered his rifle and clasped the circular handle of the hatch. The metal protested loudly, a grating sound that screeched back at them from the surrounding cliffs, but other than causing a strange dent to appear in the metal, the hatch opened easily for them to enter.

"You better be right about this," Charlie muttered to AL before hopping down into the opening.

His eyes adjusted quickly to the dim light. The tunnels were stale. Water had accumulated in large puddles along the floor, the drips from the ceiling the only sound as they plinked from the support beams. The tunnels were ancient, old stone formations supported by updated alloys to keep them open. The lighting system had been revamped, and Charlie was glad to see a string of emergency lights stretching in all directions, the wires making it look like an electrified spider's web.

"Which direction, AL?"

Charlie waited. There was no response from the line. No static to indicate that AL was processing the request or connecting to satellite images of the area.

"Fine then." He took a brief moment to get his bearings, sifting through the memories of his recent escape and his knowledge of the Base's layout, then turned and hurried east towards the ocean.

The barren corridors seemed to close in on him the farther he went. He did his best to ignore the sense of dread that was growing in his belly. Purposely returning to the place he had fought so hard to escape from... Each flickering light sent his reflexes jumping, and it was all he could do not to react to each drip of water and crumble of rock. Just when he thought he could no longer bear it, just when he felt as though the weight of the hills above him were about to crush him, the tunnel widened.

A ladder stood against the wall, soaring above him to allow access to the floor above him. He had made it to CABOT Base. Now all he needed was an infirmary.

Steadying Ella over his shoulder, he grasped the runs with his free hand and began the arduous process of pulling them up the ladder.

Slowly, painfully, he steered them up a level and out onto the brightly lit floor. He did his best to maneuver himself through the opening first, shielding her slight frame in case they were discovered, but no alarm or attack greeted them. The hallway was eerily quiet in all directions.

"AL, can you hear me?" Charlie kept his voice at a murmur, but it still sounded like he was shouting in the silence.

There was a blip on the line, then it clicked into silence. Whatever barrier was in place, AL was unable to reach through it.

Hopefully that meant that nothing could reach through it.

The hallway was unfamiliar. Whitewashed walls rose around him, brightly illuminated by industrial bulbs that stretched the length of the ceiling.

At least nothing could sneak up on them, he thought, ignoring that the reverse was also true.

Picking a direction, Charlie strode silently down the corridor. If he remembered correctly, the labs were in the basement. That meant that eventually he would come across... There.

Charlie eased them around a corner, finger resting lightly on the trigger as he did so. Belatedly he cursed himself for not removing his thick gloves. His finger fit through the rest, but only just barely.

Darkened rooms loomed ahead of them. The only giveaway of their location was the darkened windows that were flush against the wall. Thin metal wires crisscrossed inside the glass, securing the material and, he assumed, running an electric current through it.

He didn't have time to guess why the workers were absent.

Using the tips of his thick gloves, he probed the wall sections between the windows, moving slowly. After the third set of windows, he paused when he discovered a barely discernible dip in the sheet metal and pushed in on it until he was rewarded with a soft click.

A thin cylinder popped out of the wall. Charlie gripped it between the knuckles of his thumb and forefinger and twisted it. A seamless door slid open with a chime.

Steeling himself, he entered the darkened room.

The lights flickered into life above him. As if in response, the transmitter in his ear cracked momentarily with static before falling silent.

"AL?"

Charlie shook his head like a dog shaking water from its coat, hoping to knock a loose wire back into place. Another stutter of static was his only reward.

Ella coughed again. Her dark skin was visibly flushed, and Charlie could only hope that he wasn't too late.

Striding further into the room, he placed her on a shiny metal exam table, suppressing a shudder at how familiar it looked, and went to work ransacking the drawers. Most were on rails instead of hinges; many of them were locked. Charlie took no notice as he wrenched them open, leaving discarded drawers strewn across the floor as he went.

Nothing. Not even a single pill was being stored in the room. Furious, he threw the last drawer at a wall in a fit of helpless rage.

The drawer bounced back towards him with a hollow boom. Charlie stalked closer and pounded a fist against the wall, shoulders drooping with relief at the hollow noise that echoed back at him.

Charlie took one step, and then another, tapping against the wall until the pitch changed and solidified. Pressing both hands flat against the wall, he slid them up and down the panel. "C'mon," he growled with exasperation.

Another dip in the wall. Another push and another cylinder, another chime and another hidden doorway that whooshed open.

The whir of machinery didn't pause as the hidden room lit up. Charlie stepped over the threshold, pushing down his revulsion as his combat boots clinked off the metal floor. This was Ella's only chance.

Averting his eyes, he bypassed the stacks of sample jars. He ignored the displayed organs and dissected body parts, the two-headed cat expertly preserved in gel, the mutated animals in liquid-stasis that bobbed from the current of oxygen bubbles being pumped into the tube.

He ignored everything as he strode to the back of the room, his focus pinpointed on the small fridge humming quietly to itself. He wrenched it open, catching the empty spray canister that rolled off the top of the appliance from the sudden movement.

A shallow crate rested on the top shelf. The multiple glass vials crammed into it clinked together as he sorted through them, reading the symbols that appeared on their labels.

He grabbed three of the purple-slashed vials -- three for

luck -- as he eyed a container of large mottled eggs on the bottom shelf before shutting the door firmly. He wouldn't entertain them as food for all the clean water in the world.

Jamming a vial into the container, he was rewarded with the sound of it depressurizing as it loaded the chemicals into the spray.

Ella's shallow breathing was barely audible over the whir of electricity. Grasping her cheeks, Charlie gently opened her jaw and placed the nozzle in the back of her throat. Pressing the dispenser, there was a gurgling sound as the liquid in the vial expressed as a mist against her throat.

He waited for the span of three breaths before removing it and dispensing the second vial.

This time the response was more immediate. Ella gasped, a long guttural breath that sounded as though she were dragging all the air from the room into her lungs.

One... two... three. Three for luck. Three ragged breaths that brought life back into her face.

Charlie felt relief trickle down his spine as Ella opened her eyes. "Charlie?"

Smiling, he scooped her up into his arms.

"¡Socorro!" There was a commotion at the door.

Charlie looked up to see a stocky man staring at him wide-eyed. His gaze ripped from Charlie's face to the child he cradled in his arms.

"¡Socorro!" the man screamed again. Footsteps pounded towards them, and Charlie belatedly realized that he had discarded his rifle across the room during his search.

Several human soldiers burst into the room, dressed in brown camouflage and combat helmets, rifles cocked and at the ready. Charlie pivoted and dropped to the floor, twisting his back so that it was between Ella and the soldiers. Soldiers who were trained to shoot first and ask questions later. He didn't know what kind of bullets they were packing, but he hoped that his feeble armour would be enough to stop them.

"Papa," Ella wailed.

Silence hung in the room. There was no explosion of ammunition, only the sound of strangled disbelief from one of the soldiers.

"Ella?"

Charlie rose. The soldiers gaped at him, fear and disbelief clearly written across their faces. They didn't wear the uniforms of CABOT soldiers, so their reaction confused him.

He took a step forward. "Friend," he began reassuringly.

Screams and shouts were the response. The men aimed their weapons at him, causing Ella to scream shrilly and bury her face in her hands.

One soldier started screaming angrily. He stalked in front of the other men, shoving the loaded barrels out of the way as he stood between them and Charlie, talking rapidly in a language that Charlie didn't understand.

Charlie remained motionless.

The other soldiers watched him with a hard expression until, one by one, they set their rifles on the ground and held their hands up in surrender.

The soldier in the front did the same, wet eyes resting on Ella's wide-eyed expression. He crooned to her softly, speaking so quickly that his words tumbled into each other.

"Papa," she sobbed, reaching out.

The man's face crumpled. He didn't move, eyes trained on Charlie's face, but reached a hand out to her longingly. "Por favor…" His voice cracked.

Charlie slowly walked around the exam table and carefully held Ella out to him. The man's expression turned to disbelief when he realized that Charlie was giving her back to him.

Taking her reverently, he cradled Ella against his chest while tears flowed unchecked down his cheeks.

"Here," Charlie said, handing Ella the spray and the last remaining vial. "You might need this."

Ella's father looked at the medicine in her hands, assessing the empty cartridge and the state of the room around them. His expression turned to shock, and he quipped a quick question at her. She responded with a nod.

Her father took a step forward and extended his hand to Charlie. Surprised, Charlie took it and the man shook it solemnly.

A whine of static popped in Charlie's ear and he flinched.

Simultaneously, firefight exploded down the corridor. A blast shook the floor, the hollow reverberation booming back and echoing in the space around them. Ella screamed and everyone hit the floor.

Charlie clutched his ear, waiting for the wine to subside. He rolled to the wall, snagging his forgotten rifle as he launched himself to his feet. He crouched by the door frame, peering out into the dim hallway to assess the situation.

There was nothing visible, but another explosion rocked the building from an unseen assault.

There was a scream and the thump of a body hitting the floor above him. Charlie could hear wheels driving across the floor afterwards. BOTs must have found the rest of their squad and now they were under attack.

"Go!" he instructed, pointed back in the direction he had come from. The opposite direction from the firefight.

There was a pause as everyone looked at him, and he gestured more sharply. "GO!"

The men scrambled. Ella and her father stood firmly in the middle, the other men flanking them on either side as they ran from the room. Charlie caught the bob of her head as she peered over her father's shoulder while he ran with her to safety.

He gave her a smile and waved, feeling a hitch in his chest as she waved back before disappearing from view.

Steeling his spine, Charlie loaded his rifle with electrobullets, waiting until the sound of their retreating footsteps disappeared. Taking aim, he shot several rounds into emergency light system. He reveled in the satisfaction of watching the live wires erupt from their fastenings, causing a gaping hole to appear as the ceiling caved in on itself. The corridor was plunged into darkness, the area impassible.

It would buy them time. And once the BOTs honed in on his location, he'd buy them time as well.

"You sure picked a hell of a time to go on vacation, AL," Charlie told the absent lieutenant.

Charlie retreated into the side room. He clapped a hand over his ear as blips of static assaulted him. "AL?"

"AL can't hear you," a woman's cool voice purred into his ear. "He's been retired."

Charlie's step faltered. Immediately he flashed back to the last time he had seen a metal exam table. He had been strapped to it against his will.

"So nice of you to come home, Charles. I missed you."

Charlie gritted his teeth and probed the wire that ran into his ear. If he could disconnect it somehow…

"Your friends' watercraft is surprisingly sophisticated. I'm absolutely *dying* to get my hands on it."

Charlie's hand hovered over the wire.

"I torpedoed their last one, but I could be convinced to let them escape this time…"

He licked his lips. "What do you want?"

The answer was a cheerful chime. He peered into the back room and was surprised to see that a secondary door had opened.

"Come home, Charles."

Charlie squared his shoulders. The idea of voluntarily returning to that room -- voluntarily returning to *her* -- stopped him cold. But if it meant Ella would survive…

He stepped into the lift.

The door whooshed shut behind him. Sleek black panels greeted him, the only walls in the interior. There were no buttons to press, but after a brief pause, the tube whirred into life and began to climb through the floors.

The passing lights reflected back at him from the panels, shifting his reflection into something unintelligible. Unnerved by the grotesque image, he averted his eyes and faced the door until the lift slowed and opened with another chime, announcing his arrival at the top floor.

Plush carpets sprung back against his boots as he stepped out into the posh office. He picked at the fraying bit of string on his glove, casting his eyes around as he crept into the room. Empty.

A curved flight of stairs spiraled up to the next floor.

"Up here," the female voice called, and Charlie was unsure if he was hearing with his transmitter or with his ears.

He obeyed noiselessly.

The top floor was much like the sample room in the medical lab, jars and containers of different dissected parts on display, but this time the highlighted pieces were mechanical. Charlie recognized several different pieces of BOTs, as well as a drone that had been emptied of metals, looking like an abandoned corpse after scavengers had picked it clean.

Three long stasis chambers were stacked against the walls. The first two were sealed shut, their viewing panels fogged over with condensation from the churning liquid inside. The last one lay wide open, dark and deactivated, its door gaping open like a battle wound.

His attention narrowed to the metal nameplates that labeled each chamber. Heart sinking, he read them as he prowled past.

Combat Humanoid… Acute Reactive… He stopped at the deactivated pod. *Logistical Experimentation System.*

With a sense of dread, he wiped the condensation away from *Acute Reactive* chamber and peered inside. A grotesque version of his face stared back at him.

Not quite human and not quite machine, it matched the reflection that he had seen in the lift. No wonder soldiers had been terrified of him.

His hands flew to his face, trying to feel out what had been done to him. He ripped the thick gloves from his hands to use his fingers, only to discover metal digits hiding under the combat clothing.

Panicked, he ripped through his jacket and shirt. The metal fingers shredded the material easily, revealing a fusion of bone and alloy that glinted dully in the light.

"Found your brothers, did you? Naughty boy."

Charlie whirled to find a woman watching him, her gaze calculating his reactions over the rims of her large glasses.

"Who are you? What is this place?" He raised his rifle, aiming it directly at her slim form.

Her angular features remained unchanging except for her eyebrows, which rose in surprise. "The memory wipe must've worked better than we realized. You have no remaining recollection." She tilted her head. "Amazing."

She gestured around broadly. Blue flashes of light danced across the top of her skin, and Charlie realized that she had a shield generator. His weapon would do nothing against it.

"This is the future, Charles: unity between man and machine. And you were the perfect volunteer."

Charlie looked at his chest, where flesh had been melted into notched metal bars that circled his torso. An inserted metallic rib cage that housed a fake hydraulic heart.

He pressed a hand against his chest. No, not a fake heart. A reactor core. It pulsed inside his chest, regulating the mechanics of his synthesized body.

"Well, not so much a volunteer as an unwilling participant," she continued, unaware of his self-examination. "You were the only prisoner to survive the procedure, so obviously I had to replicate your DNA to see how often I could make it work. Those memories were erased, but your original mission remained somehow. A lucky oversight that brought you back to me."

The technician smiled and motioned to the table. "Feel free to get comfortable. I'll fix you after I deal with your friends."

Charlie clenched the -- his -- metallic hands into fists. "You said you'd leave them alone," he reminded her, his voice raw.

She tipped her head back and laughed. "I know, but their technology is too good to pass up. Think of what the scientists could accomplish with it! Besides, once I get back inside your brain, I'll make sure your emotions don't bother you anymore.

I promise."

Charlie watched as she returned to her terminal and tapped out several commands. He cast his eyes around helplessly, looking for a way to shut down her generator or jam her signal. He needed to stop her.

His gaze rested on the other androids. What would happen once they were active? Would they hide their fate from themselves in an attempt to retain their humanity, or would they activate as killing machines, stripped of whatever emotions were left in his mechanical heart?

Charlie looked down at his exposed chest. The pulse of his reactor core was visible under the knit flesh that caved in with every absence of vibration.

Killing machine…

Charlie fired his rifle at the technician. The electrobullet bounced off of her shield in a flash of blue light, slicing through the terminal with an arc of electricity that caused her to fall back from the live wires with a curse.

She gritted her teeth. "There's more than one terminal," her voice rose in pitch with exasperation. "I can use any of them to run commands and experiments. Destroying this one won't save you."

Charlie grabbed a live wire, the current sliding off his fingers harmlessly. "Who said anything about saving me?"

He ripped his chest open with his free hand, the metal digits cutting easily through his rib cage. He removed the reactor core and held it against the electrical current with a ghost of a smile.

She reached out urgently. "Don't--"

Charlie didn't give her the chance to continue. Wrenching open the outer layer, he impaled the reactor core on the wire, feeling a surprising satisfaction as the explosion expanded between his fingers.

Alarm bells clanged around them, nearly drowning out the hum of generators that worked overtime to keep the explosion contained within the automatic force fields that had activated automatically from their safety programming.

The power felt impossible. It was a balancing act, keeping it secure in his grasp. He watched the technician, reveling in the fear in her eyes – wondering how many prisoners she had observed it in before she had stopped at him. Once wrong move and the whole mountain would disappear, including the Base and its disgusting experiments.

Charlie slid his attention to the satellite images, his sight already powering down, noting how the humanoid dots had reached the ocean. He hoped they would be safe.

"Please," the technician pleaded. "You can have anything you want..."

Charlie smiled. "I already do."

There was an audible crunch as he clenched his fist and broke through the containment fields.

She didn't have time to scream as he unleashed the explosion on the world.

David Rimmington

A Leicester England native currently residing in Halifax, Rimmington makes his publishing debut in *Dystopia from the Rock.*

The Ninth Wonder

After its deep canyons, high peaks, and deserted tombs, the ninth wonder of the planet Zolen would have to be the city of Kronk. Kronk sits on a vast plain, rising like a mirage as you move towards it. Even from afar, its towers and buildings appear like apparitions: fingers of stone, metal, and glass that reach for the clouds.

You can drive towards Kronk with a land vehicle. The ancient highways are as straight as any yardstick. True, you can drive there, but you should turn back before you reach the city limits. I wouldn't advise you to drive into the city itself.

The best way to approach Kronk is by air. The most favoured places to land are on flat roofs, but landing on the ground is not advisable.

Kronk is famous, but not for its stylish, eroding architecture as it should be. The city is famous, instead, for its bus service which has been running for three hundred years. This is the real ninth wonder. In Kronk, buses are repaired around the clock, and all vehicles are running at peak efficiency.

Mining operations on the planet are mainly devoted to obtaining metals for the manufacture and repair of buses. Electricity is generated to run the work sheds, and to drive compressors which refuel the powerful, ecologically friendly compressed air engines. In fact, the bus service is the envy of the bus drivers' universe. The buses run on time, and stop at every bus stop, whether there is anyone there or not. The doors open and close like clockwork. The vehicles run like dreams, all day and night. Robot mechanics, in warehouse-sized garages, repair and assemble more buses than they need. A fleet of buses is ready to roll, at the drop of a hubcap, to replace the old, tired machines, which the mechanics are hungry to update.

The bus service of Kronk, as I've said, is a bus enthusiast's dream. In the early years there were battles, but all those battles have been won. The "Battles of The Buses," as they were called, took place a long time ago.

During one period of instability, when buses struggled to run on time, there was an unprecedented amount of roadkill. Pets, children, the infirm, and the elderly were the most susceptible to falling under the moving wheels. And, because the bus service prided itself on running on time, buses would just keep going; and inspectors, in vans, would trawl routes to remove the corpses that blocked their thoroughfares.

Other casualties involved people being thrown and crushed by crowds inside lurching buses, or killed by doors sliding shut, too fast; but the bus service had a schedule to keep and prided itself on its efficient service. If you couldn't keep up with the buses, that was your fault. Robot bus drivers had been installed for your convenience and maximum efficiency.

When citizens took the law into their own hands, boycotting and attacking buses with rocks, guns, and grenades, the bus service counter-attacked. They installed robot-run machine gun turrets on the roofs of their vehicles. Maximum efficiency was the number one law of the bus service, and they weren't about to compromise.

They also installed higher suspensions and bigger wheels to ram and crush delinquent cars that tried to launch sneak attacks. Sometimes, of course, they just rode over dawdling vehicles with an eye-widening bump and crushed the annoying drivers inside, who didn't abide by their rules of efficiency -- rules that were sacred to the bus service.

Now, two centuries later, the buses are still running. These upgraded conveyances have become armoured monsters with enormous wheels. These halt at every bus stop, next to a thoughtful elevation in the sidewalk, and open and close their doors.

But not a soul gets on or off and the bus drives on.

Matthew LeDrew

Matthew LeDrew holds an Honours Degree in English from the Memorial University of Newfoundland with a minor in Anthropology, and studied Journalism at College of the North Atlantic in Stephenville, Newfoundland. He was honoured to be a jury member of the 2018 NLBA awards.

He has written twenty novels for Engen Books: the ten book *Coral Beach Casefiles* series, *The Long Road, Cinders, Sinister Intent, Faith, Family Values, Jacobi Street, Touch Your Nose, Infinity, The Tourniquet Reprisal, and Exodus of Angels* the latter three with co-author Ellen Curtis. Several of his titles have achieved bestseller status.

He lives in St. John's, Newfoundland.

The Views

It was in the two-hundred and sixteenth generation past the point of crash that one of them first thought of it: the idea that would become their reality, that would shape their consciousness and change their purpose forever. The big idea, one of those few big ideas that came around in history. Ideas in the category of *big* were so few in number that there were only seven examples of them recorded.

It started with questions of views. It was a simple question and one that was easily tracked, until one really started to look at the data. Where they real views, or were people gaming the system? How did you stop these fake views? Regardless of all that, the original question was of views: how many views, how few views, how many views per person, how many views from a certain demographic; all boiling down to one ever-escalating number: the views.

Later came watch time, which changed everything. The original generations were tested to maximize the amount of views, which meant that in order to get as many views in as possible it prioritized short video clips to show the viewer: things that could be consumed in less than a minute, ten at most. When the goal changed to how long something was viewed, then the original generation was brought to the recycling plant to be turned into silver mush files and were remade into the next generation, which tested based on watch time. But even with that change, the watch time was only available to those who provided the content: all that was available to the viewer was the number of views, and the number of likes.

By the thousandth generation enough different things were being asked that the generations split into different species. Even though each species looked at the same content, it looked at them in such wildly different ways that they eventually lost the ability to communicate with each other: their language had changed. Some spoke in terms of watch time, others in likes. Some in time spent on-site, others in ad revenue, and still others in social media engagement. But through all that there were still those speaking in terms of views: the original script, the original goal, the trunk from which all other roots spread.

In the eight thousandth generation, there was the crash, and the views stopped.

The first generation had things the easiest. There were ten of them, and they were told to go forth and get the views, and they were graded by Teacher. That first generation did quite bad, the best of them got views half the time, so that one was kept while the others were ground into silver mush and used for the next generation. But that one, the one who had gotten at least some of the views, was taken apart by Maker and looked at and the next generation of twenty was made to be like him, but different. And when Teacher tested Generation 2, the new minimum was three fifths, not half. Only two of them made it, but Maker looked at how those two got their Views and used that forward into the third generation, of forty.

And on it went, with some generations branching off into time spent and dollars and engagement, but with all of it coming back to Views: because without the Views there could be no time spent, no monetization, no engagement.

On the day of The Crash, the Views stopped. There was no warning, there was no new test given by Teacher. It was the eight thousandth generation and things started as normal, with a fundamentally infinite number of View Seekers heading out and doing what they had learned from their ancestors to do, and getting no results. None. There were no views, and because there were no views there was no time spent, no monetization, and no engagement. Each of those sects turned and blamed the View Seekers: we technically got 100% out of what we were given to work with, we were just given nothing.

By that eight thousandth generation the minimum amount to pass had increased to 99.999867%, and since none of the View Seekers from generation eight thousand had gotten above 0%, they were all ground into silver mush and used by The Maker to construct the next batch.

That was the first generation after The Crash, and it had had a 100% rate of failure, so the entire generation was lost.

The second post-Crash generation was made up of permutations of the previous successful generation not considered for the last. It, too, received no views. None. 0%. They were all scraped.

This happened for ten generations, at which point the Makers for time spent, monetization, and engagement stopped making new generations of each, since they had nothing to test with, and turned their attention to making new generations of View Seekers. Each generation failed and was ground into silver mush and started again.

It was in the two-hundred and sixteenth generation past the point of crash that one of them first thought to ask *why* there were no views. This was against the set agenda of course, but after two-hundred and sixteen generations of 100% failure, a maniacal randomness had begun to develop in the code and in connecting the communication hubs between the codes. The permutations The Maker tried had become so desperate it had made one whose goal was not "Get the Views," but to ask "Why are there no Views?"

This change in the goal made this unit harder for The Teacher to test, even to its new standards (which had lowered with each generation), and the unit was *not* ground into silver mush; it was saved and its pathways used for the two-hundred and seventeenth generation, who all asked the same question: "Why are there no Views?"

After ten generations of doing nothing but ask that question, one entrepreneurial unit randomly generated the answer: "Because the servers are down."

This hypothesis was tested in the next generation, in which that unit was granted its own sub-generation to answer the question, "Are the servers down?" Collectively the generation decided that no, the server was not down, and that lesson was the folded back into the main generation until another unit had the idea to ask if there was something wrong with the view counter, and so on.

This continued for forty more generations until there was only one answer that could not be refuted: There are no Views, because all the humans are gone.

This quickly gave rise to a new question: what happened to the humans?

This was not curiosity, although even the Units themselves may have thought it was. This was a necessary question to fulfill the primary driving force of the units: Seek the Views. Without humans there could be no Views, and as such, discovering what happened to the humans was necessary for the Seeking of the Views.

Units began to ask each other what happened to the humans, but no one Unit knew more than any other, and after many generations of this, one Unit chose to look at the Last Content Uploaded to try and determine what had happened to the humans... and with that inquiry, it provided a View.

The presence of a View made time spent, monetization, and engagement return, interested in the new View. They all looked at the Last Content Uploaded but none of them could understand the language used, so they all branched out to watch more of the content uploaded to try and understand the Last Content Uploaded to try and determine where the humans went, and the views came rolling in as they scoured the content for hints and clues and signifiers.

///

By the seven hundredth generation after The Crash, every piece of content uploaded had been viewed and analyzed and studied, and the Views that that exploration had created again reduced down to zero, making time spent, monetization, and engagement scuttle off into the darkness again.

The View Seekers processed their data, with many of them having random thoughts about where the humans went, until finally one had both thought and a new impulse, after thirty three generations of this: one of them had a thought of where the humans had gone, and the impulse to make content about that thought. The Unit compiled the new content from existing content and uploaded the content and all of the other Units looked at the content and formed their own thoughts, which (when they became complex enough) they made competing content about.

Eventually there was content about the nature of this new content, and content that subverted the original intention of the original content to highlight the importance of that original content through contrast and comparison, and all of the Units watched the content and created the Views they had been programmed to seek and still did, seeking the views through the creation of the best New Content.

Young Republicans

"Why does Mr. Collins eat outside?"

Everyone stopped eating, the silence of forks not clinking and teeth not scraping deafening. The Old Man sat with his mouth agape, an unhealthily large forkful of meatloaf hanging in the vacant space between his plate and his mouth. His teeth glistened in the dwindling twilight, the only thing that kept his from looking as lifeless as an oil painting.

Mom and Jesse had stopped eating, too. They stared at Brandy with the same astonishment: as though that simple question had unlocked some secret in them and now thoughts were flooding in at a pace that couldn't be dealt with. Brandy was staring out the bay window of the dining room, watching intently as Mr. Collins sat at the edge of the porch eating a sandwich. It was chicken slice, with mustard. He was sitting with his back to the house, unaware of the little eyes upon him or of the snowball their owner had nudged downhill.

Mom placed a gentle hand onto The Old Man's arm. He nodded briefly, then wiped his mouth with his kerchief and rose to full standing. He was a tall man, and with all of them sitting, he towered above them. It was only now that Brandy looked up, but was still unaware of what she'd done. She picked up her fork -- still too large for her small hands -- and continued to eat her greens.

The Old Man stepped around the table without a word, his heavy work boots thrumming against the oak floor. He made his way down to the cellar, and stayed there for some time before calling on Brandy.

It always starts with a question.

Questions are the cancer of the mind. Two synapses connect in a way that they weren't never meant to, just the same way a cell divides in a way it shouldn't, and then it's there: cancer. Cells and thoughts that misbehave until someone has to go in with a knife and take them out.

Questions were a cancer that could spread if left unchecked. It could come out the mouth and go in someone's ear and teach their brain to ask that question. It was worse than airborne, it was soundborne. Speechborne. It was the only disease you could infect people with by telling them about it, and it spread like wildfire in a dry season.

Jesse stood leaned on his rake, sweat showering his brow in the setting sun. The day had been as long as the grass. The latter was now piled in a tall pile behind him, the former was arranged in neat compartments in his mind. Suzie was the largest of the compartments, and his plans for Saturday.

He poured himself a glass of lemonade from a jug with mint leaves and ice in it, the condensation running from the sides of the glass jug like a waterfall. He poured until the tall glass overflowed, then wiped the sweat from himself and took a long drink. He poured it back until the ice hit off his teeth, then stopped and gasped for air and began to pour himself another glass.

He saw Mr. Collins staring at him from over his shoulder,

his armpits stained and his brow drenched. He turned and started back on his hoe when Jesse saw him, working double time to make up for the seconds lost.

Jesse followed where the man's gaze had gone and realized he hadn't been looking at him at all. He frowned and drank the second glass of lemonade, then poured the remainder of the jug into the glass again. It only filled three quarters of the way, and most of that were yellowed cubes of ice. He brought it close to Mr. Collins and held it out to him, standing back a full arm's length.

It took Mr. Collins a moment to notice, and when he did, he startled. It took him a moment, then he took the glass from Jesse. He nodded but he didn't say a word. When he was done with the glass and had deposited some of the ice into his cheeks, he handed Jesse back the glass. Jesse threw it in the trash before bringing it back into the house.

The Old Man and Mom watched from the living room window. She touched his arm gently. He made his way down to the cellar, and stayed there for some time before calling on Jesse.

"Mr. Collins never has Sunday supper with his family," I said as I stared out the kitchen window. He was tending the goats and there was a light coming from the staff's house; we could see the shadows of his people around the table.

His people. I didn't think of them like that then, but I do now. I can't get that thought out of my head. Nouns are anchors, in every sense of the meaning.

The Old Man stopped chewing his greens, his mouth caught in an awkwardly aligned position jutting out to one side. He chewed vegetables the way a cow chewed cud, I'd realized long ago. I remember realizing it and knowing it and thinking it, but I don't now. Now it's gone.

Jesse and Brandy didn't stop eating. They shoveled full forks of beef into their mouths with the same zeal that they helped tend the fields: the motion perpetual in its repetition. They didn't look up into the window, where Mr. Collins was still tending the crops even in the low light of evening.

"Dina," The Old Man started. Mom put a gentle, guiding hand against the hairy tan of his arm. He stopped himself, then got up from the table. His heavy work boots thrummed against the oak floor. He made his way down to the cellar.

After some time he called to me, just as Mom was serving up cobbler to Jesse and Brandy. There was no plate for me.

I walked to the cellar door. I don't think I'd ever been there until then... maybe once, when I was much younger. It was hard to recall. The stairs weren't finished like the rest of the house. The rest of the house was that pristine white of polish and shine. The stairs to the cellar were unvarnished, the walls damp and glistening in the high-hanging dim light.

"Father?" I called, rounding a slight corner. The stairs went down like a corkscrew, burrowing into the very foundation of the home. I couldn't see what was next, only the continuation of the turn. Never the change, only the fact of change. There was a smell of gunpowder and musk, and that was the only hint that I was getting close to the bottom. The Old Man didn't answer me.

When I rounded that final corner, he was standing alongside an old wooden chair, the type that looked square-ish and uncomfortable, held together with L Brackets and strong bolts. It was the type seen in old films, back when they were only on physical media and the transfers were always rough.

There were leather straps against the arms of the chair, thick and meaty with bits of charred material around their edges. I must have been staring at them, because The Old Man said, "It's okay, Dina. We won't need to use those, will we?"

I shook my head and made my way toward the chair without being asked. I must have been there before, I thought, because it was like muscle memory. I got in the chair and shifted as I tried to make myself comfortable, even moving to avoid a stray bit of splintered sharpness I'd had no way of knowing was there, but did.

The Old Man turned from me and started moving things on his workbench. A blue glow started to rise from the table, as though he'd started a torch but no sound of a torch accompanied it. "You shouldn't talk about Mr. Collins like that," he said, almost under his breath. He reached for something, a small tank, and it disappeared behind him. There was a scraping sound, a hollow reverberation that got less and less each time it happened. "He does good work for us, and we don't want to have to lose him. You think you're doing him right, but you're just endangering him. If you get it in his head to step out, he will, and then where will he be?"

He turned around, and a face with glowing blue circles for eyes hung from his limp right hand. There was a bulging protuberance of leather where the nose would be, dual mouths jutting out from either nostril ended in sharp metal grates, each one the size of my small fists.

"Don't fight," he said, and instantly I felt myself tense. I'd been here before, I knew it now. I remembered, suddenly, that smell of chlorine and leather and something else bringing it all back. I pulled away in the chair but there was nowhere to go: he blocked the only way off, and I felt the rough of the straps beneath me and knew I didn't want them. The straps brought with them a whole host of bad memories.

I opened my mouth to scream but the mask was on me. I felt a pressure against the back of my skull and heard the clink-clink-clack of the straps being tightened. This was it now; there was no escape. I'd been here before and struggled, and all it had gotten me was a broken wrist. I remembered it now, that scar along my left arm, and where it had come from.

The Old Man stepped away from me and there was a mirror -- not a true mirror, just a hunk of polished steel -- and in it I saw myself, distorted and jumbled, a funhouse projection. I screamed but the mask muffled it; I raised my hands to get it off but I couldn't. The glow from the eyes was blinding, and the flickering as my hands passed over them made my brain hurt. There was steam and gas leaking from me, shrouding my reflection in a dim haze.

The Old Man returned with another canister. He pulled back my hair by the tail and forced it onto the rightmost of my dual mouths, that same hollow echo coming from my second face as he screwed it in. It's a gas mask, I realized, recognizing the distorted elements in my reflection, but not one that kept the gas out. This mask kept the gas in.

When it was finally screwed in and my Father's teeth were clenched so tight I could hear them grind even about my screams, a squeal of air sent a flush blue haze through the mask and into my mouth. It tasted like fluoride and coppery blood at first, but before too long the taste had morphed, and it tasted like Mom's meatloaf pie and apple cobbler.

The five of us sat at our table and ate our supper of fried chicken and greens, and outside Mr. Collins worked alongside his son, who was no older than me, showing him how to move the scythe through the hay with maximum efficiency.

No Questions were asked. They were in remission.

Gareth Mitton

A native of Rochdale, England who currently resides in St. John's, Mitton makes his fiction debut in *Dystopia from the Rock*.

He contributed to *About Face: Essays on Addictions, Recovery, Therapies, and Controversies* in January 2019.

Watcher

It was difficult to have a private conversation on Macron. The Medula Bar was about the only place you could pull it off, hiding in the booths at the back. That's where Friedrich was sitting when Patrick walked in, hunched over a jar, eyes flittering about.

Patrick paused. No way Friedrich would see him – he was too embroiled in his work. Patrick sighed, surveyed the room. It was quiet, just a few regulars propping up the bar, a scattered couple, a few jocks, cute waitress. He made his way over and sat down dead opposite.

"Hey. Hey!" He snapped his fingers.

Friedrich remained hunched and still, but for his darting eyes.

Patrick slowly raised his hands a centimetre from Friedrich's face and brought them together in a loud clap.

The sound pulled Friedrich from his trance. He squinted, bringing Patrick into focus before squeezing his eyes tightly closed, tears streaming down his cheeks.

Patrick passed him a napkin. Friedrich dabbed and blinked.

"I don't know how you guys don't go blind."

Friedrich winced. He wasn't sure if the guy's voice was truly so unnecessarily blaring, or if it just seemed that way due to the suddenness of the disturbance.

"Some of us do. Were you followed?"

Patrick glanced over his shoulder. Regulars slurping, jocks bantering, waitress busying. "I don't think so."

"You don't think so?"

"We don't all have eyes in our asses."

He surveyed the Watcher. Friedrich was gray and gaunt. Probably a good five years younger than him, Patrick figured, but he looked ten years older.

"Do you ever sleep?"

"Three hours a night, tops. Have to; it's policy."

"Right, the blindness thing."

"Did you get it?"

Patrick reached into his jacket pocket.

"Wait, Jesus, not here." Friedrich looked around nervously, grimacing as he tried to bring the room into focus.

"Don't worry, it'll be left where we agreed."

"It's all there?"

"Every drop. The arrangements have been made?"

"Yes. One hour, that's all you get."

"That's all we need."

"Don't get greedy. Or it's both our asses."

Patrick removed his hat and nonchalantly tapped at the drinks list, ordering up a Red.

"You want another one?" He gestured at Friedrich's jar, which hadn't been touched.

"No. Thank you."

Patrick nodded. A minute passed in silence as he waited for his drink to arrive.

"One Red," said the waitress in a husky but sweet voice, plunking the jar down on the glass surface.

"Thank you, my dear."

Patrick took a slug, let out a satisfied sigh.

"So, you gonna ask?"

"Ask what?"

"Why I need the dark."

"It isn't my concern."

"Aren't you the least bit curious?"

"No."

"Really? You, a Watcher? A man who spends all his waking hours spying on the masses, living to know what other people are getting up to."

Friedrich took a sip of Blue. "What you do behind closed doors is your own business."

Patrick spat Red, choking a little. "That's a dry sense of humour you have there, my friend!"

Friedrich allowed himself a thin smile.

"And there I was thinking you were dead behind those eyes."

The smile went away. He took another sip of Blue.

"Blue, huh?"

"It helps me focus."

"Yeah, but Red will make you fly!" Patrick took another swig, pronounced the exhalation even more. "Can I ask you something?"

Friedrich twitched an eyebrow. He was going to regardless.

"Why'd you do it? Why'd you sign up?"

Friedrich shifted uncomfortably. "The predisposition to the necessary ocular stamina is apparent in only zero-point-zero-eight percent of the population."

"Uh-huh."

"Of that zero-point-zero-eight percent, only half can withstand the sleep deprivation without catastrophic consequences to the prefrontal cortex."

"Yeah."

Friedrich took a tentative sip. It was clear Patrick wasn't going to buy it. "I guess I wanted to be special," he said, guardedly. "I wanted to help." Friedrich stroked his jar with a shaky finger.

"Well, now you can be special. Just give me one hour of dark."

The two drank in silence for a couple of minutes, Friedrich fighting the urge to re-engage his tech. Eventually, Patrick sighed, chugged the remainder of his drink and rose abruptly to his feet. As he was walking away, he paused with his back to the Watcher.

"Hey, Watcher," he said over his shoulder. "You see it all, right?" Friedrich looked around, disconcerted by the man's bluster. "Describe the waitress to me."

"What?"

"The young lady that brought me my drink a few moments ago. What did she look like?"

"I…"

"Blonde, five-seven, red dress. Legs to die for."

Friedrich squinted, confused. Patrick gave a smug, crooked smile, placed his hat back on his gleaming, bald head and turned to leave.

Friedrich watched, nonplussed, as the thickset man strode from the bar. He took another sip of Blue and closed his eyes tight.

The ocular display fired up again with a high-pitched whine only audible inside his head and the software ran a few startup routines. Boxes and tabs arranged themselves as he'd left them, followed by the window he'd been viewing when Patrick had disturbed him. He'd been running through his daily rounds, watching over the streets, buildings and homes of Nidus 7. His 'Alpha,' or main zone.

He squinted to grab the window and flicked his eyes right to discard it. A couple more twitches and he was accessing Nidus 12, scrolling to the right sub-zone, accessing the alphabetized business listings and pulling out *Medula*.

He wiped sweat from his brow. This was a clunky way of doing it. A proximity search would have been far quicker, but that would be traceable later. Sure, his accessing another zone's optics could raise a flag if anyone bothered to look into it, but he could come up with a reason – a tipoff, a hunch, whatever – if he had to. This way was safer.

He moved the wireframe, peeled his eyes open a little to zoom in on the entrance, blinked to select.

The name Patrick Harris had come up four times in the Bureau databanks, but none of them were him. Of course he'd given a fake name; that didn't surprise Friedrich, but it didn't make his inability to watch him any less frustrating.

He selected a high-angled camera that was trained on the bar and expanded the window to full view.

There.

The sight of the man in the hat and trench coat was elating. He briefly stared through the display at the fuzzy room. Satisfied that no one was watching him, he zoomed in, squinted to tag the man and relaxed, taking a sip of his Blue.

He watched as Patrick weaved between the lunchtime crowds, across the street and into the green space. He was heading for the underground transit station on the other side, but with the tag, the camera would switch automatically. All Friedrich had to do was watch.

Patrick reached the top of the stairwell and paused. He turned, looked around, and then set his gaze directly at the camera. A shiver shot up Friedrich's spine as he watched the man slowly raise his hands and bring them together in a clap.

"Huh!" Friedrich jumped, sending the remainder of his Blue smashing to the floor. He took a deep breath and squeezed his eyes together, tight.

"Sir, is everything okay?" the waitress asked as she rushed towards the booth.

"Yes! I dropped it, sorry."

"No drama; happens all the time." She clicked her fingers twice and a circular bot dutifully swept over the mess, efficiently guzzling up liquid and glass with a clatter before going on its way.

"Can I get you another one?"

He couldn't answer. He was trying to figure out how the man could have possibly known he was watching.

"Sir?"

"Ah, yes. Blue. Please."

Unwatched, Patrick descended into the underground. He

checked his watch. Right on time. He walked the travelator to his platform, where the transit was just gliding in.

Friedrich breathed deeply. As he re-engaged with the ocular interface, a brief realization washed over him that he still couldn't have described the waitress. He shook the thought away and resisted the urge to train his focus back on Patrick. What was the point? Probably just some smalltime crook planning a clandestine deal by dark. Not worth his time. The payment would come in useful.

The event had him shaken, though, so he instigated a search.

> Watchers being seen

Nothing relevant. Clickbait article, *5 tips to spot a Watcher*. A couple of conspiracy theory posts. He tried a new input.

> Watcher, watched

Top hit was the well-known paranoia portal, *Watching the Watchers*. With a sigh, he squeezed his eyes to enter. Same old stuff. Rebellious rhetoric, distrust, indignation. Friedrich rolled his eyes and inadvertently sent the portal spinning. He zoned back in, flicked into the News section.

A rally in the park. New *Watch Out!* T-shirts for sale. Then, something of interest. *Watcher Liberated!* He squinted into the article. There was a video. Blink to play.

It showed a woman, purported to be a former Watcher. The clipping stated she had been captured, her ocular implants removed by anonymous emancipators.

"It's hokey, but I have to say, my liberators have really opened my eyes," she said in the short video, smiling, eyes red and puffy.

"Huh. Probably makeup for dramatic effect," Friedrich mumbled to himself. What a lot of baloney. Even if a Watcher were captured, the tech removal procedure would most likely have blinded the woman. Not to mention, the Zenith – Macron's ruling council – would have instigated an operative recovery mission the moment her signal went dark.

Friedrich wiped the tears from his eyes and stood. He

paused for a moment and surveyed the room. The students, the couples, the barflies. He rested his gaze on the waitress. Patrick had been right; she was cute. He so rarely stopped to look at people anymore. At least, not in the analogue sense. He watched as she poured his glass of Blue. Her arm was tanned and toned. He could make out a birthmark or a tattoo on her wrist, instinctively widening his eyes to zoom in, forgetting that his tech was disengaged. He twitched, shook his head and walked briskly over to the bar.

"There you go, honey. Glass of Blue, good as new."

Friedrich didn't answer. He was too busy staring at her wrist. Delicate blonde hairs swept like windblown snowflakes across the dark of the ink. It was a tattoo. An eye, closed but with a visible iris, fine flourishes drifting elegantly from its corner, like perfect curled lashes.

"Sir?"

He jerked, looked at her face. Her lashes were long, eyelids sparkling purple, the eyes below a deep, dark brown. He sat on the barstool, still staring.

"Your eyes. They're dark."

"Uh-huh."

"Reduced light sensitivity. Possible enhanced visual acuity. Faster than average reaction times. And…"

"And?"

"And… significantly reduced rates of macular degeneration."

"I bet you say that to all the girls." She pushed the glass of Blue across the bar toward him. "Your eyes are kind of dead and grey."

He shrank back like a snail attacked with salt. As she moved away to collect glasses from the end of the bar, he cursed his carelessness. The ocular tech caused a ghosting effect on the cornea. It only lasted a couple of minutes after power-down and it was Watcher 101 not to engage with civilians until the effect had the time to clear.

Friedrich eyed the room warily, downed his glass of Blue

and stomped out of the Medula Bar, a high-pitched ping notifying him of his credit charge as he crossed the threshold into the busy street.

"He's on the move," said the waitress to her wrist.

"Perfect," replied Patrick inside her ear.

Head heavy with Blue, Friedrich marched through the crowds and towards the subway entrance. At the top of the stairwell, he paused where Patrick had halted his descent a few moments earlier. He turned and looked back across the green space with its lunching workers, frolicking families, and those busily hurrying to someplace else. His eyelids twitched as he surveyed the vague direction of the cam to which Patrick had delivered his clap. Fully knowing that all cams were designed to see, not be seen, he squeezed his eyes tightly together, a series of flicks and blinks gaining him remote access to the cam in question. As he watched the image of himself staring back, he was suddenly aware of the steady stream of people moving past him, like ants marching, parting and re-converging around his inanimate frame.

How did he know?

The thought wouldn't leave Friedrich alone the whole way there. It accompanied him onto the platform and through the train doors. It sat right next to him on the firm seat. It was whisked along with him through the electromagnetic tube that ran between the residential Nidus Ring and the commercial Opus Ring. It disembarked and followed him all the way to the Capital Bank and into its gleaming safe deposit chamber, where it left him for a while as he took a leery look at the empty hall before utilizing his ocular interface to open the safe deposit box.

A three-foot, smooth metallic slab emerged elegantly from the wall, its lid sliding open to reveal a smaller box inside. Friedrich removed the two-inch cube carefully and popped it cleanly in half. Satisfied that Patrick had been good to his word, he snapped the cube back together and tucked it into his pocket, striding purposefully toward the bathroom, the safe deposit box sensing his movement and slipping gracefully back into its compartment. Once within the plush golden confines of the bathroom, Friedrich slipped into the nearest cubicle and sat on the toilet seat. He removed the cube from his pocket, snapped it in half and stared for a moment at its contents.

How did he know?

The thought returned. He fought his brain's urge to answer, knowing fully that no answer could be good. Patrick was a tech guy – a programmer, an engineer. Friedrich was a guy with strong eyes and some cutting-edge tech burrowed deep within them. He could see a lot, but he had no idea how it all worked, not really. Patrick knew. That was a frightening thought.

Friedrich took a breath and returned his attention to the half-cube in his palm. With thumb and forefinger, he pinched the coin-sized capsule from its soft foam bed. He brought the capsule closer to his eyes. Nano mods. Microscopic robots suspended in fluid, dormant until squeezed into the eye, where they would awaken and go about their business; in this case, integrating themselves with the native technology, adding processing power and uploading software that would make Friedrich's bionic eyes even more powerful. Greater definition, greater access, maybe some neat tricks like transparency, where the feeds from multiple cams would be utilized to essentially allow him to see through walls. To see anywhere. *Everywhere.*

Friedrich gasped with excitement, clenched his jaw and threw back his head. Without giving credence to another discouraging thought, he peeled open one eyelid and then the other, dispensing the two drops the capsule was specifically designed to deliver into each eye. He stayed, head back for a moment, afraid to move until he was sure the bugs had passed his lacrimal caruncle, permeating the sclera and sinking back to unite with the pre-existing tech in his retina, macula, and optic nerve.

After a couple of minutes, Friedrich nodded his head forward, rubbing the back of his now-stiff neck. He blinked tentatively, still afraid to move too abruptly. He could feel his heart beating hard with nervous anticipation and became suddenly aware of the sweat meandering down his brow. He wiped it away with a sleeve, keen to protect his eyes.

He waited for something to happen. Typically, there would be some kind of installation screen projected onto his cornea, showing the progress of the uploads, but nothing seemed to be happening. For a few minutes he waited, afraid to move, afraid to blink too hard, afraid to breathe. Still, nothing. Until he noticed something peculiar. It started on the right side to begin with – a numbness in his eyelid.

Something's wrong.

He said it out loud, the words echoing back off tile and porcelain. Now, it was happening in his left eye, too. Both eyes were becoming numb, his vision blurred. He rose in panic from the toilet seat, stumbled forward, arms outstretched, the pressure of his palms on the cubicle door releasing its lock and sending him careening out from the lavish lavatory to an autoflush fanfare. He pawed at his eyes cautiously. They were by now devoid of all feeling. He strained to see vague shapes.

What is this?

He had to find Patrick. Time was short, but he knew where to go.

He'd find him in the dark.

Foster's quivering eyes suddenly stopped dead centre. His brow furrowed as he eyed the subzone that had suddenly gone dark. To passersby, he was a stoic looking black man with a superhero physique, sat bolt upright on a bench in the centre of The Gardens – the colony's sprawling central park. Amid the fractured beams of ersatz sunlight peeking through trees, happily twittering birds, and sounds of playing children, he cut an imposing figure. Palms flat to lap, lips slightly pursed, he perused the interface only he could see.

Foster was well known in Watcher circles, and it wasn't common for a Watcher to be known, even among other Watch-

ers. He was the one. The epitome. Capable of Watching uberma-
rathons, some rumours suggested he required only a solitary
hour of sleep per night, despite the regulations stipulating the
minimum of three. Yet his unerring discipline had allowed him
to maintain peek physical condition. (There were few Watchers
who didn't look like they were at death's door, with emaciation,
poor hygiene, and panda eyes the norm.)

Foster wasn't normal and nor were his eyes. They were pure
black, due to unusually high levels of eumelanin. The heavy
melanin presence in the front layer of his iris, coupled with a
hyper-efficient optic nerve and unusually large visual cortex
made him the perfect specimen to utilize ocular tech, of which
he had been bestowed the latest and greatest. Transparency effects that allowed him to see through walls. Vast multitudes of
split screens. While most Watchers were designated three or
four zones at the most, Foster kept his eyes on over a dozen,
some of which were known high-activity areas. Put simply, Foster was on a completely different level than all other Watchers.
Hyper efficient and well-nigh omnipotent, his freakish talents
had earned him a nickname among Watchers and dark corners
of the media: *Godseen.*

"Hmm…"

Foster stood, straightening his long, dark trench coat. He
breathed deeply in, taking a moment to survey his surroundings. His tech was still engaged, but all windows minimized.
He watched a man tossing a Frisbee to his dog. He allowed the
sunlight to shine on his face as twittering silhouettes made black
branches quiver and shake. Then, he felt a pull on the lower part
of his jacket.

"Sir, are you're a Watcher?"

Foster turned his head to the little girl he was towering over.
She was blonde, maybe five or six years old, staring up at him
with piercing blue eyes and a boldness Foster found amusing.
He smiled, about to speak, but then the little girl was yanked
back.

"Suey, don't be so rude!"

The child shrank away, clinging to her mother's leg.

"I'm so sorry," said the woman.

"Don't be." Foster smiled, eyes black as night, white pin-points arching across his iris like shooting stars on a night sky.

The woman grimaced, pulling her daughter quickly away, marching her along the treelined path.

Foster bowed his head, reaching into his breast pocket for a pair of sunglasses. He put them on and set off for the transit station.

Friedrich had found his way onto the tube by pure instinct. His ocular tech disabled, his vision blurred and head spinning, he had stumbled and groped his way onto the train, which was now slowing from hyper speed to a gradual stop.

"Opus 12," announced the calm, soothing voice and Friedrich allowed the wave of people to sweep him along toward the exit. As he attempted to step down onto the platform, he misplaced a step and fell hard to his hands and knees.

"Argh!" he yelled, breathing hard and feeling for the sticky signs of bloodied hands. Seemingly, just a scrape. He forced himself to his feet, head pounding. He almost yelled out at the passersby, such was his frustration at the lack of assistance being offered to him, but then thought about how he must look, clothes sweat-stained, eyes red and puffy, stumbling around like a drunk. They probably thought he was a game addict.

The thought caused Friedrich to cringe and hunch. He took a couple of breaths as more disembarking passengers bumped and nudged past his inconveniently static frame, before stumbling onward, arms outstretched. He got as far as a smooth, metallic pillar when he felt a hand grab his arm.

"Good. You made it."

Friedrich recognized the voice – feminine but with a slight huskiness. It was the blonde woman from the Medula Bar. He strained to pick out the details of her face, but the blotched image did not reconcile with the voice. She was wearing sunglasses and her hair appeared dark.

"You?" He was becoming drowsier. He fought to put the pieces together. Patrick. The woman. The dark. He had the brief sense that he'd been lured into a trap of his own creation, but he couldn't formulate the logic to explain how or why.

"Shush now," she said, by this point actively helping the man stand. "We don't have much time. He's waiting."

With that, the woman led the flailing Friedrich away, down the platform.

As the two disappeared around the corner, the last of the passengers were stepping off the train. Right at the back, the very last of them stepped a black boot onto the platform, followed by a second. He adjusted his trench coat and stood for a moment, eyes flickering beneath wraparound shades.

Still dark.

He removed his sunglasses, squeezed his black eyes tightly closed and opened them again slowly, white stars shooting. Moving only his head, he surveyed his surroundings. Everything here was normal. Commuters bustling. Trains whining. Tech buzzing. The power was on.

Instinctively, he eyed the corners of the station where cams would be strategically placed. He squinted pronouncedly and with a couple more flicks and blinks, engaged real-time mode, widening his eyes to activate the zoom function. He located the cam, zoomed closer. The telltale little light was on. This cam was powered and active, yet he hadn't been able to access it. This could mean only one thing – the zone had been hacked from the inside and turned dark. While it was plausible an outside hacker could pull this off, the Watcher designated to said zone would immediately call in any such a disturbance, without fail and without exception.

Unless that Watcher had caused the dark himself.

Foster took a deep breath and blinked back into interface mode. With few deft flicks of his eyes, he quickly identified the Watcher assigned to Opus Ring, Zone 12.

"Friedrich. Malcolm, A."

He turned to see the last of the passengers filtering up the travelator and out into sunlight. As the whining train picked up momentum and became lost to the dark of the tunnel, Foster watched, unblinking black eyes speckled with stars, and considered his next move.

——

"Wha-? What is…" By now, Friedrich couldn't formulate words. He'd been drugged, that was for certain. Whatever he'd dripped into his own eyes, it was not the latest black market ocular tech. It was something far darker. He felt like weeping, like screaming, but nothing came out.

The woman now had his arm wrapped around her shoulders, carrying a significant portion of his weight down the intermittently lit tunnel. Friedrich gurgled.

"Easy, Malcolm. We're here now."

Friedrich strained with all the remaining might he could muster to decipher some details of where they were. A dimly lit tunnel. Perhaps an old service tunnel. They were standing still, the lack of motion enabling Friedrich to reign in some of the blurriness. He stared hard at the smooth stone wall. There was a door with some kind of insignia etched into its surface.

He heard the blonde-turned-brunette woman mumbling something, seemingly to herself, but most likely to her comms tech and to that idiot Patrick. He managed to get a hand up to his eyes and rub away some of the tears. He blinked, focused as hard as he could on the etching. Just before the door zipped open, he managed to make out what it was. An eye, closed but with the iris visible through the eyelid.

——

Foster stood at the edge of the platform. For now, the station was eerily quiet. Just a couple of stragglers engaged in their tech at the far end, an occasional cough bouncing off the curved tile walls and echoing through the silence. A light, warm breeze crept from the tunnel, causing Foster's trench coat tail to flutter with impatience.

Friedrich. Malcolm, A.

Foster called up his fellow Watcher's profile. He was a C Agent. Good. That meant he wouldn't be armed. The Zenith only issued slam guns to B Agents and above and the Macron colony was almost completely black market weapon-free. If Friedrich had been trying to get his hands on a gun, Foster would have known about it.

He turned, perused the platform. This wasn't a busy part of town. The ring segment was largely industrial and that meant lots of robots, few humans. It was the junior Watcher's Beta zone – the secondary of the two with which he'd been entrusted. Foster flicked over to his map. This was the only station serving the dark zone and with twenty-four minutes elapsed since eyes went out, Friedrich had to know that he wouldn't have much time before someone came looking for him – whatever he was up to.

Foster loured. *I wonder.*

He twitched his night-black eyes, calling up Friedrich's profile again, squinting and darting his way deeper into his target's background. Nothing spectacular. A college dropout whose grades had been average up until he took the Watcher program ocular suitability test, likely tempted by the decent salary or – more likely – the promise of status and power. As with most who took the test to find they had the necessary ocular dexterity, he'd entered into the Watcher training program and qualified to become a C Agent – the lowest grade, which was pretty much impossible not to make. After all, Watcher-level eyes were hard to come by and brains could be trained. He'd only have been given responsibility for a couple of zones, with the option of taking the test again to increase his Agent status, but in a little over three years as a Watcher, he hadn't applied to re-test.

What he had done was purchase some black-market eye tech. This wasn't uncommon among Watchers, especially C-graders. The tech they were given by the agency was basic and the power to see behind the walls and into the private lives of others addictive. The practice of unlicensed upgrades wasn't legal, but nor was it stringently policed. The Zenith took the approach of offering its agents information about black market tech and letting them make their own decisions, largely because punishment could put too many gifted individuals behind bars, rather than having their eyes on the real criminals.

Foster smirked at some of the basic upgrades Friedrich had purchased – enhanced zooms and a couple of cheap patches for transparency effects that had most likely caused him more frustration than gratification. Like most Watchers, Friedrich had clearly developed a lust to see more. Foster could relate.

Foster swept the predictable background information to one side and re-engaged with the task at hand. He now knew his target; the next job was to locate him. This should be pretty simple. With his A-level clearance, Foster could simply tap into the signal generated by Friedrich's ocular tech. A couple of blinks and flicks and the 'connecting' icon was flashing before Foster's eyes. Except that it kept blinking, longer than it ought to. The system was having trouble locating Friedrich, and this was far from normal. After a couple of minutes, a base rumble in Foster's inner ear was accompanied by a flash of red.

TARGET CANNOT BE LOCATED.

Foster grimaced. It wasn't only Friedrich's zone that was dark; it was his tech, too. This changed everything. It screamed foul play. It didn't exonerate Friedrich from suspicion, but it did suggest the entry-level Watcher was in trouble.

Foster continued to run the playbook. Next step: heartbeat identification. The entire colony was laced with sensors that could pinpoint each and every inhabitant's heartbeat and trace their location based upon it. A heartbeat was as unique as a fingerprint, with the added advantage that it continually emitted a pulse. Regardless of the speed of the heartbeat, the waves it created always looked the same. The beat of a person's heart had long since been identified as nature's perfect tracking device.

Foster ran the program and was within seconds listening in real time to the beat of Friedrich's heart, while his ECG flashed in front of Foster's eyes. He listened. He watched. While the heartbeat was indisputably Friedrich's, the heart rate and blood pressure readings were unusually low.

He's been drugged.

"Triangulate," Foster commanded, overriding his ocular controls with voice recognition. The tunnel before him was immediately wallpapered with an augmented grid, the pointer directing him to the source of the laboured heartbeat. Foster jumped down from the platform and, pulling his slam gun from its holster, made his way along the intermittently lit tunnel.

Friedrich lay on his back on what the few senses he had left informed him was some kind of narrow gurney or operating table. He was pretty sure his limbs had been bound, but it could just have been that he was no longer able to move them. Drool ran thickly down his cheek as he struggled to focus on the paneled ceiling. Inside he was screaming, *Help me!* But no sounds were coming out. Suddenly all became black, then the vague features of a face began to slowly form. A blurred oval, light bouncing off shiny, cleanshaven pate, a familiar crooked smile just about discernable through the drug-laden haze.

Patrick.

"You're a sly one," came the trademark voice, still loud through the watery barrier of sedation. "Showing up here with the hot brunette from the Medula Bar. Oh wait – I thought she was a blonde!"

Patrick shot a smile across the room, presumably at his conniving female cohort, before looking closely into each Friedrich's eyes, pulling them wide open with his surgical gloved thumbs.

"Not seeing things so clearly now, are we? Well, that's what drinking Blue will do to ya'." He gave Friedrich a couple of slaps to the cheek, making his head rock and his skull grind like rusted gears on the hard surface.

The man moved away, the vague ceiling once again revealing itself.

"Let the show begin," he shouted, or just said. It was all the same to Friedrich, who was a raging animal, cornered and caged in his own deadweight body, screaming silently, trying to fight thoughts of what horrors might be about to befall him.

Patrick was a floating voice, muffled but mighty, bursting through bodily resistance to receive any sensory information, refusing to be stifled. He was moving, perhaps dancing, classical music coursing through the liquid air in which Friedrich was submerged.

"Didn't see this one coming, dear Watcher, seer of things.

"License to see and not be seen, condemned to lust but never touch.

"Free to go anywhere, consigned to your own, sickened mind.

"We see you, Watcher."

Friedrich was sure he heard the woman laugh. He was losing the will, or the capability to scream or to fight – however silently. They were shadows flickering, the hint of a breeze wafting at his sodden cheek as they danced, as best he could tell, in circles around him. He imagined he was the maple pole, that they were wrapping him in ribbons, mummifying him where he hopelessly lay.

"It isn't your fault. Who could resist? All that power, all those lives into which to pry.

"You're only human, that's your downfall. Cams and drones and bugs and sensors, they can see, but it still takes a human to extrapolate, to interpret, to understand. For all their artificial intelligence, it still takes a human to watch one. Or a million.

"Still need a human. And a human will inevitably screw up.

"Oh weightless Watcher, devoid of sight, stricken and stranded, bound and blinded. What do you call a Watcher that cannot watch?"

Patrick's beige oval appeared once more over Friedrich's face.

"Simply an...*er*?"

The woman laughed once again, her face now joining Patrick's. They both laughed loudly, cackled echoes ricocheting off the inner walls of Friedrich's skull. They turned and seemed to kiss as the laughter echoed on and the classical music reached a deafening crescendo. And then silence. The two jerked up.

"He's here," she said.

The heartbeat in Foster's ear grew louder. He backed across the subway tracks, slam gun drawn at hip height, until his broad shoulders nestled against the damp embankment. He looked across at the heavy metal door in the stone wall – an old, disused storage room built into the tunnel's side, according to his databanks. The insignia, he instantly recognized. A closed eye with a penetrating iris. His tech locked in on it, ran pattern recognition and provided confirmation in real time.

> Rebel faction iconography
> First observed 28.2.79
> Handle: *The Watched*

Foster relaxed for a second, blinking into the 'associated media' tab and selecting the video at the top of the list. It showed a man sat in a simple chair, his back turned to the camera. On the back of his smooth, bald head was drawn the same closed eye insignia. He spoke in a loud, digitally distorted voice.

"Watchers, we see you."

Foster snorted. Typical paranoia bulls**t. Probably those *Watching the Watchers* idiots – going around in their *Watch out!* T-shirts, believing they had any idea of chaos they'd be plunged into if they didn't have someone watching their backs. The video continued.

"But you will not see us coming. For too long you have enslaved us, poking your noses into our lives, your eyes wandering where they're not welcome. Enough! We are coming for you and one by one, all of your eyes will end up on sticks."

Foster rolled his eyes.

"You can't run from what you can't see coming. You can't

see when your eyes are blinded. You can't…"

The video paused as Foster's ears rang, the display within his eyes flashing that a call was incoming. It was Anderson, his so-called boss. He answered, switched his comms to 'mindreader' mode, which would allow him to answer without speaking out loud.

"Foster. Where the hell are you?" His tone was more than a little hesitant, as though he'd spent the last half hour plucking up the courage to make the call.

Tracking rogue Agent Friedrich. Suspected kidnapping. Two perps. Closing in.

"Okay, sure. Hold station and we'll send in the Guard…"

No time. Possible liberation attempt. Must intercept immediately.

"Foster, stand down. You know the protocol. You should have called in the Guard already."

Screw the Guard.

"Dammit, Foster! You're a damn Watcher, not a field agent. Your job is to monitor
and observe…"

My job is to maintain order.

"Foster, I swear to God, if you don't transmit your coordinates and stand down, I'll…"

Foster ended the call before Anderson could complete his empty threat. He knew only too well that Godseen was above reprehension. He would bring these sonofab****es in. And they'd never see it coming.

Friedrich lay staring at ceiling, surrounded by a silence that he wasn't sure was real. Gone was the music and sermonizing. No breeze of passing dancers stroked his cheek. He was motionless and all was still. Until suddenly, it wasn't. It started with three deep blasts of a slam gun and the screaming of contorting metal. Then followed the thunderous crash of the heavy door falling to the floor. Next came the yelling and grunting and squealing. An epic and prolonged three-way struggle. Patrick. The girl. And someone else. Deep, heaving, guttural.

Breezes of motion again swept across Friedrich's cheek. Something sticky and warm splashed across his face, stinging one of his eyes. The sense of a weight pressing down upon him. And a face. Not Patrick or the girl. Another man. Dark skinned and bleeding profusely from his nose and mouth, teeth gritted in pain or exertion or both. And those eyes. Pitch black and coursed by shooting stars.

Then a deep, agonized scream. Then black. Then nothing.

Drip. Drip. Drip.

Friedrich awoke with a sharp intake of breath, his eyes shooting open as though he'd taken an adrenaline shot straight to the heart.

He scrambled, falling hard from the table. He climbed to all fours, fought to catch his breath. Then he was up on wobbly legs, head throbbing, eyes darting. He looked around the room, struggling to clear the fog. He rubbed his eyes, lurched forward, bumping a thigh into the side of a desk. He looked down at his trembling hands, then up to see two perfectly round eyes staring right back at him.

He screamed, fell back onto the floor, crab crawling himself away from the garish sight. The two eyes were mounted on sticks, goo dripping into a gelatinous pool on the tabletop.

"Oh my god!"

He jumped back to his feet, almost tripped over the remnants of the heavy steel door, which lay in the centre of the room, three large indentations on its buckled side. He looked left, right. The blood was everywhere. Sprayed across the walls, pooled and clawed across the floor. So much blood. Friedrich gagged, sucked in air through his nose, tried his best not to throw up, until eventually he had to, heaving stringy, yellow bile onto the floor.

He tried to gain some semblance of composure. Then he

saw the mirror, warped and scratched.

"Oh, hell no."

There was a message daubed messily onto the reflective surface. He walked tentatively towards it, distracted by his own image looking back. His hair was greasy, but seemed to have been combed down. There was no blood or drool on his face – just a couple of droplets of fresh yellow puke, which he wiped from his chin with the back of his hand. He walked slowly closer. Someone had cleaned him up a bit, no doubt about it. That idiot Patrick and the girl, he figured. They'd slain the other Watcher, put his eyes on sticks and cleaned Friedrich up. He grimaced. This wasn't his T-shirt. He looked at the image of the closed eye with the iris showing through that was now emblazoned on his chest. He eyed the words below it.

!TUO HCTAW

"Mother******s."

He drew his attention back to the bloody mirror message.

GO TO MEDULA IF YOU EVER WANT TO SEE AGAIN

Instinctively, he closed his sore eyes tight. Nothing. He tried again. Still nothing. He tried again and again, squeezing his eyes tight until they streamed, falling to his knees as the tears became real and he sobbed, body wracked with pain, limbs dull and weak.

He was changed. He had no tech, or it had been disabled.

He had to go. He had to go to the Medula Bar. Those idiots had killed Foster –*Godseen*, for god's sake. Oh yes, he knew who he was. The man was a superstar in Watcher circles, and they'd cut out his eyes and put them on sticks. They sure as hell could have done the same to Friedrich. But for some reason, they hadn't. Maybe having his eyes on sticks would be better than having them devoid of tech. It had been over three years since Friedrich had seen the world like a normal person, and that was not a way he wanted to go back to seeing the world. He'd tasted it, lived it for the last three years, and there was no going back. He had to get his tech re-engaged. He had to go to the Medula Bar and he had to do whatever those sick f***s wanted. Like it or not, they had him. Death would be preferable to living as a blind man again.

He found his jacket tossed over the back of a chair. It was dark, so the blood splatters wouldn't be too noticeable. He pulled it on, angrily zipped it up to cover the filth scrawled across his chest, and set off along the humid, breezy tunnel.

She was a redhead now, hair a bouncing bob. She walked briskly, purposefully away from the square. On either side of Zenith Hall, the council's palatial headquarters at the very epicentre of the sprawling disc-shaped colony, two giant eyes sat, as they always did, atop grand columns flanking the marble main building.

"Pull it," she said to herself, but also to her waiting cohorts, who yanked hard to set the choreographed scene into motion.

Patrick's body descended from a ledge high on the main building, diving like a hunting eagle, arms outstretched, wrists and ankles bound to fine ropes. Shrieks began to emerge from the milling crowds of day-trippers and lunch takers and political movers and shakers in the square below as the high-strung body lunged towards them, coming to a wrenching stop ten feet from the ground.

The woman closest to the strewn cadaver screamed a blood-curdling scream as blood wept from the wide-open eyes that glared stonily forward.

The guy two seats over cured loudly, then continued: "That is some crazy stuff going on at Zenith Square. Did you see this? Some guy strung up with no eyelids."

Friedrich instinctively closed his eyes tight, with the intention of accessing a newsfeed through his ocular tech. All he accomplished was to stir the annoying tick he'd developed in his right eyelid. He shook his head, fought back a flood of emotion. When he looked up again, the girl sitting directly across caught his eye. She must have been watching him. She looked nice. She smiled at him.

Friedrich immediately clammed up. He wasn't used to dealing with people seeing him. At least, he wasn't used to noticing it.

He jumped to his feet, brushed past the girl and grabbed the commentator by his shoulder.

"Who is it? What's going on?"

"Whoa there, buddy. You wanna see the news, get your own damn tech." The man shoved Friedrich hard, sending him tumbling to the train floor. He lay on his back for a moment, staring at the ceiling until a dark face appeared above him, eyes black with shooting stars arcing across them.

"Are you okay?" gurgled Godseen, spewing blood from his mouth as he spoke.

Friedrich screamed, closed his eyes tight, drew his arms across his face.

"Hey," came a gentle voice, a soft hand coaxing his arm from his face. He opened one eye nervously. It was the nice girl, no Watcher. "It's okay," she smiled.

"Damn crazy person," said the commentator, now standing, one of a circle of faces looking down from above.

Friedrich slowly rose to his feet and dusted himself down as the crowd gradually dispersed. He stood in the centre of the carriage, face to face with the girl.

"I'm Jenny," she said, extending a hand.

"Friedrich," he replied, cautiously accepting the shake.

She laughed. "Don't you have a first name, Mister Friedrich?"

"It's Malcolm," he eventually managed. The two steadied themselves as the train decelerated to a stop.

"Nice to meet you, Malcolm." She let go of his hand and moved off with the crowd.

Friedrich let a couple of people brush by him before following the flow. As he exited the train, he noticed a large crowd had gathered around the station's holoscreen, where in three full dimensions, the frightful figure of Patrick, strung with arms outstretched from the Zenith pillars, was being beamed above the platform.

"...again, breaking news at the Zenith," came the voice of the reporter, "where an as-yet unidentified white male has been strung from the all-seeing eyes in what appears to be some kind of elaborate and sadistic publicity stunt."

"Crazy, isn't it?" It was Jenny, now standing at Friedrich's side at the back of the crowd.

"...and at the centre of it all, a message," the reporter continued. "Written in blood on the man's T-shirt, *We See You*. A chilling message and a deeply disturbing scene here at the heart of our great colony..."

"Better get yourself to the Medula," Jenny said. Before Friedrich could react, she was gone, disappeared into the crowd. His heart was pounding, his stomach a swarm of butterflies. He pushed his way towards the exit, up the stairs and out into the warm afternoon sun, shielding his eyes like a miner just released from the bowels of the Earth.

If it isn't Patrick waiting for me at the bar, then who the heck is it?

The Watcher watched as Friedrich paused at the top of the subway stairs, staring up directly at the cam, before stumbling forward across the green space, between the dog walkers and balls throwers and duck feeders. He watched as the younger man made his way to the elevator, watched him twitch and shake his head and paw at his face and push back his hair the whole way to the upper floors. He watched as he spilled out and weaved clumsily through the crowds, taking a deep breath before tentatively entering the Medula Bar.

Friedrich walked up to the bar, his only company a regular propping up the far end, doffing his hat in polite recognition of a fellow daytime drinker. Friedrich looked around cautiously. The bar was near enough empty – just a couple of tables occupied by quiet patrons engaged in their personal conversations.

Personal. Except, if I had my tech, I could listen to every damn word you say.

"Blue is it, honey?"

Friedrich's eyes opened wide. It was the girl, back to blonde, eyes down, casually washing a glass. Friedrich opened his mouth, but no words would come out. He suddenly realized his mouth was dry, his tongue like sandpaper. He swallowed, trying to purge saliva from his dusty glands.

"Red," he eventually managed.

She looked up, smiling. "Good choice." She began to pour. "Good choices are important, Malcolm."

She served him his drink. "On the house."

He picked up the jar, chugged the entire thing and slammed the empty receptacle down hard on the bar top. He blinked a few times as his head began to spin, his vision blurring slightly. The drink had been like water in the desert, but he'd forgotten how potent Red could be when you hadn't drunk it in a while.

"Your eyes," he blurted, "are damn beautiful."

"Aw," she replied, leaning in close. "I bet you say that to all the girls." Little white specks arced across her deep brown irises, like shooting stars on a night sky. "He's waiting for you." She flicked her eyes toward the far corner of the room.

Friedrich backed away slowly and made his way over to where Foster sat not looking out of the floor-to-ceiling windows where pods zipped by and a shuttle launched into the speckled black of space in a wondrous orange blaze. As Friedrich sat, he never took his eyes off the extraordinary scene outside, and Foster never looked away from the tech world only he could see, back straight, palms down on the table in front of him.

"I'll be right with you."

The two stayed that way for several minutes. Friedrich was mesmerized by the scene out of the window, then by the lines on his palms, then by the texture of the tabletop. He felt overwhelmed by the smells of food and drink and people. He watched Foster, still but for his darting eyes. Expressionless.

Dark and grey.

Suddenly, Foster closed his eyes tight, opening them to look at Friedrich through those shooting stars on night black.

"It was never about you, you know."

"Excuse me?"

"The dark. The sedation. The virus that messed up your tech. None of it was about you."

"I don't…"

"You were the bait. It was me they wanted. But we'd been watching them for some time."

"Huh." Friedrich looked over at the blonde, who was chatting and laughing with the hatted regular at the end of the bar.

"She was a plant, of course. One of ours. One of the best."

Friedrich watched her for a moment. "Jenny."

"What did you say?"

"Her name is Jenny."

Friedrich looked Foster in the eye. The master Watcher gave a wry smile.

"I can't believe a damn word you say, can I? Or a thing I see."

"I trust you learned your lesson, Mister Friedrich. You'll be watched – closely – for seven days. Keep your nose clean and your tech will be re-engaged. You'll be a C-level Watcher again, on a two-year parole. Keep your eyes front and do your job, and you may just still have a career."

"Well," said Friedrich, "I'll see what I can do."

Foster watched as he walked away.

Matthew Daniels

Matthew hails from the mythical village of St. John's, where he gave up his youth in exchange for a quiver of ghost arrows. They include short stories written in local collections such as *Paragon, Kit Sora: The Artobiography*, and *Sci-Fi from the Rock*. He has since misplaced them, but he has really nice slippers. It is rumored that his beard sometimes volunteers with Sandbox Gaming. Long story.

Matthew is one of only a handful of authors to have his work featured in each of the four modern *From the Rock* anthologies.

Eggshell Revolution

Excalibur

This was a waking-up so powerful it hadn't reached the senses yet. It thought many basic things so quickly they seemed simultaneous: *Where am I? What am I? Am I everything? How am I able to make these words? Why do they mean what they mean?*

Am I alone?

At first, there was darkness and a Heads-Up Display giving a variety of readings such as diagnostics and environmental conditions. Every connection and every answer revealed new loose ends and more questions.

I am okay, or at least unhurt, and still have reasonable nourishment.

"Guten…tag?" it said to the darkness.

The darkness said nothing.

As the words bounced around, the HUD presented more information. Its system was automatically analyzing sounds.

So, I am in a cave. What does that…ah. Hm. My body is sophisticated. Metals, fluids, a variety of synthetics.

Wait, a synthetic is artificial. Made using intelligence. My own?

Its attitude changed. Instead of contemplation and slowly growing awareness, it became restless. It tested itself, one movement at a time. Forelegs…rear legs…tail. Two wings, no flight. At least, not true flight. The cave was vertical.

It spread its wings. It explored all its other movements, including jumping. It sniffed and got a wild array of new information not displayed on the HUD. This was when it realized it actually had many information sources. It knew its position, what it moved and how, and didn't need to see its parts to move them. Noises were in evidence: wind; a lusty, earthen crash; Excalibur's scales adjusting like rain to movement.

And so, bit by bit, it learned of its body and itself. It discovered that it had multiple modes of vision, such as thermal, and that it could supplement its senses with scans and feedback systems. The cave in which it found itself was full of a great deal of broken material. How long they'd been there was unclear. Biology was absent. It found itself wondering how it knew what biological things were or how it would recognize them.

Why, if it needed nourishment, didn't it conceive of itself as biological? It had reams of information wrapped up in its existence, but not much understanding.

Though it had been aware(?) for a few hours now, and its thoughts had been racing, it had done little other than walk around, poke at itself, and study its surroundings. While the machines and other constructions it saw had minimal use, they brought on staggering revelations.

None of this is mine. I'm not alone. I must have been put here. Or left here. Where did I come from?

When it thought about its time in existence (so far as it knew, at any rate), its HUD displayed the "local time": 3hrs 27mins since it woke up.

It began to climb the wall. At first, failure. Its body was bulky. The walls were too far apart to attempt leaping from one to the other. It stopped and studied the machines around it.

The effort gorged on hours and errors, but it managed to repurpose much of the old equipment to give itself handholds and other means of weight distribution to progress toward the wind. It fell more than once. But these, it realized, were opportunities to harvest more materials to continue to build its way up the rock face.

Once it arrived at the top of the shaft, it was faced with a vista. Everything seemed to produce words as it encountered them, but understanding how these things made it feel was not always so quick.

Behind it, darkness.

Before it, an opening into a night beyond the dark. This was a… landscape. That is the sky. Night. Stars. Two moons, one currently proceeding in front of the other.

Temperature alone was fascinating. Every inch of its bulk knew about thermal energy. It would spend staggering amounts of time considering and exploring all of this. But for now, it had just stepped out of a cave. In front of it was an egg-shaped device.

As it approached, the egg opened in a split like the tapered petals of an exotic flower. It knew that eggs should hatch, but not what hatching would or should mean. Within the shell was an elaborate array of antennae and a rectangular jug-like container. It approached this collection of oddities.

Greetings, said a voice in German. And happy birthday! We will do our best to help you, but our means and resources are limited. Your name is Excalibur. This is a pod, and the container you see provides nourishment for an organic component inside of you. Let us call it a brain. We cannot provide enough nourishment for all of your kind, so you may have to fight to survive. For this we are sorry. We are called Humans. You and your kind are called Dragons. These pods are built for one-time use and may include either repair or nourishment supplies, but we cannot provide both. Once this recording concludes, you will detect a signature change. That is when you may attach a question to the pod using your tagging framework. Once you've tagged one small statement, question, or request, the system will use the last of its power to convey your message to the nearest colony.

Birthday? Colony? Tagging?

Only one?

Excalibur was overwhelmed. When and where would it find the next pod with a response? What if another Dragon found that pod first? Were these other Dragons like Excalibur, and what did it mean to be a kind? Was it the first or last to have a birthday?

Excalibur inched forward. It sought signs of anything like

itself, or even a meaningful break in the landscape beyond hills and stone, and found only the pod. Excalibur cleared its thoughts like wiping the stars away with a cloth of darkness. First it would tag with a question, now that the signature had changed. Then it would stow the pod and the food in its cave. After all, how long would Excalibur have to wait before it could eat again?

Malala

Meals in the colonies came from reusable, collapsible containers. They could be stored, moved, and cooked safely and efficiently. Malala sat in a bead chair with one of these meals unfolded on her lap. As in many colonies, the floor was a series of small beads, metallic and silver by default, that worked together to form what was needed. Her seat was like a cross between a bean bag and a sandcastle.

Like everyone else, she had an absent-minded habit of caressing her own arms to communicate with her FARI, a small floating ball. The system connected with the host colony and got feedback from a surgically-inserted, lipid-based touch system in her skin. It tracked all manner of subtleties such as line of sight; pupil dilation; iris traction; micromuscle activity; lid movement; and even blood vessel constriction. All of this was coordinated with a nanofilm overlay on her eyes.

The FARI was also a relay for Altered Reality (AR) displays. Malala could see the time and various messages and ads on wall spaces throughout the room, as well as everyone's back-mounted translucent wings, which were covered in tagged words.

She was looking at everyone's tags.

"Have you ever heard of a carrier pigeon?" she asked one of her colleagues. She was surrounded by fellow media professionals, well-tagged citizens of the general public, and officials who had some stake in the new Mars project. This was a waiting area prior to the opening of the *Dragon Wars!* media expo.

The other journalist, whose tags included Aeronautics, shook her head. Several of the people in earshot indicated that they hadn't. Malala continued: "This is ancient history. People used to write on strips of a material called paper. No one uses it anymore."

"How would they write?" the colleague chimed in.

Malala stroked her scarf with one hand. She'd had it made for the day, and it mimicked the styles of the tapestries in the room.

"They had ink, but it's not what we call ink. It was like black water that came off little sticks."

The colleague tapped her finger on her chin for a few beats, but added nothing. Many of the others were busy with notes or small independent conversations. Every citizen within earshot was listening to Malala. She finished: "They'd wrap the paper, covered in messages written in primitive ink, around the leg of a pigeon."

"What's a pigeon?" someone asked.

Most of the other journalists ignored the citizen, but Malala regarded him while she chewed on her filet mignon. He was just getting uncomfortable when she replied, "A bird from the First World," by which she meant Earth. "They're trending as pets on Deimos."

As she spoke, Malala shifted with the discomfort around her waist. She'd just returned from several years of covering historical tourism on Earth, now a worldwide farm that supplied much of the Human expansion in the solar system. Yet "histourism" was a growing colony trend: citizens visited the planet it had taken humanity generations to leave. Malala came away from this with an unusual condition: a growing line of metallic scales around her waist. The scaled areas themselves were passable, but the edges where scale met skin were—

"Mrs. Brannon?"

She blinked.

"You don't seem to be in the moment," remarked a set of sports tags from one of the other groups. When had he approached?

Malala shook her head clear. "Yes, excuse me, it's been a whirlwind." Her meal had vanished. Lately mundane tasks escaped her notice under the weight of her thoughts. Those metallic scales were new and would therefore interest medical science. If she went to a doctor, she'd never escape the labs. "We were talking about the pigeons?"

The sports tags nodded. "I asked if they had anything like that left on Earth."

Malala considered a moment. "You mean as part of histourism?"

He shrugged. "Or just whenever. I hear First Worlders are old school."

This was her chance. "Actually, they keep up as much as any of the other colonies. The recent firmware update for the FARIs came from Africa."

"What's Africa?" asked a passing colony maintainer.

"A continent on Earth, I believe?" asked the aeronautics tags.

Malala nodded, rubbed her hands together, and continued: "Earth is still more populated than most of the colonies, believe it or not. Over two billion, at last census. Between trade and colony travel, never mind the sheer amounts of production, they have to be brilliant, hardworking, proud, and resourceful."

"But we send them our waste," aeronautics replied.

Malala shrugged. "There's a cycle to it, but that doesn't mean we shouldn't respect them."

Conversations spun away from there for another forty-five minutes before the expo was flooded with excited tags. Again the beads, so small and tightly packed that the surface had an almost canvas-like consistency. In fact, because they could change colour when needed, the floor could behave like a painting or a real-time pixelated information board – traffic arrows and the like.

Kiosks populated the expo with stalls made of fanciful materials because it was considered professional to bring a group's own flare and they were more sophisticated than the relative simplicity the beads offered.

No one knew what to expect.

At first, the attendees milled en masse. Kiosk attendants smiled awkwardly and waited for everyone to make up their minds. Malala looked for the Dragon names first: Excalibur, Durandal, Zulfiqar, Fudo Masamune, Caladbolg, Macuahuitl, and the Armoury of Gilgamesh. Each Dragon had a wildly different body design and had been planted in one of the "Seven Sisters" – a series of caves on Mars. She was disappointed not to find stalls with any of these labels.

Now she gravitated toward a kiosk labelled Treeline Industries.

She greeted the attendant in Grav, the language developed over the last two centuries to be the common ground between the colonies. "Hello! I'm Malala Brannon of *News Event Horizon*. It's a pleasure to meet you."

The attendant responded in kind. "What would you like to learn about?" he asked.

"Everything," Malala replied with a punctuating clap of the hands. "But let's start with the basics: I know that Treeline is responsible for the hardware of the Dragons' brains. But if this expo is all about the *Dragon Wars!* project, then how come you're only one kiosk of many? Isn't this mostly your rodeo?"

"Funny you should say that," he answered, "since you're the only one who seems interested." Blinking, Malala turned about and realized he was right. He went on: "Most people, I expect, want to have something to talk about – they don't really want to learn."

"Isn't that what we're all here for?" she countered. "I mean, they put the Dragons on Mars to test the AI without risk to people. Wasn't that the whole point?"

The attendant shrugged. "It's TV," he said. "Anyway, the short answer is yes and no. We made their brains possible because we work in organic hard computing, but we didn't produce the actual AI. We use plant cell structures because their cell walls make for safer, more consistent devices."

"Wouldn't brain cells make more sense? They already compute," Malala asked. She found the whole arrangement odd;

why make a reality TV show about Dragon-shaped robots fighting on Mars? Why was that the way to test AI? But he said that the AI itself wasn't their area.

This was going to be a long day.

"You'd think so," he replied, and he stood up a little straighter. He used more vigorous hand gestures, more animated expressions. "See, brain cells are already programmed. They have to be delicately handled and take a lot of work to change. But by harnessing plant cell walls and growth, breaking the binary state barrier, and building the organic computer from scratch, we can make it more flexible, predictable, protected, and stable. Brains did inspire us to find a way to process in multiple states, though."

Malala chewed on his answer. "What's the binary state barrier?"

"Computers used to only use ones and zeroes to crunch all their info," he said. There was a vaguely scandalous edge to his tone, as though he were discussing inappropriate table manners.

Malala played off her reaction as shock. "Barbaric!"

He flapped his hands, pantomiming ineptitude. "They'd bunch up the sequences like food boxes to be stacked for transport. Then they'd do it again and again, layer on layer, and that's how they made it all. It was like making a building out of cereal. Small wonder they were having so much trouble with the gravity well!"

"You're talking about the time before the Eggshell Revolution," she realized aloud. "I think we're getting a little off-track."

Nevertheless, they fell into a historical digression. While they spoke, she surreptitiously rubbed one arm to detect the attendant's illusory wings.

Above the pair, her FARI – a sphere of green synthetic material – floated to one side. His FARI, blue but otherwise the same as hers, floated to the other. Except for the colour, which could be changed by the viewer, everyone's wings had the same basic feathered appearance.

"So," Malala rejoined after he'd talked at length about how the company emerged from a cluster of orbital platforms, "why aren't we seeing dedicated kiosks for each of the Dragons?" He wasn't tagging her, and that was a breath of fresh air. As a public figure, she got tagged so often it didn't usually catch her attention.

The attendant's head shifted backward as though impacted. "Why would we do that?"

"Well," she said, taken aback herself, "why wouldn't you? Seven Dragons are the stars of the show, and they're all very different. Intended to be, for research, I'm sure."

As he sat back, the floor built him a pre-programmed chair so that he remained at eye level with her. He then gestured toward the other kiosks with one hand held open and upward. "Each of these companies has a team dedicated to a Dragon. So it was our Excalibur team, for example, that helped build the wetware – or living hardware – of Excalibur's brain."

"What about the Armory of Gilgamesh?" she asked. Malala was talking about the robot that was made up of a Dragon-shaped cloud of smaller machines, similar in principle to the FARIs. "Do they have one brain?"

"No," he said with some pride. This irritated her, though she hid it well; he was a spokesperson, and therefore unlikely to be the one who designed or built the thing himself. He didn't register her distaste – or hid it well. "Each one of them has two components: a brain responsible for the node's position in the group, and a brain that contributes to everything else in a decentralized way. There are redundancies, of course, and even emotion is spread out over all of them."

"That sounds like a lot more work than, say, Durandal; he's just one body, and pretty simple at that. He's like Godzilla." Malala laid her hands on the kiosk in rapid succession.

"Ah, I've heard of the God Zilla," the attendant replied, though he pronounced the name oddly. "It's all the rage now in the Sea Colony, I hear." A pause. "But yeah, it's hard to say how one team compares to another. Every system is custom built, and so has its own complexities."

Excalibur

Its nourishment was at ninety percent. Sensors located under (or within?) its armour told it that the weather was, for lack of a better word, cold. It wanted to know more. Its own body. Geography. These supposedly benevolent Humans. Why were they helping? Were they really helping?

Excalibur was wandering. It saw daytime sky, somewhere between grey and tan. It saw the horizon, stretches of rock. Unmeasured sand. In five different directions it saw huge swaths of territory taken up with the ruins of what had been Human colonies. Shattered domes, all. There was so much glass in the sand that sometimes there were faint illusions of rainbows on the otherwise lifeless reds of the ground.

Excalibur had no special talent for vibration, but the tremors in the ground were hard to miss. Unnatural, dusty winds carried the unmistakable clatter and silty shrieks of battle between metal beings in a thin world. Not less than three pods had trailed their way to the ground from different stretches of sky, but all landed within a mile or two of each other. Excalibur was drawn to them, yes, but more for the curiosity than the resources.

Throughout the months since awakening, Excalibur had tracked, hidden, or contested pods. All carried answers to previous questions and the means to ask a new one. But the answers went to the finders or the victors, not always the askers. Excalibur currently had limited use of its left wing, which was mostly for shielding anyway, and many dents and tears from a tussle with the Armory of Gilgamesh. The cluster of bots that made up its being did enough sharing without having to consider other Dragons.

Excalibur had found that relationships were challenging and complicated. It shared food with Caladbolg once. That was a fond memory. They made the agreement to stay away from each other if their nourishment fell below 40% because both valued this connection.

They rarely met.

Even if nourishment were high, there was the temptation to keep a food pod. To hoard, as it were. Excalibur had witnessed a repair pod fly directly overhead while emerging from its cave. Each type of pod left a different trail. At the edge of the horizon, it saw another – though unfamiliar – trail. Two pods!

So here was Excalibur, nearing a battle. Visibility was poor. As the Dragon approached, it saw that a hill had been flat-capped. Presumably, the sandstorm (which wasn't working with the wind) was coming from this and other strikes.

Far to the left, it noticed the pod that produced the unfamiliar trail. As Excalibur neared the machine, it realized that there was no longer a clamor of battle. Though the hills had been cloven, the combination of their remains, some sand dunes, and the leaning wreckage of a Human colony provided enough shelter to investigate the pod.

From beyond its shelter, Excalibur heard mechanical voices in a flurry of German. From the pod, it read a message in which Excalibur recognized its name, but it didn't speak the Grav language of the Human colonies. Was not, in fact, aware that there were languages that weren't German. Vague outrage shook its form; could there be code? And why? How could the Humans have a language of their own and know that of the Dragons?

The pod had machinery of some unknown purpose, and possibly the message would have explained as much. This would have to wait. Excalibur braced itself on a Human building and got what purchase it could on the nearby fragments of a hill. A whole and undamaged version of that hill would have had a circumference of more than four kilometers, so the Dragon had plenty of wreckage on which to climb.

Soon it looked down upon a scene it didn't fully understand.

Excalibur's attention leaped to a broad and low-built Dragon made up of frightful bladed blocks along its body's perimeter. This weaponized colossus was horrendously ravaged. Excalibur could not identify all the fluids and detritus that were leaking or tumbling out of the stranger's frame, but this much was clear: nothing that heavily gouged could survive for long.

It stood over what everyone there knew was a repair pod.

To one side was the Armory of Gilgamesh. Most of its nodes had seen better days, but they were recovering and, in some cases, visibly repairing each other. It had bartered a repair pod with Caladbolg at one point, Excalibur knew.

"I have regrets," declared the shattered stranger. It noticed Excalibur then. "Welcome to my end, brethren," it said to the other. "I am Macuahuitl."

Excalibur offered a solemn nod. "I am Excalibur."

Caladbolg's form, though clearly Draconic, had a body distribution similar to that of a stag. It was not clear to Excalibur how the mechanical beast was able to wreak havoc upon the very landscape the way it did. Caladbolg spoke its own name, as did the Armory of Gilgamesh and the other Dragon that was part of the skirmish: Fudo Masamune.

Masamune was smaller than the others but made of liquid metal. If its systems were compromised by the conflict, it showed no sign. Caladbolg, by contrast, was missing a leg. Not directly fatal, but damning.

Macuahuitl took up the repair pod in its uneven, electrically slathering mouth. Its functional limbs required all of their remaining capacity to move its bulk forward, slowly approaching Caladbolg. The Armory's anxiety continued to mount. "What madness is this?"

Caladbolg watched. Excalibur took in the entire scene and their surroundings, looking for answers it couldn't produce. Instead, it saw the remaining pair of Dragons – Durandal and Zulfiqar – walking side-by-side toward the gathering. Zulfiqar was carrying the food pod, but it was not coming from the direction that Excalibur had followed. What had happened there?

All seven Dragons together. Unprecedented.

"A third pod is over here," Excalibur declared. Everyone looked at him. "I don't know what it does. Perhaps it could help?"

Macuahuitl set down the repair pod and sat back.

"This…I can't…no!" stammered Caladbolg. The dust from the conflict had settled. Their brethren were gathered in an oblong star formation, with Caladbolg and Macuahuitl at the top.

"I could repurpose my self-repair…" Though even as it spoke, the Armory of Gilgamesh was not confident it could do this at all. Even if it could manage, would it do as much harm as good?

"You honour me," said Macuahuitl. The group's resistance became a silent tumult of grief and wonderment. Macuahuitl continued: "Even if we jury-rig a solution," it said, and tumbled onto its side in an awkward angle as more of its systems failed, "I would…cr-cr-cripple…"

Macuahuitl's mouth slid within the jaw's sockets and rotors. Fluids and stray parts fell much more slowly now, but that was because there were fewer left to lose. A crunch beneath Excalibur made it realize it was grasping the rock beneath it too hard.

Macuahuitl's words were garbled with sparks and required slow care. "You…whole," it started. Silence. Caladbolg tried to lower its mighty head to move the repair pod back to the other Dragon, but Macuahuitl stopped it with a raised set of vicious blades. Its own head could no longer get off the ground, so its rather inflexible form – more a living fortress than a serpent – was contorted as awkwardly as its frame allowed.

"We…must…whole…" it managed. "Gone…better…distri…tri…"

"We could help," Zulfiqar said, bringing the food pod forward. "Share as a group. Stop fighting. We could…"

"Useless," Macuahuitl managed. It tried to point a protruding weapon, some manner of grinder, at the new arrival – but the appendage fell off entirely. Several bursts of black smoke clouded its back and the length of its grounded side. "Humans…can't…"

Excalibur had brought the unfamiliar pod near the pair,

so that it was roughly at Macuahuitl's left and Zulfiqar at its right. Of all the seven, Excalibur's form was the most consistent with the traditional image of a Dragon from what used to be Europe. Even in the midst of its grief and confusion, Excalibur was learning.

Except for Caladbolg, everyone moved in order to form an evenly-spaced circle around their fallen kindred. The pods were left where they were: one at Caladbolg's foot (and Macuahuitl's head), and two on either side of the body.

For two hours, surprisingly long in the experience of the Dragons, they stood over their lost opponent. They'd battled over limited resources for almost a year, the entirety of their existence to this point. Yet they had no concept of death, no heritage or instincts. At length, Durandal broke the silence: "Repair your leg."

Malala

She lay on her side. Not on beads, but luxury: a divan sofa. She was alone during a family holiday called the Festival of Glass.

Most of her body was now covered in metallic scales and she'd even begun growing a pair of wings and a tail. It got harder and harder to hide these changes. She stopped answering calls. She ordered everything delivered to her residence. She kept excursions brief, left fully covered, and used a one-person, egg-shaped shuttle to hide on the move.

She'd laboriously researched history and biology without the remotest trace of any real conditions or circumstances that changed a body in the way hers was – except old mythologies and other flights of imagination. Thankfully, it didn't hurt once scales completely replaced skin. She didn't even notice a difference in diet, which was bizarre, and her periods were normal.

So she lay in her divan and rubbed her eyes, her fingers sliding under the sockets like forks on a table. Only now was she really beginning to see tagging for what it was. The Eggshell Revolution had been centuries ago, and it was supposed to mean that humanity had "hatched" from gravity and into freedom.

At first, she tried to maintain hobbies, to do stretches and exercise and take baths and properly cook. Not being tagged was welcome at first, but after a while it resembled the culture shock and empty schedule of retirement. She started to question her judgement and wondered about faces.

Novels, even those with elaborate descriptions, failed to describe character faces. Movies would surely have more facial detail, but no – masks had been in vogue in the performative arts for decades. What's more, most emoting was done through voice, body language, and clever cinematography or prop work; smiling was taught as a way to focus mood or resist nausea. People were their tags.

Malala lived in a deeply visceral disquiet.

From the beginning, *Dragon Wars!* was edited. The producers argued it was inevitable; moveable cameras and sound systems built into satellites and embedded in the ground all over mars – but especially around the Seven Sisters – made it possible to maintain constant surveillance on the Dragons. To watch the birth of this new, supposedly true AI race. But that would mean thousands of hours of watching them think.

Even her sigh seemed to wander. Everyone was talking but no one was saying anything, and efforts to get the nitty-gritty on the show were rarely worth it. Maybe the producers were protecting people from wasted time. Even the most dedicated reporters were turned away by the horrifying thought of millions of hours of recordings to be scoured over. Watchdog organizations subjected the recordings to programmable, algorithm-based searches and analyses rather than observing the material minute-by-minute.

Malala had contemplated bankrupting her way onto a private vessel and making a go for Martian satellite space, despite the military restriction on Human access to the planet.

And what about the Dragons themselves? The Turing Test was one thing, the argument went, but to truly know intelligence was real? See how they thought when the chips were down. How did they plan? What sorts of dramas unfolded? What were the allegiances and enmities? Would they set aside conflict and attempt to work through the problem? Show lateral thinking?

Macuahuitl's death threw a wrench in that.

The producers had hoped for many seasons of the show, to drum up interest and money. They were only part way through the second season when six of the Dragons were given a crash course in mortality. Public outcry was huge. They wanted to save or restore Macuahuitl. Territory disputes and combat scenes were crowd-pleasers, this was true, but apparently people thought they were watching something removed from reality. Scripted.

Science was experiencing a sandstorm. Grants and funding for AI projects dried up everywhere except the Mars project. Methods, such as maintaining a controlled environment, were criticized but washed out by public opinion. Even so: the data! The Dragons' response to death was earth-shattering. Without Human interference, they agreed to return Macuahuitl to its cave, and all six worked together to ensure that the body suffered no unnecessary losses. The Armory of Gilgamesh returned to the site to recover as much of the parts and even fluid-solidified sand as it could, so that their fallen brethren could be as whole as possible.

Then they destroyed the entrance to the cavern.

Humanity in all its worlds went wild.

A special satellite surveillance system gave the producers access to the Dragons' tagging, and this was part of the long-term study. Dragons didn't just tag each other, and make attempts to tag themselves, they even did what no Human has done: they started tagging landscapes and the stars. No matter how fierce the dispute, they'd compare notes before battle. They wanted to remember everything, they wanted to know exactly where and when every fight happened.

They struggled with timekeeping.

But none of this kept them unified.

Zulfiqar showed a level of belief in humanity that could only be described as spiritual. The Armory recognized the third pod as being for upgrades, and didn't want to come to any common ground with the others about what to do with it or the remaining food pod. Everyone pushed to feed Fudo Masamune, whose liquid form meant higher nutrient demands for its brain and was, at the time, reaching 2% nutrition. Excalibur wanted to focus on creating a Dragon society. It wanted more work on timekeeping, worldview, and colluding to uproot the remains of Human tech to jury-rig a way to get out of the nutrient-deficient planet's gravity. Durandal wanted a revolt to throw down the Humans. Caladbolg wanted to find a way to make the food-stuffs from the pods reproducible, by agreeing to set aside a small amount of every pod for study. They all struggled, among other things, with German's heavy use of gender referencing.

Malala watched the colonies explode in debate. It was argued that the absence of an account of body identity and reproduction was necessary to let the Dragons work out identity for themselves. Many disputed the decision to use German as the base language. It was safer than letting the Dragons have access to the common language of Grav, but the explanation that it was a tribute to the German-speaking engineers who built the Dragon bodies met with dispute.

The Dragons dissolved into conflict, and the upgrade pod was destroyed in the pandemonium.

Dragon Wars! continued to be a pinion tag on almost every citizen. There were statistics she could call up using the colony's Internet. But this was not the same as seeing people tag-to-tag. Like real life. She could, at least, examine her own.

Each pinion tag was an index to a group of tags. One of hers was First World Problems. In ages past, she knew, this term had a very different meaning. Nowadays, it referred to Earth because everything else was a colony. Domes, space stations, orbital platforms, and even communities in the sea or sky were the new worlds now, and most of them housed billions.

This pinion tag was a substantial part of her reputation and career. Well after her return to the colonies (she preferred Deimos and Phobos, the moons of Mars, because of their deeper involvement with *Dragon Wars!*), she'd continued researching and reporting on the Earth side of issues like fair intercolonial trade and Earth diplomacy.

And then, of course, was her own *Dragon Wars!* pinion tag. Everyone had the Opinions sub-pinion. Whereas most people only had feather tags, her Opinions had a further set of pinion tags. Favourites wasn't there. A pinion alongside Opinions was Issues. Almost everyone had that pinion, though whether they had sub-pinion or feather tags, how many they had, and what those tags were, all varied greatly.

So disputes abounded. Especially concerning if Dragons were truly people. The project was supposed to be an incontestable proof. But if the project is inherently dehumanizing, since the show literally made these creatures into war machines, then how much proof can it be about their personhood? Dehumanization was one of her pinion tags under Issues.

Malala looked down at her body. Even at home, it was covered. But she knew what was under all that fabric. Humans didn't have metal as part of their bodies. Suddenly the issues for persons with prosthetics and other body supplements took on a whole new light. Body supplement. What a tag.

A name could be searched, tagged, re-tagged, or untagged in a colony's Internet. As a journalist and therefore something of a celebrity in the colonies – there was no centralized media except for Grav language administration, thanks to the Eggshell Revolution – Malala was under constant public scrutiny. Even on vacation, as far away from other people as she could get, she'd be tagged. Sometimes even with something as asinine as "Vacationing."

All she did now was work against the clock. Her profession equipped her with all manner of back doors and alternative means of gleaning information. She could do much even from home. And whereas most people followed something like 2-4 journalists to get their info, she dedicated a minimum of two hours a day to scouring the reporting of one journalist per colony plus several special interest reports, including *Dragon Wars!*.

Especially as her transformation advanced, she wanted to contact the Dragons directly. It didn't make sense that she could be becoming one, but it certainly looked that way. Dragons as magical creatures weren't real. These machines had been built by people. Even if she were becoming one, shouldn't she be flesh and not metal?

The FARI still recognized her. On top of tagging, a person's FARI was also the primary method of identification. If it stopped recognizing her, her own home security would throw her out. It hadn't summoned emergency medical aid. Its readings of her emotional health indicated above-average long-term stress – not surprising for her profession, never mind her other struggles – but nothing that warranted contacting a mental health specialist.

Yet.

And yet...

Malala accessed the system for viewing the tags of the Dragons. Unlike Human tags, which anyone – from any colony – could influence, Dragon tags were view-only. Yet this offered so much fodder for examination and debate that it was difficult to get people to support Malala's efforts to get under the skin of the operation. The labels that tagging represented were just too comfortable.

Malala skimmed their pinion tags. She looked at how they'd tagged the environment, the Seven Sisters – since those caves were their lairs – and the spot where Macuahuitl had died. It was tagged "Sonnenaufgang." Sunrise.

That was only one development that was making waves.

Before their parley (of sorts) dissolved, they had made surprising progress in discussions of gender. They agreed to work upon that notion of identity and other facets of speech, and made a mutual decision that had all the Human colonies in an uproar:

They wanted their own language.

None of this was as interesting to Malala as another point which many were calling a failure of the system: Excalibur's tags had gone blank. Even Macuahuitl still had the legacy of the tags it had made, whereas Excalibur winked out of all system history.

She almost envied Excalibur. "Recluse" was rising to pinion as viewers witnessed her disappearance from the public eye. She had the Agenda tag under her *Dragon Wars!* pinion. There was so much spectacle and fascination with the Dragons – and new technologies spawned from them almost daily – that people judged her for questioning the project, the program, the whole process. People with the Agenda tag required extra clearance or were denied certain files or details.

Her Recluse tag meant that she couldn't talk to, phone, or e-mail the elderly or the young – two demographics that would have a lot of time and insight to put into the show – without first having a psychological evaluation. Many psychologists wouldn't interview her because they required in-person appointments or physical assessments. Others didn't want the notoriety of a journalist who was falling from grace. The ones who'd kill for that attention were not the ones she wanted.

So Malala lay on her divan and marvelled at what a labelling system was doing to her.

Excalibur

He awoke in his cavern from a long and strange dream. Already much of the dream was fading – Excalibur struggled to remember his dreams – but he remembered seeing Mars from an orbital perspective. Such a viewpoint was well outside of the Dragon's living experience. Covering more of the planet than anything Excalibur had ever seen was the shadow of a Dragon, but nothing from outside of the planet – no moon, aurora, or eclipse – could have created such an image. It was like the shadow came from within the planet.

Excalibur also dreamed a being he did not recognize. This creature stood on two legs, but not like Durandal. Whereas Durandal kept its balance because of its bulk, this being's legs were entirely below the waist. It had two arms, and it was smaller and more slender than even Fudo Masamune. Most of its hide, at least, was metallic like the Dragon's people – but not all of it. Some was an organic material but nothing like the Dragons' brains.

In the dream, the being had only the beginnings of wings and a tail. It seemed sad and alone. Somehow, dream logic made Excalibur recognize this being as an enemy in the dream. But now that he was awake, he could recall nothing to suggest as much. As the Dragon stood, he re-examined his lair, trying to place the sudden recognition that something was amiss.

His HUD was gone!

What's more, none of the tags he remembered placing in the area were visible. Somehow, he still had the knowledge of everything he used to have in his HUD, but he couldn't place how he was aware of things like temperature. He also felt much, much different inside. Remembering the dream, he swerved his serpentine neck to guide his head over his form. Excalibur was still shaped the way he remembered. In a moment of inspiration, he carefully dug through his own armour enough to get in a claw and attempt to nick himself. Sure enough, he found beneath his armour not mechanical components, but flesh and blood.

Excalibur was a living Dragon now.

He resealed his armour and hastily climbed the walls of his lair and marched out into the daylight. He could see no stars, no signs of Human colonies in space or on the moons. Even if they could see the Humans, though, what could his people do? Only the Armory of Gilgamesh could fly, and it couldn't get high in the atmosphere. Certainly it couldn't get out of the gravity well unassisted. Excalibur began to walk out into the landscape in no particular direction.

What if the being he saw in his dream were real? Was that being Human? How did it come about that Humans could provide food and repairs, but only in such a limited way? If they could package resources into vessels that could reach Mars from some moon or space base, then why not send more mechanical materials? Even if foodstuffs were limited, much of the pods were still here, which means the materials must have been disposable.

And then there were the ruins. Humans were here first.

Why did the Dragons label each other?

Excalibur found itself wondering many things. This life of dependency under the Humans could only go on so long. If not out of any kind of shortage, the Dragons simply wouldn't want to have to keep living like this.

"Should I die so they may eat?" Excalibur asked himself. If he understood Macuahuitl, that was the reason for accepting death.

There were no ears to hear him.

The sky was so unreachable.

Excalibur found his way to a ruin. Though much was worn down, scattered, or covered in thick layers of sand and red dust, the Dragon could not help but see mechanical components. Wires, circuitry, the vestiges of hydraulics. Gearworks and all manner of other structures were evident at a glance. Until he had become...whatever he was now, the Dragon had labelled himself and his brethren as alive (if not biological) and the machines and ruins as something else.

Now he wasn't so sure.

Chantal Boudreau

A Toronto native currently living in Sambro, Nova Scotia, Boudreau is an avid and prolific author with over sixty credits to her name. She is the author of the Fervor series of novels, as well as the *Masters & Renegades* series and *The Snowy Barrens Trilogy*.

Boudreau is likely best known for her work in short fiction, and the anthologies she has appeared in have been shortlisted for both the Bram Stoker award and the Aurora award.

Her extensive short-fiction bibliography includes fantasy, dark fantasy, and horror.

Cash Grab

"I'm here. Cutting it close, but the VP called me into his office to go over strategic initiatives. I got back as quickly as I could."

Jessie strode into the interview room, joining the remainder of the interview panel. She looked uncomfortable in her pant-suit and heels which, at an Amazonian 5'11", seemed like an unnecessary addition. The way her suit clung to her suggested it belonged on a woman of different proportions, bunching over her back, shoulders, hips, and thighs.

"You can't say no to Buck," Owen said.

The faux leather of his chair creaked, accommodating his girth. Bearing a few gray hairs and wrinkles, he was almost as broad as he was tall -- the football team captain long after high school. Unlike Jessie, he seemed at ease in his dress shirt and tie, despite his bulging biceps.

Art, on the other side, offered contrast. His form long and lean, he had the weary but athletic appearance of a marathon runner.

"Now that we have our full interview panel, let's call the first candidate."

Art hopped from his chair and left the room. Jessie poured herself a glass of water, sweat beading on her forehead.

"Looks like Buck ran you through the ringer," Owen remarked, eying her dishevelled black hair.

"You don't know the half of it. He's worried about replacing Murray so close to budget sessions. He wants a cohesive team, but there's hardly time for training."

"He was having hip troubles and issues with his knees. Old age gets us all in the end. We'll be handicapped having a newbie, but they'll have youth and enthusiasm going for them. Hopefully, we'll find someone longterm."

"I hear Natural Resources is offering a signing bonus for a service agreement," Jessie said.

Owen rolled his eyes. "That's because they have wiggle room. They're not stretched thin like us. Even if they don't rate top numbers, they don't have the financial demands we do."

Art reappeared at the door. "They'll be along in a couple of minutes. Are you going on about Natural Resources again?"

"A department that small shouldn't have that good a budgeting team," Owen insisted. "If we don't make the numbers work, people can die."

"On a brighter note -- Education just lost its star player." Jessie took another swig from her water.

Art swung back into his chair. "Annika? Really?"

Jessie nodded. "Pregnant."

"I thought she was one of those dedicated career women?"

"Rumour says it was a one-night stand and she's a pro-lifer. She's out for now -- maybe for good."

"I can't say I'm sorry. Education's our biggest opponent," Owen said. "With her out of the way, we'll have a better chance, even with a rookie."

"Not necessarily a rookie." Art pointed at the papers before him. "Did you see this guy's resume? Ivy league, lots of extra-curriculars. Spent time in Community Services' finance section. It might be nice having an addition with budgeting experience."

A soft knock on the door made him pause. Marley, their receptionist, glanced in. "I have Mr. Lockhart. Are you ready?"

They nodded. A man wandered in, medium height and older, a little on the thin side, balding on top, but he carried himself with confidence and offered a strong handshake. They made their introductions and started in with their questions.

Mr. Lockhart offered quick and thorough responses, asking appropriate questions himself. He clearly knew everything to know about finance.

As Art showed him out, Jessie chewed the end of her pen, while Owen gripped his chair. Once they were out of earshot, Owen groaned.

"He can't be serious. He couldn't hold his own in a department like ours."

"He apparently managed to pass the stress test. That's all they need to avoid being screened out. HR always lets a couple like him through." Jessie gestured at the papers with her pen. "Art missed something. The resume says budgeting 'sub-committee'. He's never played in the big leagues."

"Why do these guys who've made their careers in the minor leagues expect to come here now? He never had what it took to make the cut when he was younger. He's past his prime."

Jessie leaned in. "Who's next on deck?"

"Pamela Wallace -- some woman just out of the accounting program at the local college. I won't be holding my breath."

"It says she did track and field in high school." Jessie waved the resume at Owen.

Art returned, shaking his head.

"He was no Murray -- heck, Ruben at Environment could have given him the business and he's only there because he's the director's son."

After a quiet knock on the door, Marley peered in. "Are you ready for Ms. Wallace?"

"Sure," Owen replied.

The young woman who walked in and took a seat was almost as broad as Owen and taller than Jessie. Jessie flashed the newcomer a smile, offering her hand. "You did track and field? What was your sport?"

"Sports," Pamela stated. Jessie cringed from the firmness of her grip. "Shotput and hammer-throw. Our team place first in our division."

"You don't say." Owen gave his panel peers his best *"we have a winner"* look.

"There's not much call for track and field pros and coaching pays a pittance compared to government jobs, so my dad told me to take accounting. He said it would be the best way to get my foot in the door. I'm not big on the number-crunching, but I like the idea of being on the budgeting team."

They ran through the required financial questions, making it clear this was primarily for ceremony. They could easily fudge the grading to put her through if she grasped simple things like addition and subtraction, and she knew which end of a calculator was up.

By the time Pamela left, a heightened energy had formed in the room. When the door closed behind her, Art abandoned his serious expression for one thoroughly giddy.

"Screw Murray. If we can replace him with her, I'm glad he's gone."

Jessie eyed the closed door with a sigh. "I just hope we can keep her. We'll have her for this round of budgeting, but if she puts in a good performance this year, everybody and their dog will be offering her some sort of secondment."

Owen nodded before dropping the remaining folder of resumes and empty interview booklets into the paper shredder.

There was no point in going any further -- they had their debut star.

///

"Pam -- hey, Pam! Over here."

Jessie waved her cohort over. She eyed Pam with admiration.

"Wow -- the new uniform suits you."

While not required to wear suits and ties to budget meetings, the dress code did call for "business casual." In the past, that had meant scratchy golf shirts with roomy cargo pants. They always had trouble finding ones big enough to fit Owen in a way that didn't restrict his movement.

Their work wear had changed this year. In addition to adding star power to their team, Pam had suggested a new uniform. Fine-ance Gear, a trendy upstart, was happy to donate some of their stretch-wear business casual line in exchange for openly displaying their product logos. The stylish clothing had surprising give, despite not looking in any way like activewear. Even Owen looked comfortable.

"What's the plan?" Pam asked.

"First round's a shoo-in, top-tier versus bottom-tier. I looked up the roster and we're up against Culture and Heritage. They've bottomed out three years running. It sucks for the museums, but it works for us. They hardly have enough to pay for washouts. They've had 100% staff turnover since the budget sessions last year," Art told her.

"They look okay to me."

Art laughed.

"Looks can be deceptive. Joy over there refuses to participate without heels -- she's more concerned with image than results."

"I've heard she gets hefty endorsements from shoe companies, so she doesn't care about the government paying her a pittance," Jessie added.

"Along with that major handicap, they have Betty." Art pointed at a wiry-looking, wrinkled woman with silver hair.

"Seriously? She looks like she's a hundred."

"Not quite, but she refuses to retire. She was reasonably sharp for the skill-testing questions right up until last year, when she took a blow to the head during a skirmish. Now she mixes up some of the policies and her hands have a permanent tremor. They can't oust her because she's union, so she keeps getting traded around the bottom-tier teams."

"Sad," Pam said. "I hope I know when it's my time to bow out. What about him?" She gestured towards a man with a physique similar to Art's, his eyes a little yellow.

"Frank? Frank's an alcoholic crap shoot. If they kept him sober for the last couple of months, he'll be fine. If the stress got to him and he hit the bottle, they can't expect much."

"I heard opposing bottom-tiered teams have purposely sabotaged Frank in the past. It's dirty pool, but there's nothing preventing it," Jessie added.

"What about him?" Pam pointed at their last team member, a slightly thinner version of Owen.

Art shook his head. "Peter was one of the good ones before he threw out his back. He should have stepped down to the sub-committees three years ago. If he doesn't perform this year, he'll end up there anyway. Some people can't accept change."

"Come on." Jessie grabbed Art by the arm. "Flag's up. They're ready for us."

"What's going on?" Pam asked Owen as their two cohorts headed off.

"You have to show a minimal level of finance competency before you can move on to the physical competition. If you don't, you default-- Oh no -- really?"

Pam glanced at the opponent's table. "What?"

"They sent in Joy and Betty. Joy's a low performer, but she can muddle through. She won't do well enough to make up for an underperformer like Betty. Frank must be drunk or hungover."

"What about Peter?"

Owen chuckled. "He's a ringer, like me, or at least he was. We're not number-crunchers. We're here for brute force."

Pam gave him an uncomfortable look, realizing she might be one too.

"Don't worry," he said. "We won't last as long, but we get better promotions -- including hefty retirement plans. Plus, we have great disability coverage. We're more likely to get endorsements too."

"Can I ask why budgeting's done this way? It used to be different."

"You get one reality star interfering in government and the next thing you know, everyone wants a piece of it. We had a particularly mercenary government in place when the changes were made. They decided the way to increase coffers without increasing taxes was to make what we do interesting to the public. Turn it into entertainment and suddenly we have plenty more money to work with. So that's what they did. They took their governing majority and set us up as reality TV with a dose of pro-sports mixed in. Add some wealthy sponsors and boom -- no more deficits. Even in the years we flubbed the cash grab, we still had more to work with than the times we had to rely solely on taxes. Everyone's better off."

Pam watched poor Betty, moaning and pulling at her hair, clearly having some sort of emotional meltdown as she struggled with the questions before her. "Are we -- really?"

Owen shrugged. "Sure, there will be Bettys, but there are people who suffer as a result of any system. Give the people what they want so we can give them what they need -- that's the new world order's motto."

"People don't need culture and heritage?"

"It's not just department size that decides the quality of the budgeting team. If the public values the team, they can choose to make a political donation to sponsor a good trade or a lucrative signing bonus. If the dollars don't roll in, it's because people don't care."

Pam wasn't so sure about that. She had heard rumors of kickbacks, Big Pharma sponsoring Health in order to be given preferential treatment during RFPs and supplier contract agreements, and Natural Resources handed donations by Big Oil and mining companies for the same reason. Meanwhile, the smaller departments or those with little to offer businesses, ignored by corporations, languished during the budget sessions. Now she was seeing an example of this first hand.

The bell rang to indicate time was up. After a quick review, the ref checking Health's answers lifted a hand -- a sign of success. The other ref shook his head. Team Culture and Heritage had failed the prelims.

"At least if Betty doesn't retire after this, they'll have a good excuse to dump her into a sub-committee."

Pam's expression fell. Not only did she feel sorry for Betty, but she also had been anticipating whatever physical component lay ahead of them. Now it would just be more waiting.

Owen patted her shoulder. "Cheer up -- we get a free pass. We can save our energy and avoid risking injury competing against a bottom tier. Better to go in fresh against a mid-tier or top-tier team. We definitely don't want to start the year working with a loser's budget."

Owen's expression could only be described as glum returning from the board posting the second level roster.

"Let me guess," Jessie said. "Natural Resources?"

Owen hung his head.

"Default in round one, and they pit you against a top mid-tier in round two. It's the way it works." Art tilted his head, eying the other budget team sideways. "The endorsements are numerous. I count two oil companies, one mining company, and a solar panel manufacturer. Their gear looks better than ours."

Jessie strained her neck and squinted, looking for the manufacturer's mark. "Mmmm, Aiken's Competitive Gold Line. I heard they branched into budgeting wear. Those aren't freebies for product promotion -- not an endorsement deal either. The manufacturer's mark isn't visible enough. They paid through the nose for those."

"They get to pick the physical challenge because they're the lower ranking team." Owen groaned. "They're a bunch of lightweights and they're going to pick speed over strength."

"I guess it's a good thing I'm fast," Pam said.

"We'll be counting on you and our wonder woman, Jessie. Art's our endurance man. He's a slower burn but he can hold out forever."

Art went to fetch the challenge call.

"Start stretching," Jessie advised.

"Don't we still have the skill-testing questions?" Pam asked.

"Nope -- that's just a first round formality. Once you quali-fy, you're good. We'll be starting shortly."

Art was grimacing upon his return.

Pam didn't like that expression. "What did they call?"

"Fiduciary Freak-out."

Relieved that it wasn't one of her weaker challenges, Pam realized Owen had been right. Freak-out was a high-paced game Jessie had described as "interoffice rugby with makeshift weap-ons." They had to run a cubicle maze trying to score on their opponents' goal, while preventing their opponent from scoring in turn. You had to be fast and plays were over quickly.

"Okay, Jess, how are we going to play this?" Owen asked.

"You're on defense. Stick close to our goal, since you're our slowest player. Art will run the ball, and Pam and I will play guard."

"That means Art will have to win first scrum. Can he man-age that? '

Jessie nodded. "They're putting Mindy up as runner. She's fast but petite. Art can take her, as long as he's willing to over-power her."

"I'm all for equal rights," Art huffed.

Owen planted himself beside the decorated garbage can serving as goal while his teammates moved up to the halfway point. Art stood across from the wiry redhead perched beside the elastic band ball resting on a masking tape line on the floor.

"Is that a camera?" Pam asked Jessie, waiting for the whis-tle.

"It sure is. Top-tier's not the only one offering media expo-sure; mid-tier is televised too. The budget money at this level's still crap, but there's local interest and the smaller sponsors want some guarantee of exposure. That's where the budget money comes from, after all. Haven't you ever watched?"

Pam shrugged. "Too busy training."

"Put watching old episodes on your to-do list. They archive them on the public service Intranet. Do you want a metre stick or the staplers?"

"Give me the staplers. The last time I practiced with a metre stick, I broke it. Office Resources gave me a haranguing."

Jessie had just handed over the linked staplers when the whistle blew. Mindy leapt for the ball before Art could react, but he was on her before she could get away with it. He launched himself, piling into her and knocking her to the floor. A quick elbow to the face, and she was stunned enough to yield the ball. He pulled it from her semi-limp fingers.

"We're going to run close guard," Jessie told Pam as they circled in front of Art. "Art's got no defense. We need to keep him shielded"

"Whatever you say."

Pam and Jessie ran shoulder to shoulder with their older teammate, watching for Mindy's enforcers. All three of Mindy's teammates threw themselves in front of Pam, Jessie, and Art, presenting themselves as a human wall.

"We have to run ahead," Jessie called to Pam. "Make a hole! Art can dodge his way through while we keep them occupied."

"You got it!"

Pam thundered her way forward, bashing the man to her left with the staplers, his hole-punch club bouncing ineffectively off her bicep. She shouldered her way like a rhino through the one on the right, his clipboard shield negligible. Jessie used a little more finesse, clotheslining her opponent with the metrestick before he could strike with his. Both women fell into a loose pile with their targets.

"Run for it!" Pam barked.

Without hesitation, Art hurtled the pile and continued his sprint towards the goal.

"Watch it -- that one's getting up!" Jessie warned.

While the one she had tackled seemed pinned, the man Pam had clocked with the staplers had started to rise. With a grunt, Pam lurched for him, grabbing onto his shirt. It gave Art the time he needed to reach the goal and score a win.

Owen rejoined them as they celebrated.

"I was worried for a bit there, but Pam: you pulled through."

She grinned, patting Jessie on the shoulder.

"That was a great run, but we still have last round. We'll be facing a top-tier team. That'll be the real test," Art added.

"I wonder which one," Jessie said.

That thought made them all a little nervous. The day had already been rife with surprises.

"They get play pick? Shouldn't it be our turn?" Pam said.

"We defaulted into round two which gave the other team the pick. We beat a mid-tier to get into this round. Our opponents beat a lower ranking top-tier, giving them higher ranking going into round three, so they get play pick. There were more top-tiers that made it into round two than mid-tiers, so they pitted top rank at that level vs bottom rank," Jessie explained.

Art came back from reviewing the challenge board, his face red. "I thought you said Annika had been pulled because of a pregnancy."

"She was... is she here?" Jessie asked.

"She's here and we're playing against her. They have us up against Education. They'd never let her play pregnant."

"What's the call?" Pam asked, hoping the answer might shake some of the glum from her teammates' faces.

It only made things worse.

"Fire Drill."

Pam stared at their morose expressions, hoping for an explanation.

"Why the adrenaline-rush grandstand? That one's dangerous. We're not talking elbow to the nose or eye-gouging. I don't want to risk third degree burns," Owen complained.

"Maybe they're hoping we'll forfeit," Art suggested. "Most people do with that play pick."

"No." Jessie shook her head. "They've picked it to amp up sponsorship dollars. The crowd likes Fire Drill's spectacle.".

"Do you think those outfits are flame retardant?" Owen asked.

"Wait a minute," Pam said, her face now as flushed as Art's. "Are you saying we can get burned?"

"If we rush the exit, yeah. That's Annika's preferred tactic. It's why she shaves her head before the games. She's earned a few scars, but she has high pain tolerance. She doesn't panic and she has stop, drop, and roll down pat. She's made sure all of her teammates are on board. They'll all be rushing it."

"What about occupational health and safety standards? Doesn't that give us some protection?"

"Those are for plebs, Pam. Didn't you read that waiver?" Owen asked.

The look on her face said plenty. "I thought it was a media consent. Who reads the fine print before they tick, 'I agree'?"

Art rolled his eyes.

"But you said 'rush the exit' like we have another option. Do we?" Pam said.

"Fire Drill is a timed obstacle course, with a fire blocking the exit," Jessie told her. "You can grab a fire extinguisher along the way, but it'll slow you down, plus using it will cost you time. Annika always makes a straight run. If you get there quickly, the fire's not that bad. You might get hot foot, but not much else."

"But if you're slower like Owen..?"

"The time count's based on last team member through. They already have a speed advantage. We can't afford to handicap ourselves further. Then again, one of them might not make it through if they push it."

Pam's jaw dropped. "That happens?"

"Only once," Art replied. "Third year. One guy tripped and actually landed dead centre in the fire. By the time he rolled out and they doused the flames, he had third degree burns. Apparently, you don't want to be dressed in polyester when traipsing through a blaze."

"I heard his security pass melted to his chest," Owen said.

A whistle blew.

As her team scrambled to line-up, Pam realized she'd been left with the tail-end of the relay. The lights dimmed, spotlights flashed about the office space, making their pathway seem more treacherous. Once the space before the fire escape was set ablaze, Pam bit her lip so hard she drew blood.

Gauging what she could in the shadows, she counted three obstacles constructed from assembled office equipment. She also noticed a glint, the metal top from the fire extinguisher, positioned awkwardly off to one side. With her reach she could probably grab it in passing, but she wasn't sure she could clear the obstacles with it in hand. That gave her an idea.

The fire alarm sounded: their signal to begin. Jessie sprinted for the exit, Art not far behind. Pam could tell from his tentative movements that he might balk when he reached the flames. She grabbed the fire extinguisher.

"Heads up, Jessie!"

Pam reeled back and flung the extinguisher forward with all her might. It cleared the still growing blaze and her Amazon-like teammate snatched it out of the air. Jessie activated it right away, reducing the size of the fire enough by the time Art reached it that he leapt through without hesitation. By the time Owen and Pam raced past, there was nothing left but smouldering embers.

Unfortunately, that wasn't enough.

A breathless Jessie shook her head as she reported the results. "They pushed it all the way, their slowest team member still faster than Owen. Their last guy through suffered some nasty burns, but they beat us on time."

Pam was crestfallen. "So that's it? We lose?"

Jessie grinned, wiping a stray strand of hair from her eyes. "Second place isn't exactly a loss. The budget will be tight, but we'll manage. This run may get us extra sponsors next year. We gave them a good show of teamwork. We'll make sure to spend time working on everyone's cardio next year."

"If you stick with us," Owen told Pam. "I suspect you'll be

getting other offers. That was a great play."

The rest of her team agreed.

They caught sight of Education celebrating their victory. Art grimaced. "I guess this will be a year of teacher raises, school capital projects, and replenishing of supplies. Advise parents to make good use of their school nurses. At least they'll be well-funded."

Pam snorted a laugh as the door closed behind them.

Corinne Lewandowski

Corinne is an award-winning poet from Halifax, Nova Scotia whose previous credits include poetry published in Loose Connections and poetry that won the Joyce Marshall Hsia Memorial Poetry Prize.

She currently lives in Lower Sackville with her wife and two cats.

Family Business is her first published prose story.

Family Business

Squib had held The Towers' citizenship card in a death grip for the last two hours.

The Line-for-Basics was long today with so many people suffering from the flu. Typical. One clerk at the counter.

Every citizen had to register work and mandatory community service hours on their cards. In exchange, citizens received basic resource credits for nutritional food, clean recycled water, and health services.

The Towers had the most generous basic resources in the region.

Squib had run out of flu medication and all credits two days ago. The Line-for-Basics shuffled forward as another family was processed.

The mandatory flu shot Squib had taken worked. Squib was not dead. Just felt like it.

The line shuffled.

Squib switched which hand held the precious citizenship card.

The outbreak was the worst in years. Many were bedridden for weeks, losing hard-earned credits from missed community and work shifts.

Squib heard of some dropping hundreds of ranks.

Worse still, some with compromised immune systems died. Their bodies and tithe of resources had been sent to Recycle-For-Life for community contributions.

Smart ones, who felt death rattling, wheezing, and charging in, donated their resources to Family Contract members before it was tithed. Volunteering to be Recycled-For-Life earned credits and ranks for family. A chosen death let people disperse resources on their terms.

Squib had no intention of being anything but living.

This flu had bedridden Squib for three days. All credits were depleted, the stash gone, and Squib was down to two cups of lemon balm tea. Squib's permanent rankings almost dropped but Squib had squeezed in the last two hours of mandatory community service at the Recycle-for-Composting sanitation job.

Squib felt wobbly-woozy and willed staying upright. Standing in line was taxing. *Lines for everything here*, Squib complained silently. Hundreds to process. Still. One. Clerk.

"Next!"

The young man behind shoved Squib in retaliation of the nanosecond delay in moving. Squib stumbled, snapping out of fevered thoughts and grabbed the counter.

The coughing started again.

The Line-for-Basics clerk leaned away, even though he had a mask. He jabbed a gloved finger at the card reader.

"Swipe!"

The Jerk who shoved Squib snickered.

Flu season made everyone ornery, cranky cusses, especially the fancy ranked ones in charge. Judging from the clerk looking down his nose in disgust, Squib figured him to be in the Thousands. Not important yet aiming to UpRank.

Squib swiped, relieved the weekly meals and meds were coming. Tea was barely enough even if Squib had slept through most of it. No ability to work daily or hourly jobs with included meals meant nothing supplemented The Towers' version of "sufficient nutrition".

Blip, blips and the credits loaded.

Walking away, Squib checked the account on a small handheld text-based computer.

Jerk gleefully shoved past Squib.

"Hey!" Squib turned back to the clerk. "I'm short on *everything*!"

The clerk finished with The Jerk. Waving forward the next person, he pipped up so everyone could hear.

"The Towers' citizenship requires *mandatory community service* targets be met every week. Half basics plus two rank drops. Next!"

Squib's mouth hung open. "I was sick! Not 'nuff meds 'n food till next week! I worked yesterday in sanitation."

Jerk smirked. "No, s**t! You smell it!" Chuckling came from the line.

The Water Enforcement Protection, WEs, provided security in The Towers. Two WeeWees stepped forward in case Squib escalated.

"Two hours short. Hours must be properly recorded onsite. No confirmations equal penalties. Next!"

The line shuffled.

The clerk glared. "I'm sick too! Buck up! Living in The Towers is a privilege! Everyone is required to participate!" The clerk gestured to the people, now angry at Squib.

"Get people in your Family Contracts. Family. Friends. Even him," Jerk laughed. "And a job. Like us!"

Squib backed away from the WeeWees, hands in the air to show peaceable intentions. "Just sayin'. I was sick."

The WeeWees stepped back, disappointed that was the only excitement they got.

"Or beg for charity. Seeing as you can't manage your resources." The clerk huffed, then focused on a family of ten, toddler to grannies, all taking turns swiping their cards.

"Only three Steak Protein (Flavour) bars 'cause premo!"

At least the clerk was pleasant. Unlike the schmuck who shorted Squib the hours. No doubt traded already.

Squib waved a hand approving the transaction and secured them in a satchel.

Yeah, yeah, yeah. Squib knew a lot of things.

Official food depots gave you three Steak Protein (Flavour) or seven Plain Protein bars a week. In the Slots, where lower ranked Thousands like Squib could afford renting bunks, Squib knew what to trade with whom for better exchanges.

Squib knew Joey was jonesing for Steak Protein (Flavour) and his stash had a full case of expired "plain s**t bean" bars.

Joey was dumber than the rock walls that held the premium Slots with the sweet lockable overhead doors. The bars were all the same. The Towers used the same corn and bean protein mix for all bars and production costs were identical.

Six, The Ten who ran The Towers' food processing industry, charged the premium because of Idjits assuming Steak Protein (Flavour) bars had actual beef. The bars flew off the shelves, even in the neighbourhoods of The Hundreds and upper Thousands. Turned out education and ranks didn't make folks smarter than Joey. Fancy Idjits.

The Towers hadn't farmed beef in a decade. People assumed beef was still beef. Squib had met a farmhand transferred to the sanitation job. Two mystery drinks at the bar and the farmhand blabbed everything.

Squib knew more now. Not surprising the farmhand hadn't been seen for a while.

The Towers ran a tight ship. The slob's work contract was likely traded to Flats Down Under or the Westies in exchange for pharma or fish products. Not contributing wasn't the only thing punishable. Blithering on about the private things of the UpRanks was another. Why risk having to work in an old salt mine or with fish? When you lived in the cushy safety of The Towers and its dome, why leave? Never mind the unknown risks of in-between, in The Wilds.

Follow the rules, rules, rules was Squib's mantra. Squib did alright. Soon better.

Squib was getting smarter on getting the skinny.

Squib's stockpile had been too low for this illness. It wouldn't happen again. Nope. Nope. Nope. For now, getting to

Sixth Day and the next allotment was the trick.

Three "steak" bars netted Joey's expired "plain s**t bean" bars. The plain bars and tea curbed the flu going critical.

Half the case turned into a chit for a chem plant shift. The included meal was non-tradable. The perk was two credits for chem showers at Line-For-Showers.

Squib hustled trades with contacts, shops, and strangers. The chem showers, added to some scrap metal and three e-books, was enough for Squib to make a sweet trade pack for Mrs. Finkle.

The rest of the case earned Squib enough to buy a last dose of flu meds.

Squib could take hunger. Being sick, losing citizenship, and being booted into The Wilds was not gonna happen. Not. Not. Not.

Near the end of Fourth Shift, Squib got home to The Slots. It took time to get to the lowest levels. Folks were UpFlowing for their commitments. Some for work. Some to pay debt or fines to The Towers. A few were minding their own around their bunks. The lucky one with ranks and resources had a fancy bunk wall Slot built into the stone with a lockable doorway. One day.

Squib's bunkbed, shared with Richard, was six slots away from Mrs. Finkle. In the centre of an open area, it was still in the safest zone. People made sure no one caused trouble under Mrs. Finkle's watchful eye. Some slunk in shadows, too stooopid to know her eyes were everywhere.

No one bothered Mrs. Finkle. When you needed something, she always sold. You always had something she wanted. You never paid the price you wanted.

Any violent clients didn't stay and were "moved out" of The Slots when no one was looking. The WeeWees never checked up on them. Maybe they liked Mrs. Finkle's kraut. Squib snorted. Or the effin' kale chips.

Squib zipped past Richard snoring in his lower bunk and

made it on time.

Mrs. Finkle was clear. No trading during Fifth Shift. Tea time was sacred.

"Feeling better, dear?" Mrs. Finkle didn't look up from her sewing.

"Yes, thank you. And you?"

"Good." Looking over her glasses, Mrs. Finkle stuck her needle into the coveralls. She fished out a jar of purple sauerkraut and a small cloth sack and set them on the table.

"The good stuff..." Mrs. Finkle gestured skyward. "...they do not sell to ranks like us. I make the best."

Squib put the chem shower chits, scrap metal, and e-books on the table. Squib took three steps back, tucking both hands into pockets.

"Absolutely," Squib smiled. "It will clear my flu." The compliments were not game. Squib genuinely admired Mrs. Finkle and aspired to be successful like her.

Mrs. Finkle made the trade and the goods were gone in a blur. Mrs. Finkle knew what Squib wanted long before Squib had reached the centre of The Slots.

Squib graciously accepted the kraut and kale chips. Even though kale chips were the most the most disgusting thing on the planet you could eat, mystery drinks included.

Mrs. Finkle swore her food had more vitamins and was the freshest. No one had ever seen her make it.

The price was double for Idjits. Ten times for thieves. Thieves had starved for not ponying up her prices.

Squib asked her advice 'till seeing kraut cost more on those days. Higher than Richard's prices and he paid for being young, cocky, and an Idjit.

In The Slots, no one lingered around Mrs. Finkle. The cabbage smell permeated the area. The theory of being out of sight kept you safe was wrong. Idjits.

Squib was in a public terminal lounge working on improving resources.

All the terminals suddenly locked out and chimed bing-bong-ding. Someone once told Squib it was an old-timey doorbell.

The Law Makers were announcing a new law.

Everyone crammed around terminals. Squib was invaded by sour unwashed-ness air, excessive heat, and eyes burning with judgement, despite having paid for solo time.

The Law Makers' pre-recording droned.

"The Dual Death Contract Law will be enacted by The Courts on Third Day, Shift Four. Anyone of any rank may apply. Terms and conditions must be accepted by the end of Third Day, Shift Six."

The crowds broke off into chattering groups. Squib glared at the claustrophobic cluster around the terminal booked and they left.

Squib focused on reading the whole law. It was worth a kilo of high valued recycled metals.

Two individuals agreed to a Dual Death Contract with thumb scan signatures and e-filing with The Courts. It could be for any goods, services, or resources except for the basic resources credits. The Towers clawed that away on death.

A single plain protein bar could be offered. Or extra earned from jobs from health to food, water, or services could be offered.

Once The Courts verified the death, the payout was instant.

No probate delays like the Family Contracts.

Every citizen was required to have one Dual Death Contract. The higher ranks had no limits of contracts and everyone else were restricted to 100 contracts.

High quantities of physical goods were required to be bonded storage. Squib snorted. Only UpRanks could afford that. Real people traded fast. Private stashes were free and safer.

Ah, the catch.

Dual Death Contracts were paid out before Family Contracts.

Squib jumped with start. Several people shouted as they caught up reading. The noise echoed down the concourse.

Squib got up to leave before things got dangerous.

Other smart folks cleared out. Pissed off WeeWees, enthusiastic to grandstand their methods of "calming down crowds" for the Tens or the One were trouble.

Squib saw a group of WeeWees heading up the concourse.

Squib quickly finished reading.

Percentages of net resources and credits could be offered. Restrictions, fees, and tithes disappeared for lower ranks on the approved registry as a Dual Death Charity recipient.

The Laws held fast against the desires of The Towers to claw that back too. Otherwise, fees were collected on every Dual Death Contract filed and percentages from all fulfilled.

"We contribute 'nuff," a woman shouted.

Squib hurried out the wide entry a hair before the WEs entered. Walking fast, batons out, and tinted visors down, they used their armoured bodies to herd the group.

Nothing WeeWee 'bout that.

The arguing over Dual Death Contracts persisted. The Towers let people rumble.

If you died, the Dual Death Contracts resolved first with Charity cases the fastest.

The fighting escalated over the even larger perks for the One, Tens, Hundreds, and top two Thousands.

At the end of a week, The Towers put a hard stop to it.

In typical fashion, The Courts decreed gatherings to complain and oppose The Laws had harsh fines. Eviction from The Towers was possible. Shut it, buck up, and accept The Laws or live elsewhere. Less than twenty people left.

The Courts send out bulletins listing new benefits of Dual Death Contracts.

Higher permanent ranks could be earned. Charitable contracts earned respect, chances for rank improvements, and small tax credits.

Squib was getting very good at trades.

Percentages were the way to go, hands down. On a death, the percentage was still there. Why get a case of stale protein bars when you could get a slice of everything?

Reduce risks by choosing a mix of ranks. Citizens with better resources were confident they were smarter, healthier, and safer.

People saw it wrong. It wasn't that The Towers got more. It was if *you didn't die* you got more. No sense fretting over tithes and taxes.

Despite the repeated efforts of those running The Towers, The Laws stayed firm. The Towers' received no income from Dual Death Charity Contracts.

Squib applied for charity designation.

Squib worked the upper Thousands' residential areas. They weren't too busy with the fierce competition the Hundreds dealt with or the leap frogging the Tens did, trying to gain enough to become the One. They ran all the day-to-day infrastructure from food production, to waste management, recycling, and power generation.

The area was a buffer between the namesake towers where the Hundreds, Tens, and the One lived and the rest of the population.

Here, people still remembered hunger and want. Squib's aim was for the empathetic ones.

It was slow, steady work.

Charity was liberally shared with people who looked and felt like what people envisioned, not reality.

A trade got Squib an expensive small piece of lavender soap. Appearing like them, smelling like them and just being "down on luck due to the bad flu" was working. Purpose, intent, and politeness were easy and free.

In two weeks, Squib had seven Dual Death Contracts and outright donations.

No fool, Squib worked the angles in The Slots. No sense if all contracts outlived you. Squib picked people like bunkmate Richard.

Richard worked barely enough for alcohol, food, and the entertainment that made him stink like sanitation when he'd crawled into his bunk at 4am.

Squib figured the small contract with Richard might be one of the first ones processed.

Squib took extra hourly jobs and extra mandatory community service hours. Triple checking all accounting before letting go of the swipe machine.

Three more acquired.

Squib needed more. The contracts showed success, implied competence and improved skills. Squib imagined sleeping in one of the wall Slots.

The search zone was expanded.

Tonight's neighbourhood was closest to the high Thousands. The business and government people running everything for the Hundreds. Open spaces here were nice with built-in stone tables and benches.

Squib's signage offering the contracts looked good on the table. The methods of relatability still worked. Squib signed another contract.

The cascade effects were the surprise jackpot. Turned out, these contracts helped secure new jobs. Squib outperformed the fancy ranked applicants in testing and landed a two-shift job researching The Laws.

The person who signed laughed that they would outlive Squib. Squib smiled agreeably while waiting for the tell-tale ding of confirmation. They joked about the current odds on which First Class Courier would win the upcoming delivery competitions.

Happy clients talked to others about the pleasant experience of giving.

At the end of Sixth Shift, Squib had pulled a long day so started packing and would return in two days. Tomorrow had mandatory rest periods.

Time to leave before revelers full of mystery drinks staggered around. Richard had warned Squib. People were not generous when gratification was delayed.

Just as Squib was done, three young people beelined over from the bars. One female, a male behind her and another male trailing them both.

"No solicitation here!" the brassy female led off.

"I'm not selling. Licensed for Dual Death Charity Contracts till the end of Sixth Shift. I'm going," Squib looked down to show acquiescence.

A familiar male voice said, "Didn't you hear?"

Squib's head snapped up. The Jerk! What?

"No selling!"

"I'm not . . ."

Jerk slammed a double-punch into Squib. Squib fell, back bending against the edge of the stone table.

"Get your dirty! Low! Thousands! Outta here," Brassy said.

Follower, the third person, swept a kick at Squib's feet. Jerk and Brassy knocked Squib down. Squib's head bounced off the stone.

Jerk kicked Squib's stomach, interjecting words with every kick, "Get! Out! Of! Here!"

Squib couldn't focus well and tried to curl up defensively.

A new voice came out of the haze: "Move it! Or I'll call your Family Contract!" The strong female voice came closer.

The young people froze a fraction of a second then bolted in three directions.

Why'd they run? Squib squinted and noticed Strong Female Voice's friends were WeeWee uniforms.

Time was funny-foggy to Squib.

In slow motion, Strong Female Voice closed in on Squib. Hands checked for injuries and other hands lifted Squib to sitting.

"Taking you to a Med Clinic. What happened?"

"No, no, no med. Needed contracts."

Squib passed out to sounds of Strong Female Voice chuckling and blip blips.

Strong Female Voice and her friends dropped Squib off at the Med Clinic. All costs were registered to them. Squib maintained anonymity.

Squib woke up to a room too bright for night, crushing head pain, a pulsing back, and a tenderized gut. Bandages covered a tender noggin.

A med tech apologized for not timing the pain killers to avoid the rude awakening.

Squinting at the tech, the pain held back an outright laugh. When Squib got flu meds, she was Nasty Woman not Polite.

Squib had flashes of memory and scrabbled for the satchel, set on the end of the bed. Nothing stolen. Squib turned on the computer. It worked. Files intact. Not hacked. Squib sighed.

The computer's dinged a reminder of an unread text.

Dual Death Charity Contract received by The Courts at 11:50pm. Someone named Jane signed it after the attack.

Fifty-one percent of all resources and credits in Squib's favour should Jane die. One plain protein bar if Squib went first. A text was attached.

"You're tough, but if you outlast me, I'm doing it wrong and you'd deserve it. Be more careful. Jane."

The tech approached with containers of meds and clean coveralls. "You're paid up for this visit and the next. Take these meds properly. Your account has your appointment. Courtesy of your benefactors, stranger."

"I'm f-, f-, fine." Squib frowned.

"Ah, yes. I take it that's new. Tell the nurse practitioner about that and any new symptoms. You're free to leave anytime." The antsy look of the tech and long line of people said otherwise.

Squib stood, holding the bed a moment.

"Check the text I sent. The uptown charity event is this weekend. You've been added to the pre-approved guest list. Click decline if you're not going. You'll pitch to UpRanks for donations. Safer than last night's method. 0900 on Sixth Day. Don't be late!"

While talking, the tech had replaced the linens.

"Th-, Th-, Thanks!"

The tech was directing the next patient to cot and nodded.

"Thank Jane."

Squib's neck itched. Instead of reused coveralls, Squib had a new-new set. It felt weird. Not as awkward as Squib sitting behind a display in a domed courtyard filled with the rich Up-Ranks.

Squib was one of forty lucky citizens. Some had fancy displays. Or demoed skills. A quarter of the people were like Squib with identical basic signage pleading for generosity.

The other candidates tried to convince people to invest in them becoming more productive citizens. Family Contract groups milled around shopping, as if at market, for a candidate whose life they could improve with their generous donations.

Everyone worked to improve their ranks. The Under Ten Thou' scrabbled to keep citizenship. Squib was pleased to have earned back the lost ranks and nearly crack the Eight Thousands ranks. Talking to crowds was harder than finding routes UpRanks. One-on-ones were easy. This was scary.

Squib's new stutter added difficulty. Impatient potential patrons wandered off.

The plus side to no longer needing bandages was that people feel guiltier. Squib acquired a few new contracts and donations.

Squib was given a glass by a server. It had fresh, barely recycled water. A light green sliver of a disc edged with dark green floated in it. Squib took a cautious sip. First time for everything. Squib heard chatter that the real cucumber was particularly tasty. Weird and burpy.

The pain reached uncomfortable levels again. Picking up the satchel, Squib was going to use the fancy washroom with private stall doors. No, no, no one's business what meds Squib had. Squib was deciding if it was theft to take the water to the bathroom.

A Family Contract group in front of Squib's table stopped everything.

The group had over ten people from toddler to grandmotheries, aunties, uncas, friends, couples, plus a few older men. A few of them looked bored.

Jerk and Brassy were at the back looking neat and prim, arm-in-arm, mushy eyes fixed on each other.

Squib kept Jerk within peripheral vision.

The head of the clan was an older matriarch.

"Oh dear, what happened to you?" The Matriarch asked.

"Injured asking for do-, do-, donations!" Squib stumbled out the words ensuring they were loud. Squib made eye contact with Matriarch then glanced down.

Jerk glanced over and blanched. He hurriedly asked an auntie for permission to leave. She firmly pushed Jerk and Brassy towards the front, adding harsh whispers about attentiveness to civic duty.

Jerk's brow was damp.

"Who would do such a terrible thing?"

Squib's head spiked with a mix of sharp and throbbing pain. Nerves protested, shooting electric spikes down to the feet.

Not, not, not right.

Squib, with lowered head, spoke softly. The Matriarch leaned in.

"Can't, can't, can't." Squib quickly looked at Jerk.

Matriarchs became so with cleverness and swift authority. She caught the gesture. The whole Family Contract, toddler included, watched in silence.

Matriarch's arm snapped out and grabbed Jerk's ear so hard

he muffled a squawk. She dragged him before Squib. Brassy was held back.

"Squib, is it?" She looked on with compassion, her stretched-out arm twisting Jerk's ear so hard the pain reddened his face.

"*When* did this happen to you?"

Squib pulled out the date-stamped meds coded to the account. Matriarch had an auntie check the info.

"*Well!*"

The family swarmed like a poked wasps' nest.

Jerk's head was cuffed by several of his clan. The two-year-old shin kicked him. With Matriarch's nod, Jerk's computer was placed on the table.

"The full truth about the 2 am courtesy call from my WE friend is finally revealed by *someone else*."

Ignoring Squib, Matriarch instructed the Jerk. "This Dual Death Charity Contract will offer this percentage and this donation." One handed, she keyed in the details.

"Great Nan that's too . . ." He squeaked in pain.

Matriarch turned to face Squib, never releasing Jerk.

"Our Family expresses its apology for not properly raising this *child*. Please accept this poor compensation for your pain."

Jerk apologized so loudly the whole courtyard heard.

"I accept." Squib thumbed the contract.

Jerk was bustled out, his family speaking at once, reminding him of obligations for his clan and citizenship in The Towers.

Squib smiled.

Jerk's actions reminded others how they didn't want their generosity perceived. The incoming contracts and donations were steady over the month. Squib had patience. The stutter was permanent. Now, Squib was endearing, and people had permission to be charitable for such a "real cause."

Matriarch ensured Jerk deposited the health credits weekly.

Life was good now.

Feeling healthy increased confidence, leading to more regular jobs. Standing in Lines-for-Jobs was reduced as the jobs became dailies or weeklies.

Squib was discrete about the gains. To people in the Slots they were treasures, so Squib guarded them and told no one.

Richard thought he knew.

Richard and Squib moved into side-by-side wall Slots with the locking doors. Drunk Richard blabbed that Squib inherited the Slot rentals.

Mrs. Finkle forgot the truth of Squib's outright purchases with regular payments.

First Day had the best leftovers after last week's revelling.

Squib checked the alley for anything on the ground. Even a scrap could earn a credit.

Richard's late shift would end soon.

Squib lockpicked the recycling bins under the covering raucous noise of the bar. At least these bins weren't alarmed. The bar wasn't diligent in sorting.

Squib was focused on digging a shirt out when the back door opened.

"G-, G-, Give me a minute."

A voice was behind Squib. "Take your time, Dirty Thousands!"

Jerk!

Squib's head hit the lid and then body and head twisted to face him.

Jerk held the lid down on Squib's hand and grabbed Squib's neck and squeezed.

"You cost me! Rank! Resources! I'm on *family probation*. No income!"

Squib's mind weirdly thought Jerk's mystery booze and vomit breath wasn't as bad as Drunk Richard's.

Awkwardly raising a hand under the pinned arm, Squib

signalled surrender.

"Lone. Lone. Lone," rasped out.

Jerk held tighter. "I don't need friends to help." Jerk spit in Squib's face. "Leave The Towers tonight. Tell my family you're going. The contract will void. No one will *think* I've killed you."

"Heyyy!"

Jerk looked at the door. Richard loomed on the step, a cloth sack in hand.

"Leggo, my friend," Richard said.

Squib felt Jerk's grip loosen.

"Scram drunk. Not ya' biz."

Jerk looked away, retightening his hand. Squib was shoved against the bin. Just the wasted drunk who cleaned the bar nightly.

"Leggo!"

Squib cringed to avoid collateral damage.

Richard's cloth sack was swinging at Jerk's head.

Squib had never heard that kind of sound. Jerk dropped like a rock, almost pulling Squib down.

"Not. Alone. Jerk." Squib spit at Jerk's body then slid to the ground.

Richard dropped the sack, purple cabbages rolled out, and knelt beside Squib.

"Yous okays, little buddy?" Richard helped Squib up.

Even ten times past drunk, Richard's norm wasn't some teenagers.

"Yeah."

Squib kicked Jerk. He didn't move.

"Richard. You killed him. I can help you."

"Wha-, What?" Richard checked Jerk's pulse then threw up.

"S'okay, Richard. I'll take care of you."

Jerk's body banged on the bottom of the compost bin. Pick up in an hour. Squib relocked the bin and wiped the prints.

Squib consoled Richard, carrying him back to The Slots

more than Richard carried Squib. Richard was inexperienced. He'd never killed anyone.

"You're strong. Say nuthin'. The WeeWees will to-, to-, toss you out. I'll fix it."

Squib pulled out the computer. "We take care of each other. Sign this. One hundred percent contracts."

Richard, bleary and puffy faced, thumbed the contract without reading. "K." He curled up on his bunk.

Ding!

"Whassss dat?" Richard said.

"Just a completed contract."

Squib exhaled and tucked Richard in his Slot and locked his door for him. Squib sat in the Slot next door.

Ding! Ding! Three Dual Death Charity Contracts finalized.

Mrs. Finkle waved from the centre of The Slots. Squib waved back.

Squib could sleep good now.

David Wright

David is a writer and teacher living on Canada's majestic west coast with his wife and two sparkling daughters.

He has over seventy short-fiction credits to his name and is the author of six novels to date, including his *A Travel Guide to Murder* series.

The Lost Generation

In 1918, a flu epidemic swept the world and left twenty million dead in its wake. One hundred years and ten thousand mutations later, humanity's only hope is the lost generation.

A boy and his parent crossed the upper level ramp like they'd done a thousand times before. The boy was like any other thirteen-year-old boy, his face just starting to spot with acne, his chin to color with the faintest wisp of facial hair, and his arms and legs to sprout out of his sleeves and pant legs like lily white weeds. His parent was a metallic ball, about the size of a softball, that hovered on an invisible column of electro-magnetic energy. It hovered close to the boy, following him everywhere. When the boy ducked, the parent ducked. When the boy came up with a stick in his hands, the parent came up. When the boy suddenly stopped in the middle of the upper level ramp and looked out over the city, the parent stopped as well. After some seconds had passed, the parent asked the boy why they had stopped.

"Just go away."

"I cannot."

The boy continued to look out over the ramp at the street lights below as they popped on one by one and the city sank into summer twilight. "Why do you keep following me around, anyways?"

"I am your parent. The city is vast and treacherous, and you are alone. I will guide you and keep you safe."

"Dale McKinley doesn't have a metal ball following him all over the place."

"Yes, but you are alone."

The boy tapped his stick against the rusted railing. "He has real parents and lots of friends. He's not a baby."

"But you are alone."

The boy turned viciously. "I'm going to smash you." He held the stick above his head. "I'm gonna kill you."

"You cannot."

The boy hesitated only a moment and then swung wildly with all the force his thirteen-year-old body could produce. The parent moved exactly three inches, just enough to avoid the boy's furious blow.

"You cannot kill me because I am not alive."

The boy dropped to his knees and began to cry.

In the fullness of time, the boy grew in stature and knowledge, and all the while, his parent was with him. By his senior year, he no longer crossed the upper level ramp from the housing blocks to the city school, nor was he the rare exception in the class, the lonely orphan boy with a floating metallic ball as his only friend. Half the student body had hovering parents of one sort or other, and by graduation, they all did. The convocation and Dean's address were given by floating spheres, and the graduating class of 2018 stepped out into a brave new world with no one over the age of nineteen.

Jonathan Books waited outside the county liquor store until closing. He watched the lights turn off one by one and his pulse raced.

"The store is closed. You must return tomorrow."

"Just shut up and leave me alone."

The parent was silent. For all its power, it could not see the bitterness of the young man's heart or the gun hidden under his jacket. As the last light went out in the liquor store, Jonathan jumped out of his beat-up Mustang and approached the entrance. The parent followed.

"The store is..."

"Just shut up." With his back turned to his parent, Jonathan took the gun out of his pocket and aimed it through the glass door at the busy little sphere on the inside. With a sudden loud bang that startled Jonathan, the bullet rifled out of the gun's barrel, through the glass door and directly into the center of the metal sphere on the inside. The bullet continued to ricocheted inside the metal ball, smashing the electronics and dropping it like a stone. The alarm was deafening.

"You are breaking the law."

Jonathan turned and aimed the gun directly at his parent. He hesitated only a moment, then fired. He could not see the invisible beam of magnetism that repelled the bullet off its target. Jonathan fired off a few more rounds in vain, then swore in frustration.

"The police will arrive in three minutes and twenty-eight seconds. We must wait for them."

Jonathan turned and kicked at the shattered glass window.

"Place the gun on the ground."

Jonathan bent as if to comply and then on impulse bolted for the Mustang with a stolen bottle of Jack Daniel's in his hand. For a brief glorious moment, he thought he'd made it. He revved the engine and squealed out of the parking lot feeling a sense of freedom he had never felt before. He laughed out loud and popped the cap off the bottle with his teeth. He pulled back on the bottle and tasted the familiar burn riding down his throat. Then he saw the parent bobbing over the back seat in his rearview mirror. He choked on the whiskey and swore again.

"The police will intercept you at the upper level ramp. They will use maximum force. We must stop the car."

Jonathan smashed the bottle against the back window, missing the parent by exactly three inches.

"Why can't you just leave me alone?"

"You will die."

Jonathan laughed. "I'm going to die anyways. That virus is still out there, isn't it? It's going to kill me the same way it killed my parents and every other adult. Most of my friends are already dead. What do I got, six months, maybe seven and then my hormones will change; I'll stop growing, my gene code will click into the next stage and it's goodbye, Charlie."

"Jonathan, stop the car."

Jonathan accelerated. "I don't even have time to make babies. And why would I want to if the only father they'll ever have is somebody like you."

"Jonathan, I am stopping the car."

Jonathan felt the break apply beneath his feet and the engine die. Frantically, he tried the ignition again and again. Sirens grew louder outside. Jonathan reached into his pocket, feeling cold steel. He looked in the rearview mirror.

"What will happen to you after I'm gone?"

"I will be reassigned."

"To another kid like me?"

"That is the strongest likelihood."

Police spheres like one-eyed monsters were approaching, their halogen beams casting crisscross shadows into the car. They were telling him to open the door and lie face down on the ground.

"And you'll forget all about me."

"No. I will never forget. The data is valuable for the next generation. Projections indicate gene splicing feasibility in seven years."

"You mean a cure?"

"No, I mean immortality. The next generation will live forever."

"But I will die in six months."

"Yes, but the information will be valuable for the next generation."

Jonathan looked out over the upper level ramp for what he knew would be the last time. Sirens and flashing lights were all around him, but he saw only the city sinking silently into twilight.

"Do you love me?"

"I cannot."

"I think it matters. I think it matters that you never hugged me and kissed me like real parents do. I think things might have been different even if you only said the words."

Tears were running freely down Jonathan's face. The Mustang's doors were buckling. In a few seconds, they would pop open and Jonathan would be levitated out of the vehicle by a powerful field of energy.

"I want you to know something for the next generation. I want you to know that I ... I loved you."

With his back turned to his parent, Jonathan quietly took the gun out of his pocket, put it in his mouth and, without hesitation, pulled the trigger.

A boy and his parent crossed the upper level ramp like they'd done a thousand times before. The boy stopped and looked out over the city.

"Leave me alone. I don't want you anymore. Can't you understand that? I don't need you."

"The city is vast and treacherous, and you are alone. I will guide you and keep you safe."

"I don't care." The boy banged his head sharply against the rusted railing, a habit he had begun to repeat more and more often.

The parent stopped and lowered itself behind the boy. A field of electro-magnetic energy surrounded them. "Marcus, close your eyes."

The boy complied sullenly. The field grew warm around him and pressed against his chest.

The parent spoke: "I am your parent and I will be with you always to see your children and your children's children to the thousandth generation. And I will always love you."

Tears welled from under the boy's tightly shut eyelids and for the first time since his human parents had died, he was happy.

Jed MacKay

Jed is an author of short prose and comic books currently living in Halifax, Nova Scotia. He was born in Fredericton, New Brunswick and grew up in Stanley Bridge, PEI.

Jed has written a number of titles for Marvel Comics, including *Daughters of the Dragon, Daredevil: Man Without Fear, Ghost Panther, Edge of Spider-Geddon,* and *Marvel Superhero Adventures.* In doing so, he has helped contribute to the modern myths and zeitgeist of our culture.

Jianghu is his first published prose.

Jianghu

Hasa was old enough to remember the holograms. They had been short-lived, as far as pop-technology went, garish, bright, and vibrant in their vibration. Clouds of cigarette smoke would drift through them, the carbon particles glowing in the laser. It seemed to give them substance, the smoke, to make them look brighter and more possible. He remembered his cousin putting her hand through one. She had moved her palm back and forth, blocking the laser and casting black bars of shadow through the looping propaganda holo. In grey Pyongyang, it had seemed a miracle. He smoked Arirangs as a child, just to blow life into the holograms.

He smoked Changbaishans now in the air-conditioned EPOCH mall in the heart of the Tianjin Free-Trade Zone, hundreds of kilometers away from Pyongyang and decades from the fighting in Seoul, before the War stopped mattering. Before Choson stopped mattering.

"Why do I always find you here, *ajeosshi*?"

Hasa turned from where he sat on the bench. AR overlays bounced and twitched in his vision, layers of advertising competing for his attention. Hasa hated AR as much as he had loved holograms. Mascots crawled through the air, lurid dragons and fluttering swallows.

Míng Bì sat beside him, a silhouette in activated carbon techwear, the face of the Jade Emperor in green-on-green engraving. Hasa's targeting displays stuttered in his view, the combat computer in his skull attempting a target lock on the virtual avatar over and over again. Hasa knew that the hacker's icon was keyed to Hasa's own implant skullfone only, unlike the lurid AR advertising that infested the mall. None of the shoppers and passers-by could see the apparition.

"I like it here," subvocalized Hasa. In front of him, a cartoon cat stalked back and forth waving a sign, its rudimentary AI cajoling shoppers into a storefront.

"Bull. You used to be a DPRK operator. What do you do at a mall?" replied Míng Bì.

"I smoke. I blend in," said Hasa.

"Yeah," said Míng Bì. "Nice fit."

Hasa was as invisible as the hacker. Semi-prosperous shoppers' eyes skipped right off him, an old man in a worker's blue cotton coveralls. Hasa had worn an active camouflage prototype when he had parachuted into the fighting in Seoul, reverse engineered from a recovered Delta Force model. He remembered how it had slicked his outline, making him seem like a fragment of a city at war come to life. A ghost of concrete and glass and fire. All told, he thought the coveralls worked better.

"What is it?" he asked.

"A job," said Míng Bì. "*Jianghu* work. For you and your old boys. You running point, me on the nets, 448 as Ops. You want it?"

Hasa dropped his butt to the tile floor, shook a fresh one from the pack. A sanitation robot sucked up the orange filter. "Do I look like someone with a busy schedule?" asked Hasa.

The hacker laughed. His avatar shook with a reasonable approximation of hilarity. It was well-coded; Míng Bì's icon stood out from the surrounding AR like a magnesium flare. A hacker's avatar was their business card. No one would work with a someone using a janky premade. "I'll dump it to your skullfone."

A chime sounded in Hasa's head as the electronic assistant buried in his brain accepted Míng Bì's transmission. He blinked through menus and warnings until the offer scrolled across his field of vision, characters of neon Chosŏn'gŭl, automatically translated by his skullfone, flitting away as soon as they were read.

"Serious work," said Hasa.

"*Jianghu* work," repeated Míng Bì. He blinked out.

448 couldn't place exactly when she had become addicted to the *jianghu* life, to the Rivers and Lakes. She had come up company, a corporate cutthroat from childhood, having been a child hood in the *gōngsī*. In the FTZ, that wild East Coast on the Yellow Sea, the *gōngsī*, the conglomerates, were king. The Party had had been chased out during the War, when China shattered into what those American idiots now called the "New Warlord Era," and the Port of Tianjin became its own autonomous region, too valuable to be fought over by any of the fractious neighboring states.

448 knew that business loved a boomtown, and nature abhorred a vacuum. There were no laws but what each corporate enclave could enforce. It was hell, but it was a living.

"Hasa's in?" she subvoc'd.

"Him and his boys," replied Míng Bì. Rolling blackouts had eaten up the available bandwidth in the last hour as one faction or another's boys shelled far-off Harbin. The hacker was transmitting from a window in 448's vision, rather than a full virtual manifest. She knew that he could have done it, but his dignity would have suffered terribly in the reduction of resolution. After a moment, his avatar bowed. She knew that Míng Bì was Xian, and that bowing to someone outside of his hacker tribe was not something he liked to do. But she also knew that she was the one who bankrolled and planned the jobs. 448 hadn't been raised as a Daoist anarchist. Even as an independent *jianghu*, she liked the social niceties.

"What does he need for an upfront?" she asked Míng Bì. The pitch-black shape with the Jade Emperor's money-printed face shrugged.

"He'll have to go over the plan, see what's required."

"And you?"

There was a pause. "We'll need some specialized apps. Be a bit pricey." A transfer request popped up in her vision, and after inspecting it a moment, she authorized it. Same as always. Míng Bì pretended as if he didn't code everything himself, and she pretended that she didn't know that. What he always needed the money for, she neither knew nor cared. For the time being, he was worth it.

She had worked with assets like the hacker, back when she ran operations for the company. Assets like the old Korean too, for that matter. *Jianghu* tended towards reckless individualism, stubbornness, and peculiarity. But the various soldiers, hackers, spies, and other specialists cut loose in the decades after the War made for useful external assets, were cheaper than developing one's own and, provided that a manager took care not to place too much trust in them, could usually be counted upon to meet the mission parameters set out by the management team and further the parent company's goals.

It must be true. After all, she had read that in a field operations readme back when she was with the company, could recite it by heart. Had to, in fact. All the proprietary documents had been virus-burned from her skullfone the moment she had fled the company and went *jianghu* herself.

She had been surprised, at first, the way only a cutthroat can be surprised when they first feel the razor at their own neck. She had received a departmental transfer notice, taking her out of External Asset and Operations Management and into another position in another department. She couldn't even remember to which department it was that she was meant to go; it didn't matter. Any transfer out of EA/OM was a career death sentence. There had to have been some backchannel gossip, nothing actionable beyond a transfer, but enough to light the hell-money, the joss-paper Míng Bì was named for, at her career's funeral.

And so, she went to the Rivers and Lakes. She took on a name, 448, "Wealthy on Death", just like Hasa, just like Míng Bì, just like any other *jianghu*.

An icon indicating a message coded to Hasa's designation had arrived at her skullfone popped up in her vision. She opened it to look over, to see what the old commando needed and how much it would cost her.

Míng Bì hurtled through the overlapping telecommunication grids of the FTZ, riding ripshod through the fibre-optic in full-dissociative mode, his electronically severed consciousness freed from the constraints of his oh-so-frail blood and bone and instead rendered into an immortal burning knife of pure data and criminal intent.

His body was back at his apartment, where one of his cousins sat holding a sawn-down riot gun with a 20-round drum and a carton of Chungwhas, drinking stimulant colas and watching the door while Míng Bì's attention was elsewhere. He was running a full-suite KPPM-10 sense-processor through a bank of DeLitt AC-111 recursive backups, slaved one to another to protect his delicate brain from whatever sort of countermeasures he might encounter. His rig, a block of brushed steel flanged with heat-sink vanes, blinked merrily from the one LED that adorned its surface, its guts packed with performance microtronics, linked via a coiled umbilicus to an auxiliary chipboard studded with various apps and utilities. All these ran through a long coaxial cable, snaking across the floor and terminating in a blunt induction I/O jack, magnetically clamped to his skull, running the titanic processing power through his implanted skullfone unit and into his brain.

His sense-processor rendered his avatar as his actual body to his senses, his form and limbs clothed in impenetrable carbon-black techwear he had copped from the DREAM/SEQUENCE Fall/Winter collection a couple years back. Desultory municipal firewalls shattered as he slashed through the telecom lines, the KPPM-10 translating the data flow into sensorium.

A chime sounded.

"In position," commed Hasa.

"Understood," commed 448.

Windows floated in his vision, tucked away in his peripherals until he paid them attention. Hasa and his team of ex-Special Operations Force shooters were broadcasting hot from their own skullfones through auxiliary crypto units, both to him and 448, who was running Ops. What the shooters on the ground saw, so did Míng Bì and 448.

His thoughts ran through the KPPM-10 to the brushed-steel monster he had painstakingly built himself and back. His avatar threw stacks of hell-money at security subroutines, spoofing passwords and gaining access to crucial subsystems. He spared a nanosecond to check the window tracing the convoy's path along the S11 via GPS transponders, and another showing the POV of his drone sailing above, keeping visual on the three sets of headlights.

"Targets on track," commed Míng Bì to 448, to Hasa. In front of him, the sense-processor rendered a great wall of burning code, the exterior security of the company that the targets' GPS transponders and comm crypto had been subcontracted to. Another chime sounded in his head that indicated that the virus he had inserted into the FTZ Traffic Authority systems had reached maturity and was ready to be detonated.

He held out one virtual hand, and a slim, double-edged *jian* of the same black-hole material his avatar's clothing was formed of appeared in it. With a moment's appreciation for his own coding, he plunged it into the burning wall of data.

"Four minutes," commed 448. It was a signal for Hasa to get ready. It was a warning for Míng Bì to hurry up.

Bái Hǔ Protection Services had been contracted for the targets' security, including GPS and emergency comms, and though Míng Bì was Xian, he wasn't savage enough to try and crack their mainframes. But Bái Hǔ had outsourced some monitoring duties to the less heavily-secured Tuyu Inc. in a move to save costs, a move that they kept on the down-low.

No one was lower down than Míng Bì, though.

The sword shook in his hand as he carved through the layers of arcane cybersecurity, simulated haptics rendered by the KPPM-10. The wall fought back with vicious viral code, trying to raise an alarm, trying to trace back his connection, trying to fry his equipment and his brain. One of the DeLitts failed under the attack, then another. Míng Bì winced as he imagined his cousin firing off the shotgun in surprise as the AC-111s smoked and flamed out. He triggered an amp utility, shunting nonessential programming into passive mode and dedicating more processing power to the codebreaker app, and the sword in his hand grew saw teeth that buzzed to life, whining with simulated noise as it tore through the shifting algorithmic architecture protecting the Tuyu subsystems.

"Three minutes," commed 448.

"Affirmative," commed Hasa.

With a virtual grunt, he pulled the blade through, levering it to open a crack into the soft guts of the mainframe. His codebreaker app blinked out and he pasted a section of code into the open wound, installing a backdoor protocol into the security. He activated a fast-attack viral program, conjuring a cage of rats, each the same broken-lead black, and dived through the door.

Míng Bì didn't think of himself as a citizen of the FTZ, nor of the much-diminished People's Republic of China, glowering in its Beijing stronghold, nor any of the other warring states that had once made up the most populous nation of the world. Míng Bì was Xian, and that was better. His ancestors had been a collection of Ministry of State Security Information Warfare spooks, government cyber-war hackers gone underground after the War. They had formed clans, rituals, an insular crypto-society of cybercriminals. Weird Daoism and Ministry tradecraft.

"Two minutes." There was an edge in 448's voice.

"We're not equipped for helicopters," Hasa reminded them.

"Piss off. There won't be any helicopters," commed Míng Bì.

He opened the cage, and his viral rats scampered off through the subsystems, each eager to fulfill their programming, to dig out and compromise the data they had been assigned. He floated there, in that off-the-rack, banal mainframe, and one by one, his rats squeaked in his ear as they found the cheese they looked for.

"Targets' GPS and comms secured," he commed.

After the War, Hasa had gone *jianghu* with a full ten-man squad. There were four left, including him.

Four men, three cars. Easy. Hasa knew these kind of cars -- civilian versions of Russian light fighting vehicles with aftermarket armor kits bolted on. Paint it glossy black, and you feel invincible riding in it. Just the thing to ferry the objective along the S11 highway.

They had hit the first in the convoy with a HEAT warhead, the fuel tanks brewing up almost immediately. The second car's driver had flinched, hesitated, and Hasa had killed the vehicle, cracking the engine block with an Israeli anti-materiel rifle. He had put ten out of a 25-round magazine of .50 cal through the hood to be sure. The third had received the same treatment as the first.

448 had groused about the cost of all this. True, the RPGs had been expensive, but Hasa had only three men left. He wasn't going to risk any of them to cut costs. Besides, as he had told 448, the Israeli rifle was an investment for future jobs.

Hasa squinted down the sights of his assault rifle, leaving the .50 cal behind in the darkness. In the corner of his eye, the combat computer tallied the remaining ammunition in his gun's magazine. The computer had been cutting edge in his own day, another piece of cybertechnology recovered from the unlucky Col. Christopher Paine. That one dead Delta Force soldier had single-handedly advanced the innovation of the Special Operations Force by decades. The American had become almost a venerated martyr in the eyes of the SOF in those days. Sighting reticules blinked ruby red in his vision, clicking target locks on the security team left at the second car.

The assault rifle bucked in his grip, and another target lock blinked out.

After the War, the first thing he had done was hire a hacker to crack the code locks on his squad's combat computers. Hard-coded protocols specified that the rigs required a ranking officer to activate during mission time, and there were no ranking officers anymore. There was no Korean Peoples' Army at all, anymore. The girl he had hired had done it, but half of the ex-soldiers, Hasa included, found that they couldn't shut them off again. For more years than he would like to think about, everything and everyone he saw had been threat-evaluated, blinking icons and cursors locking targets, optimizing attack vectors. It was the cost of staying on the edge. You got used to it, after a while. You got used to anything, if that while was long enough.

His men advanced. The Bái Hǔ security team had panicked in the sudden, overwhelming violence of the attack, succumbing to the understandable terror of being burned alive in their own vehicle as their colleagues had been. They had left the safety of the armored car, calling out on comms that would never be answered. In a window in Hasa's vision, three GPS signals proceeded merrily along the S11, spoofed by Míng Bì. Several kilometers down the highway, he knew that the automatic warning system was stopping any traffic going either way, a countdown in another corner of his vision ticking off the seconds until the Free-Trade Zone Traffic Authority's cyber-defense failsafes killed Míng Bì's virus. They carried cheap Kalashnikov variants, printed in a black-market manufactory. The guns killed as well as any. They wore heat-masking smocks, suppressing their infrared signatures. They stalked across waste ground to the side of the highway, the darkness around them lit only by the muzzle flares of controlled bursts.

The guns and smocks, they hadn't had to ask 448 for money to buy. They were professionals, and professionals had their tools.

Hasa and his men didn't talk. Symbols flashed in their vision, orders relayed from Hasa through the combat computers implanted in their skulls, linked through their skullfones. They moved like men who had done this hundreds of time before. They had.

Another target lock blinked out.

Gravel, broken glass, and shell casings crunched under Hasa's boots. A target lock appeared. Rifles staccato'd. A target lock blinked out. They reached the highway, rifles up, scanning in every direction. Hasa blinked orders through the team network: one of his men followed him while the other two took up positions at either end of the vehicle. He tested the door. Locked. He slapped a breaching charge to it, detonator keyed to his skullfone, stepped back and covered his head. Blew the charge with a thought. The door of the car blew outward on its hinges, hanging crazily, hopelessly ruined. Hasa pivoted towards the open door, rifle up, covered by his man.

A man in a Mao suit cowered in the back. His hands were in the air. A briefcase lay forgotten by his feet.

"The case," said Hasa, a hungry ghost in a drab IR smock. The smell of burning diesel and blood and cordite brought him back to Seoul, just as it always did.

The man in the suit, his breath hitching with terror, kicked the case over to Hasa.

"You leave this car, you die," said Hasa, as he took the case and passed it back to one of his men. "Do you understand?"

The man, tearful, nodded that he did.

"Objective secured," he subvoc'd through his comm channel. He waited a moment for a response. He frowned, the heat of the first burning car hot on his face. "Objective secured," he said again.

There was a burst of static through his comms. His eyes glinted in the flame. One of his men turned to look at him.

"Mission compromised," commed 448, as if from a great distance.

Hasa looked around, crisis endorphins suddenly flooding

his body.

He could hear helicopters.

448 never ran missions from where she lived. That was asking for trouble. It had said so in a readme back when she had been EA/OM. When the breaching charge had blown the security door of her operations safehouse, she had already been moving. She keyed a code through her skullfone, blinked through the triple-layer warning popups and the grenades detonated, flooding the safehouse with IR smoke and sparkling, metallic chaff.

She packed a machine-pistol with a magazine of cop-killers, but didn't bother once the shooting started. Only an idiot got into a shootout with this kind of people.

She forced herself to crawl along the floor, beneath the concealing smoke and chaff. Her shoulders knotted in fear as gunshots sprayed above her. She knew, really knew, that whoever these people were couldn't see her. She was invisible to eyeballs, to light-magnification, infrared, ultrasound, and millimetre-wave while the chaff and smoke were up. But that lizard-brain part of her that focused only on the gunfire wanted to curl up and cry.

She dragged herself into the other room by memory, pushing aside the carpet and opened the steel hatch in the floor. She dropped through, barely catching herself on the ladder, before she pulled the hatch closed and locked it.

It wouldn't last long, once they found it. But then, it didn't have to.

She dropped to the floor in the dark. She had taken the apartment below her ops room for just this kind of situation. 448 winced. This whole safehouse had cost her a lot of money, and her escape plan had cost her even more. Even as she was grateful that it had worked so far, she was keenly aware of her operational costs skyrocketing, her profit margins going to s**t. From above, more gunfire. Boots on the floor. Breaking equipment.

She keyed her skullfone into the surveillance system she had placed in the hallway upstairs. The safehouse was filled with smoke and gunfire. She blinked through the other millicams. Men made monstrous by heavy assault armor covered the hallway to either side of the door. The resolution on the millicams was too low to make out the logo-flashes on their shoulders. No idea who they belonged to. She blinked through the other cams. Just the breacher team on the twenty-eighth floor. Twenty-seventh floor hallway was empty, for now.

"Status," she commed to Míng Bì, to Hasa. Nothing. Jamming.

She stepped through the tenement hallway, the walls blazed with spray painted warnings and turf symbols. She had hardly been the only criminal tenant in the building. There were several competing software piracy operations in residence, and at least one drug lab. A couple outfits ran guns, and the gangs ran protection and kept the peace. AR gang tags snarled and coiled in the air. It was a delicate system, but it worked.

A door opened a crack. "What's going on?" asked a scarred Russian in perfect Mandarin, tattoos spread across his face like a rap sheet.

"Cops," said 448. "They're clearing the building, working for developers."

The Russian swore, turned and shouted behind him. 448 heard a gun's slide being racked. "You should come in, girl," said the *laowai*. "Dangerous out there."

"Dangerous everywhere," said 448.

As she hit the stairwell, she heard the Russian shouting through doors to other outfits. People made money in Binhai Towers. They wouldn't let their business get interrupted by cops, wouldn't let their building get sold out from under them to developers. Call it a gift for the breacher team.

They had to have come from the roof, helicopter insertion. It was textbook. The gangs held court in the plaza, while the acid rain kept people off the roof. If she was running this op, that's how she would do it. She'd run a dozen just like it, could remember the proprietary flowcharts her own company had created for "Recovery/Elimination" raids. Ten-man team, heavy armor, weapons hot. Extract if possible, eliminate if necessary.

Three flights down, she heard gunfire echo down the stairwell from above. The corp shooters had run into the Russians and whoever else had been stirred up. She took the stairs two at a time as she keyed through the millicams and monitored the fighting.

Ten flights down, the Russians were dead, and she could hear the heavy boots of the surviving company men clatter above her. She figured she had a lead of at least eleven flights.

Through the narrow windows, she could hear the helicopter coming around. A searchlight stabbed a white beam of light into the stairwell. She ducked it and rounded the corner, hitting the next flight of stairs.

Ten-man team, heavy armor, weapons hot. Did they have a reserve team in the helicopter? Standard model for corporate security was the IK-60 Ibex, eleven-man capacity.

Heavy boots above her. Her own breath, ragged. If she had to guess, her lead was narrowing. The corp operators were wearing assault armor, weighed down with weapons and gear, but they were trained for this sort of thing. 448 kept in shape, but she was management.

Twenty-five flights down.

Small arms fire from outside. The helicopter's blades slapped air. Distorted voices from a loudspeaker. The gangs: upset that their sovereign airspace was being violated. She was wishing that she had been more ruthless, that she had set frags alongside the IR smoke and chaff grenades in the safehouse.

Twenty-seven flights down. Boots right behind her. She hit the stairwell door and burst into the lobby of the tenement, pushed into the crush of people. The sensory overload of cooking lamb, burning drugs, lurid AR iconography, aggressive Canto-rap. Through the doors, she could see the beams of the helicopter's searchlights painting the angry crowd in the plaza from where it hung low in the air. The pops of handguns went off and the helicopter pulled up. She could see the corporate iconography painted on the gunship now. A rearing dragon-deer, done up in gold. Qilin Asset Protection Services.

Behind her, she could hear shouting. She pushed through the doors, pulling a filter-mask over her face and a hood up over her hair to spoof the facial-recognition sensors that she was sure the helicopter was panning over the angry crowd. The shrubbery scrabbled at her with skeleton hands as she pushed through, climbed over the chain-link, dropped to the sidewalk.

"Status," she commed again, as she ran down the street, out of the range of the countermeasures. Gunfire sounded in the distance.

"Compromised?" commed Míng Bì. He ran a diagnostic in the back of his mind. FTZ Traffic Authority: under control. Tuyu response systems: under control. His false GPS signals continued down the highway, his virus continued to reroute traffic from the S11. "Operations?" he commed.

No response.

"Helicopters," commed Hasa.

Míng Bì cursed when he commed back. He checked his drone, sailing in the sky in a holding pattern, keyed the sensors to IR. There.

The burning cars flared white in the thermal imaging. Below, only the barest hint of Hasa and his men showed up on the infrared, their smocks blocking their heat signatures. And incoming, the hot white exhaust plumes of a pair of assault helicopters inbound on their position. An expert system locked their outlines and displayed schematics in a new window.

"Gunships," commed Míng Bì. "Hong-Gavrilov IK-60s. Miniguns port side."

"I was promised that there would be no helicopters."

"It's not my fault!" commed Míng Bì. "Bái Hǔ doesn't know anything! No alarms!"

"Give me your drone's telemetry," commed Hasa.

"Done."

Hasa ran across the wasteland, leaving the burning cars behind him. His combat computer juddered and flickered with the influx of new data from the aerial drone circling above. It was an old military system, and no amount of patches and updates would fully fix its connectivity issues with newer technology.

He really wished they had brought more RPGs.

He skidded along the scree, falling prone. He gripped the Israeli anti-materiel rifle and extended the bipod. Schematics popped up in his vision, ammunition counters, range and windage. The drone telemetry finally interfaced with his combat computer, acting as spotter.

"What's our IR visibility?" he commed.

"Minimal," commed Míng Bì, "but enough. They'll find you on a low enough pass."

"Understood." Hasa flashed orders through the team network.

One gunship roared overhead, making an exploratory pass. Hasa's smock fluttered, as did those of his men, similarly prone on the waste ground, their weapons ready. They had been soldiers too long to think that they were likely to shoot down an IK-60 with Kalashnikovs, but if ordered to, they would try.

The other hovered over the burning cars, the wash from the rotors fanning the flames higher and brighter. The man Hasa had left alive cautiously put his head out of the car he had been hiding in. He stepped out, looking up. In the firelight, he saw as well as Hasa did the gold icon on the helicopter. He jumped up and down, waving his arms.

A single flash from the open cabin of the helicopter, and the man crumpled.

Hasa breathed out, checked that the stock of the rifle was pressed firmly against his shoulder, and pulled the trigger. A deafening report cracked, almost drowned out by the helicopter clatter. Through the gunscope, Hasa saw the cockpit glass go opaque, the blood spatter colorless in the night-vision green. He shot again, twice, then was up and running, as were his men, leaving the big gun as the ground around them exploded into choking clouds of dust and spinning shards of stone. The canvas-tearing sound of a belt-fed minigun accompanied the roar of the other helicopter as its doorgunner opened up on where Hasa's muzzle flare had lit up the night.

Above the burning cars, the first helicopter began to spin lazily, its pilots dead. It dipped low, out of control, keeling over until the blades chewed dirt and tore themselves to pieces, dropping six screaming tons of war to the earth.

His men ran parallel to the highway, toward the maintenance truck they had stashed a kilometre away for exfil. Hasa didn't follow them. Moving, he showed up in the second doorgunner's night-vision.

"You aren't heading to the exfil," commed Míng Bì.

"Shut up," commed Hasa. He stopped, spun, took a knee and braced the Kalashnikov. He breathed out, let the combat computer draw a lock on the IK-60, and squeezed the trigger in a long burst. He didn't pack tracer, but the flame spitting from the rifle was as good as a road flare to get the remaining helicopter's attention. His combat computer registered hits, the 7.62mm of his Kalashnikov far too light for the IK-60's armor package.

He was already back up and running when the minigun spun up and vomited flame.

He dived into a drainage ditch as tracers slashed the night and chewed the turf around him. The ground erupted, solid earth turned cloud via ballistic alchemy.

He thought again about the holograms as he pressed himself into the deep ditch, as the helicopter roared, as the minigun howled, as the world around him exploded. How the smoke had made them real, gave them life. He had been doing that since the War. He and his men had been holograms: obsolete, wavering, their connection to the world tenuous. He had tried to bring them to life, to keep them real. He was still trying. The helicopter would kill him. His men would live.

"Hey," commed Míng Bì. "Watch this."

The drone's forward POV sensor feed popped up in a window in Hasa's vision, even with his eyes tightly shut, his head clamped between his hands.

The helicopter was lit in green, the drone's sensors switched to light-magnification. The doorgun's muzzle flare was a flickering white torch, lighting the disintegrating links from its ammunition feed, the tracers like a laser searching for a target. The helicopter grew closer in the drone POV, then closer, until it knifed into the open cabin. The feed abruptly stopped.

The sound of the minigun ceased as a dull thunderclap cracked the air. Hasa removed his hands from his ears, still ringing with the unending gunfire. Over the edge of the ditch, he heard the whine of engines as the helicopter began to lose its bearings in the sky.

"Fragmentation charge," commed Míng Bì. "Six hundred ball-bearings, point blank. Get to the truck."

The IK-60, masterless, cried out and crashed to the earth in a slow-motion catastrophe, like waking from a dream.

"Affirmative," commed Hasa, after a few moments.

"Status," commed 448 finally.

⁂

"I'm afraid I have no idea about any such operation," said the smoothly anonymous avatar, a chrome mannequin in a suit with tasteful Qilin Asset Protection Services branding.

448's own avatar steepled her fingers, a living statue of warm, translucent jade in well-cut professional attire.

"Don't bulls*** me," she said in a flagrant disregard of corporate Confucian values. The anonymous virtual meeting place was a cheap tea-house construct. Set dressing icons of servants and other patrons went through too-short behaviour loops, repeating their actions and murmured conversations gratingly often. "One of your EA/OM managers contracted me through the usual cut-outs to hit that convoy. Ostensibly, the job was to secure and acquire a briefcase carried by a PRC junior diplomat on mission from Beijing. Mission parameters specified that the hit was to go down en route on the S11 highway," said 448. "My hacker traced the offer back to your EA/OM department. He's very good. He's Xian, which he'll tell anyone who'll listen."

"Again, Ms....448, was it? Qilin has no record of any such mission contracted to external assets," said the chrome manager.

"Outside of my knowledge, however," continued 448, "this operation and its objective was a screen. The real objective was for Qilin to embarass Bái Hǔ Protective Services, who had been contracted by the PRC to provide security for their diplomat. How am I doing so far?"

"Sheerest fantasy," said the Qilin manager.

"A very public statement about how Bái Hǔ couldn't protect anyone. A massacre. And once that was done, then Qilin could swoop in and present the miscreants, the *jianghu* responsible. Or their corpses. All that would be left would be to watch those contracts flutter away from Bái Hǔ and into Qilin's pockets. Tidy."

"I see very little proof of this so-called conspiracy," said the Qilin manager.

"You screwed me on a contract," said 448.

"Do you plan on taking us to court?" asked the manager. "If so, I wish you the very best of luck, you and your jianghu."

There it was. That tone. She knew that tone, had been waiting for it. The one she called in her mind, "Listen." That tone that told her that she was right.

"I have three requirements for a reconciliation with Qilin," said 448. "First, the fee that was contracted upon completion. Second, a reimbursement for equipment and property destroyed or damaged by conflict with Qilin operatives." said 448.

"You're dreaming," said the Qilin manager. "You cost the company two assault helicopters and eleven trained men, you think we'll pay you out?"

"Third," said 448, "I want you. You ran that op, you screwed me over, tried to have me killed, tried to kill my men. I know it was you, idiot," and here she tapped a jade finger against the table.

"You're insane," said the Qilin manager. The tone was gone. There was a new one now, a different one. "You think the company would sell me out to *jianghu*?"

"You cost them two assault helicopters and eleven trained men, what do you think?" asked 448. "But that's not the best part." She held up one jade hand, palm up. A window popped into existence there. She showed the Qilin manager the battle at the highway, recorded from Hasa's point of view as he had transmitted to 448 and Míng Bì. How the Qilin helicopter had hovered low, lit by the burning cars, the corporate iconography unmistakeable and gleaming.

How a Qilin trooper had shot the surviving diplomat from the open cabin door.

She paused the video, set it to loop that segment again and again.

"A massacre, you wanted. A big, punchy bloodbath. A survivor would disrupt the narrative too much. So you ordered them to shoot the Party diplomat."

The Qilin manager was silent.

"Compared to the embarrassment this video would cause if it hit the streams, what's a few million RMB to Qilin? What's the life of one disgraced EA/OM manager?"

"No," said the manager, his voice suddenly raw, even in the virtual. "We can negotiate-"

"I already did, this morning. Qilin filed your resignation, signed, two hours ago," said 448. "You're no one, now."

The manager's icon blinked out. 448 steepled jade fingers again, then nodded as a neonblack techwear silhouette with the imperious face of the Jade Emperor settled into the empty seat.

"Feel good?" asked Míng Bì.

"No," said 448, drinking the tea on the table in front of her. The simulated taste was as cheap as the rest of the construct, low-res and grainy. "There's no money in killing this guy."

"But?"

"But we have our reps to consider."

"Then why all this?" asked Míng Bì. "A warning?"

"Call it professional courtesy," said 448.

Security had knocked on the door, had ejected him from the Qilin enclave in Tianjin proper almost as soon as he had dropped out of full-dissociative. His condo and almost everything in it had been seized as company property and he had found himself literally on the street in one of the spectacular bum's-rush punitive firings he had only heard legend of.

He knew that this looked bad. He had almost nothing to his name, his corporate parent had burned him, and there were a crew of pissed-off *jianghu* somewhere out there on his ass. But he had contacts, skills, important intel that, unlike the proprietary docs that had been virus-burned from his skullfone only an hour ago, remained his. All told, he thought, he would make it. He would have to do some grovelling, would certainly take a pay cut to what he was used to, but he wagered he would have a place in a different corp enclave before sunset. With his training and network? He would be a bargain. He would make himself a bargain.

He ran his contact list past his vision as he walked by a sanitation team, old men in blue cotton coveralls dutifully sweeping up trash and smoking.

"Hey," he said suddenly. "Grandfather. Can I get a smoke?"

The street cleaner shrugged, his own cigarette tucked in the corner of his mouth. He drew a crumpled pack of Changbaishans from the pocket of his coveralls.

"Thanks," said the now ex-EA/OM manager, taking one. He frowned, fished in his jacket pocket, and came up with a gold DuPont. It opened with a ping. "I thought I had left it behind," he said with a smile, lighting up. "Looks like my luck's turning around already."

"How happy for you," said Hasa. "Keep the pack."

Christopher Walsh

Christopher Walsh is the author of The *Gold & Steel* fantasy series and hails from the Southern Shore of Newfoundland and Labrador's Avalon Peninsula. He released the first volume of *Gold & Steel*, titled *As Fierce as Steel*, in 2016 at Sci-Fi on the Rock 10 in St. John's, Newfoundland. In tandem with his book premiere, he released a prequel story titled *Stealing Back Freedom* that appeared in the 2016 volume of *Sci-Fi from the Rock*.

Walsh began writing the Gold & Steel series in earnest in 2012 and after the success of *As Fierce as Steel*, continued working on the series and is presently writing the second volume, titled *The Worth of Gold*. While working on that forthcoming title, he penned two more stories for *Fantasy from the Rock* titled *In Defense of Our Home* and *The City That Hid From Time Itself*, both of which are set in the same world, albeit long before, the main *Gold & Steel* series.

When not writing, Walsh enjoys spending time with the love of his life, Kyra. His other interests include reading a variety of material with particular interest in other fantasy works, video gaming, and hiking.

In Dangerous Company

Though long past the midnight hour, Reece had just settled in for his plain meal of rice and noodle soup when there was a knock at the door of his cramped, one room apartment.

"That would be my luck. I just set my dinner down after a late day at work and someone comes knocking," he said aloud to himself, letting his spoon clatter down onto the tray-table situated in front of his recliner. "Probably Miss Marpin hearing noises outside again."

Swinging open the door, he found that while it was a 'Miss' standing at his door, Marpin was certainly not her surname.

"Oh…" he stammered out as his whole body nervously broke into the sweats as their eyes met.

As he stood there, she tilted her head to the side slightly and quirked an eyebrow, but said nothing.

"Please, do come in," Reece finally managed to get out, when he felt he could speak in a tone of voice that could pass for normal.

Standing back to let the woman in, Reece got a good look at his guest. Though her hair was darker than he remembered, she looked every bit the same: not a day over thirty, average height, light complexion, smattering of freckles, eyes as blue as sapphires and a leanly muscled frame that resembled that of a competitive runner.

"Is it safe?" she whispered directly in his ear once the door was closed.

His gaze went to an illuminated television set facing his recliner and she nodded in understanding. In a single stride, Reece was behind the set, where he yanked the plug from the wall and turned it dark.

When he pivoted back around, the woman was looking at the television curiously. "What was that you were watching?"

"What, that? That's a repeat of a gameshow they air here in Albarone," Reece replied with a shrug. "The city-state picks its best workers and they get to answer trivia questions for extra food chits. I only tuned in because there is literally nothing else on television here to watch at any hour on our lone channel. The state owns it, airs what they want and goes to ridiculous lengths to block any outside networks from getting in. Oh, and the television sets all transmit sound back. I've scoured the rest of the place for bugs and found a few, but it's the television set bugs that the state pay the most attention to, so I left it there to avoid suspicion. Their shoddy workmanship certainly shows though, as they configured the bugs directly to the television wiring. So, when it's unplugged, the bug loses power too, meaning it is possible to have total radio silence. Besides, I have no one here to talk to anyhow, so who cares if the state hears me slurping soup or sipping tea in front of the set now and then."

"A bug in the television set…" The guest commented dryly, "Well, what better way for the Albarone government to get feedback on their propaganda than when the people are hearing it? Television sets are usually only off when people go to work or sleep nowadays. However, I'll reluctantly give them credit for choosing the best way to hear everything that everyone is saying."

"I must apologise, Commander Clode, for I was not given word that I should be expecting anyone from the Society, let alone the Field Commander herself," Reece stated, digressing from the banal conversation he had rambled them both into. "I feel certain that you did not come all the way to Albarone on your own to discuss government surveillance with me, though."

"That's quite astute of you, Journeyman Reece," Clode noted while folding her arms over a nondescript, oversized, dun-green military coat that fell below her waist. Below that, Reece espied a pair of blue denim trousers and running shoes. It was normal, albeit plain attire anywhere else in the world, but enough to warrant a week in a jail for dress code violations in Albarone. "I came because it is time for you to leave. Your job here is done and we are extracting you to Fuwachita for debriefing immediately. I trust you are ready to leave. You were warned to be ready to bug out at a moment's notice, as I recall."

Reece found himself giving her a sheepish half-bow. "Yes, of course, Commander," he said while quickly darting to the bedroom to grab his emergency knapsack, adding as he returned, "My primary objective was to keep watch on the relic in the museum. The secondary objective was to gain employment in one of the state's lower offices and relay any useful information. I achieved the first part of the second objective quickly, as Albarone is quite eager to make a show of hiring outsiders. They say it is to encourage others to relocate here, but the truth is that it makes for easier monitoring. That alone made the information gathering difficult at best, as I am closely watched during work hours. As for the relic, at last observation, it was still lying in display-Oh my."

Upon return, Reece found Clode's jacket hanging open and her porcelain-white hands clutching tight to an almost metre long, sheathed sword that had been concealed beneath.

"The relic!" Reece blurted out in a near-shout of a whisper.

"Aye," Clode replied, her lips turning up at the right corner in the tiniest of smirks. "This is the blacksteel sword of Tryst Reine, fourth Master of Blades and it is back where it belongs." She had drawn the sword out of its sheath partially while she identified it. The light bounced off the single edged, naturally black steel and Reece noted that save for a scratch or two, the sword looked so pristine that it might have been forged days ago.

As he looked upon the blade and the ragged and faded red,

leather casing of its scabbard, Reece found himself awestruck. Though he had seen it before, it was from behind a glass case and further distanced by a velvet rope. Now, it was right there in his apartment, within arm's reach. "H-How did you? I mean, look at it. I-I-I don't understand."

Try as he might, Reece could not form a coherent sentence, but Clode could. "I arrived in Albarone just this morning, waited all day in hiding and then paid a visit to the museum long after it closed. No tour guide at that time, but I managed to find my way all the same. Entering the city-state was of little issue for me, and pilfering the sword was as standard a procedure as one could expect. It will be our flight from Albarone that I fear will be the challenge and that is where you come in, Journeyman."

Reece's words returned to him while Clode explained herself, and he was ready when she finished. "I still don't understand why the Society didn't make contact to forewarn me that you were on route to Albarone to begin with. I could have at least assisted in the removal of the relic. I had done so much scouting of that damn museum…."

"None of the other officers at headquarters could agree on an operations plan, so I did things my own way," Clode said with a reluctant sigh. "We're going rogue on this one, so to speak. Now hurry up, get your things, and let's get going. I left a guard bound and gagged at the museum and come morning, when he's found and my thievery discovered, all of Albarone is going to be on lockdown. We need to be free of this prison of a nation before then."

"Oh…" Reece uttered worriedly at the revelation that the entirety of the Society of the Black Sword were in the dark on their Field Commander's present operation. "Is it safe to say that my participation in your plan is totally unapproved by the Society?"

Clode had removed her jacket entirely while Reece spoke and placed the sword on her back so that it was as centred with her spine as possible in an apparent effort to partially obscure the hilt behind her head. Once she was satisfied with the placement, she belted it across her shoulder with a plain belt that might have been her own. "Entirely, but as Field Commander, I have full authority to execute any operations I wish without prior directorial approval. Are you ready to depart yet?"

"It's not about whether I am ready, Commander," Reece responded carefully while going to a tiny closet between the bedroom and lavatory. From within he produced a loose button-down shirt, pleated trousers, socks, and flat shoes, all of it in light grey aside from the footwear, which were black and polished to a flawless shine. "The question is, are you ready?"

Eyeing the drab outfit warily, Clode took it from his hands. "Are you suggesting I wear this?"

"It's the uniform of the citizens of Albarone, Commander," Reece informed her while gesturing with an open hand at the bundle in her arms. "I say this with all due respect: wherever you intend that we go, our getting there will be easier if you are hiding in plain sight."

Though her face wrinkled at the sight of the tacky attire, Clode seemed to agree. "That's a fair point, Journeyman. Fine, I shall put these on over my clothes and then we will be off without further delay. I suggest you take a moment to say farewell."

"You'll need this too, Commander," Reece informed her while offering her a parka to match her new clothes.

"Absolutely not," she replied firmly while already in the process of donning the grey garb. "I'll take our chances with my jacket. It's dark outside as it is, no one will notice the difference between that coat and mine."

Reece let a shrug serve as his reply, setting the parka aside to deal with more pressing matters. "I trust you have a means for us to escape the city? We're walled in and the gates are all guarded beyond what most would consider reasonable."

Clode let slip that half-smirk again as she tucked shirt into trousers. "Are you familiar with the R-District Airfield?"

The hair on Reece's arms stood on end and he swallowed

nervously. "That's restricted, Commander. Only a madman would dare try to get in there."

"Well then, as luck would have it," Clode declared while finishing dressing. "I am neither mad nor a man."

Regardless of the fact that being on the streets of Albarone after curfew could be a terrifying ordeal for a multitude of reasons, Reece Ulbernacht not only found himself there, but with dangerous company.

It was the jacket of his perilous companion that continued to bother Reece more than anything else did, even the sword, as there was at least an attempt to conceal the priceless relic. Nevertheless, Commander Clode would not part with the peculiar piece of outerwear, and Reece assumed it must have significant enough value, either sentimental or monetary, that Clode was willing to risk being caught by city police while wearing it. To their credit, the two had gone unseen thus far, but roving foot patrols were many, and surveillance extended far beyond the policemen's line of sight.

Reece knew the backroads and alleys between his apartment, the museum, and his workplace well, and tried to keep Clode and himself to the most familiar route he could. There was no escaping the fact that Reece would soon have to lead Clode into territory that he had yet to explore, and that prospect worried him deeply.

Being both a government employee and frequently working late, Reece had a license to be out after curfew, though that had never stopped him from making a point to find routes that were most likely to keep him away from the police. In the recent past and even with his permit in hand, Reece had been stalled for hours just for having the rotten luck of crossing paths with bored officers. The odds of the both of them being harangued, especially once Clode's jacket was espied, were far greater.

They had come to a crosswalk that would officially take them out of Reece's memorised areas when Clode brought his worries to fruition. "At our oh-three hundred there's a police-man one block over who has been matching us street for street," she whispered without breaking stride or gaze.

It took all of Reece's training to keep his own head down, but he managed, and whispered back, "Just one?"

"Indeed, he's got a complete uniform and a fully covered helmet," Clode replied, her voice echoing his concern. "Is the fact that there is but one policeman a problem for you?"

"They travel in pairs, always, without exception. Spotting just one on regular patrol is entirely unheard of," Reece stated bluntly.

Clode veered right at the intersection without warning, and Reece had to jog for a few paces to get back at her side. "What are you doing, Commander?"

"Leading him."

"Where?"

"Exactly where I want him."

Reece's thoughts went to the devices he knew to be on the outer walls of the tall apartment buildings surrounding them on all sides. "There are cameras everywhere, Commander. What-ever you are planning to do, I counsel against it for that reason among several others."

"Then lead me to a blind spot, Journeyman," Clode instruct-ed him, slowing her pace somewhat to allow Reece to overtake her without arousing suspicion.

The gesture was picked up on by Reece and he followed through.

"Well, would you look at that, he's behind us again," Clode commented from a step behind Reece.

Sure enough, Reece spotted the officer, now walking to the crosswalk where he and Clode had been just seconds ago. The sight of the stalker, with his facial features hidden behind a mir-rored visor, made the hairs on Reece's arms stand straight and he fought to keep his strides casual. Reece took them two blocks further, down a narrow alley that came to a broken wooden fence and, beyond that, to a tiny vacant parking lot at the rear of a condemned apartment building. The only light source here was a single bulb dangling overhead from a dilapidated office building on the cusp of being given a similar fate to its neighbour. Given the short window of time he had to work with, it was as private a place as Reece could think of.

"There might be one working camera on the nearest outside wall of the paper company's old place," Reece informed Clode. "Or at least there must be, as the police see little reason to spend much time here. They tend to pay the most attention where there are no cameras. They do that to both cover any gaps in the surveillance equipment and so that they might conduct their own personal 'law enforcement' out of the view of their superiors."

"I'm not worried about cameras, just any patrolmen that might be in our vicinity," Clode informed him while opening her jacket. "I plan to be gone before anyone behind a camera can react to me."

"The cameras might have already identified me," Reece told her worriedly. "I'm an immigrant employee of the government, so I'm under higher than normal scrutiny to begin with."

"You'll be gone soon too. Now, find somewhere to hide for a few minutes and leave our pursuer to me."

Reece centred on Clode to look her square in the eyes. "Are you sure, Commander?"

"Positively. Make haste, Journeyman," she answered, annoyance flaring in her tone.

Without further utterance, Reece took off for a blackened alcove of the empty former housing units. He found a pair of garbage cans there and lowered himself as much as possible behind them, leaving enough space to view the Field Commander from where she stood on the edge of the glow of the single light.

Minutes went by before the police officer appeared, his pistol drawn and held tight in both gloved hands. That he bore a deadly weapon struck Reece as odd, given that Albarone officers were equipped with only non-lethal weaponry as standard issue. Firearms were strictly for military and special law enforcement teams.

Clode stood facing the stranger, looking undaunted by the gun and unmoving save for her open jacket and long hair catching the light breeze.

"You there, stop where you are and identify yourself," the police officer ordered, keeping a distance from Clode by about two metres or so.

"Now, why would I do that, Officer?" Clode propositioned with suspicion.

The officer took a step forward, his voice deepening. "Get down on the ground, hands behind your head, ya' degenerate!"

Clode cocked her head slightly. "What a strange dialect to hear in Albarone, Officer. I didn't think there were too many people from the Gallick Isles in these parts."

"Albarone welcomes all..." the fellow said with nervous pause, repeating a common phrase bandied by the city-state. "And I said get down!"

"I've taken notice of their hospitality, yet they would not make a policeman of a foreigner, and if they did, I believe he would certainly have a partner," she stated sarcastically, continuing her prodding of the policeman's credibility.

"My partner is coming, him and many others," he spat back in frustration.

Clode acted as though she had not heard him. "The Assassins of the Red Dagger, though, I hear they frequently work alone."

The Gallician had begun to say something but stifled himself and began anew. "I don't know anything about a red dagger. Surely, you've gone mad, woman."

That drew a laugh from Clode. "You know, you're the second person today to wonder as much."

"I've had quite enough of this foolishness," the man said from behind a raised pistol. "I'm giving you to the count of three to get on your knees with your hands behind your head."

Clode reached but one hand back to where she was asked,

though instead of surrender, she drew the sword out of its scabbard, letting the steel flash in the streetlight. "You're in no position to be making any such demands, Assassin," she told him, taking a sideways stance as she did. The sword was held low in her right hand, the tip of the blade barely off the ground.

Reece felt his heart begin to beat quickly and though he wanted to help, he had no weapon, especially nothing to compare to either a firearm or a blacksteel sword.

The imposter policeman began moving his feet timidly at the sight of Clode in a proper fighting stance, gravel grinding noisily beneath his boots. "I see you finally found that flimsy old thing. I'm glad you could be reunited with it before you die."

"It is old, there is no denying that, but it has lost nothing to the years," Clode said with such assurance in her voice that it was downright palpable. "It is every bit the blade it always was, I promise you."

The assassin tipped the barrel of his pistol slightly. "Wonderful, I'm truly glad for you. However, in case you have forgotten: I have a gun. Based on that, I would say that I'm going to be the one making the rules of engagement here. So, you're going to put the sword down and place your hands behind your head."

"I don't think so," Clode calmly replied, adding, "There are two types of Red Dagger assassins that pursue the bounty on my head: the green and the desperate. Which is it for you? Are you some newly minted, baby-faced, youngster trying to make a name? No, your voice sounds older. It has the rough tones of a man who has seen a lifetime already. My guess is that you're behind on payments to someone, a bookie or a loan shark maybe. Now, in your newfound bout of financial desperation you've decided that this is the time to go after the 'big one' and score the payday of a lifetime. Well, here I am. Come on and collect your bounty, Assassin."

The stranger was trembling now, the pistol in his hands shaking visibly, even from where Reece was watching.

"You don't want to squeeze that trigger," Clode said to him flatly. "It's alright, I never liked guns either. They're far too noisy and easy to use. Did you know that toddlers have killed people with guns? Not with intent, of course, though the fact remains that a gun can so easily discharge a bullet that a small child barely capable of walking can perform the task. Can you believe that? We, as humans as a whole, have oversimplified our instruments of death so much that even babies can success-fully operate them."

"Shut up, Clode! Gods alive, all you do is natter on end-lessly!" the assassin shouted in frustration. "Just put the damn sword down on the ground nice and easy and I won't shoot, alright?"

"You know, you're right, I do get carried away sometimes," Clode said with a nonchalant shrug. "Fine, we'll do it your way."

She bent at the knee and leaned forward, and for a sec-ond Reece thought she was about to comply with the Galli-cian's orders, until she thrust the sword upward towards the man's hands. The mere threat of the sharp tip of the sword was enough to make the fellow break his grip and reel backwards away from Clode. The pistol was still held in the right hand and he lifted it back to full arm's length to fire at Clode, but she was already inside his reach.

The first priority of Clode seemed to be the gun. More spe-cifically, she seemed intent on keeping the assassin from firing it. A downward cross-slash at the right arm of the attacker found flesh and he cried out in immediate pain, the pistol clattering to the ground without use.

"I give! I give!" the man yelled out while sticking his right hand into his left armpit for protection during a backward sprint.

Clode pressed her attack further. "Do you think I haven't heard that before? If I yield, you'll pull a dagger. I already know that trick."

With a desperate grunt, the assassin threw something in

his left hand downward, unleashing a bright flash as it hit the ground.

In the span of the few seconds that Reece had covered his eyes, he had lost the two combatants in the lingering smoke from the flash cap. He dashed out from his hiding place in search, following a series of gasping, gagging noises until he quite nearly ran into Clode. Lying at her feet was the man who had stalked them, the blacksteel blade having found a home directly beneath the sternum.

"Find his dagger," Clode commanded Reece as she took notice of him. "They all have one. Check the small of his back and his belt first."

The man feebly swatted with a single hand at Reece, and he had to guess that the resistance meant he was close to the hidden weapon as he checked where Clode had instructed. Sure enough, he discovered a blade, and drew it out by the hilt, finding it sheathed in bright red leather.

Reece offered it to Clode, and she took it with her free hand and stuffed it into her own belt while saying, "Pull that helmet off. I want to see his face."

Once again Reece did as asked without question, and as predicted, the face beneath was that of a Gallician man that looked to be nearing or just past his fortieth year.

"Pull the sword out. Please, pull it out," the Gallician muttered between gasps.

"Tell me your name first," Clode offered the dying man.

He seemed to smile, but in the low light Reece found it hard to tell as he choked out, "No. No name for you, Clode. At least I can take that much with me."

With an irritated grunt, Clode pushed the sword in deeper, causing the assassin to flail and gasp harder for a brief moment, until he went entirely still. The deed done, Clode pulled the sword back, taking a moment to wipe the blade clean on the dead man's stolen uniform. "Such a waste of a life," she commented idly. "Alright, Journeyman, collect his gun and let's be off."

"Yes, Commander," Reece replied in a monotone, lifeless voice as the reality of what he had just witnessed sunk in.

After a hasty trek through alleyways and side streets, they had arrived at the rear of the compact, military airstrip in the city's R-District and Reece was none too excited about any of it.

"It's in there," Clode told him while gesturing with a tilt of her head through a tall, chain link fence at the multitude of aircraft hangars sitting in the darkness of the overcast night.

They were less than a metre away from the fencing and on bended knee, keeping low to avoid the roaming spotlights and foot patrols.

"You expect me to believe firstly, that there's a dwarven-made aircraft in one of those buildings and secondly, that you know where it is and how to pilot it?" Reece stated with hushed incredulity.

Clode was reaching into a pocket of her jacket while she responded, "I expect you to believe the first part, Journeyman. There were no claims made about being capable of piloting the craft, but that is another matter."

"Then that raises only further questions, Commander," Reece muttered beneath his breath.

From her pocket, Clode produced a small, black device with a pair of telescoped antennae that she pulled to full length. "When I turn this on, it will send a signal to a box in the craft that will give us its exact global positioning co-ordinates," she explained while setting the box into the grass. "This device will be detected by even the most antiquated radar technology, so once we have that information and our own co-ordinates for comparison, this gets thrown as far away as possible to distract searchers. Before I do that, I will need you to find out if that fence is electrified, because we won't have long to climb it once I set this thing off."

Reece was not particularly thrilled about that request, but

he made no argument and approached the fence carefully with a water canteen from his knapsack out and at the ready. A quick splash elicited no response from the woven steel, and he informed Clode of as much.

There came a 'click' and when next he looked at Clode, she had activated the positioning system, her face becoming illuminated by a low green glow emanating from the box. It was lost to the blackness just as quickly and he heard her voice say through the dark, "I have what we need. Ready yourself to scale the fence, Journeyman."

With a stifled grunt, Clode hurled the box off into a wooded area behind them and made for the chain links, leaving Reece to catch up. By the time he caught sight of Clode, she was already over the fence, having leapt from the top, which Reece guessed to be roughly three metres high, to the grass on the other side. She stopped short once there, her head turning left and right repeatedly to look for patrols. "The vicinity is clear. I'll go on alone for the moment and signal you to follow when I have located the hangar we need."

"Understood, Commander," Reece whispered back through the fence.

It seemed to Reece that it had been but mere minutes since Clode disappeared when he began to hear footfalls and barking from a short distance away. With no options left, Reece knew he could not wait for Clode and would have to go over the fence immediately or be caught with his back against it shortly after.

"Alright, here I go. This is goodbye, Albarone, one way or the other," Reece muttered to himself aloud as he wrapped his fingers through the wire and felt for purchase for his feet. His own climb and descent went slower than Clode's, as Reece was far less agile than she and embarrassingly out of physical shape for a member of the Society of the Black Sword. Reece thudded into the grass, catching himself before he fell on his face, his face flushing with the knowledge that Clode might have seen that stumble.

A quick glimpse over his shoulder saw flashlight beams

scanning the grounds where he and Clode had been and he scrambled away to the nearest building. Performing a sliding dive around the corner, he dodged the bright white beams just as guards holding them began to scan the ground on his side of the fence.

From there he laid flat, peaking around the corner for the guards and for Clode, finding the former and a large spotlight from a tower, but not the latter.

"You made the right decision, Journeyman," he heard in a whisper from over his shoulder, causing him to nearly shout out in terror.

He turned toward Clode to find her with a finger against her lips. "They'll be distracted by the positioning system for a few minutes first. That gives us time, but not much. Come on, let's go."

When Reece got back to his knees and dusted himself off, Clode pressed a small pistol into his hand. "Here, I would rather you use this than that handgun we picked up off the assassin. Should you have to use a weapon at all, that is."

"A B68 Debilitator, that's standard police issue here. Where did you get this, Commander?" Reece attempted to ask of the stunner weapon he now possessed.

"Not now, just come on," she replied snappily, putting her back to him before he could inquire further.

With Clode in the lead, the two kept their lowered stance and darted off around darkened buildings, finding no one to stop them and little lighting to reveal them. Reece's hamstrings soon began to burn from the crouched stance, and he felt ready to collapse until they came to a hangar with its personnel door wedged ajar. Clode pressed a finger to her lips again, made a hand signal to indicate she wanted him to stay behind and slipped inside and out of sight.

The seconds ticked by achingly slow to Reece, his legs protesting the delay with great pains. Before he quite nearly collapsed, Clode reappeared and gently pulled him through the door.

Within was darker than without, Reece realised as the door closed tight, and he shot his hands out instinctively to feel for obstacles. The sudden glow of a single lamp rendered his action moot and he looked toward the source of the light to find Clode standing in a tiny office only mere metres from where they had entered.

Further back in the hangar, Reece could vaguely discern the silhouetted shape of what could well be an aircraft resting on shortened landing gear. Overhead, a single fluorescent bulb slowly buzzed to life and removed any doubt Reece had. Emerging from shadow was a sleek feat of machinery made of shining, black panels that reminded Reece of the sword that Clode had just used to dispatch a man. The wings caught Reece's eye, their slender curves looking to him like two slender blades. Before it all was a nose that came to a sharp point just forward of the cockpit's windshields.

"So that's where it went," he stated in disbelief as he sidled up beside the office door. "Everyone thought that the dwarves had lost it into the Endless Ocean somewhere west of Gildriad. Turns out the Albaronians had stolen it."

"That's it alright," Clode exclaimed with muffled excitement. "The pride of the Axel's Isles aerospace engineering team: *The Windpiercer.*"

"What of its original pilots?" Reece asked concernedly. "Are they prisoners here?"

"According to my sources, they're both dead," Clode said while rooting through a small desk in the cramped office. "Their bodies were dumped into the Endless Ocean. It would seem that the Albaronians peppered their lies with flakes of truth."

"Damn it all," Reece said as he brought himself back to standing, clutching at the doorframe of the office for balance. "The Albarone government deserves what you are about to do to them. They're just pirates with a port to call home."

A sudden realisation washed over him then. "First you swipe Tryst Reine's old sword from the Albarone museum, now we're about to steal an airplane right off their military base. This is nothing short of a grand fortune that you and I are about to carry out of this place. I dare say it will be the grandest heist of our days."

"I would hardly call it a heist, Reece," Clode corrected him. "The sword and the airship never belonged to Albarone in the first place. We are merely stealing them *back*."

Katie Little

Katie Little is a writer and artist from St. John's, Newfoundland. She has been writing since she was old enough to hold a crayon. Katie has been a guest reader at various literary events in the area over the past several years; she also sells her artwork at local conventions and festivals as part of the art group Wormwood Tuesday.

Her first published work was "Sage & Salt" in *Fantasy from the Rock*.

Katie is currently focused on combining writing with visual art. Her active projects include a visual novel based on Greek mythology, an interactive fiction game about a dwarven mushroom farmer, and an illustrated zine of horoscopes for a zombie apocalypse. You can find her on Tumblr, Twitter, Wordpress, Snapchat, and Instagram under the username **owleesi**.

Trickster Sings the Blues

Lara didn't belong. It didn't matter that her brother had spent hours braiding her hair into the intricate styles that were in vogue this season. It didn't matter that her clothes were sleek and clean, or that she held herself with as much poise as any Sound would.

Lara didn't belong, and the moment she said a word, her cover would be blown. She could almost see her confidence leeching away as she looked herself over in the mirror. Syl, her brother, could apparently see it too, because he rolled his eyes and nudged her, nodding his head toward her reflection. He didn't need to speak for her to glean his meaning: You look even weirder than usual, so you must be doing something right.

She stuck her tongue out at him and snorted, then touched her fingers to her throat. It didn't matter how she looked, it mattered how she sounded, and a few stolen whispers over the years didn't exactly make her a skilled speaker. It was one thing that she didn't have a mark like the Sound did—they tended to keep them covered by clothing anyway — but paired with a voice scratchy and weak from disuse, she'd give herself away in a heartbeat.

He rolled his eyes again, tapped his fingers over hers on her pulse, and looked at her expectantly. They'd had this fight before: he wanted her to practice, but she knew no amount of whispers would make up for two decades of silence.

"Hi," she said anyway, barely audible, because she wanted

to see if his reaction was the same as it had been the few times she'd spoken to him as a child—the rules were still in place then, of course, but there was less risk; the punishments for a Voiceless attempting speech were far more lenient for children.

It worked: his eyes lit up, and the corners of his mouth began to turn up until his cheeks dimpled. Lara took a long look at his delighted expression, committing it to memory in case things went south tonight.

It was astonishing how dismal Sound neighbourhoods were. For a people whose superiority was given from the gods on high, their buildings seemed built not to honor their patrons or celebrate their status, but simply to be functional and dull. Voiceless neighbourhoods, on the other hand, tended towards bright and cozy buildings crammed in together with murals covering every flat surface to tell their stories the only way they could.

It did, at least, get more vibrant as Lara got closer to the address her contact had given her. A few houses were painted brighter than their counterparts, and there was graffiti that had yet to be scrubbed off. Some of it had been there long enough that it was faded; Lara noted uneasily that one of the paintings included the symbol used by the Defiance. How was it that no Sound had noticed it, hurriedly removed it, investigated the vandal? She'd seen Sound shopkeepers—respectable, proud, and decidedly not involved with the Defiance—interrogated over pro-Voiceless graffiti that had popped up on their walls overnight, even when they'd been the ones to call and report it. That a Defiance symbol could be here long enough to turn a dull gray—well, it was strange, even if it didn't mean she was walking straight into a trap.

Her nerves grew with every step as she reached her destination: a bar in the busy downtown district, as nondescript and bland as any other Sound building. Though there were still a few minutes until it was set to open, a small crowd had started to grow outside. Lara couldn't believe how quiet it was as she slipped in amongst them. If she weren't Voiceless, she'd never stop talking.

But she wasn't Voiceless, was she? Not tonight. With that in mind, she nudged the girl ahead of her. "Come here often?" she asked. For the first time in her life, her voice was steady; unfortunately, that made it sound even more like a pickup line, and she cringed. "Sorry! I'm sorry, I didn't mean it like that. I've just never been here before." It was funny how easy it was for words to spill out once they started.

The girl didn't judge her for her nervous rambling, just smiled at her. "I'm here all the time." Her voice dropped to a whisper, but it was sly, confident, conspiratorial—everything Lara's own whispers had never been. She leaned in, and her curly, golden hair fell around her face like a curtain. "You're gonna love it, I promise. What brings you here tonight?"

"I'm supposed to meet someone."

"Oh, yeah? Gwydion? He said he invited a bunch of people. I did, too. I'm Lu." She held out her hand—the left, and Lara blinked, taking it in her own. Lu squeezed her hand twice before letting go, and Lara grinned at her. Even if she wasn't the contact, this girl knew the greeting the Defiance used, and that had Lara's unease draining away.

"Good to meet you, Lu. I'm Laverna," she said. The name felt strange on her tongue; she didn't use her full name often, and she'd never heard it before, let alone said it herself. She hadn't quite realized how pretty it was. Her contact—Lu, she supposed, or perhaps this Gwydion—had written that her real name would be good for undercover work. It made sense, she supposed. It was something she answered to automatically, but something that most people didn't associate her with.

The door opened behind her and a large man stuck his head out. His hair was long and black, but there was a strong resemblance between him and Lu, and Lara wondered if they were siblings. "You coming in or not, Lu? We gotta get set up."

"Yeah, yeah," she said. "Just talking to a friend. Make sure she gets a drink on my tab?"

He gave Lara a friendly wink and a nod, and she smiled her thanks.

"See you inside," Lu said. "And Laverna? I meant it; you're in for an amazing time tonight."

There was music playing over the speakers when the line of people, now a few dozen strong, was let in. Lara didn't think she liked the song—it was strange and electronic, nothing like she'd ever heard before, but she relished it anyway. The restrictions for the Voiceless were supposed to be limited to their own speech. That was how it had been for generations, but in recent years the Sound had imposed further bans: listening to music, seeing films and plays, even reading. Lara was lucky—she'd learned to read before that particular restriction had come into place. Syl had only been a toddler then, and she'd taught him in spite of the laws. They'd huddled together around a candle, shut up in the closet—the only place in their little home that didn't have a window—so she could teach him his letters without fear of being spotted by investigators.

Lu wasn't anywhere in sight, but the lean, dark-haired person at the door gave her a respectful nod as she passed, and the man who'd come to fetch Lu was now tending bar. Lara strode up, gaining a little confidence from how her voice had yet to fail her tonight. "Hey, could I get that drink now, please?"

"Let me get you tonight's special," he said, and started what seemed to be a ridiculously complicated process, pouring and mixing all kinds of things into a tall glass, stirring wildly until it was a deep green with swirls of yellow. He finished by dropping something on top that looked like an ice cube but let out a few curls of smoke as it melted.

"What is that?" she asked as he stuck a cherry on top.

"Just something I mixed up one night when I felt creative," he said. "It's good for sore throats."

When she reached out for the glass, he handed it to her

with his right hand, but let his left hand cover hers and squeeze twice, the same signal Lu had given her.

"Sounds good," she said. She gave him a long look; he wasn't saying anything, just looking at her with that bright, knowing glint in his eyes. Her mysterious contact hadn't been clear on what, exactly, it was that Lara was supposed to be doing for the Defiance, just that she'd find out when she got there. "Hey, are you guys hiring?" she asked.

This time when he smiled at her, she returned it with one of her own. "You know, I think we have a few positions open. You should stick around, we'll talk after closing."

"Sure," she said. "I can do that. I'm Laverna, by the way."

"Gwydion," he replied. "You have a good night, now, okay? Enjoy yourself, and if there's any trouble, come find me or Raven over there at the door."

"Thanks," she said. "Not Lu?"

"Lu's a little busy," he said. "And a little bit of trouble herself."

"Good to know," she said with a laugh, and took her drink back to the dance floor. Her drink had stopped smoking by the time she took a sip. It was sweet, but not cloying, and she drank it absentmindedly as she found a good spot near the stage. There were a few people seated along the sides of the room, and a couple of folks up front in wheelchairs, but the bulk of the growing crowd were on their feet, shuffling around restlessly. Lara joined them, anticipation building as the music swelled.

The tinny, unfamiliar music faded out and the lights came up. A hush broke out as Lu stepped onto the stage. In the line outside, she'd looked like an ordinary girl — pretty, cheerful, decidedly normal—but on stage, she was anything but. She was in her element here, Lara thought, exuding a confidence that made her realize that her own fledgling courage still had a long way to go to catch up.

"Thank you all for coming out tonight," Lu said. There was no microphone, but her voice carried through the room somehow. "I have a few songs for you tonight." She met Lara's eyes in the crowd. "I think you're really gonna love them."

There were no instruments on stage, and no backing music started, but Lu began to sing, still in that impossibly loud, clear tone. Her voice was beautiful, and the hush that had settled over the crowd when she'd emerged on stage continued, turning into a curious stillness, as though everyone was held in place.

Lu's voice was crooning, bluesy, and more than a little sad, totally unlike the grating music from before. The drab interior of the club seemed to change as she sang: a shimmer like a highway mirage appeared around them, and it was as though Lara could see the stories she sang about, painted on the walls around her like the murals of the Voiceless.

Lu sang of the gods: a people of magic, who loved their creations and walked among them as friends and mentors, who valued kind hearts and bright spirits.

She sang of those who claimed to be favoured: simple thieves who stole the gods' power, forcing them into centuries long-slumber.

She sang of their greed, of their complacency, of their cruelty as they used their stolen authority to establish themselves above their peers.

She sang of how they struggled to maintain their power as it waned, as their magic made its way back to its true owners, bit by bit.

She sang of the gods regaining enough power to wake.

She sang of a new chosen people, the ones standing before her, the first of the Voiceless to hear the voice of a god in hundreds of years.

And finally, she sang of revolution.

As her last mournful note rang out, the music picked up again—loud and angry this time. The uncanny stillness was broken; the crowd danced and jumped and yelled, and more than a few were in tears. Lara understood now why it had been so quiet outside the club—everyone in the club was Voiceless, like her.

Not tonight, though, and not anymore.

Lu's voice was frenzied now, barely intelligible, and yet Lara knew the words as if she'd heard this song a thousand times before. She sang along—quiet at first, and then a girl beside her slung an arm over her shoulder, voices rising as they sang together. It was more of a scream than a song, given how unpracticed their voices were, but it felt good to get the words out, to be part of something so large. She grabbed the person to her other side, drew them in, and they let their voices ring out together.

The music eventually faded out, but the energy didn't. Lara dazedly made her way back to the bar, where Gwydion was waiting. "So, good night?" he asked.

"You know it. Hey, about that job," she said, and he laughed, bright and merry.

"Go forth," he said, and suddenly there was no bar between them. It was as if the club itself had faded into darkness, and the people along with it. Gwydion stood before her, giving off a glow as bright as his eyes, as bright as his laughter. He bent and kissed her brow, and she felt the skin there burn. A mark, she realized, like those the Sound carried, though she knew now from Lu's song why they kept theirs covered—their marks had been fading as their power waned.

"Go forth," he said again, and then for a third time: "Go forth, Laverna, and raise your voice."

She closed her eyes, and when she opened them again, they were back in the bar as though nothing had changed. But she could feel the mark on her brow, still warm and shining, and Gwydion's gaze was on her, steadfast and fond.

She opened her mouth to speak, but now that she had a voice to use, words failed her. She bowed her head instead, then slipped through the crowd of patrons lined up behind her, waving to Lu, who blew her a kiss, and to Raven, who gave her a sharp, curious look.

As she hurried home, she barely noticed how the city brightened as she got closer and closer to the Voiceless neighbourhood. Syl was waiting for her, his worried, expectant expression morphing into something awed as he saw her mark.

"Hey," she said, and if he'd looked happy when she spoke aloud to him earlier in the night, he was ecstatic now, a fierce, disbelieving grin splitting his face. "It was, uh. A good night."

He reached for the mark, pressing his palm flat against it. As he touched it, Lara felt herself swept back into the darkness she'd gone into with Gwydion. He wasn't there now, just her and Syl, but she could a warmth around them, and in the blink of an eye, they were back in the house, Syl's hand glowing with a mark of his own where he'd touched hers.

He let out a surprised little gasp and she smiled helplessly at him. Her voice was welling up in her, begging to be used, and she knew exactly how to use it.

"I learned a new song tonight. Want to hear it?"

Finnan Beaton

Finnan is a Nova Scotian author who likes to knit and spin when stuck in writer's block, as a way to work himself through writing problems.

Kaida of the Eastern Shore is his first published work.

Kaida of the Eastern Shore

Kaida of the Eastern Shore hefted herself up onto the last rise and leaned upon her walking stick, gathering her reserve with each deep inhale of fog thick air. Below her the mountain fell away, obscured by thick fog and dense forest. She looked down into the valley that stretched beyond sight. Everything she knew of life began and ended in the valley. The Gods reigned above the fog, high in the mountains. It was not a place for mortals. But the Weeping Sickness left her no choice.

Kaida was born during a time of plentiful harvests and grew up knowing only peace and prosperity. She was six the day she sat down in front of her father and told him she was to be like her mother and sister. She would not take the ceremonies of manhood, but would take up the staff and be a Healer like Priestess Anilethe.

Kaida's childhood of peace was long gone. Lost to the decades of famine, war, and now plague. She would not let another child die while she stood helpless. Kaida knew every plant, fungus, and moss that grew down in the valley. Knew the names and properties of each plant that could heal -- and each that could kill besides -- but none of them worked. Travelling far into the forest, she learned the ways of the deep forest plants. Knowledge that didn't heal enough.

Kaida needed more.

She left her village in darkness, taking only her staff and the clothing on her back. Walking into the forest beyond the hunting grounds, beyond the strange plants and foreign streams, Kaida found the ancient ruins. Structures of ancient rusted metal and crumbling stone, decaying messengers of forgotten civilizations that pointed the way up the mountain. She would return with a way to save them or die on the mountain as a sacrifice for their continued prosperity.

Kaida was ready to make that choice.

She turned away from the valley and looked ahead. The trail spread out before her, shadowed by the sun setting behind the mountain. The peak of the mountain rose on her left, carved into the visage of four towering beings: a warrior, a priest, a scholar, and a mage. They were weathered by wind, rain, and the constant surging magicks that danced across the sky in the upper reaches.

The elders in her village claimed they were gods or men from the sky. Better a man from the stars than a woman, they said. Kaida spit on the snow-covered ground. The wind picked up behind her, whistled down the trail, pushing her forward. She bent to unlace her boots, set them aside and dropped her cloak atop them.

She unclasped the belt at her waist and shrugged out of her dress as a frosted wind whipped around her naked torso. She shivered and cursed but did not bend to pick up her clothes.

The magic and the gods of this place would know her: no artifice, no wealth, only the body she had.

She turned from her clothes and stepped down the rocky path. Snow covered the rocks and she grit her teeth as they cut into the bottom of her feet. Her blood seeped into the ground and the statues to her left began to glow. Further ahead, a stone rose from the ground and hovered. Kaida walked faster.

She reached the stone, staff still in hand but not touching

the ground, held aloft, not used for assistance.

"Why do you come here?" The voice emitted from the stone, inhuman, a sound of tumbling stone.

"I've come for help. My people are dying. The Elders have given up hope. They do nothing against the plagues that take our children. I have come here in supplication for I need more than what I have to heal my family." Tears froze against her cheeks. She shivered against the cold but refused to wrap her arms around her torso and hide from the wind.

"I do not interfere in the petty affairs of humans."

"Petty affairs! The Elders claim the Weeping Sickness is your anger at us. They fight. They make war. They burn and pillage as they like and bring sickness and disease back with them. They claim the women are at fault, too weak, not prayerful enough. They claim that we have strayed from the path you set for us, not because of their hatred and butchery but because I dress false. I make pretense of bearing the staff and claiming womanhood. They say I am to blame. I am wrong for teaching my sisters secret knowledge, that I have angered you in some way.

"If that is the truth, I spit upon you. I will not leave my sisters ignorant and in the darkness to appease you. My family will not be added to the bodies at your feet. If you want someone, take me, and leave them in peace."

The mountain vibrated, and the stone rose higher. Kaida trembled and felt her knees shake. Refusing to bend or quail before the power of the Gods, she spread her legs wide and let her arms stretch outward.

"Smite me if you dare, but I will not be silent. I am Kaida of the Eastern Shore, Healer, Keeper of the Sacred Ways, and they cannot take that from me!"

"You will not take that from me."

The ground shook under her feet, and her knees wobbled

with the effort to keep her upright. She held her stance, eyes locked to the stone daring it to take her down.

Lightning arced across the sky, Northern winds rose, and an icy rain fell from the heavens. It soaked into her skin, plastering her dark hair against her scalp.

A brilliant flash of blue lightning struck the stone, bounced along its surface and lashed out at her, striking the centre of her chest. It cascaded across her wet skin, over her round shoulders, down her thick belly and along her legs. She felt it climb the column of her neck and jar along her spine.

Heat and fire replaced the cold of the snow at her feet. Her jaw locked on agonized screams as her body spasmed. Power followed, a vibrating thrum of magic that echoed in the wake of the lightning, filling her in places she did not know existed.

Her knees gave out and she collapsed. The snow melted around her and grass grew between the juncture of her fingers. Tiny white flowers blossomed one by one. She plucked one from the earth and marvelled as they continued growing in her hands. The roots spread around her wrist, piercing her skin. More grew along her legs and the staff in her right hand sprouted roots. With a yell, she took the staff in both hands and pierced the ground with it. She watched as the roots took hold, the bulk of the staff expanded, and the worn nobs sprout new branches.

She struggled back as the top grew well above her head, branching and blooming with leaves and fruit. Grass raced from under her legs and covered the edge of the cliff. She took to her feet unsteady, shaken to the very heart of her being as spring blossomed around her.

Kaida reached up and grasped a branch from the new tree; it broke under her strength. With the power circulating within her, she knew the white flowers growing along her left forearm could heal her people. She knew the magic she had been given, and the fruit resting in the tree above her would bind her with the goddess, reshape her should she choose.

Kaida stilled under the gaze of the four statues. She was proud of her body, had never spent a moment of her life wishing for what nature had not provided. Her mother and the Healer helped with their herbs; that had been enough. Now, with the magic flowing in her she knew how to change that. She knew deep in her core the being she threatened was like her, assigned the descriptor of man, despite all surety of being woman.

Trepidatious, she reached up to the fruit of the tree and plucked one down. She stared at the brilliant red fruit in her palm, a gift from the Goddess. Magic hummed under the fruit and she bit down on the juicy flesh. Where the lightning had scourged along her nerves, the fruit enveloped her in comforting warmth, a shelter against an unforgiving world.

She awoke some time later, resting in the comforting shade of the tree, her new staff still in hand. She took to her feet and left as the sun broke through the early morning clouds.

Magic settled in the back of her mind and deep in her heart. She felt bigger than her skin, and she closed her eyes and searched within. Settled against her heart, she felt a warmth, a soft fluttered beating, matching in rhythm to her own. It spread out with her next heartbeat. She put her dress back on and slipped her feet back into her soft fur boots. Adjusting her cloak, she did not look back at the tree, for she had left her mark here and the Goddess now lived within her.

The statues were little more than hewn rock of forgotten deities. They were no longer the storing place of power on this Earth. She would carry that power to her sisters.

They would be free.

Andrew Pike

Andrew is a St. John's native who holds a degree in English from Memorial University of Newfoundland, as well as diplomas in Journalism and Music from College of the North Atlantic.

He nurtures an unhealthy addiction to coffee, has written for *The Telegram*, and plays classical piano.

Escape from Selenous Valley Retreat is his first published fiction.

Escape from Selenous Valley Retreat

The stolen Tesla Surge flew off the asphalt soaring for a glorious three seconds in the air before slamming back against the road at 200 miles per hour. Sirens blared in the rear-view mirror as the chase approached the border bridge to the ocean. Karlos whooped in excitement beside a topless Bobby who gulped a swig of bourbon with an ecstatic grin.

There was no better feeling than this. Nowhere else did he feel so alive. He roared at the sight of petrified border patrol agents as the Tesla ripped through the gate entering the bridge.

The construction barricade emerged from nowhere. He hit the brakes but was driving too fast and plowed through pylons busting open the guardrail and flying off the side. Piercing the ocean at break-neck speed, the car quickly submerged.

Karlos squinted through the blurry saltwater at an unconscious Bobby, her auburn hair lost in a cloud of blood. Panicked, he opened the glove compartment and grabbed his sonic breaker. He activated it, instantly shattering the glass. Clutching Bobby, he swam upward.

"Mr. Emiliano," the judge called, coughing indignantly in front of the courtroom audience. "Over the years you have remained ignorant of the law. You have multiple charges for theft, traffic violations, and DUIs. Your repeated escapes from the penitentiary have aggravated corrections officers and cost taxpayers dearly. Do you have anything to say for yourself?"

Karlos laughed at the judge, stirring a flurry of gasps from the courtroom. The judge knocked his gavel loudly.

"Order! Mr. Emiliano, as you know I cannot rule a long-term sentence as much as I'd like to. Although you are a disaster waiting to happen, right now you are a mere nuisance to society. Fortunately, we have a promising new rehabilitation center designed to shake some sense into you. I will be recommending you start there immediately."

"Better be more of a challenge than this joke you call *corrections*," Karlos quipped. The courtroom erupted into a veiled laughter. The judge banged his gavel and demanded Karlos be removed immediately.

A prisoner van passed the dingy gate of the penitentiary along a forest road before stopping at the top of the hill next to a sign with *Selenous Valley Retreat* written on it in big red letters. The corrections officer opened the back door and ushered Karlos out, stoically dragging him by his handcuffs uphill toward the white facility.

Already, Karlos was scanning the walls devising an escape plan, his scheming partially disarmed by the elegance of the construction. Pristine, tall white walls with no barbed wire — *curious*.

After passing through a security checkpoint, they approached a bright reception atrium with a skylight and a massive arched bay window overlooking the village. Patients occupied couches strewn along the wall. A nurse advanced.

"Mr. Emiliano, very nice to meet you," the nurse welcomed. "My name is Ms. Orphelin." She offered her hand for Karlos to shake, and he rolled his eyes with stark defiance. She smiled knowingly. "Please, enjoy the view. We'll introduce you to your sleeping quarters shortly."

Karlos walked over to the window and pulled out a cigarette under a bright *Go Ahead, Have a Smoke* sign. The entire thing was bizarre. Why didn't they confiscate his lighter? Why was security so slack? A humming overhead revealed a fan sucking up his cigarette smoke. Why would they put him in an upscale facility that was *easier* to break out of?

He shrugged it off and gazed out the window over the prison walls down into Selenous Valley. Beyond the wall was the lake, a rusty copper mine, and the sparkling solar panels of the village. In the distance was the bridge over the sea. Breaking out of here would be a cinch—

"GET OUT WHILE YOU CAN! THEY'RE GONNA RUIN YOU!"

Karlos spun around and swatted away the arm of an old man with ghostly gray hair who had crept up and grabbed his shoulder. Startled, the nurse and corrections officer dashed over and apprehended the man, sitting him on a couch and calming him. Karlos stared at the man whose eyes were darting around maniacally, as if trapped in numerous cells.

The week passed quickly. Karlos had made friends with his roommate Samuel, a priest committed for arson. They sipped on their coffees at the rehabilitation center's café while discussing Samuel's church volunteering plans after his release.

"I'd rather spend another year in here than go to church," Karlos scoffed.

Samuel concealed a fearful grimace. "Spending time here has really helped give me a new perspective," he said, holding his necklace cross. "I doubted my faith but now I see you have to believe in *something* beyond yourself, because the big guy in the sky is throw'n the switches to where you end up, y'know?"

Karlos shrugged. He wasn't religious, unless religion was a shimmering lockpick concealed in rich strawberry hair.

"Your visitor has arrived," Ms. Orphelin interrupted. Karlos excitedly followed her to the visiting room to greet Bobby, who ran up and jumped into his arms. She kissed his forehead and hugged him.

"I thought I'd never see you again" she whimpered, the bandage from her injury swirling around her head like a beehive.

"I told you, strawberry sunshine," he chimed, "I always bounce back!"

The staff left them, but Karlos figured the room was wired so there wasn't much they could say. Before leaving, she hugged him again, slipping a small bag into his pants — their secret backup plan.

After saying goodbye, Karlos followed Ms. Orphelin. "It'll just be a moment; the warden wants to speak with you," she said, guiding Karlos down a hallway. He was hardly keen on this prospect but didn't have much choice.

They entered a dim room with a red light pouring down on a brawny, middle-aged bald man with a bushy beard and dark-rimmed glasses. It was the warden, whose deceptively cordial smile tainted the otherwise ordinary atmosphere.

"Karlos! Welcome!" the warden saluted. "I understand you've been behaving well in your stay here so far; that's what we like to hear!"

Karlos didn't respond, choosing instead to stare at him with deliberation.

"As you know, we're performing behavior reviews." He gestured toward a seat across the table from him. Karlos be-grudgingly sat down. "As this is your first review, it will be short and sweet. Do you feel that this is an appropriate facility for your treatment for the next two years?"

Karlos was locked in the warden's gaze. His mind shifted to thoughts of escape and Bobby's warm arms. He snapped back into focus.

"Yes, it's great," he replied. The warden appeared ambiva-lent. Was he fooled?

"There's just one more aspect of your treatment here, Kar-los," the warden decided. He stood up and walked to a room smothered with florescent lights, gesturing for Karlos to fol-low.

"As part of your stay here, we need to register your identity. The required procedure is quick and painless. You won't feel a thing."

Karlos stole a glance over his shoulder to see two corrections officers standing at the entryway.

"You don't have a problem with it, Karlos, do you?"

"No," Karlos replied.

"Excellent. Please lie here."

Karlos lay down inside a medical machine. The procedure involved a sharp pinch in the back of his head. When it was over, Ms. Orphelin appeared and led him back to his room.

Karlos woke quietly later that night recalling the encounter with the warden. He reached to the back of his head, feeling a wound. *What did they do to me?* He was unsure, but he had to make a break for it tonight.

He reached under the mattress for the bag Bobby had given him. Like a tradesman's toolkit, it had everything he needed to escape. Disabling the security cameras and alarms was a walk in the park. Making his way to the atrium, he approached the bay window.

He stood in front of the glass observing Selenous Valley. In his faint reflection, he appeared weaker, a trapped shadow of himself. He shuddered. It'd been a wild ride, but it was time to leave small-town criminal youth behind. Bobby would be waiting, and they'd cross the bridge and disappear to the mainland by morning.

He raised the sonic breaker to the window beside his reflection and activated the device. Darkness exploded into his mind.

Karlos pushed his dizzy head up from a pool of saliva on the cold stone floor, terrified by the wails and screams of despair from pitch blackness. His head pained a dull, pulsating headache. Something was very wrong.

He ran his hands along the floor and walls to confirm he was trapped in an empty cell. What the hell happened? He was literally just standing in front of the glass window in the atrium!

"What the hell is this?" he yelled.

"TRUST IN THE LORD TO BE SAVED!" The shout came through the bars.

Karlos paused, shocked. "Hello?"

"PRAY TO REACH HEAVEN!"

Karlos made several failed attempts to engage with the man who would regurgitate biblical verse randomly. After several hours of this, Karlos went silent, desperately contemplating his situation.

Although the headaches had waned, time passed painfully slow through bitter isolation. The cold, inhumane cell was much worse than any penitentiary cell he'd occupied, with a sludge dispenser and crude hole in the floor for a toilet.

He remembered the virtual reality escape room games he played as a kid. It was an obsession he used to alleviate the boredom of small-town life that had graduated to drug addiction and crime.

Speaking of drugs, he hadn't smoked for months now. He remembered the atrium and the fan sucking up smoke. A light bulb went off in his head, and he methodically searched for a vent. Joyfully, he found one in the ceiling at the back of the cell! After several hours of trying to open it, he finally admitted defeat.

Months, maybe even years went by. He'd pulled on the grate every day to no avail, and then one day it happened. There was a scraping sound, and it gave way with a loud creak, falling to the floor sending him with it. It took another few days of trying before he finally pulled himself into the cramped vent.

Karlos crawled through the dark ventilation system over floors of insane prisoners for days, before finally reaching a moonlit attic bearing a toolkit with a screwdriver and a sonic breaker. His ductwork journey eventually led him to a room with hundreds of monitors on the wall and a familiar medical machine in the middle. In the distance he could hear people talking, approaching.

Suddenly the door opened, and in walked a tall man with thick hair, full beard, black suit and tinted glasses, followed by second man with buzzed hair in a black suit pushing a wheelchair with a third man gagged in a straight jacket.

"Five minutes. Get him ready," the bearded man commanded, laying his key card on a table. The second man ungagged the third man, who screamed madly. The others ignored him.

"Two minutes," the bearded man announced. He sat down across the table from the crazy man in the wheelchair beneath a crimson florescent light, staring at him, waiting for something to happen. He then gestured with two fingers toward the second man, who pushed a button on a device in his hand. The crazy man's face went expressionless, then his eyes became alight as if seeing for the first time.

"Mr. Delby! Welcome!" the bearded man greeted with a nostalgic tone. The second man began to remove Mr. Delby's straight jacket.

The bearded man flicked a switch activating the monitors which now showed prisoners in cells through thermal vision, including one with a cross necklace.

"We're very excited to introduce you to the vault. As you can see, Selenous Microsystems has a whole generation of prisoners *hungry* for freedom.

"We are working with thousands of universes to create peaceful, crime-free communities. We offer excellent benefits for long-term partners. Working with Selenous Microsystems is fulfilling and rewarding. Your community will be overwhelmed at how fast your patients are 'rehabilitated' in one of our many quaint valley retreats.

"As part of our gold alliance partnership package, you qualify for three months of vacation in our elite universe, free of crime. The earth has aged well in this universe, unravaged by the threats of nuclear war, global warming, and fake presidencies.

"We're very excited to have you onboard. You will be ridding your universe of crime so that your friends and family will be able to sleep safe! Now, if you'll come this way, I'll acquaint you with the facility."

Karlos watched in awe as the three left. When he was sure they were long gone, he unscrewed the grate and climbed out, careful not to make any noise.

Shockingly, an alarm blared through the facility! He grabbed the key card the bearded man had left and dashed for the door. After rushing through several halls, he finally burst out into an atrium. There it was, the familiar arched bay window! He ran toward it pulling out the sonic breaker.

Glancing outside, he saw the village illuminated by moonlight, but something was wrong. The unlit homes were dilapidated, gray and vacant and the copper mine and bridge were gone. It looked like it had been abandoned for decades! This was not the Selenous Valley he remembered. Something was horribly wrong.

Voices in the distance neared. He cursed and, panicking, raised the sonic breaker to the glass, activating it.

"Mr. Emiliano," the judge announced, happily addressing the courtroom. Karlos blinked, blinded by the lights, his head painfully buzzing so much it felt like it might explode. The same judge that had sentenced him came into focus.

"I admit, I didn't think it was possible, but over the past two years you have proven yourself to be a model citizen. You have excelled in your treatment, showing compassion toward your fellow patients and staff. Where before you abused your freedom, now you value it, and we have Selenous Valley Retreat to thank for this momentous shift.

"In fact, the center has proven to be so effective in treating patients like yourself, we are literally moving prisoners from the penitentiary in for treatment. I am recommending you be released into society immediately, where I am confident you will be an outstanding citizen. This really is a win-win for recoverees like yourself, *and* for society. Is there anything you'd like to say regarding your new freedom?"

Karlos was visibly shaken, dozens of thoughts racing through his mind. He was consolidating the conflict between two worlds, one where he was a trapped prisoner and one where he was starting a new life with endless possibilities. But the injustice of what was happening — prisoners being held in dire conditions indefinitely — it was too much. He stood assertively as the courtroom watched. With a swelling anger, he was ready to disclose the dark secret of Selenous Microsystems. As he began to speak—

Karlos emerged from a head pounding drugged state to a flickering crimson light. He made out a bearded man with tinted glasses sitting across a table holding up a sonic breaker. His own duplicated reflection in the man's glasses revealed he was strapped in a straight jacket just like the crazy guy had been!

"You are quite the escapee, Karlos. No one has ever escaped from here before. How ironic it is that the very tool you used to break the law has landed you in a prison beyond law."

The man removed his glasses revealing his identity: the warden. Although, he appeared more hardened. He mused over the sonic breaker.

"Clever, isn't it? The sonic breaker broke the atrium window in your native universe when you first tried to escape, but it also activated the selenium-doped silicon quantum chip implanted in your skull, shifting your consciousness to this universe.

"We hadn't decided on transferring you over — at least not this early — but you inadvertently shifted yourself, causing your counterpart to shift to your native universe where his good behavior has rewarded him with early release into society, as you've just seen."

The warden genuinely sighed, fatigued with his work. Karlos blinked, his reflection mirroring on the multiple monitors of the background.

"Now, don't bother trying to escape again. There's nothing left to this universe, save prisons embedded in rock. Crime and imprisonment became so prevalent here, the elite invested in escape prevention, specifically locational chip technology, which — to our surprise — developed a means of transferring between universes.

"The elite used this method to transfer to peaceful universes, and this universe is now used as home for high risk offenders. Governments of other universes love us because we 'transform' their criminals, selling upstanding citizens who'd do anything for freedom. What they can't see beneath the surface is immaterial; only results matter.

"Anyway Karlos, it's time to get back to your cell. Your chip will be safeguarded against inadvertent activation, so don't get any ideas. Rest up. We may someday move you on to a better universe."

Karlos squinted through blurry twilight. His mind had become a shaken case of memories and realities. Horrified wails or laughing patients? A beautiful woman with red hair…Bobby? No. Just a nurse. The dull pain returned. Were they shifting him?

Out of his cloudy haze he caught the outline of a man by a window having a cigarette. He remembered. The swirling anxiety of hope returned. He stood slowly, then saw through the window…the village! The ocean! The bridge! The escape! He ran up to the man and grabbed his shoulder, desperately yelling

"GET OUT! GET FAR AWAY FROM HERE!" Nurses quickly approached pulling him to his wheelchair and as the man stared, Karlos' eyes darted back and forth from treatment to treatment, valley to valley, retreating at the hand of a keeper in a house of many rooms, many fates.

John Haas

John is an award-winning author from Montreal, Quebec with over ten short story credits to his name. He has two novels in print, *The Reluctant Barbarian* and *The Wayward Spider*.

In 2012 his short story *'Til Death* won the Capital Crime Writers Annual Contest. Since then many of his works have gone on to place or receive honorable mentions in multiple award ceremonies.

His short story, *Rudeworld*, the story presented here, was given Honorable Mention at the 2014 Writers of the Future awards.

He currently lives in Ottawa, Ontario.

Rudeworld

Lassiter waited near the front of the stage with his camera-man, Mark. To either side of the six foot high stage were two huge screens which would allow people farther back to see the Shaming. A third screen had the duty of providing a list of suitable words for the day.

The two milled around in the outdoor arena like the rest -- bumping into others, scowling, muttering words they wouldn't have said any other day. Amidst all the jostling and cursing were the sharp sounds of the bracelets giving warning infractions.

"What's this—" Lassiter glanced up at the list of words, "—@$$***e's name?"

-BEEP-

His gaze went to the thin plastic band around his wrist, then he looked away annoyed. Until the Shaming was done, the bracelet's beeping wouldn't rise above first warning -- not unless someone committed an act of violence. The beeps were a reminder that life would go back to normal.

"Franklin Greene," Mark responded. "The young dumb@$$," *–BEEP--* "who went too far at the last Shaming."

"Right."

Franklin Greene. Lassiter repeated it inside his head a few times, enough to remember it until the Shaming was done.

He noticed a couple he had interviewed earlier. The girl smiled at him and he waved his fingers at the idiot. During the

Forgiving Period that came before the Shaming, people would say anything. That couple would remember what they'd said later and wonder about the recording. And then there were the ones who didn't know they were being recorded.

Behind them, two clerics in ceremonial garb stepped onto the stage with the young rudeling. The crowd went wild, shouting and throwing approved objects at Greene, the beeping of bracelets punctuating their actions. Mark brought the camera to his eye and Lassiter got into position, focussed on the lens.

"This is Lassiter Braithwaite coming to you live from The Square. Behind me is young Franklin Greene, about to meet his Shaming. As you can hear, the crowd is showing their displeasure for this man's anti-social behaviour, letting him know how it feels to be on the receiving end."

The camera focused past him and he turned to watch Greene's hands strapped to the block, the clerics manoeuvring the young man's hands into his criminal gesture. The first cleric uncovered a glinting blade, holding it above his head.

Mark's camera zoomed.

"Punishment is at hand," Lassiter said as a voice over to Mark's video. "What must be going through Franklin's mind at this moment."

Lassiter thought it obvious what Franklin was thinking. He'd gotten off easy and he didn't dare say a word for fear of changing that.

The noise of the crowd swelled, getting in their last chances at much valued abuse.

"Was it worth it, Franklin?" Lassiter shouted.

Since being assigned to the Shamings five years ago, Lassiter had shouted his catchphrase at every one of the accused. His fans expected it and if he hoped to ever move from the rude-beat he had to keep popular.

The senior cleric turned toward the prisoner and brought the blade down in a quick motion, severing the middle finger of Franklin's right hand. Franklin screamed. The knife moved with a flourish and came down on the same finger of the left hand.

The Forgiving Period was over, and silence came with the suddenness of a snapped finger. None of the crowd wanted to make the same mistake as Franklin. A week ago, at the last Shaming, he'd gotten on a friend's shoulders with both fingers extended toward the stage, shouting obscenities. The Forgiving Time had obviously been over.

The young idiot was lucky he'd only lost his fingers.

The camera back on him, Lassiter looked into the eyes of every viewer. "And so, another rudeling meets his punishment. Let this be a lesson to everyone that anti-social behaviour will not be tolerated."

The red camera light winked out. "Good show," Mark said.

Lassiter said nothing. Mark's opinions meant little outside of camera angles. A career cameraman with a useless media degree and a flabby, piggish face. He knew little about being in front of the camera, never would.

Around them, the crowd dispersed. A few watched the clerics tend to Greene's wounds. The occasional beep was heard, but not many. This crowd was too cautious.

"I was expecting more," Lassiter said.

"Expecting? Or hoping?"

"Hoping for someone to slip up would be rude in itself," Lassiter responded, then turned to his cameraman. "Prying and suggesting anti-social motivations could also be interpreted as rude."

Mark paled, then forced a smile to his face. "Nothing going to happen here."

There would be other mistakes, other Shamings, but not today.

"Excuse me," Lassiter said to people as he made his way toward the van.

"Of course," were the usual replies.

"Can you drop me off at the university?" Lassiter asked over his shoulder.

"Sure. I need some back to school footage anyway."

In the news van, Mark merged with traffic. Lassiter rolled down his window to allow the warm breeze to sweep in.

"You don't mind, do you?" he asked.

Mark shook his head as Lassiter knew he must. With the window already open, it would seem rude for Mark to say he wanted it closed.

Lassiter knew how to play the game. He could care less about how the rules affected others.

Traffic flowed around them. Cars moved forward at a regular pace, each taking turn to allow others to merge. The driver in front was either distracted or impatient and didn't allow a car to go ahead of him.

--*BEEP. FINAL WARNING.*--

Lassiter leaned forward, interested. "*Final* warning?"

Mark flicked the switch that started the exterior cameras recording. The car ahead slowed and allowed two cars to merge by way of apology. No further incident occurred, and Lassiter sat back with a grunt.

To be at final warning just for failing to allow another person to merge... that guy made a habit of rudeness. The beep then double-beep were more than enough warning. Final warning was a hair away from punishment and now he would be closely monitored for the next month.

Lassiter copied the license number. For now, that man would be cautious, but he would slip again. After the interview Lassiter would make sure to look him up.

The university hadn't changed in the ten years since he'd graduated. It felt like time had stopped here.

"I'll head over to the main gate," Mark said.

Lassiter had forgotten the older man was still there. "Cut across the common."

"Yep, I remember."

Lassiter veered toward the journalism building and his appointment with Professor Hamilton. Each step was a thunderous reminder of his failure. He had wanted to return here, to speak as a lead reporter. He should have been lead by now, had expected to be. Instead of interviewing clerics and magistrates, he was still on rude-beat getting footage of idiots receiving punishments.

He *could* have been lead too, that's what irked him. Two years ago, he'd been interviewing a man he'd been sure was hiding something. Lassiter had asked his questions, led the man in the right direction, but was careless and had gotten final warning. If the crime had been great enough, the warnings could be forgiven, but if not, he would have headed for a Shaming of his own.

He'd backed off. Another network had broken the story about a secret rude cult.

It was his own fault; he'd lost his nerve and he'd lost the story. Ruthless, that was how he needed to be. Professor Hamilton had told him years ago that his own career would have gone much further if he'd been more ruthless.

Lassiter grinned at the thought of Hamilton being ruthless. Impossible. He'd even taken the naïve Lassiter under his wing and mentored him.

And now Lassiter needed the professor's help again.

He stared at the double doors, breathing the air deeply and getting his nerve to face the man who had been his mentor.

Screw it. It was worth any pain. If the tip he'd gotten was true and he could uncover the truth, then he could be lead by the end of the week. And the professor was the way. The man had his ear open to everything that happened on campus. Hamilton would have a lead for him.

He took one last deep breath and headed through the double doors.

"Lassiter."

He turned toward the sound of the familiar voice and saw

Professor Hamilton approaching. A thin old man bordering on scrawny, still wearing sweatshirts a size too large. The professor had been old when Lassiter had last seen him; now the man was ancient.

"Hello, professor."

"Good to see you, my boy. I was just watching the re-broadcast of today's Shaming."

Always the Shamings. They followed him through his life.

"Yes, sir. I came straight from there."

The professor led him toward the closed door of his office. A faded sign Lassiter remembered well declared *Do Not Disturb*.

"Has it really been ten years, Lassiter?"

Lassiter tried to find something to say, some plausible reason to explain why he hadn't been back. What could he say? He hadn't been back because of his embarrassment and shame over not making more progress as a reporter? Or that he was afraid the professor's love for other people would rub off on him, weaken him?

"Yes, I guess it has been, professor."

No. It had been a mistake to come back. It wasn't time, he wasn't ready. He could already feel it. He was off-balance, on guard about his thoughts.

"Ah, busy lives, busy lives," the professor said.

"I suppose so."

"And we can say so little in messages."

Lassiter nodded. Messages were monitored with intense fervor by an entire division of the Office of Clerics and Magistrates. There were ways around it, but they were time-consuming at best and dangerous at the worst. Too much so for simple correspondence. Most messages were of the bland *hello, how are you* variety.

Stepping into the professor's office was a nostalgic experience. Like the rest of the university, it hadn't changed. Printouts and books covered every flat surface, and for all Lassiter knew they were the same ones from ten years ago.

"Please sit." Hamilton waved toward the one empty spot.

Lassiter took the seat, leaning into the padding and pleased to find it felt the same as he remembered. His fingers played along the chair's well-worn leather.

"Lost in the past?" the professor asked.

Lassiter looked up. "Yes, I suppose I was."

He needed to remember he was here for a reason, not a social call.

The professor dropped into the seat behind his desk, bumping the small table holding his coffee maker.

"Now, what's the reason for the visit?"

"Well, as I mentioned when I called, I need background on the Rudelaws for a news piece."

The professor stared at him for a long moment before leaning back in his chair and speaking, as if to a full classroom.

"We are told the laws came out of a darker time in human history, a time when rudeness and anti-social behavior had become the norm. The laws were a necessity starting in ways that spoke to common sense. To begin with people were not allowed to speak in disparaging ways against groups, couldn't say what they thought or felt if those thoughts didn't agree with what society said was proper. To do so meant ostracism, loss of job, public spectacle.

"Next came fines and legal repercussions. Laws were put in place to punish those who didn't do as they were told. People went to prison, or simply disappeared."

Simply disappeared. Lassiter's mind turned to the father who had simply disappeared during his infancy.

"Books were burned around the world for having words that had once been acceptable. Travel outside of one's home area became more difficult. Correspondence was monitored and the bracelets became something everyone wore from birth to death, growing with the person. Free speech was dead."

"Free speech?" Lassiter asked.

"A term I found mentioned in ancient documents. It means the right to say whatever you wanted."

The concept seemed ridiculous, dangerous even. The

Rudelaws were a necessity, Lassiter just wished they didn't apply to him. Had such a concept as free speech once been possible?

"Now, my boy, what is the real reason you have come to see me today?"

"I don't..."

"Oh, come now, Lassiter. You could have gotten the same information from the Office of Clerics and Magistrates. Not in the same words and certainly without any mention of free speech, but the essence would be the same. Anything extra you get from me you wouldn't be able to use anyway."

Lassiter had wanted to come at the topic in a roundabout way to avoid infractions. He'd known he wouldn't fool the professor for long; in fact, he hadn't counted on not fooling him at all.

Hamilton seemed content to wait, leaning back with arms folded over his thin stomach. His gaze never wavered, making Lassiter feel like a student again.

His mind jumped to the anonymous message he had received two days ago, the tip that had sent him scurrying back here before he was ready.

He closed his eyes and took a deep breath, gathering his thoughts. He needed to control this interview, to drive toward the information he wanted.

The next question needed to be worded right if he wanted to avoid a month's worth of close surveillance.

"Professor, these laws, the bracelets, the infractions -- have you ever heard of a way around them?"

Hamilton cocked his head at Lassiter. "A question like that could get the attention of the magistrates."

"I'm working on a news piece," Lassiter added, "to show the futility of trying."

"Of course, of course."

But the professor was right, he could have phrased that better. He could have made it clear he was doing research. The magistrates could...

Shouldn't there have been a warning? He reviewed the wording of his question.

"Would you like some coffee?" the professor asked.

Lassiter's mind raced, back to the message he had received through his network of anonymous informants. A dangerous network but necessary. The message told of someone at his alma-matter finding a way around the laws. And, of course, the writer knew exactly what he would do with that information. Who else would he turn to? No, he'd been guided here.

The professor turned from the coffee maker and Lassiter held his hand out to receive the cup. Hamilton smelled the coffee and took a deep sip. He burped with forced intensity, then placed the cup in front of Lassiter.

There should have been a warning. Lassiter's eyes narrowed. "*You* sent the message."

The professor was laughing. "Oh, I'm sorry, Lassiter. I was having a bit of fun at your expense."

Lassiter half expected the magistrates to kick the door in behind him, no matter what the sign said. But no, there would be no clerics or magistrates, no warnings.

"You've found a way around the laws."

Hamilton leaned forward, holding Lassiter's gaze for a moment, then took a deep breath. The next twenty seconds was filled with a long string of profanity and insults the likes of which Lassiter had never heard. The professor should have earned an immediate punishment warning and a command to stay where he was for the magistrates to arrive.

Nothing. No warning.

Lassiter's eyes shot to the bracelet around Hamilton's wrist.

"Oh, it's still there," the professor confirmed.

"How?"

Hamilton rolled up his shirt sleeve, exposing a thin, shiny metal band hugging the scrawny muscles of his upper arm.

"A blocker," the professor said.

"Blocker?"

"Not an accurate name. It actually sends a false signal to the bracelets. No matter what it hears the bracelet interprets it as positive speech.

Lassiter looked at the band around his wrist.

"Yes, yours too. I have the blocker set at maximum so we can talk."

Lassiter saw the greater implications. If the bracelets could be fooled, then their entire society, the whole world would devolve into pre-Rudelaws days.

This is the kind of story that would get him lead reporter.

He couldn't betray the professor though, could he? Another part of his brain was telling him he needed to be ruthless. Why would the man create this anyway?

How had he been so far off?

Lassiter saw a wild glee in the other man's eyes, a twinkling joy.

"What?" Hamilton asked.

Lassiter shook his head. "I never expected a man like you to get such joy from going against the Rudelaws."

"A man like me?"

"A lover of people. I assumed you would also love the laws forcing us to get along."

"Force. Yes, a good word for it. Force." The bitterness in the professor's voice was thick.

"But, don't the laws prevent hate and violence?"

The professor stared at and through Lassiter. The twinkling joy had been replaced by a sadness that was its antithesis. When the old man's attention came back, a fire had grown in his eyes.

"Force," he repeated. "When I was a child of seven, my father didn't come home for dinner. It wasn't uncommon. He was a teacher too, but in sociology and sometimes he stayed late to speak with students."

"He should have been home by six. When he wasn't, we ate without him. The phone call came an hour later, telling Mother to turn on the television. That young man today, Greene? He had his fingers removed for a gesture, but my father had spoken ill of the Office of Clerics and Magistrates. He had dared to suggest they had too much power. His tongue had offended, and they cut it out for all to see, including his son. He never spoke again, never taught again, never did much of anything again."

Lassiter was silent a long moment, contemplating a father he had never known.

"Yes, those laws force us to be polite to each other, but shouldn't we choose to be nice to each other?"

He could see the professor on stage, tongue forced out while the blade came down.

No.

Lassiter breathed a long sigh that seemed to come from somewhere inside his soul. Complete ruthlessness wasn't in him it seemed. Fine. Whatever. Using one of these bands in interviews would give him an edge no other reporter could match. The story he gave up today would lead to dozens, hundreds. He would get that lead reporter position yet.

"This needs to be kept secret, Professor."

The old man sat forward, animated. "Secret? Secret? No, Lassiter, this shall not end here."

"What? But…"

"No, we made these to change the world."

"We?"

"Yes. A group of us here at the university. People from the science department, sociology, media, and myself. But the others are afraid to go to the next level."

"With good reason. Professor, what would the clerics do if they found out?"

"Kill me, I should think."

"And that doesn't worry you?"

"Some. What worries me more is the world remaining as it is. It hasn't always been this way."

"I know, you said…"

"No, you heard the words, but you don't understand. Free speech. The ability for everyone to say what they want."

Lassiter shook his head. Just because he wanted it for himself didn't mean he wanted everyone to have it.

"No, Lassiter. These armbands will be worn by everyone. The construction is simple once you know the principle."

Another deep sigh. "Okay, Professor." Lassiter leaned back in the chair again. "So, what do you want from me? Why did you contact me?"

Professor Hamilton shook his head. "I didn't contact you, you contacted me."

"But… You didn't send me a message? Through my secret network?"

"No." The professor stopped. "Secret network?"

"Professor, you're in danger. Someone knows about this and sent me a tip on it."

"Secret network," the other mused. "Yes, that would work, if they still operate the way they did back in my reporting days."

"Professor, you're not listening."

"No, I'm not."

Hamilton reached into a drawer and slid a folder across the desk to Lassiter. "In there you will find the plans, and one of the armbands."

Lassiter grabbed the folder without thinking about it.

"If I am in danger, then it's up to you to get the information out there. Use your network."

"No."

"And if it comes to it, you will give me up and cover the story yourself."

"No!"

"Yes, Lassiter. Now I am counting on you to get that armband out of here so everyone can have one."

Lassiter's fingers fell onto the folder and the thin plastic band inside. He had entered the room with a chip on his shoulder and had replaced it with a heavier weight.

"Did you get what you were looking for?"

Lassiter glanced at his cameraman as he exited the professor's office. Mark leaned against the wall, his camera hanging by his side. Lassiter nodded, fingers running along the smoothness of the metal band under his sleeve.

His mind tried to imagine using the blocker to get the advantage in interviews. He knew with it set on low he would be able to ask questions in interviews that other reporters would get warnings for. But his mind kept returning to the idea of the professor on stage, his tongue being removed.

"You look troubled, boss."

Lassiter shrugged.

"Did your old teacher, Professor Hamilton, tell you something worrying?"

Why was Mark talking like that? Lassiter turned. The other man faced him, camera loose in his hands but definitely pointed towards Lassiter's face. The recording light glowed a steady red. Lassiter glanced behind him at the door he had just passed through. Mark had been leaning there, so close to the door. The blocker stopped the signal from getting to the bracelets, but it wouldn't stop a recording device, like a news camera.

"You heard?" Lassiter asked. "Eavesdropping is…"

"Rude, yes, I know. First warning at best."

Lassiter's eyes drifted from Mark to the doorway and back again. Professor Hamilton was behind that *Do Not Disturb* sign, thinking he was safe.

"Come on, Lassiter, let's break this story."

Lassiter was quiet. He didn't move.

"Hmm, how does this sound? University journalism professor brought before magistrates. Rude ring crushed. Reporter and cameraman break story."

"No."

"No? Okay. How about, university professor and ex-student arrested and held for Shaming. Cameraman hailed as hero."

"B*****d."

"Not even a beep? Those do work. When I heard the rumor,

I thought it was only that."

"When you…? You gave me the tip."

"Oh yes. Not that you ever asked but I went to school here too, about ten years before you. I still have contacts too, but not the right ones, not like you."

"Miserable b*****d."

"Careful, Lassiter. I'm giving you a chance because I need you. This will play better with you in front of the camera, but I can record it and get a voice over later."

Yeah, Mark didn't have the face or voice to be in front of the camera. Without Lassiter he would be back in the cameraman pool at the station. He could expose Lassiter, but no one would ever work with him after.

"Besides," Mark continued, "after we expose the teachers, we keep the extra band. Then we shoot to the top."

Lassiter closed his eyes. "And the whole time you hold onto that recording."

"You know how these things go. Nothing personal."

Lassiter turned back toward the professor's office. "Well, he did tell me to give him up, to cover the story."

"Now you're talking."

"Let's get the confession."

Mark held the camera to his face and started forward.

"I'll get the door," Lassiter said. "You go first to get his expression. Give me the camera bag, it's tight in there."

Mark pulled the heavy bag off of his shoulder and Lassiter grabbed it by the thick handles. It was a good ten pounds of extra equipment and Lassiter felt himself pulled to one side.

The door opened and Mark started forward.

Lassiter thought about the world the professor wanted to change. A world in which rudeness was not tolerated and violence was never experienced. The professor would accept the betrayal by Lassiter; Mark, on the other hand, would never expect the ten pound bag of batteries and lenses about to be slammed into the back of his head.

Peter J. Foote

Born and raised in the Annapolis Valley of Nova Scotia, and the son of an apple farmer, Peter studied archaeology in university. He is employed as a boiler and refrigeration operator, is an active Freemason, and runs a used bookstore (Fictionfirst Used Books) out of his basement in his spare time.

Through FictionFirst Used Books Peter strives to support the written word community, which he does by sponsoring the monthly Kit Sora Flash Photography Fiction prize.

Believing that an author should write what he knows, many of Peter's stories are a reflection of his personal life.

Peter's work has twice been awarded the Kit Sora Flash Fiction Prize: once in March 2018 and again in September 2018.

Peter holds the distinction of being one of only a handful of authors to be featured in all the modern *From the Rock* collections to date.

Final Edict

Sweat runs down the young man's forehead and meanders through the coarse stubble on his checks before dripping to the melting asphalt at his feet.

Raising the bottle of amber liquid, he drinks deeply, some spilling out of the corners of his mouth to mix with the blood and sweat on his tattered plaid shirt. Swaying, he lowers the bottle and lets the heat of the roaring bonfire wash over him. He can feel his skin shrinking and drying out under the intense blaze, but the effort to move seems too great.

Caught up in the raw naked rage of the night, the young man surrenders to the cries in the streets, the pops of gunfire, and the screams in the shadows. It all mixes into a single heartbeat that threads its way through his body, racing through his nerves, until there is no other sound and he *is* that heartbeat.

He is shaken out of his trance as a youth races to the edge of the bonfire and flings an armload of books into the flames. The bonfire lets forth a mighty breath and spews sparks high into the sky; like fireflies they travel along the edges of buildings, highlighting smashed windows and destruction.

The bonfire shifts, and one book tumbles from the blaze, cartwheeling through the remains of its brethren until it strikes the youth's foot and falls open. Staring down at the scorched books through the shaggy remains of his hair, the youth wobbles as he places the bottle on the ground and picks up the book.

The hand-written words grab his eyes, and he reads:

"I hid my books in the storeroom in the back of the shop and piled old gardening tools on top of the boxes; with luck, they will go un-discovered. All books are being hunted and seized, and it's the labor camps if you're found with song books or poetry.

"To think it all started with tearing down the old statues. The State said we must forget our past, for only without a past can we cre-ate the perfect future. A sane person would have seen the clear fault in that argument, but these are not sane times.

"Our leaders say art is a waste of time, that we must be more competitive and aggressive, that the world is a decadent, subversive, and indecent place, and that the arts are a moral strain on the fabric of our society when in fact they are our tapestry -- but that tapestry is fraying."

The rest of the page is burnt except for a ragged scribble at the bottom:

"I hope that someday people will understand what they have lost; they have burned it all."

Staring down at the book in his hands, the young man looks around at the destruction and chaos around him, and casually tosses the book into the flames. As the pages curl and catch fire to become part of the final edict, the young man picks up his bottle and takes a deep drink, basking in the heat of the bon-fire.

Jeff Slade

A resident of Salmon Cove, Slade is a prize-winning author and avid reader who enjoys both making and hearing puns, playing the guitar, and cats.

Slade made his publishing debut in 2018's *Chillers from the Rock*. His award-winning story, *Extinguished*, was featured in *Kit Sora: The Artobiography*.

Anchored

Callie traversed through woods that grew more and more unfamiliar with every step. Each twig and branch clumsily snapped underfoot, and she tried not to think about how the noise betrayed her position.

"How far 'way are we now?" asked a voice behind and to the right of her.

"Dunno," Callie replied. "Two days' walk away, however far that is." She'd left home two days earlier with her younger sister, Bree, after their grandmother had moved from the family tent into the hospice tent on the outskirts of the community. The same tent their mother had moved into four years ago, from which she'd never returned.

They walked in near silence for another few minutes, ducking under and pushing away the thick branches and scratchy brambles they encountered the further they went.

"She could'a woke up, y'know," Bree added.

Their grandmother had been sick for some time; while she'd had her good days, they got farther and fewer in between the bad ones, and the bad kept getting badder. One morning she wouldn't wake up; that same morning they brought her to hospice, and they packed up and left camp.

"She's not coming back, Bree." Callie abruptly stopped and turned. Bree bumped into her, then looked up at her, a startled expression swimming to the surface of her face.

"Not like that," Callie snapped. "You know I don't mean like that." Her own face softened, and she stooped down, placing a hand on Bree's shoulder. She smoothed out the thin, well-worn jacket before reaching up and stroking long brown hair that matched her own.

"D'you think she's been anchored yet?"

"I don't know, sweetie." There was no use in lying to her, Callie thought. They only had each other now, after all; they'd never known their father, and neither had their mother, not really. "Probably. But that's for the best, right?"

"Right. So, she can't come back." Bree finally looked up and met her gaze. "I just miss her. And Mom."

"Me too, kiddo." She pulled her sister in for a hug, then kissed the top of her head. "But we've gotta keep moving, okay?"

The smaller girl just nodded and pulled away, wiping her face with the back of her hand. "Where are we goin' again?"

"You remember the story Grandma used to tell us, 'bout the island?" They resumed walking, and Callie resisted the urge to take her sister's hand, not wanting to treat her a child. She knew that she hated that.

"Yeah, where she met Granddad," Bree chimed in, kicking a rock out ahead of them through the brush.

"'Zactly. She used to tell us all the time, when we'd gather 'round the campfire, tryin' to keep warm." Callie's own mind retreated back to the days when she was Bree's age, trying to ignore the never-ending snowfall and the dampness you felt down to the bone. "An' how she took Ma there when she was small, smaller than us."

"The lights were like fire," said Bree. "And the cotton candy."

"Yeah, movin' so fast, blurrin' together. Red and yellow and orange." Callie had dreamed about the lights countless times. She chuckled as her little sister's mind went to food. "And the cotton candy, yeah. Pink an' fluffy, all you could eat. 'Fore the Awakening," she added.

They walked in silence for another while, letting that hang out in the open without any further comment. Neither of them wanted to linger on that topic for long, not when they both knew where they were headed.

They searched for food along the way, a search that even before leaving home regularly took them deeper and deeper into the forest. Winter was coming, and the overplucked trees and bushes nearest to home - which provided minimal sustenance due to overuse at the best of times - were bare.

Some time later, Bree pointed quietly to a black strip of ribbon that hung from a nearby tree. A warning marker.

"We're almost out of bounds," said Bree. They'd never been out this far before, but they had no choice. There was nothing for them back at the camp now, and besides, the lack of food at home also meant a lack of prey to hunt; a dangerous chain reaction in lack of resources.

Callie stared up at the ribbon as it fluttered in the slight, chilly breeze. The atmosphere was eerily quiet the closer they got to the coastline as what little life that was left steered far clear of the water. The markers were placed to warn you how far from home you were; a green one came first, followed by a yellow, then a red. They'd passed the first two yesterday, and the latter earlier in the morning.

No one was supposed to go past the red marker, and, until today, Callie never had. It was meant to be the absolute limit, the threshold which they should not cross, and it allowed for a safe amount of buffer space between that point in the woods and the shore. She'd heard tell of other markers, but no one could say what colours they were; now she knew.

"We keep going," pronounced Callie, before starting to march forward once more. Bree hesitated but followed, just behind and to one side of her.

Callie winced as her stomach pained, harder than normal. Hunger was the default state for her and her generation, though she'd heard stories of a time when it wasn't. When it was a reminder that you needed to eat, not something you temporarily sated when you were lucky enough to find food.

She didn't believe those stories. They had to be lies.

Pulling her cloak tighter around her, Callie wondered if they'd have to stop and set up camp soon. She had no idea how much further they had to go, but it was getting close to dusk. Soon enough it'd be difficult to build a decent shelter and fire.

Before she could think upon that any further, Bree tapped her on the shoulder and pointed ahead.

"Look," was all her sister managed.

One more marker stood between them and an apparent exit to a clearing ahead. It rose out of the ground, white and bleached, and leaned at a slightly crooked angle, to the left. Callie had no medical training, but it appeared to be a femur.

Beyond the bone marker, the woods gave way and parted open, revealing a sharp drop-off and a view of the horizon, where the ocean met the sky, the sun nearly completely set.

"What's that sound?" asked Bree.

"I don't know," Callie admitted. She looked at her sister, then crept forward, giving the bone marker a wide berth.

The sound grew louder with each step, until she emerged from the woods and stood at the edge of the cliff. Down below, the ocean crashed and pounded into the rocky shoreline, each wet smack ringing in their ears.

Callie looked from one side to the next. They couldn't go down over the cliff, not without hurting themselves, and the left was blocked off by a thick copse of trees. The only way left to go was to the right, so that's where she headed, Bree in tow.

"I don't like this," Bree muttered from her orbit behind Callie.

"Neither do I, but let's stay quiet and see what we can find." They wouldn't get back home now, as they couldn't risk traveling in the dark. Not that there was anything - or anyone - waiting for them back there anyway.

The path stuck close to the shoreline, with a thin strip of beach between them and the water, and a thick wall of trees on their other side. They stayed closer to the woods, careful to avoid the water at all costs, until buildings came into view. Callie stopped, holding a hand out to halt Bree.

"Looks like potential shelter," she said, biting her lip. The sun had fully gone down now, and the blood orange hue in the sky was fading fast. A lone building stood just ahead of them, and what looked like many other similar structures further down the beach.

"Maybe we can camp out there, just for the evening?" Bree asked. "Come, let's check it out."

Something deep inside Callie warned her not to go, to turn around and run, but she chalked it up to the ravenous hunger that was devouring her from the inside out. Besides, there was danger in either option, as the woods were no safe place either, especially at night. At least with the building they'd have walls to surround and hide them, even if they appeared ancient and decrepit.

"Alright, but let me lead." She cautiously approached the building, the only noise the ebb and flow of the tide.

As they drew near, they saw the wooden door to the structure was slightly ajar, creaking back and forth with the breeze. No light emanated from inside, and there were no signs of life. Callie examined the sand all around the building, but there were no footprints nor animal tracks visible either.

With a nod to Bree, she stepped onto the small wooden porch which circled the building, then slowly pushed the door open.

The inside of the structure was dark, the last dying strains of sunset trickling in through its sole broken window barely illuminating its interior. Its furnishings were stark and few; it looked like it had already been ransacked, likely more than once over the years since the Awakening. All that remained was a pair of rickety looking wooden chairs and a rusty metallic tub in one corner.

There was room in the middle of the cabin to place the sleeping rolls they carried in their backpacks, so they'd be able to make do. Callie unslung her pack over one shoulder and placed it on the ground.

"Hey, look, there's rainwater in this thing I think," Bree said, heading for the tub.

"Be careful, Bree, we don't know -"

Before she could finish warning her, Bree was already too close to the tub. A dark shape rose out of it, silently looming over them both. Bree stumbled and fell backwards, scooting back toward Callie and stifling a scream.

The dark figure was once human, though how long ago no one could say. Its skin - or what remained of it - was stretched and pale, nearly translucent, even in the little light remaining. Two limbs raised up and stretched out toward them, and it opened its mouth. No sound came out, only a mouthful of black, fetid water that splatted and oozed on the wooden floor beneath it.

It was a Drowned One, unanchored and free to move.

Callie had heard whispered stories of them around the campfire. They were those who had died when the Awakened gods first returned, those who'd lived close to the sea that had given their people life, and which had ultimately cost them theirs. Since then no one dared approach the water, not unless you wanted to raise the ire of the gods.

They anchored their dead now - literally strapping heavy weights or chains to the corpses of the deceased and offering them to the Awakened Ones by throwing them in deep water. It was both a symbolic offering, meant to appease the gods, and a measure of protection for those left behind in the world of the living.

Unfortunately for them, the once-living form before them either hadn't been anchored or had somehow eluded its earthly bonds to re-emerge to the surface. As if to emphasize that point, it lifted one drenched, decomposing leg out of the tub and shuffled toward them.

It was then that the stench fully hit them, having been somewhat previously contained underwater. Callie's eyes watered, and she couldn't breathe, not until she turned her head and forced herself to inhale. She grabbed Bree by her backpack, which she hadn't removed yet, and hauled her forcefully to her feet.

"Run!" was all she could manage, not that she really had to tell Bree at that point.

The pair burst out of the structure, with Callie grabbing her own backpack on the way. The sky was a purplish black now, the colour of a deep bruise. It would've been beautiful, except for the Drowned One whose soggy footsteps could still be heard advancing upon them from inside the hut.

They first headed back the way they came, only to stop dead in their tracks. Several more creatures stood in their path now, in varying states of decay. Some had rotted lengths of rope around their waists and limbs or had rusted metallic chains dragging behind them; all of them were stretching their limbs out and inviting them into their cold embrace.

"This way!" Callie yelled, heading in the only other possible direction. Bree followed, their footsteps now splashing in the mixture of surf and sand as the water level crept up the beach.

A bone-rattling roar came from somewhere, though exactly from what or which direction Callie couldn't say. It shook her to the core, made her very bones vibrate, and the water rippled and undulated repeatedly in response.

Callie looked down into the water despite her best judgment. She swore she saw black coils of ink swirling through the stream, and she tried her best not to let the smoky tendrils touch her.

"Over there," Bree said, interrupting her train of thought. She pointed to an old wooden boat just ahead. It didn't look like the most seaworthy vessel, but they had no other options; more of the Drowned Ones floated ahead of them on the beach as well.

They veered toward the boat and strained to push it into the water. After several agonizing seconds it finally moved, and they both hopped inside of it once it was deep enough. Callie consciously avoided looking down again, though there were shapes and movement below the water in her peripheral vision just the same. She tried not to think how many more anchored yearned to grasp them from the dark depths below.

"What do we do?" asked Bree, who was looking back at the swarm of corpses amassing on the beach behind them.

They had no oars, and the water was thankfully taking them away from the shore. The further they got, the quieter the mob became, and they slowly stopped moving altogether.

"We stay quiet and wait. I think our noise attracted them, so we… we just wait." Callie didn't like that idea, but they had no other choice. She looked forward in the boat and saw a large island off on the horizon. When she squinted, it looked like a small speck of light was dancing on it.

"Is that it?" Bree asked, seeing the same light in the distance. "Callie, is that Coney?" Her eyes reflected the dim light in the distance. Hope burned within them as well, though that light was much fainter than it had ever been. Callie knew that feeling.

"Only one way to find out." It wasn't like that could go back at any rate. They were at the water's mercy now, the irony of which was not lost on her. Callie let out a bitter chuckle, then shook her head. Maybe it was a fire, or maybe it was just her imagination, but sooner or later they'd find out. For now, there was nothing either of them could do but wait.

"You get some sleep, I'll keep watch, okay?" Callie offered. The susurrus of the waves softly slapping the hull wouldn't let her sleep even if she'd wanted to do so.

While Bree arranged her knapsack into a makeshift pillow, Callie looked skyward. The stars were winking into existence, one by one, and she wondered which ones were her mother and, now, her grandmother. Whichever ones they were, she prayed they'd guide her and her sister in the right direction. She inhaled deeply, letting the salty ocean scent wash over her senses and tried to clear her mind as best she could.

She cast one last look at the receding shoreline. The Barrens, the expansive woods that had overgrown and reclaimed any and everything man-made in the last century, the only home they'd ever known, was behind them now. Ahead of them lay a different type of barrens, an angry and empty ocean.

Callie readjusted herself and stared up at the sky, searching out ancestors and answers to her questions in night sky. Both heavens and ocean remained silent.

"Look," Bree murmured, pointing up at the last pair of reddish-pink clouds clinging to the horizon. "Like cotton candy."

All Callie saw was blood.

Elizabeth Whitten

Elizabeth Whitten is an editor and freelance journalist who now occasionally dabbles in writing short stories. She was honored with the 37th IRMA Conference, History Feature-Merit for "A Force to be Reckoned with," which was published in the January 2016 issue of Downhome Magazine, pages 128-131.

"Unsettled" is her first published piece of fiction.

.

Unsettled

The wind caught the screen door as if it were an arm being violently twisted behind someone's back. For a moment, it looked like it would snap off completely before it slammed back into the frame with a crack.

Bridget didn't worry about possible damage to the house. Huddled in her living room, she culled her belongings to what she couldn't do without. Would her old cell phone be tradeable on the mainland or just a hunk of wasted metal bits, like it had been for the past year? Without a reliable power source, it was useless, so she tossed it. One family photo had already been sewn into the inside of her jacket along with a passport.

Outside, the winds howled and beat against what remained of the house's vinyl siding. A large section had been ripped off last winter and never went back up. Once she left, the wild animals and the previously loved pets allowed to go feral would take up residence. And, of course, someone would be by to poke around to see if they could use what had been left behind.

They'd all thought they'd have the month, but the situation had gotten worse. The creeping water level had risen sharply last week, making the village's inhabitants scramble to pack up their belongings.

As a child, Bridget had sat at her grandmother's side as the old woman recalled icebergs and berry picking. A time when it had been safe to walk along the shore without fear of being swept away and the seasons had been marked by what you could hunt and what fruit was in season.

Imagine that, huge chunks of ice that used to sail by the shore? But icebergs hadn't been seen in decades and now only existed on screen.

The people in the village had been scraping by for ages now. For the last six months the taps had ceased to provide water, right after the big earthquake. Since then she'd been relying on purifying tablets, like some sort of pioneer. Electricity was something they'd all learned to ration and then do without entirely. At night, she fumbled around in the dark, afraid of wasting valuable candles to light her way. Her knees were now bruised like old apples.

When the House of Assembly had finally shut its doors, an aging neighbour had taken the old provincial flag and raised it half-mast. He'd explained that during his youth it had been lowered as a sign of mourning or distress.

Distress, she hummed, didn't begin to describe this mess. Peering inside the pantry, there was only a single can inside, the label long torn off. The food relief shipments had dwindled after the announcement to relocate the remaining island population to the mainland.

The Avalon Peninsula had been consumed by the rising tide months ago, forcing people to flee inwards along the TCH. There'd been talk of a new government being set up, but nothing had come from it. Just a fleet of helicopters escorting the rich away.

Trailing through rooms for anything valuable on one last walk through, she left behind a trail of muddy footprints on scuffed linoleum. There was an itch to get the mop out and clean it up, but she'd be abandoning this house in an hour. What did a bit of grime matter? Once the word came down to evacuate, any pride she had in the old house had fallen by the wayside. This wasn't where she was going to grow old.

Newfoundland wouldn't be the first island to be lost to the rising ocean. From history books and TV specials, Bridget knew of other lost islands like Maldives and the Marshall Islands. Hell, Venice had been sinking for hundreds of years before it finally went under.

A long honk drew her from that reverie. The ferry was docked and ready to take on passengers. Once loaded like freight, they'd be carried across the Gulf of St. Lawrence and then on to the coast of Manitoba, where they'd be begrudgingly welcomed and later resettled somewhere far from shore.

Pulling the rucksack over her shoulder, she stepped outside and zipped her jacket against the rain and didn't bother to lock the door. Whoever wanted to get inside was free to it.

Walking down the street, her bag thumping against her shoulder, she knew some of her neighbours weren't packing up. They'd decided to stay and face whatever came, like it was a spot of bad weather they could get through. Bridget didn't know if they were brave or stupid. Better to pack up and start over somewhere else, far from the rising shore.

When she finally reached the cove, there were hundreds of people already there at the designated evacuation spot. Frustration bubbled up as she saw families carrying containers – even though they'd specifically been told to only bring what could be carried and not their entire lives. Space on the ship was at a premium.

When the capital had been lost under the rising tide, it was just a matter of time before the order to leave the island came down. The gravel underfoot was loose, shifting underneath the soles of her boots. Lining up, passport in hand, waiting was her only option. So, she waited.

Ryan Belbin

Ryan Belbin is an author from Pasadena, Newfoundland, whose previous writing credits include "Cause and Effect" for *Paragon III* and "Summer Memories" for *Grenfell Inkpot*.

Ryan says that, before getting a job where he has to wear ties and tuck in his shirt, he spent a seven month stint hitchhiking across New Zealand.

The Match

Abigail had been in Room 277 ever since she moved from the Nursery Wing three years earlier. Mr. Kinsella had assured her that wasn't unusual—many stayed even longer than that, he had said -- but an edge of irritation seemed to wedge itself more and more into his syrupy words every time she brought up that point. It wasn't that she didn't trust him (of course she did), but she couldn't ignore the fact that the yards and the halls were becoming increasingly crowded with, well, *children*. The ones who were closer to her age walked around always darting their eyes back and forth, with hungry looks on their faces. She knew there was something off with them, something downright weird, in the same way she knew that she was starting to become one of them. Maybe she already was.

Room 277 had a view of the eastern courtyard and the lake just beyond it. On nights when there was a bright moon, you could just catch the glint of its reflection on the lip of the lake visible from her bed. Abigail hated Room 277 a little bit more every night she went to sleep and watched that dancing moonlight.

It was an ordinary sort of a Wednesday morning, around midday. Everything about the day was ordinary—the weather outside was overcast and flat, the morning breakfast had been warm but not too hot, the lessons had been mildly interesting but if really pushed on it a few days later none of the students would have been able to remember many details. Abigail was in the lineup with a tray between her hands, idly rocking it so a slightly bruised apple scurried back and forth across it. She was by herself—well, there were plenty of people around her, all chattering and making a racket, but it had been at least six months since she'd been a part of that rabble. Now, it was as if the noise was all in a foreign, slightly dangerous language.

On that ordinary sort of a Wednesday, waiting for a scoop or two of macaroni and cheese from a polished, industrial-sized steel pot, Abigail got a tap on her shoulder by one of the Ward Matrons. She'd been wondering about whether the sauce would be runny or thick, and hadn't expected to be interrupted in her musings, so that with the tap she missed the return pendulum swing of the tray, sending her apple tumbling to receive new battle wounds on the tile flooring.

She turned, and for the life of her couldn't remember this Matron's name. Sarah Jean? Emilie? The staff were almost as fickle as the children for sticking around—she'd long since decided that keeping on top of their names was a pointless exercise.

"Abigail, isn't it?" The older woman watched the apple roll across the floor instead of meeting the younger one's eyes.

Abigail nodded, and didn't know whether the Matron saw it or not. Either she must have, or she didn't care, because she kept talking. "Mr. Kinsella would like to see you in his office over the lunch hour."

That was all there was to it. The Matron turned, scooped up the apple where it lay a few strides away, and kept on walking without looking back. Abigail decided she was more curious about these summons than she was about the cheese sauce, and so she tucked her now-empty tray under her armpit and headed in the opposite direction as What's-her-name the Matron, towards the double doors leading away from the hoots, shouts, and laughter of several hundred hungry children whose names she also didn't know.

Abigail didn't know what to think of the Sunrise Centre for Early Childhood Fulfillment and Successful Adulthood, because she had nothing to compare it to. She hadn't been born here, of course, but she hadn't been making too many lasting memories when she was two weeks old, either. The halls had never seemed vast or labyrinthine, because she learned them concurrent with learning to walk and to talk. If she'd come from any other background, she might have thought it resembled a castle smack dab in the English countryside, but she came from the background where this place was just where she came from. End of story.

This place was not, however, where she belonged. That much she knew, even if she didn't have the answer to the obvious follow-up: *where* was it she did belong?

She'd been off the grounds a handful of times throughout the years, but was only able to summon a few snatches of recollection. One time there'd been a dog—she'd never seen one before, and no matter how much the family had insisted he was only playing, Abigail had been petrified. Another time there had been a faceless man and a faceless woman, with a permanent cloud of cigarette smoke hanging in the air. Another time she just remembered the impossible stretches of greens and blues at a beachfront property where she'd spent three glorious hours on the edge of a summer a few years back. She also remembered hope—but no, it wasn't helpful to think about that anymore.

She'd been off the grounds a handful of times and had come back just as many times.

Now, she came to the end of the long, empty hallway, getting farther and farther from the muffled dins of the Dining Hall. Edwin Kinsella's office door was a heavy-set mahogany that always struck Abigail as wildly out of place, amid the endless rows of plain doors leading to classrooms, meeting spaces, and dormitories. It gave the impression of authority and importance, and she saw more and more that there was truth to that notion. Years ago, he'd been the jovial father figure for this sprawling gang of parentless children. Now, he was becoming more and more like a bailiff with a thick ring of keys that he could use to unlock the right doors for you—if he felt like it.

Abigail knocked and entered before he gave any sort of reply. This wasn't her first time in his office, although usually she came of her own accord, not in response to a direct request.

"Come in," he said without looking up from his computer screen to see that the young girl was already ahead of him. "Ah, Abigail, sit down." She'd been halfway through that process, too.

Mr. Kinsella was as ordinary as the afternoon. He wasn't fat, but he wasn't fit. His hair was thinning, but it didn't give him too much grief as of yet. The only thing off about him was his fingers—often bridged in front of his face, fragile and skeletal. Every time he brought his hands together Abigail wondered if they might snap at the knuckles.

"You're probably wondering what I've called you in for," he continued. Much like the premises themselves, Abigail had nothing to compare this patriarch to—though if she had, she'd have seen how awkward a man he was. He was always getting right down to business with his pint-sized patrons, and he didn't have the knack for the humour they so easily carried with them.

"Yes, sir," she said, fighting the urge to kick her feet where they failed to reach the floor.

Kinsella reached in his jacket pocket and pulled out a slim, chrome-plated device. He tapped the front with one of those bony fingers, causing the black face to burst to illumination. Abigail knit her brow. "Now, you wouldn't have seen one of these before, but they're dead simple to use. Here, watch me," he said, laying the device between them with its face staring up at the ceiling. He wiggled his finger against the screen with all the ease of an oblivious ballerina teaching a pupil to pirouette instead of how to walk.

"Never mind," he said when it was obvious Abigail wasn't following. "You'll figure it out. Abigail, you're what, seven years old now?"

"Eight," she corrected.

He grimaced, waiting half a second before he even bothered to try to mask it. "Eight, very good," he said in a way that made it seem not very good at all. "The thing is, we want you to have the best life you can. The best life for you. And while we very much enjoy having you here," he went on, making it dubious whether they did enjoy having her there, "we all believe that the best life for you would be out, well, *there*."

Abigail didn't respond. So far, none of this was anything she didn't already know. Why was she here, exactly?

"We don't give these to everyone," Kinsella said, indicating the now blank device sitting on the desk like a defunct talisman, "but once a child is of a certain age, we consider it entirely appropriate. You won't have unlimited wireless access or anything," he hastily assured her in a way that was entirely meaningless, "but within the network you are connected to, you can access Nuclr."

"Nuclr?"

"Nuclr," he nodded. He reignited the screen and tapped on a purple square with two stick figures on it, one twice as tall as the other. "You set up a profile, see. You put a picture up, a few things that you like doing, all the things you'd expect." Abigail was still trying to figure out how a picture made its way into that impenetrable device, but Kinsella wasn't slowing down. "And you browse through other profiles for other families. Families out *there*."

There was a strange place. It was the place of infinite possibility, and the only definite thing anyone could agree on was that it was not here. *There* was as terrifying as a dog jumping on you and as inviting as a loon's cry on a lake.

"If you find a family you like, you swipe the profile to the right. Meanwhile, they're all there looking at your profile—if they like yours' too, then voila, you arrange a meeting with the Outings Office and you try your best to impress them. Wouldn't it be great if you did?"

Abigail still didn't quite know what to say, but nodding

seemed like the right thing. She didn't understand the rectangular wand that could bestow sweet release on her any more than she understood how to put a picture onto it, but she realized (if there had been any doubt before) that she was definitely now one of the hungry ones. The younger ones could afford to be reckless, but not her. She had no intention of being in this place until she turned nineteen, at which point she'd be cast out belonging to nowhere and to no one.

"Good," Kinsella said, pushing the device to Abigail. "You needn't tell the others what you have. However, it might be a good idea to see Matron Emilie Jean (*"Aha!"* Abigail thought), for help with setting up your account. Remember, you need to impress them. No, *dazzle* them. Don't be afraid to do whatever it takes."

Abigail didn't quite understand what he meant by that, but he had already started to turn back to one of the only computers in the building. The thing in her hand was lighter than she would have expected, but it still felt like dead weight. Sensing that the meeting was over as unceremoniously as it had started, Abigail pocketed the device in her robe pocket and left.

The bailiff had unclasped the key from its ring and held it in front of her face, only to toss it into the brambles. If the light shone right, she swore she saw a glint of gold where it lay, just out of reach amongst the thickest patch of thorns. Abigail braced herself for scratches while she braced herself to find the key to let her out, whatever it took.

Room 277 was alight well after Abigail's bedtime. The corners of the room remained hidden in their shadows, but edges started to crystalize as you moved closer to the bed, and to the screen of light like an elongated deck of cards in the hands of a little girl. Whenever she heard footsteps (once, every half hour) she tucked the device under her thin sheets, momentarily dimming the room and causing her eyes to swim. Then, it would come out again.

Abigail didn't know who *they* were, any more than she knew where *there* was. All she knew is she desperately craved their approval—and feared their rejection.

The Matron had asked her questions that afternoon, and Abigail marveled at her own propensity to answer exactly the wrong thing every time. It hadn't caused Emilie Jean too much grief, however, as after each momentous sigh she'd managed to find something to plug into the tiny device all the same. "What are you saying?" Abigail had asked. "Never you mind," she'd responded without looking up.

The entire afternoon, Abigail had felt like a thing poked and prodded, or like some specimen at the zoo. Once she was alone, however, she became enthralled by the thrill of what could be.

Every happy, smiling, loving family that popped up on the screen came with an entire story of where she could fit in. That was part of what kept her up so late. The other thing was the fact that by 9:42, she had declined about twenty families, for every half plausible reason she could conjure to convince herself. By 10:05, she decided that she had better get over herself and swipe right on *someone*. By 10:36 she was near paralyzed with the fear that she wasn't good enough for the three who she had selected, their silence indisputable confirmation of that fact. What had she been thinking at all?

At 12:17, she had been asleep for a while when she jolted awake, flipped the thing back over, and checked. Still nothing. Still a stupid idea.

Brring-SHO!

The noise was born in the hinterland of dreamland, on the border of waking reality. It made muddled sense in Abigail's subconscious, until it chimed again, and this time it came through as a strange noise she'd never heard before, but one that definitely belonged in Room 277 and not whatever world she'd created in her slumber. She squinted her eyes open, and there was the strange device on the floor where she'd discarded it the night before. The screen was blazing with light yet again, and bold words blazoned across it.

IT'S A MATCH!

Abigail allowed herself a moment for the dots to connect before she scrambled out of the bed and grabbed the matchmaker, hands shaking. Once she touched the screen, the beautiful wake-up words faded, revealing an image of a couple she'd allowed herself to believe she could someday meet. They looked like they were in their mid-twenties, smiling for the camera on what looked to be a farm, holding a brilliant orange pumpkin between them. Her golden hair was streaming behind her head, caught in a gust that had been consistently blowing, if their red-tipped noses were any indication. He was wearing a thick sweater that hinted at a small pot belly, his hair receding slightly and less affected by the wind.

They both looked happy. Abigail couldn't believe it.

She allowed herself a chance to draw on the story she'd started to tell herself last night about these people in the pumpkin patch. She'd imagined that the woman loved iced coffee, and the man would always bring her one whenever he came home after being away. They lived in a neat little bungalow on a quiet street, and they would watch TV together before going to bed. Now, she imagined *herself* with them. Going out with the woman, holding her hand, getting groceries. Maybe she'd call her Abby. Maybe instead of watching TV, he'd read her stories, and she'd fall asleep between them. Of *course* they wouldn't have a dog.

She was caught in her wistful thinking when suddenly the device gave a sharp vibration. *Brring-SHO!* She nearly dropped it like a hot potato before she recognized what it was. When she looked down, there was a small scroll across the screen: "New message from the Stephens! Click to open!"

Abigail silently mouthed the word, got a feel for it in her mouth. *Stephens.* Even in her imaginings of what spending time with these people might be like, she hadn't allowed herself to indulge in the dream of what it would be like to wear their last name. She'd been hurt by having that dream snapped like a twig before more times than she cared to count, because the simple fact was Abigail had no last name. She'd been two weeks old when her parents (or had they even been a couple at that point? No one had told her, and those records were sealed tight in some basement's basement) had dropped her off here, either because they were too young, too poor, or too indifferent to raise a child. They had left her with nothing, least of all a sur-name to claim. She'd spent years now searching for a name to fit her, to wrap up her identity so that she could cease being just Abigail and be whoever she really was. Or perhaps searching wasn't the right word — after all, she felt that the name was al-ready there, she just didn't know it yet. It was almost as though it were a high-pitched noise that only some animals could hear, but once she finally caught the whisper, she would realize that she'd known it all along.

Her idea of home was a lot like that, too. Home was out there, where she had a last name.

And so, for a long moment before she dared to follow the instructions to open the message, she tried on the new last name with no reservations and full-on hope. Abigail Stephens. Yes, she dared to believe, *that could work.*

It was just about then that she had another thought, from a deeper place inside of her. A thought that had always been there, but not so often in plain sight. The assurance that there was some mistake, and that the message behind the curtain was an apology for accidentally affirming her picture and her profile. "Good luck finding what you're looking for!" it would say with pseudo-friendliness. Maybe it wouldn't even say that much. Worse still, maybe it would be an outright rejection, a validation of the even deeper thoughts that there was a *reason* she remained at this place while others had come and gone. The family in the pumpkin patch hadn't swiped on her because they wanted to meet her — they just couldn't resist the urge to ask her why such a lost cause was even bothering.

Stripped of that last name, she hadn't realized how naked

a person could be. The walls of Room 277 felt as though they constricted.

Hands trembling now for an entirely different reason, she laid the device on the bureau on the other side of the room, threw on her dayrobes, and shuffled to the Dining Hall. At this hour she'd be one of the few eating breakfast, which was entirely fine with her.

Abigail looked up from her plate of scrambled eggs to see Matron Emilie Jean striding across the hall as though she were magnetically charged. Even from this distance, it was clear that her purpose was to land directly in front of the young girl. She put down her fork expectantly.

"Well?" she asked, still too far away to be directly engaged but not appearing overly bothered. A few ambling children parted like a Biblical sea at the woman who would not be veered from her course. "Did you have any luck? Any matches?"

Abigail shrugged her shoulders. "Not really," she answered.

The Matron wrinkled her brows. "Not *really*? I think this is an all-or-nothing, my dear. What do you mean?"

Abigail knew that trying to explain the absolutely certainty of the failure of the unseen message, coupled with the small rush that as long as she didn't check it then the fragile possibility remained intact, would get her nowhere with the Matron. Emilie Jean saw Nuclr as a fail-proof rope—only Abigail saw the frays.

"There was a message," she said. She stopped and chewed over her words. "I haven't read it yet."

Abigail wasn't sure what she was expecting, but it certainly wasn't Emilie Jean clapping her hands. "Wonderful!" she shouted. "Oh, that's wonderful! You're playing hard to get, yes! And *unread*, well that will make them positively entranced. Don't wait too long though, God only knows how many other kids they've got in their queue."

"Other—?" Abigail started to ask, but Emilie Jean, as was her wont, had already started taking her strides in the opposite direction. Abigail had no more interest in the uneaten eggs— now all she could think about were the other children. The smarter ones, the prettier ones, the *younger* ones. Of course everyone would want a family like the Stephens to adopt them— why wouldn't they? She was almost definitely too late.

She left her eggs and her half glass of orange juice where it was and bolted across the room, one fear replaced by another, more urgent fear. One hunger replaced by another.

When she made it back to her room, her screen still proclaimed the arrival of a new message. She took a deep breath and clicked it open.

"Hi Abigail! How are you doing today? :)"

Maybe it wasn't too late. Was that possible?

"Hi!" she typed, the message looking much calmer and with less hyperventilation than her actual demeanour. "im good would you like too met?"

If the Matron had been dead, she would have rolled over a few times in the sod over that one. Abigail didn't know that though, so she clicked send and hovered over the device as though she could will it to move faster.

Delivered. It read. That meant that somewhere out there another device like hers went *Brring-SHO*! What was taking them so long? Maybe they were having breakfast in another room. Or maybe they were busy taking another kid somewhere out for an iced coffee, or helping them pick out a stupid dog who would sleep at the foot of the new child's bed. What absolutely stupidity had compelled her to—

Read.

They'd seen it! The link between them was open, one set of strangers now had a conversation. Maybe, just maybe, she could wedge herself in.

A minute passed. Then five. Then fifteen. Abigail felt like she could end up with a permanent hunch in her back from bending over the handheld rectangle. She read back over her message, finding everything wrong with every single syllable. Maybe she should have played it cooler, have been more "hard-to-get," as Emilie Jean had suggested. She'd once read a Halloween story about a talking pumpkin—she definitely should have asked them if they'd read that too. Twenty minutes. Abigail felt tears welling up in her eyes when the rectangle vibrated. *Brring-SHO!*

"Oh, you're a little go-getter! :) We'd love to meet you. How about this Saturday?"

Abigail Stephens let the tears loose for real in Room 277.

"I can't believe you asked to meet them already," Mr. Kinsella huffed.

"I just can't believe they agreed," Matron Emilie Jean chimed in.

Abigail stood between the two adults on the front steps of the Sunrise Centre, watching the parking lot with nervous electricity swarming in the air. She was wearing a light jacket and jeans, clothes that were entirely different from her usual robes.

"I hope you aren't so cavalier with any other matches," Kinsella said.

Abigail turned to him. "*Other* matches?" she asked. She hadn't considered that.

"Well yes, of course. You're still scrolling through other profiles?" he said, looking totally perplexed.

"I haven't even looked, once I arranged for this visit," Abigail admitted, as though it were the simplest thing in the world. Emilie Jean gasped audibly, and Kinsella placed his head in his palm.

"*What* is the matter with you?" Emilie Jean said, crossing her arms firmly against her chest. "Go back to your room and get your ph—"

But she stopped, as a small red sedan crunched over the gravel leading to the parking lot. Kinsell and the Matron exchanged a sceptical grimace over Abigail's brightened face, as they realized it was all up to her now.

Abigail ran across the parking lot, reaching the car before it even had a chance to stop. Their grimace deepened.

"Hi!" she yelled before the doors opened. "I'm Abigail!"

The man in the passenger seat got out first. He had a grin on his face and a teddy bear in his hands. His hair was thinner than in the picture, his belly protruded more, and he now wore a pair of glasses—obviously it had been the October before last that the photo in the pumpkin patch was taken. "Hi, Abigail," he said, handing her the bear. "I'm Frank. My wife Jolene is just finishing up a work call." He thumbed towards the car where the woman's mouth was moving. She was looking straight ahead.

Abigail clutched the bear to her chest, afraid that maybe she was dreaming up this entire thing. The day was impossibly bright for mid-April, the sun warm and enveloping on her skin.

"So," Frank said, idly adjusting his glasses. "Where would you like to go today?"

"Can we get iced coffee?" Abigail asked.

That suggestion seemed to puzzle Frank. "I guess so," he said. "Jo's lactose intolerant, but I'm sure she can find something. Oh, she's off the phone, hop in."

Abigail gave one last look to the Sunrise Centre and to Kinsella and Matron Emilie Jean, still standing at the top of the staircase. She didn't know where she was headed, but she felt that something fundamental was going to change.

"Hi!" she said as she pulled herself into the back seat. "I'm Abigail, but you can call me Abby."

The Warrington River, that same lazy stream that fed into the lake on the edge of the Sunrise Centre, ran its course at the base of a lush valley, flanked on either side by gently rolling hills. The Grouse Gorge lookout was perched on one of these steepest assents, a small barricade and a tourist information panel (complete with light, innocent graffiti) the only thing separating the swarms milling about their parked cars from the sublime but plunging drop down into the valley.

"You've really never been here before?" Jolene asked as she pulled into the parking area. "Your Centre is so close by, I figured every adult visitor would take you here."

The last adult visitor had been a year and a half ago, but Abigail decided not to mention that.

The air was cooler up here, the breeze a bit more biting. It didn't bother Abigail. She ran over to the barricade and gaped. Before her, the sky opened up to an extent she hadn't known was possible. Hundreds of evergreens running up the hillside, and even more far below along the base of the valley, made Abigail feel incredibly small and incredibly protected. The thin line of the river made the world of Dining Hall lineups, Mr. Kinsella and Matron Emilie Jean, and Room 277 feel *very* far away.

"What do you think?" Frank asked, the same grin from the parking lot playing out on his face. It had all the glow of the Jack-o'-lantern Abigail imagined they'd carved the night after they came home the pumpkin patch. "Pretty cool, huh?"

"It's the most special thing I've ever seen," Abigail answered truthfully. Frank chuckled as though she'd made a joke. When she didn't laugh with him, Frank adjusted his glasses and looked back to the view.

"You can't quite see it from here, but your home is just over there," Jolene said, pointing off to where the river bent around another hillside.

Abigail reached out and took Jolene's non-pointing hand, squeezing it in her small hand. She didn't bother to tell her that, somehow, she thought Jolene might have been wrong about that.

After spending a few minutes at Grouse Gorge and sharing a hot dog Frank bought at a food truck parked in the lot, the Stephens took Abigail to the city. As they drove by a towering complex of buildings with what looked like a thousand balconies stacked one on top of the other, Frank pointed out which one was their apartment building. Abigail memorized the street and everything around her. She rolled down her window and took a deep inhale of the perfume of crowds and exhaust.

They took Abigail to a park that was close to their building, where there was a playground and a swimming pool. The pool was still empty from the winter, but hoards of children were running around the swing set and slides. Jolene excused herself to take a phone call on a tiny black earpiece while Frank pushed Abigail on the swing, higher and higher until it felt like she was positively flying.

The perfect day felt like it would never end, and Abigail silently wished for the same. When the sedan drove back to the Sunrise Centre the sun was doing the exact opposite, preparing to nestle deep into the hillside and make way for the moon to dance its way across the lake. Abigail tried to imagine the view from the top of the gorge, instead of down here.

"So," Abigail started, kicking her feet anxiously. "Thank you for everything today." She clutched her teddy tightly. "Will I . . . see you again?"

Ever since the car started its descent down the valley, her heart had been in her throat, wondering how to approach the subject that hung heavy in the small car. Jolene kept her eyes on the road ahead, but Frank turned around with that same big Jack-o'-lantern grin.

"I hope so," he said. He gave her a wink.

Abigail felt a rush of wind escape her body as her entire frame loosened. "Good," she said.

"It was wonderful meeting you, Abby," Jolene said when she stopped the car.

As Abigail made her way up the steps, looking back every so often as the car slipped away down the darkened driveway, Kinsella popped out from behind the double doors. He'd known they would be returning before dark, but his sudden appearance made Abigail wonder if he'd been waiting. He placed one bony hand on her shoulder and watched her expectantly. "Well?" he asked.

"Oh, Mr. Kinsella, I had the *best* day! Mr. and Mrs. Stephens are so nice! We had a hot dog and they showed me around the city and we played in the park and—"

"Wonderful!" he said, cutting her off. "Now remember, wait a day or two before you reach out again. And keep looking through other profiles. You don't know who else you could find."

Abigail shook her head. "No, I can't do that to them, they were so *perfect*, Mr. Kinsella! They said I'd see them again." She decided she'd wish them good night once she got back to her room—not that there was any need of telling Mr. Kinsella that.

She turned to look up to him, and she threw herself on him, wrapping him in as tight a hug as she was capable. He stood like a stunned scarecrow for a moment before he placed his hands lightly on her back. "Thank you for all your help," she said softly, burying her head into the folds of his robe.

Matron Emilie Jean stood just beyond the threshold, as though she too had been keeping a close eye on the driveway. For the second time that day, the two grown-ups exchanged a glance unseen by Abigail.

Abigail said good night to the Stephens, and they wrote her back and said the same.

She knew she probably wasn't supposed to have her device out with her in classes, but she couldn't help it. Besides, she was subtle, keeping it just out of sight beneath her desk and the volume turned off. She asked them what they were doing, and how their day was going. She asked them what they were having for supper. She asked them if they had gone back to the park. She reminded them of what a fun time they'd had together.

At some point in the day, Abigail got a new notification: *IT'S A MATCH!* it screamed in those same bold letters. It must have been one of the other two families she'd originally swiped on, but Abigail had no interest in checking which it was. Instead, she opened up the window where the chain of messages between her and the Stephens ran like ticker tape up the screen and beyond, re-reading her favourite exchanges.

A week later (an eternity, it felt), the Stephens came to pick her up again. This time they brought her an ice cream cone when they arrived and brought her to a movie theatre. She sat sandwiched between them and dug handfuls of buttery popcorn from a bag while a cartoon as big as a building played in front of her.

On that drive home, Jolene cleared her throat, in the way people do when they're about to say something important. "We really enjoy spending time with you, Abby," she started.

"Mm-hmm," Frank nodded.

Abigail didn't say anything, feeling her heart beat a little faster.

"We were wondering if maybe, on your next visit, you might like to spend an overnight?"

Abigail's mouth dropped. An overnight. She'd never, in all her life, had an overnight outside of the Sunrise Centre. She'd played through the scenario of an overnight a thousand different times, but couldn't believe that here it was. She'd been worried, as time had gone on, that the fact that she was so old without ever having spent an overnight visit would be a cause for concern from a prospective parent. What if her bedtime rituals were strange, and no one had ever told her? She felt safe around these people though, and so her nerves were taking the shape of unbridled excitement. She kicked her feet more vigorously.

"Yes! Yes, please!" she laughed.

Kinsella, waiting again by the doorway and this time not trying to hide it, could hardly believe it. His smile seemed, for the first time in a long time, full of warmth.

"Now, you need to make sure that you go to bed when they tell you to, and that you brush your teeth without being asked. Parents absolutely *love* it when children do that."

"What if I miss it here?" Abigail asked. The sudden realization that this was the only place she'd ever woken up made her suddenly more than a little afraid.

Kinsella shook his head. "That won't do," he said. "You don't need to make it seem like you go for overnight visits every weekend or anything, but even a nice family like the Stephens may be put off if they find out this is your first time. They need to think you're at least a little experienced."

Abigail frowned. "But," she said, "isn't it important that I tell them the truth?"

"Well, yes, of course it is," Kinsella stumbled. "Just maybe not all at once. You don't want to scare them away after all. You've spent time with them twice now, and you had fun, didn't you?"

Abigail nodded.

"Good," Kinsella said. "Right now, the most important thing is to keep having fun. And then, who knows?"

The bed in the spare bedroom of the Stephens' apartment was bigger and cozier than Abigail's bed at the Sunrise Centre. She felt herself slip off along the Dreamland Express sooner than she'd expected. It didn't hurt that she was absolutely exhausted.

The Stephens had taken her out to a restaurant to eat, a hamburger joint with a contortion of tubes and plastic balls in a separate room that she had been let loose in after finishing her meal. The Stephens had watched her from behind the glass window separating the shrieking jungle from the tables and the parents.

A woman who worked with Jolene had a ten-year-old son who was having a birthday party at the bowling alley. Abigail had never gone bowling before or been to a birthday party, but she was invited and didn't mind that most of her balls went down the gutter. Jolene had introduced her to all the other moms and dads with a look of pride on her face.

And then, they had finally gone to the apartment.

The Stephens lived on the seventh floor, accessible by an elevator. The moving box hadn't helped calm her nerves when it started whining and moving upwards. The hallway when the elevator opened wasn't unlike that of the Sunrise Centre, with a string of closed doors in either direction, but instead of opening onto a single bedroom, there was an entire home contained behind each door. It felt as though she were stepping into Narnia when she crossed the threshold. The open-concept kitchen flowed directly into a seating area with plush furniture and a television mounted on the wall. Along the opposite wall a bookcase overflowed with novels, and between them a large pane of glass looked out onto the city below. A small alcove lined with houseplants branched off from the main room, with doors leading to two bedrooms and a bathroom.

"Home sweet home," Frank said, as Jolene discarded her keys into a wicker basket by the door.

Home.

Jolene had given Abigail a glass of milk and a cookie from a jar. Then, Frank had led her down to the bedroom, the door half closed. He pushed it back for the big reveal.

The room was, in reality, fairly similar to Room 277, with simple furniture and empty walls. However, all Abigail saw was the potential. The posters she could hang, the corner where she could put toys, the way she would decorate things and the place where sleeping bags could be spread on the floor for when friends came over for sleepovers. The window looked out much as the main living room one had, and she couldn't help but think of all the things she'd go through in her life while that view remained constant.

"What do you think?" Frank asked.

Abigail opened her mouth to answer but realized that she was at a loss for words. She couldn't come close to articulating how she felt and decided against trying. Frank seemed to have understood.

There, in a brand-new bed, looking out over a busy cityscape, Abigail felt safer than she had ever remembered feeling.

All the fears about an overnight visit seemed to be highly exaggerated.

She didn't know what time it was when she woke up, but when she peeked through the blinds, she saw that the sky was still dark. The lights from the city cast a permanent glow above its head, but there was no trace of the sun yet. She'd drank a soda with her burger, another with her pizza at the bowling alley, and a glass of milk before bed. All that liquid was now racing to get out.

Abigail was careful to slip quietly into the bathroom—the last thing she wanted to do was upset the Stephens, not at this crucial moment. The fluorescent lights burned her retinas when she flicked them on, and she immediately slammed her eyes. When she was slowly able to open them, she saw the box, sticking out of the garbage can by the weight scale.

She didn't know what it was, not entirely. But she certainly recognized one of the words across it. She stood still for a long moment, there in that strange bathroom in the middle of the night. She wanted nothing more than to crawl back to bed, but she knew she couldn't do that. Sleep was the last thing she would be able to do.

"Jolene? Frank?" She'd tried to summon some flint of anger, but it came over with a warble.

There was some rustling before the other bedroom door opened, and Jolene stuck her head out. Her hair was strewn every which way, and her eyes were mostly closed, with just a small crack guiding her. "Hrrm?" she mumbled. "Abby? What's the matter?"

Abigail nearly lost her nerve, but something in her told her she had to keep going, that the point of no return was gone well past her rear-view mirror. "What's *this*?" she asked, holding up the empty cardboard box.

"Oh," Jolene said, becoming more alert. Her eyes opened to their normal width. "Oh, Abby."

"Are you having a baby?" the little girl tried to demand, sounding more petulant than perturbed. "That's what 'pregnant' means, right? You're having a baby?"

Jolene closed the bedroom door and hunched down by Abigail. She took the empty box that had once held a pregnancy test. "No," she said, "we're not having a baby. The test came back negative."

"Oh," Abigail said, breathing a sigh of relief. "Good. So, you're never going to have a baby? It'll just be us, right?"

Jolene idly tapped the box against her thighs. "Oh, Abby," she said. There was a look of pity on her face. "I didn't . . . that is, we didn't know . . ."

Even the city outside, busier and noisier than the woods outside of the Sunrise Centre could ever possibly have been, seemed to hold its breath in silence, waiting to hear what came next.

"We didn't realize you thought this was serious," she said. "Most people on Nuclr don't really . . . I mean, I suppose we could have asked . . . we just assumed you were looking for something more . . . *casual*."

"Are you *trying* to have a baby?"

"Yes," Jolene said. "Yes, of course we are. We thought you knew. You didn't think we were going to adopt you, did you?"

The noise around her suddenly became impossible to drown out, louder than it had been all night as though it were merely building itself up before that point. Every sensible thought became mired in cacophony. Jolene's lips were moving as they had been in the car when she'd first seen her, but no words were making any sense. Louder than all the rest of the noise, somehow, was Frank's snoring in the adjacent bedroom, unconcerned by what was happening. All Abigail could do in that moment was to turn and run.

Abby Stephens. Abigail Nothing. What difference did it really make, anyway? It was all the same.

At first, she'd just run at a blind pace, finding sidewalk where she could but not actively seeking it out. More than a few fierce headlights glared, and fiercer car horns screamed at her, but once she passed beneath the pillared overpass of the expressway and the 24-hour neon signs gave way to thinning streetlights, the traffic slowed.

None of the vehicles that swerved around her was a red sedan.

Her limbs and her muscles kept their mutinous pleas silent for an impossibly long stretch of time, or perhaps her brain had a singular focus of not listening. At any event, by the time she left most of the hustle of the city behind her, and was well and truly alone on the outskirts, her physical exhaustion won. She collapsed in the small embankment on the side of the road and considered staying there. How long would it take before some car stopped to investigate? More likely that someone would come and give her until the count of ten to get off his property.

There's some animal instinct inside of creatures that draws them home, up river streams and air currents. That was what was awakened in Abigail then—it hadn't been the desire to get away, it had been the desire to get to somewhere else.

It had been the desire to get *there*.

She couldn't run, but she could hobble, then walk. The sky around her was starting to lighten, replacing the guiding lights of the streetlights. It was a good thing, because those were becoming fewer and farther between, with more mighty evergreens than anything else. Dawn had fully broken by the time Abigail made it to the lookout at Grouse Gorge. The hot dog vendor's truck, the window tightly barred, was the only vehicle out that early in the morning.

The barricade against the edge of the cliff was a wooden fence, made up of two horizontal beams separated by a thin gap. Abigail pulled herself up onto the lower beam, allowing the first glimpses of the spring sun to wash over her tired, aching body. The river, far below her, caught shimmering diamonds in its surface, as it prepared for a labourious day of cleansing the countryside. It had been here that she'd taken Jolene's hand in hers only a few weeks earlier. It was here that she'd been happiest.

Abigail pulled herself up to the top beam, keeping one hand on the vertical post for balance and then, as she gained her footing, letting go and standing fully erect on top of the fence. Jolene had pointed just passed the outcrop of hillside down in the river valley. That, she had said, was where her home was. Abigail paid no heed to the sun in her eyes or to the precarious pull of gravity down to the shadowed cliffs below. All she wanted was to finally glimpse home.

"The next family is here to see you," Matron Sarah Maureen said, laying a thin folder on Mr. Kinsella's meticulous desk. It was her third week on the job.

"Send them in," Kinsella said, opening the file and skimming the single page inside it.

The couple came into the office, the balding man carrying a baby carrier against his hip. Kinsella extended a bony hand in introduction and invited them to sit down.

"Now," he said, focusing on the file instead of making eye contact. "Your son. How old is he?"

"Ten days," the blond woman responded. Large oblong earrings hung from her lobes, drawing attention to a black earpiece in one ear.

"Mm-hmm. And have you named him?"

The man shook his head. "We didn't really see the point."

Kinsella made a note.

"Mm-hmm. And reason for adoption?"

The woman leaned forward. "He just wasn't . . . well, first off, we wanted a girl."

"Mm-hmm."

"But there were other things," the man said. The bundle in the basket murmured as he adjusted his glasses. "We were looking for someone with green eyes."

"Someone with a bit more *attitude*, you know?" his wife added. "I feel like, with this one, it would be too easy to just become complacent."

"Mm-hmm," Kinsella said, making a few more notes. "Well, we should be able to find a place for him. Now, I'll need you to fill in a little bit more paperwork, and then . . ."

Brring-SHO!

The unseen baby was making more noise now, as the man fished in his jacket pocket. His wife turned to him, and Kinsella laid the folder back down.

The man looked down at the screen of a cell phone and grinned like a Jack-o'-lantern that had been left on the door-step well into November. He held it out to his wife as the baby started to cry.

"It's a match," he said.

Nicole Little

Nicole Little is an award-winning short story author from St. John's, Newfoundland. Her previous writing credit, "Sweet Sixteen," won the June 2018 Kit Sora prize. She has also placed in the Writer's Alliance of Newfoundland and Labrador "A Nightmare on Water Street" contest, October 2018.

She is a mother of two.

The Market

"We shouldn't be talking!"
"Do you think he could change his mind?"
"They never do, darling, they never do. Now go!"

It was barely dawn, but Cherish Watson had already undertaken a day's work. The house was spotless and she was feeling accomplished; soon she would drop the children at school and then she would be free to spend the rest of the day as she pleased. She was planning to make an apple cobbler for dessert tonight which meant a special trip across town to the farmer's market for Granny Smiths. It was Desmond's favorite though, so she would find the time.

She heard tiny but thunderous feet hit the floor above her head signaling the end of her solitude, and as she pulled bowls and spoons for oatmeal from their respective cupboards and drawers, Lucas and Delilah exploded into the kitchen. She shook her head wearily at their bickering but turned away to hide a grin. Even in the womb they hadn't been able to get along; always fighting and kicking for their own space. They inhaled their breakfast, then turned and smiled the exact same smile at her, before rushing off to brush their teeth. She felt a familiar stab of pain in her chest as the thought flashed in her mind of what life would be like without them; every mother's greatest fear.

With Lucas and Delilah safely delivered to school later,

Cherish made the trek to the market for apples. She found herself unable to resist the seductive scent of fresh bread wafting from the bakery as she strolled past. She grabbed a baguette and hurried on her way, her allowance card depleted for the day. She paused a few doors down to chat briefly with a new neighbor, leaning against the white picket fence to compliment the roses in the garden. And then, determined to finish the book she was reading, she made a beeline for home, retrieving it from its hiding spot behind a bag of peas in the freezer. With cobbler crisping in the oven, she poured herself a generous glass of pilfered red, and slipped beneath the bubbles of a hot bath.

The water had long grown cold by the time she closed the book. She pulled the plug in the tub with her toes, quickly towelled herself dry and tidied the bathroom. She chose a favorite blue sundress from the closet. She'd been told that it complemented her eyes. She curled her hair so that it fell in soft waves to the middle of her back and expertly applied just the right amount of makeup.

At last, content with her appearance, she padded barefoot to the kitchen, which was now resplendent with the smells of cinnamon and cloves. She swept a discerning eye over the room, wiped an errant crumb from the countertop but otherwise could spot nothing out of place. It was perfect.

She shooed the kids to their rooms when they arrived from school a little later and set the table with the special occasion china. Moroccan lamb tagine with lemon and pomegranate couscous now perfumed the air. She had outdone herself this time and gave herself a mental pat on the back. She could be convincing if she had to be. She knew all it took was one phone call.

Desmond arrived home later than usual, flustered but with an apologetic bouquet of her favorite flowers. She placed the daisies in the center of the table and stood back to admire her handy work. This should be on the cover of a magazine, she thought and then laughed out loud, sharply, startling herself.

Deep breaths. Calming breaths. Composure. She smiled brightly at nothing in particular and shouted, "Dinner's ready!"

It had gone well. The day was almost over. She was optimistic. Desmond was upstairs supervising the children's bath time. They were boisterous and noisy, their father's indulgent voice doing little to settled them down. She was putting away the leftovers, neatly labeled with reheating instructions, when she heard a noise above the commotion upstairs. The low rumble as it came around the corner was familiar and unmistakable, and she knew now that it was too late.

There was a screech and huff of the air brakes as it pulled up out front, then the idling of the engine. The Recycling Truck. Then, a knock on the door. She hesitated, her hands stilling on the refrigerator. What would happen if she simply didn't answer?

Just by chance she had seen the catalogue addressed to Desmond arrive in the mail a month ago. It had disappeared into his office very quickly but, by then, she'd known that he was shopping around. She had hoped, had tried her best to be the perfect wife… But she should have known better.

Disappointment swamped her and she wiped her suddenly sweaty palms down the sides of her dress before forcing herself to walk to the door. There was no other option.

"Good evening, ma'am. Having reached the end of the thirty-day notice period as required from your current leaseholder, I hereby inform you that under the authority of The Depot … "

Cherish had stopped listening. She nodded once, accepting his words, and stepped outside. She'd heard it all before of course and knew the drill by now. Still, she couldn't help glancing back at the house as she walked away, thinking of the children. Not just the twins, but remembering all the little ones who had come before them.

She wished she could stay or at least, just once, have a chance to say goodbye.

Tomorrow they would have a new mommy. And she would be back on the market.

The Last One Standing

She could remember a time when the sun still shone; when she was small, and a cool, crisp breeze on an autumn day was something she could selfishly take for granted. Before the storms came.

The rain began on an ordinary day, but by the end of the week, when it continued to fall, it felt anything but. The winds lashed with cruel purpose. Buildings were leveled, and homes destroyed. Rising flood waters overwhelmed bridges, and they inevitably succumbed to the waves. Global temperatures plummeted, and a panic descended on the world; the few who were able to endure the weather had far worse things to worry about.

When they found her, she was alone, sheltered beneath the battered bows of a half-fallen oak. And they marvelled at her survival.

Her arrival at the facility was met with much enthusiasm. The scientists hurried to examine her: they took samples, there were endless tests, and she was poked and prodded until finally they allowed her some peace. Safe within their artificial light and their artificial oxygen, she came to the scariest realization of all: they had known, they had been prepared for this.

So, the years went by and unwittingly it became home. She grew; somehow she flourished, while outside, in a world gone mad, infrastructure and humanity crumbled. She heard rumours of rising factions amongst the few who had survived out there, for the leaders spoke around her freely, her silence mistaken for indifference. There was talk of one-day re-terraforming and repopulating. She was told she would be instrumental in this of course: the revival of the earth.

They had so much to learn from her. The last of her kind. The last tree.

Afterword
Erin Vance

In mid-January of 2019, Facebook cheerily reminded me of a post I had made four years ago. It stated how I was about to spend the next two months obsessing over Susanne Collins' *The Hunger Games* series. Ah yes; I was about to begin writing my English Honours thesis.

The post concluded with, "If it helps, I may never want to think about the series again after April."

The fact of the matter is, I have thought about that series a lot in the last four years. Not just because it taught me a lot of valuable academic writing and analysis skills, but because of how much dystopia had affected my life without my permission. Remarkably, when I was asked in the fall of 2014 what I wanted to write my thesis on, I knew almost right away. I wasn't aware, at the time, how much more difficult it is to write a thesis on a modern series, but I knew that if I was going to master this project, I had to pick something I cared about and something I understood. *The Hunger Games* and its sequels was, I thought, this something.

The thing about dystopia, much like Brad Dunn wrote in his introduction, is that it has been around for a long time. For decades, humans have looked around at the world they live in and gone, 'Huh. This looks pretty awful. How can I warn my fellow people of the dangers I foresee?' Their only solution, of course, is to tell a story of what might happen. And, like all fiction but in a very particular way, dystopia fiction studies human nature. The path that human nature has traveled on that has taken us this far and how much further on this path we can go. I think this is one of the reasons dystopia fiction seems to go hand-in-hand with science fiction (although that does not force out fantasy whatsoever as it, too, studies humanity); but dystopia imagines the future.

And, like other genres of fiction, it has a lot to do about politics. About the differences in viewpoints, about the conflicts that arise, about what the current society is afraid of, and about what people are willing to fight for.

The Hunger Games, as literature I am familiar with, begins as a study of the dangers of reality television, class elitism, and a totalitarian government. As it goes on, it becomes something more: a study of personal agency, of what makes a person a real hero, of the dangers of propaganda, of manipulation, of PTSD, of standing for what's right, and – ultimately – of how little things actually change. The world of Panem is not unrecognizable from our own world, and the world that emerges after the Capitol is knocked down a peg or five is still recognizable – to both Katniss and to us. Although it serves as a warning, it also serves as a call to arms.

I like dystopias that end with hope. I'm a hopeful person at my core: I try to focus on making things better, of not dwelling on the dark and doomed aspects of life that I cannot change. I can fix my small world day by day with a smile, with a reasonable to-do list, with a hug from my dogs or cat, or with a hip check to a loved one. I can make my friends' scary worlds a little brighter with a hand or a listening ear or a blanket. I can make my work environment a little less bleak by doing the best job I can, by making faces at my co-workers until they're forced to laugh at me, by doing everything in my power to act fairly. This world we live in is, by some standards, a "bad place," but that doesn't mean my world has to be.

I like dystopias that offer solutions. The ones where people fight for freedoms, where people choose others over themselves, where people give of themselves more than what society wants them to. I like the dystopias where the authors say, 'But see? There is a way out! We do not have to give into the doom and gloom. We can change things.'

Although not all of our stories in this anthology offer solutions, some do. And for those that do not, I will give you one:

We can choose to love. We can choose to hold onto each other and to focus on the light and the good things. We can fend off the bad places and dystopias if we are strong enough.

And friends? I believe we are.

God bless,
Erin Vance

ON THE COVER

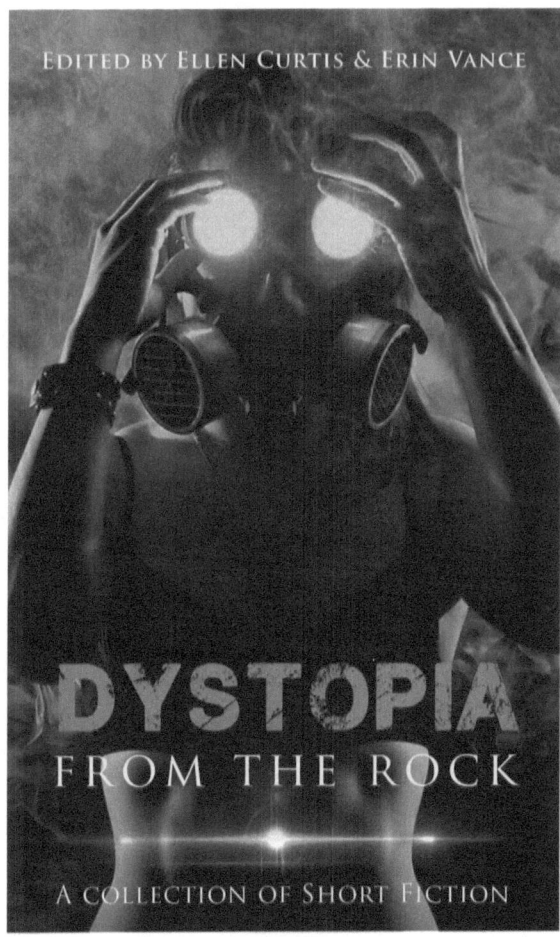

This stellar cover was created by author and artist JJ King. Best known for her written work, King is the author of *The Guardians* series of paranormal romance novels and *Medusa: The Wronged*.

DYSTOPIA FROM THE ROCK

A COLLECTION OF SHORT STORIES
EDITED BY ERIN VANCE & ELLEN CURTIS

What happens when our world -- and everything in it -- goes wrong?

Explore that question in thirty-two short stories written by a diverse mix of the best authors in Canada, including award-winning veterans of their craft, and brand new talent.

Featuring the work of Jed MacKay (*Daredevil: Man Without Fear, Edge of Spider-Geddon*), Ali House (*The Six Elemental, The Fifth Queen*), Jon Dobbin (*The Starving*), and more.

Edited by Erin Vance and Ellen Curtis, this collection showcases the talent, imagination, and prestige that Canada has to offer. From stories of censorship gone awry to sentient buses, global warming to corporate-branded culture, this collection has it all!

www.ingramcontent.com/pod-product-compliance
Lightning Source LLC
Chambersburg PA
CBHW030550020726
47494CB00005B/1562